THE ORACLE

REVELATION: PART TWO

THE VALENTINI FAMILY

SERENA AKEROYD

Serena Akeroyd

Publishing Ltd.

FOREWORD & TRIGGERS

LOVELIES,

Are you ready for war?

Please be advised that this story picks up IMMEDIATELY after The Consigliere. :)

While a pain kink is difficult to understand for some people, masochism is a part of the BDSM umbrella for a reason.

Aurora is a masochist, *not* a self-harmer.

There is a distinct difference between the two.

Don't yuck someone else's yum—her kink might not be your kink and that's okay! <3 Now, give Aurora and Hunter a chance to show you why it works for them.

If you'd like a recap of character names and organizations, click here. (The link takes you to a chapter within the book.)

Much love and happy reading,

Serena

xoxo

Triggers:

- BDSM,
- References to sexual assault,
- Self-harm,
- General violence

VALENTINI FAMILY

THE CROSSOVER READING ORDER WITH THE SINNERS & VALENTINIS

FILTHY
FILTHY SINNER
NYX
LINK
FILTHY RICH
SIN
STEEL
FILTHY DARK
CRUZ
MAVERICK
FILTHY SEX
HAWK
FILTHY HOT
STORM
THE DON
THE LADY
FILTHY SECRET
REX
RACHEL
FILTHY KING

REVELATION BOOK ONE
REVELATION BOOK TWO
FILTHY LIES
FILTHY TRUTH

RUSSIAN MAFIA
Adjacent to the universe, but can be read as a standalone
SILENCED

BON VINUTI A LA FAMIGGHIA!

Luciu - Loo-cee-you
Custanzu - Cust-an-zoo
Giovi - Gee-oh-vee
Buttana - whore/bitch
Vicchiareddu - old man
Bona sira - good evening
Figghiu ri buttana - son of a bitch
Porca troia - Goddammit
Pezz'i miedda - piece of shit
Miedda - shit
Famigghia - family (Sicilian spelling)
Grazii - Thank you
Se - Yes
Capisci? - Understand?
Russu - red
Tuttu boni? - Is everything okay?
Vinnitta - vendetta
Chista è da me - you're mine
Culu - ass
Matri - mother

Patri - father
Soru - sister
Frate - brother
All'asilo - in Kindergarten
Tesoro - treasure
Talè - What are you saying?
T'avissi a mettiri na màschira - You ought to be wearing a
    mask (phrase, meaning to hide one's embarrassment.)

To Trever,
My little fur ball.
You broke my heart.
Why did you have to leave us?

PLAYLIST

If you'd like to hear a curated soundtrack, with songs that are featured
in the book, as well as songs that inspired it, then here's the link:

https://open.spotify.com/playlist/5cT02Widx3DOMLnVUYAxzV?si=
3fd6873696534061&pt=99fb89f981112e43ebc183c6431c301f

1

AURORA

FOO FIGHTERS - TIMES LIKE THESE

HIGH DESERT CORRECTIONAL FACILITY, LAS VEGAS, NEVADA

"PARA BELLUM, SORU."

For an ancient family such as mine, one that originated from Sicilian royalty, a motto like, '*Prepare for war*,' was fitting. I just hadn't expected to hear it uttered from my baby brother's lips this morning. Not without his usual glib delivery.

"Keep on driving, bitch. Don't stop until I say so," a random fuck had snarled at me before I'd heard Custanzu's warning when I settled in my car.

That sweet, sweet serenade had been compounded by the digging of the tip of a gun into my spine through the soft cushion of the driver's seat.

The wielder of said gun hadn't identified himself as belonging to a particular faction, and because I was Aurora Valentini, I had a lot of people who disliked me, so it would have been helpful if he had declared his allegiance to whichever penny-ante organization he belonged.

The gun dug into my back again as the stranger spat, "Get fucking moving, bitch."

"You know, you shouldn't always listen to someone's bad press. I might not be a bitch," I drawled as I scanned beyond the parking lot.

Guards at the correctional facility where Alberto De Laurentiis was held were currently dealing with a lockdown situation. Alarms blared loud enough that they were hurting my ears even from this distance, and prison officers were running around like headless chickens in response to the 'Prisoner down' radio alert.

My fear was that Alberto was the prisoner down.

The reality was that I could be the next person to die at High Desert.

"Would you prefer 'cunt?'"

"Cunts take a pounding and survive," I retorted, the strategist in me racing to pin this hijacking on a faction—knowledge was power. "So, yes, I'd prefer that."

I'd just received what I assumed was a proof of life video from Stan, and from the lack of incoming calls from my twin, I'd hazard a guess and say I was the only one who'd received the file—not Luciu. That had to mean the kidnappers knew he was away and that I was in charge.

And this guy in the back of my car hadn't referenced Stan's words at all. Hadn't shoved my face in them. Hadn't been smug in victory.

So, *two* enemies?

I was in Vegas. I'd just seen the last Don of the Camorra in prison. It'd fit that this was a Camorran problem.

My brother's kidnapping, on the other hand, was a *Cosa Nostra* problem.

One shaped like the Messina and Puglisi families, I thought.

Unaware of where my deliberations had taken me, the hijacker prodded me in the back again. "Get moving, *cunt*."

"That's where you and I have a problem," I informed the stranger, making no move to switch on the engine. "This isn't my first trip to High Desert Correctional Facility and I know that once you get me away from this built-up area and out onto the highway, you'll be putting a bullet in my head and burying me in the desert."

"What?" he sputtered.

"If you'd prefer a Sicilian translation," I said silkily, my hands tightening on the steering wheel. "I'll happily oblige."

He dug the gun harder into my back. "Just get fucking moving."

Taking note of the desperation that had begun leaking into his voice, I smiled.

He wanted off the prison grounds where the alarms were blaring because a prisoner had been killed. Logic dictated this man was the murderer, which made me the unfortunate getaway driver.

No one used me.

No. One.

I just had to get to my guards.

Plan formulating, I fastened my seat belt because, *safety first*, and I started up the engine. I gave no sign as to my intentions, no sign as to the fury bubbling in my veins.

After I turned onto the stretch of road that led to the US-95, and spying no traffic from either direction, I hit the gas.

Hard.

The guy prodded me with the gun. "The fuck do you think you're doing?"

My eyes were glued to the speedometer, watching as we hit seventy miles per hour in a delightfully short span of time.

Making a mental note to applaud Hunter on his choice of vehicles, I called to the backseat, "You're going to shoot me while we're traveling at… eighty-five miles an hour?"

Ninety-five now.

A hundred.

One-ten.

The speed made my heart race more than the hijacker's presence in the car had. I almost let out a woot as we reached a second, smaller correctional facility at the end of the road before we turned onto the highway.

That was when the moron came to my aid.

He sat up and maneuvered himself between the seats. His hand moved, the gun shifting from the middle of my back to my temple.

For the first time, I saw his face in the rearview mirror and I recognized who it was—the weedy prison guard who'd escorted Alberto from the visiting room.

Anger had me putting the pedal to the metal. Releasing a whoop, I silently dared him to pistol-whip me when we were traveling at these speeds.

"Slow the fuck down," he ordered, panic streaming into his voice.

We'd just hit a buck twenty.

One-thirty.

"Gladly."

I slammed my foot on the brakes before the exit a thousand yards away, and that was when the laws of physics and his skinny ass did me a solid.

His screech was almost musical as momentum pushed him between the seats. Any bulkier, and he'd have gotten wedged between them, but instead, he was flung forward. Not far, he didn't go sailing through the windshield—a crying shame—but his head did collide with it.

A satisfying spider's web of cracks spread from the point of impact and he was out like a light.

I had no idea if he was dead or not, didn't care either way, but if he wasn't then the Camorra could interrogate him to figure out who the hell had sent him to take out their last Don.

Ignoring the distinct aches on my shoulder and hip where the seat belt kept me from sharing a similar trajectory as this prick, I hauled his bony ass backward by snagging a hold on his shirt collar and dragging him away from the console.

There was no traffic, oddly enough, but I took off and didn't stop until I reached my guards' ride.

Pulling up behind them, I got out from behind the wheel, wincing at the ache in my hip, then rushed over to the driver's door and knocked on the window.

"There's a guy in my backseat. You need to deal with him."

Both men—ketchup and mustard around their chops from the hot dogs they'd picked up from only God knew where—gaped at me.

My cell phone rang before I could ask them if they shared an IQ with the unidentifiable meat in the hot dogs they were eating.

Spying the number I'd dialed barely ten minutes ago, I almost ignored the hacker's call but self-preservation told me that wouldn't be the wisest decision.

"I thought you were about to board a plane, Lodestar."

"I boarded, and I saw what you just fucking did. Jesus Christ, Valentini, didn't Bert tell you the plan?"

My temper surged to life again. "You mean whatever the hell that was was *planned*?"

"Yes," Lodestar hissed. "Is Crayon even alive after you went all *Fast and Furious* on him?"

Crayon?

"Don't know. Don't care. He shoved a gun in my back, Lodestar, and he called me a cunt. I didn't think he was asking for a ride—" My brain screeched to a halt. "You *know* him?"

"You were supposed to take him where he wanted to go," she shouted. "You were his ride out of there! Can no one do anything right? Do I seriously have to manage every goddamn cog in the machine?"

"I didn't get a memo about being someone's getaway driver. Why the fuck did he hold me at gunpoint?!"

"He's a little paranoid."

"*A little?* Understatement. He held a gun to my temple!"

She sniffed. "So he has an attitude problem."

"You can say that again."

"He's a genius at his art. That comes with a high price tag."

His art?

The urge to scream was strong, but it'd get me nowhere. That was, however, when the silence hit me. The distinct lack of traffic was borderline creepy. Like something from an episode of *The Walking Dead*.

"Are you the reason there are no cars on the road?"

"Yes," was her sullen reply. "Fuck."

"Who is Crayon to you?"

"Oh, just an awesome sniper that was doing this job as a favor to me, Valentini. You've probably fucked with his twenty-twenty vision if he isn't dead already." She blew out a breath through her nose. "I don't believe this. What the hell am I going to tell his mother?"

"His mother?" That wasn't a story I needed to know. "We were just on the phone. You could have told me what was happening. Why didn't you?"

"Because I got my final boarding call. How was I to know that when I sat my ass down, they'd say my flight was delayed—"

The guards were gaping at me as if I were insane, and I didn't blame them. I felt like pulling my hair out.

"What do we do with him, Lodestar?"

"Gee, I don't know. Take him to a fucking hospital, maybe? So we can salvage this mess?"

"Your mess," I corrected. "If I'd been clued into the plan, I'd have been able to help. Or advise."

"You had to look clean. If the cops come sniffing, which they won't, you still need to be as pure as the driven snow on the off chance they do. That was the crux of Bert's whole plan."

That fit seeing as he wanted me to be his grandson's wife. But, still… What the hell was going on here?

"This is *Bert's* plan?" I demanded. "Not a plot by the *Reyes Dorados*?"

My question had the guards finally putting the hot dogs down and back into the wrappers.

"Of course, it was Bert's plan. Aren't you listening to me?" She huffed. "Now, are you going to deal with Crayon or what?"

Though she was annoying as hell, to the guard in the passenger seat, I directed, "*You.* Take the guy in my ride to a hospital. Say he was in a car accident."

"Because a fucking headcase was behind the wheel," Lodestar intoned in my ear.

"You," I said to the driver. "You can take me back to the *palazzo*." To Lodestar, I retorted, "Next time, key me into the plan so I don't take things into my own hands." When I cut the call, I stared at the guards who'd yet to obey. "Well?!"

"We need to call this in, ma'am. Get approval—"

My top lip curled into a sneer. "You don't need approval for this. You do as I fucking say and take me to the *palazzo—*"

"Not the airport?"

"No. Change of plans." I scowled at them both. "Why are you still in the car? And where did you even get hot dogs from? Did you leave to pick up takeout? I'm sure that'll look good to your underboss." I pointed a manicured nail at the guard who was *still* sitting in the passenger seat. "Get the fuck out of this car and take the guy to the hospital. Now," I barked, watching with satisfaction as he finally complied after I rounded the fender.

When he jumped out, I heard him mutter, "Bitch," under his breath.

I rolled my eyes at the supposed 'offense.' He wasn't even the first prick to call me that *this* hour.

"You really want your ass beating for dereliction of duty today, don't you?"

He ducked his head, but not before I saw him scowling at me.

Ignoring him, I leaped into his seat and spat at the driver, "Get me out of here."

Finally, my authority wasn't questioned; the hot dog wrapper was tossed over his shoulder and we drove toward Vegas.

Now that I was back among 'friends,' I had to save my brother's ass.

First things first, I needed to watch that proof of life video and scan it for clues, then I'd call Hunter.

Two heads were better than one on a matter like this, particularly in a territory that wasn't my own.

If that meant showing him more trust than I gave my brothers when the time came for my plots and machinations, well, after watching the video and seeing the state of Stan, it was tough shit.

Those fucking *pezz'i miedda* would pay for treating him like a punching bag.

I was the queen of vendettas, after all, and they'd just painted a target on their foreheads.

2

———————

HUNTER

"THAT AURORA VALENTINI'S something special, Don."

I cut Brunu a look, seeing he'd waded into Bert's old office with a cup of espresso in one hand, his cell in the other. "Get out. I'm still pissed at you for showing those pictures to the council—"

He scoffed, "That was Paulu, not me. And I wasn't talking about that. I was talking about this."

My Capo passed his phone to me and I stared at the pictures on the screen. Blood and… Was that a nose?

"What am I looking at?"

"No idea. Don't know who it is either. I'll speak with the guard who called it in.

"Nino ain't the sharpest knife in the drawer but he's good with his fists and quick to react. *Usually*. That's why I put him on her detail." He grunted. "Trust him to fuck up this time.

"All I pieced together through his whining was that he and Ricardu were trying to do their jobs and wanted to call it in but she wouldn't let them until he got away and that she's the psycho behind this." He waggled his phone at me.

Scrubbing a hand over my face, I muttered, "He's saying Aurora did this?"

"Apparently."

"When?"

"Somewhere between High Desert and where her guards were parked."

My mouth gaped. "Who the fuck would she get into a fight with in a prison—"

Brunu's cell buzzed before I could finish the question. I shoved the phone at him to let him answer it while grabbing my own so I could call her. She didn't pick up.

Studying the time, I frowned. Her plane wasn't due to take off for another forty or so minutes.

"Where are you?" I barked when she eventually deigned to pick up the damn phone.

"On my way back to the *palazzo*," was her grim retort.

"What the hell's going on, Aurora? I just got shown some pictures—"

"Fuck the pictures. Stan's been kidnapped. I've been consulting with—"

"Stan's been kidnapped?" I shouted. "You buried that lede, Rory! You're coming back here, not heading to New York?"

"Yes. How did he get to the airfield last night?"

"I'll look into it." My jaw worked. "We'll figure this out, Aurora. He's my family too."

A soft breath whispered in my ear. "Why do you think I'm coming back to the *palazzo* and not flying straight to the city?"

It wasn't the time for smiling, but my mouth twitched.

She was letting me in.

Aurora was the most capable woman I'd ever met. Her efficiency and cunning were borderline terrifying. She didn't need my help but she was including me.

We were going to do this together.

"I checked with the airfield, and he didn't land there like he was supposed to so I think he must have been kidnapped before take off. I'll forward you the proof of life video I received." She swallowed. "They've beaten the everliving fuck out of him, Hunter."

"He'll be fine. You know he's built like an ox. All those carbs will act as a cushion. We just have to bring him home."

"Yes. We do." She clicked her tongue. "Do you have eyes on the Vitales?"

The Vitales were *Cosa Nostra* exiles back from the days when her grandfather had owned Manhattan. After his murder and the Fieri takeover, they'd established themselves in LA.

"Their territory borders the *Reyes Dorados*, and they're always getting into beef with them that we wade in and sort out, so yeah, we have eyes on them. Why? You think they're involved?"

"We invited them back to New York this spring and asked if they'd sit on the council. What they wanted was to stay in LA and for us to help fight the Camorra—"

"'*Fight the Camorra*,'" I derided. "We're helping their asses. There's this strip of land between their mutual territories and it's where they both deal drugs.

"If we don't keep them from killing each other, it'll rain down Alphabets on us all."

"Not arguing with your grandfather's methods, Hunter. Just saying, Vitale was pretty pissed in Manhattan. He wanted help because his eldest son got murdered."

I scraped my hand over my jaw. "Shit. I remember Bert saying something about that now. It was earlier this year—"

"I'm still wicked pissed about my grandfather being murdered and I never met him," was her cool retort. "I think we know bad blood lasts longer than a few months."

I grimaced. "True. I'll check out the eyes we have on the Vitales."

"Check high up the ranks. The family will be involved in this if it's for honor."

"They wouldn't have bad blood against you."

"No, but the Messinas and Puglisis hate me, and maybe they promised the Vitales help fighting the Camorra if they did the grunt work here in Vegas."

"The Messinas and Puglisis—Stan's mentioned them to me a couple times. They give you crap, don't they?"

"Just a little," she drawled. "Sexist jerk-offs."

I tapped a few keys and pulled up the tag on the car she'd been driving earlier. "Why are you heading to the hospital? I thought you were coming to the *palazzo*?"

"I am. The cars had to split up. By the way, the guards you used to escort me to the prison are fucking useless. They left their position to go buy goddamn hot dogs, Hunt—"

Rage filled me, and my growl stopped her rant in its tracks. "I'll handle them."

"Thank you. A guy was waiting in my car at the facility; I dealt with him. One of your guards is taking him to the hospital because apparently, he's a *friend*, and the other guard is driving me back to the palazzo."

"Someone tried to hijack your ride?" I replied, astounded by the prospect. "And, wait. A friend of whom?"

"I'll explain when I get there."

On the brink of telling her that I wanted to know what was going on now, not later, I shut my trap when Brunu put his hand on my shoulder. As I turned to look up at him, I noticed his expression was somber.

"One second, Aurora," I said apologetically. "Brunu, what is it? What's up?"

The man who'd acted as my grandfather's fists for the last three decades stared at me bleakly. "Bert's dead."

3

AURORA

11 MINUTES - YUNGBLUD FEAT. HALSEY.

ALBERTO DE LAURENTIIS was a stranger to me.

I'd never met him before today.

Until this morning, I'd held him responsible for his inactions against our enemies, the Fieris, when they'd overtaken the *Cosa Nostra*, executing my whole family in the process and laying the blame at an innocent man's feet.

But he was Hunter's grandfather.

Alberto had been chivalrous and kind during our meeting, respectful of my position, uncaring that I was a woman—dare I say he'd been forward-thinking?

He'd been cunning too.

Sly.

I appreciated those traits in a person because I shared them myself.

I knew he'd leave a gaping hole behind him—my poor Hunter.

His silence was telling. Brunu was muttering something, something I could barely hear in the background, but Hunter, while still on the line, hadn't said a word since the news had dropped.

Every now and then, I heard the clack-clack of fingers on a keyboard, but aside from Brunu, there was peace on his end.

It was a testament to our current relationship that I didn't try to worm out of the conversation. Anyone else, I'd have given my condolences and would have hung up.

But this was Hunter.

He needed me.

I didn't know how to be needed in this way, but for him, I'd figure it out.

"How much longer until we hit the *palazzo*?" I asked the guard.

"Forty or so minutes."

Too long when he needed me right now.

"Go faster if you can."

The guard nodded. "Will do."

"Hunter? I'm coming. I'll be there soon. I promise."

I didn't *do* reassurances. I didn't do promises, even. But this was Hunter. He changed everything.

So I stayed on the line with him even though neither of us said a word to each other, and while I needed to be working on tasks to bring Stan home, hitting up friends and foes alike for clues, I sat through those endless minutes with him because he'd lost his grandfather today, and if anyone understood what it was like to grieve, it was me.

I'd never known mine, and I'd uprooted my life for him when I'd learned what he'd endured at the hands of the Fieris.

Hunter had the right to go to war, but the only problem was, of course, that he'd be going to war *against* Alberto… Because, according to Lodestar, *Alberto* was the one who'd had himself killed.

When we pulled up outside the *palazzo*, I rushed toward the portico. The guard on the door opened up for me, and though I figured Hunter was in his quarters, I queried, "Where is the Don?" to be on the safe side.

"He's in his office, ma'am. I can't leave my post or I'd guide you but—" He gestured with his arm. "Go down there. It's the door at the end."

"Thank you."

"My pleasure, ma'am."

Following his directions, I burst inside the office at the end of the hallway, not bothering to knock.

Brunu had jerked into a standing position at my barging in, but Hunter hadn't even looked up. He was sitting behind the desk—*his grandfather's desk*—and his elbows were on his knees, his back bowed as he stared at the floor.

Not bothering to give the room more than a cursory glance, I dismissed Brunu. "Leave us."

He blinked, mouth opening like a guppy, then he shot Hunter a look. What he saw had him obeying my order.

Once the door closed behind him, I strode across the rug, rounded the desk, and crouched in front of Hunter. My knees burrowed into the soft fibers as I slipped my arms around his neck, nuzzling my face into his throat. His arms were in the way, and he was so stiff, so unresponsive at first that a shudder of fear whispered through me—the fear of rejection—then, there was a blur of activity.

Suddenly, I wasn't on my knees anymore. I was sitting on his lap, straddling him, legs dangling either side of him in a position that wasn't exactly glamorous as he threaded his arms around my waist and held me so close that it was difficult to breathe, so tightly that I knew I'd have more bruises than just the ones from my seat belt.

It was perfect.

With his face burrowed into my chest, I pressed my chin against the crown of his head as I held him to me, just as fiercely, just as wholeheartedly.

He didn't cry—his cheeks were dry—but his grief was so raw that it was tangible. I stroked my fingers through his hair, trying to offer comfort where I could, just relieved that I was here and not on a flight to Aspen.

It was at that moment that I recognized I loved him.

I'd loved D.

I'd loved Hunter as a friend.

But this was more.

This was different.

I wasn't holding him like I'd hold Hunter the friend.

I was holding him like…

God help me.

...he was my world.

As the revelation wormed its way through me, I knew it was too soon, too rash, too ridiculous, but that didn't loosen my embrace, nor did it make me rush through this. I had so much to do, was being pulled in so many different directions, and even though my brother was in danger, I couldn't tear myself from Hunter. Couldn't hurry this along.

I might regret that later, but right now, I didn't.

I pressed a soft kiss to Hunter's temple. "I'm here. I'm here. I'm not going anywhere."

He stiffened at my words but didn't reply. His head rocked from side to side before he slowly pulled back. I half-expected him to move in that same blur as before, to haul me off his lap and encourage me to take a seat on the chair behind his desk, but he didn't. He stared at me through heavy lids, his thick lashes acting as a barrier. His hands and arms, however, remained wrapped around me.

His tone was sterner than expected. "What did he want to speak with you about?"

There was no point in lying. "He's arranged for us to marry."

Hunter's mouth didn't gape like mine had done back at the prison. He didn't even jolt in reaction. He just sighed.

"He loved you very much, Hunter. That was clear to me. H-He wanted the best for you, said that you'd wanted me for years, and he wanted to make sure you got what you deserved."

He stared at me, those beautiful hazel eyes still shielded. "I wonder who'd have won a game of chess between the two of you."

His words took me aback. "You're not surprised."

It wasn't a question.

"Bert is..." He swallowed. "*Was* a very outrageous kind of guy."

"I can tell by his choice in decor," I said wryly, my lips tipping up in a small smile.

Even the one-second glance around this office when I'd entered the room had revealed to me that Alberto thought good taste began and ended at the Moulin Rouge.

Silence was Hunter's only response. His gaze remained locked on me, and no return smile was forthcoming.

I was used to him staring at me. I didn't think he knew he did it a lot. But I wasn't used to *this*.

Somber.

Sorrowful.

Grief-stricken.

Haunted.

They were words I could use to describe the emotions in his eyes, but there was something else beneath it all.

Fire.

Only, it wasn't heat.

It was all-encompassing.

It had me shifting against him—not to arouse, but with uncertainty.

That fire would burn me alive, just not in a sexual way.

At any other given moment, I'd have laughed at my fanciful thoughts.

Instead, I found myself drowning in that continued stare.

"Hunter?" I whispered, needing to break him out of this disconcerting stasis.

"You're mine, Aurora."

My eyes flared in shock. Not because those words were new to me after yesterday, but because of the timing.

"Yes," I said simply; not a single part of me needed to battle his claim.

"We'll get married before you leave Vegas."

"What?!"

His jaw creaked. "I'm not leaving you unprotected. I won't tether you to the city—"

"Good thing because I wouldn't let you," I grouched.

"—but you're not going anywhere without my ring on your finger. Do you understand?"

"Hunter, this is insane. You just lost your grandfather—"

"Yeah, and Stan is only fuck knows where. People get stolen from us. Sometimes, we can steal them back. Sometimes, we can't."

He wasn't wrong.

Damn.

But—

"We're Catholic," I retorted, well aware that was a weak argument. "There's protocol. Banns—"

"Not in Vegas. Those who matter on the West Coast will know who you belong to before you leave—"

"Are you being serious?"

"I've never been more fucking serious in my entire life." His arms moved from around my waist, and his hands turned, shifted so that he was cupping my cheeks. "You belong to me."

Though the words sent molten lava running through my veins, I couldn't stop myself from countering, "*You* belong to *me*."

"Exactly." His smugness told me I'd walked into that trap.

Flustered, I muttered, "You're only doing this because of Alberto."

"I'm doing this this quickly because of him, sure. I should have known he had plans in motion when he presented Reilly fucking Green to me a few nights ago."

That name rang a bell. "He told me to ask you about him before I left."

That had him grunting. "Of course he did."

I bit my lip, and knowing there were more important things to discuss than a stranger I'd never heard of before, I reached up and pressed my finger to his mouth to stall him. "Tell me about him another time. I need to share something with you."

He narrowed his eyes at me. "You're not leaving Vegas without my ring on your finger, Aurora."

I huffed. "Fine."

He jerked back in his seat. "Fine?"

"Yes." I whipped my hair over my shoulder. "But I don't like your tone. You could at least have gotten down on bended knee."

"That's not what this ceremony is about. The official ceremony, I'll do it right."

My mouth pursed at how bizarre this *fait accompli* of a conversation was. I understood why he was surprised at my *laissez-faire* attitude; I kind of was too.

This was Hunter *and* D though. I'd have been insane not to snap him up as quickly as he wanted to snap *me* up. But…

"We've barely spoken in years, Hunter. You might change your mind—"

He jerked me into him, not stopping until his forehead and mine were touching. "I haven't changed my mind in twenty-two years, Aurora. If you thought sliding my cock into your cunt was going to do anything other than bind us tightly together, you were mistaken." Then, his teeth nipped at the bottom lip I kept biting. "Were you?"

It annoyed me how shaky my voice was when I whispered, "I-I don't know." A strange pain blossomed in my chest, one that neither of us had the time to really dissect through open discourse. "You might come to hate me. You didn't want Sunny at the end."

"I wanted Sunny, but Sunny came with baggage that I couldn't fix. She didn't communicate, and she kept shit from me.

"Even after all those fucking years, she still used a voice modulator and wore a mask. She needed a real Dom and, even if she'd have been willing to bridge the gap between online and real life, I wasn't willing to be that for her because I was waiting for you.

"It was tough to look past those things. Impossible to fall into anything when there was so much she kept pushing between us.

"But I liked Sunny. Do you think I'd have stuck around if I didn't? And these past six months, we've been texting more, haven't we? It's always been easy between us when you're not all up in your head."

His words resonated, but… "I'm a bitch."

His lips curved. It wasn't like his usual smile, but the warmth there made me shiver. "Yes."

"I'm opinionated."

"Good."

My cheeks flushed. "I bust balls," I croaked.

"You don't bust mine."

"That's debatable."

He snorted. "You busted the balls of 'friend Hunter.' Not 'husband Hunter.'"

The tiny shiver of before manifested into a full-on tremble.

He knew it too.

His fingers moved to cup my throat. "Someone likes the sound of that." One set of digits stayed there, the other moved down my chest and settled above my heart. "I've never wanted you to change. I like your ornery ass. You think I haven't seen the worst of you before today?"

"I never said that," I groused. "I said that you hadn't seen it for a while."

"I want your worst and your best, Aurora. Nothing else will do."

God, did he hear the things he said?

Did he plan them or something, knowing they'd annihilate me?

I studied him again, saw that same branding, blazing fire in his eyes, and I nodded.

Some, not all, of the tension in his body faded away, while his mouth remained a taut line as grief tore at him, but he turned us in the desk chair and, as if nothing had happened, said, "I think you're right about the Vitales."

Though the change of subject came as a shock, it registered that barely ten minutes had passed between my storming into the office and him getting on with business.

"I have to tell you something else about Bert," I warned him as I tried to shift on his lap so I could worm my way out of this ridiculous position of sitting on him like I was a little girl, but his hands grabbed my hips, keeping me in place.

His scowl had me huffing again. *And* staying where I was.

"What?" he demanded.

"He arranged his own murder."

His mouth twisted. "Are you certain?"

"Yes."

His eyes closed and he released a shaky breath. I didn't think he was going to say anything, so I reached up and cupped his cheek. The tender move had the heavy lids shielding his hazel irises peeping open.

He looked broken. He looked unsurprised.

It tore at my soul.

"I should have expected that," he said gruffly. "How do you know for sure?"

"Because I was the unofficial getaway driver for his murderer, but no one keyed me into that fact so when I got into my car, and I had a gun shoved in my back, I retaliated."

I knew Hunter, ordinarily, would have found that amusing. Instead, his gaze dark, he stated, "I saw the aftermath."

"That moron guard sent you pictures?" I sniffed at his nod. "He was nice and bloody, wasn't he? I didn't care if he survived the trauma to the head at the time but Lodestar sounded like she'd be angry if he died—"

"Lodestar?"

His stillness had me shutting up. "Lodestar," I confirmed. "I met her at the prison. She helped Alberto."

"Of course she did." He released his hold on my waist. "The bitch could have told me."

"I don't think your grandfather would have wanted anyone else to know. I think he wanted to go out on his own terms." I stroked my thumb along the sharp line of his jaw. "My great-uncle was sick in prison, Hunter. They don't look after geriatric prisoners in the system. I can't blame him for wanting to control his fate."

His hand clenched into a fist on my thigh. "We need to bring Stan home."

"We do," I confirmed, shooting him a wary glance. "Hunter?"

"Yes?"

"May I stand, please?"

That cold fire raked over me again. It shouldn't have felt as good as it did, but maybe that was the masochist in me. I liked a lot of pain with my pleasure.

"You may."

He helped me straighten up and then pushed himself into the desk so that he could run his fingers over the keyboard. A few taps later and pictures came up on his monitor.

Placing a hand on the desk, I studied the footage that popped up.

I recognized the Vitales from the council meeting earlier this year. The older Vitale, a hotheaded prick, was jumping into an SUV with his son—he'd also attended the meeting, but he'd been respectful. Junior didn't look pleased about the current situation.

Dissension in the ranks… *Interesting*.

Two other men were riding alongside, and I knew they were low-level grunts but they were also blood—nephews of old man Vitale that I recognized from my dossier on them.

"You have tags on their rides?" I asked.

"Most of them."

Another few clicks and he showed me a map of Vegas. A bright red line appeared on the screen.

"That's them?"

"It is. Look where their end destination was."

A private airfield.

"Their car's still there?"

He nodded.

"Is the plane?"

"No. Flight logs show they were traveling to New York."

I sneered. "Of course they were. Do you know where they landed?"

He zoomed in on a different map, and I saw they'd landed upstate.

Eyes narrowed, I muttered, "Any footage of the disembarkation?"

"No one got off, but a couple guys got on board."

More taps. More screens popping up. I scanned the footage and saw some faces I recognized—Messina and Puglisi embarking the plane.

Stan was still on the jet at that point. As Hunter said, no one had disembarked yet according to the time stamps.

"It's as you suspected?" he asked quietly.

"Yes. The Messinas and Puglisis are involved." Mind racing, I turned to him. "I never get my hands dirty."

"Do you want to start now?"

"Not particularly, but a show of strength…"

"You don't always have to spill blood to ram a message home," he informed me, his voice wooden. So un-Hunter-like.

Even on edge and pissed about the betrayal, that tone registered. It hurt me because I hurt for him.

I was accustomed to being torn in many different directions, but this was harder than anything I'd ever dealt with before.

I wanted to comfort him, but my brother was in danger.

I wanted to hold him and help him, talk to him about his grandfather, and share memories, good and bad, to ease him into the process of grieving.

Only, Stan could die if I messed around.

The *Reyes Dorados* had played their hand last night and were in need of retaliation.

Alberto, well, whatever game he was playing, that was going to come to a head at some point even if he was no longer in any danger...

Hunter's grief had to wait. Oh, how I resented that on his behalf.

Cautiously, I placed a hand on his shoulder. "I'm here for you, Hunter."

His throat bobbed but his fingers didn't stop racing over the keyboard. "I know you are."

"Do you?" I moved my hand higher, cupping his jaw and smoothing my thumb over the side of it where I could feel his gritted teeth.

He cast me a look. "I do."

Slowly, I nodded. "This is Camorra and *Cosa Nostra* business, Hunter. We're in this together."

He dipped his chin. "They're going to regret the day they were born then, aren't they?"

Unable to stop myself, I smiled and, simply, said, "Yes. Yes, they are."

4

___

HUNTER

THE POLICE - EVERY BREATH YOU TAKE

IT WASN'T fancy or big like Luc's wedding.

It definitely wasn't fit for a Don and a Consigliere, especially when they were from two different factions and this was a merger.

For all that, it served today's purpose—a wedding in a time of war.

Brunu and one of my Stidda, a *stiddari,* Adrianu, acted as witnesses while Aurora and I exchanged simple vows in Bert's office.

Once the officiant disappeared, the promise of a bullet to the skull if he shared this news with anyone, I turned to Brunu and Adrianu, stating, "Inform both councils but keep it under wraps. If I hear a whisper of this being spread to anyone other than council members, I'll make them wish they'd never been born."

Brunu shrugged, but amusement made his eyes glitter. "Whatever, boss."

"Sure, Don," Adrianu intoned, studying Aurora like she was a cobra on the hunt for its next victim.

"It's not official if no one knows about it," Aurora pointed out.

"It's official with the councils. That's what matters." I raised a brow at her, knowing the answer without having to ask it. "Do you want your council to know yet?"

Her mouth tightened. "No."

It went unspoken that she wasn't ready for her brothers to know either.

But that was okay. She was mine. That deal was sealed. We had time.

Though my glance was pointed, and it made her nose crinkle at the bridge, I continued, "Mostly, I want the councils to know that if the *Reyes* screw with you again, it's as their Dona, and that means we *will* be going to war if they pull any more stunts like last night. If you're not my bride, I can't make official moves. Fuck that shit."

Though something shifted in her expression, Brunu stalled her from making a response by stating, "Good thinking, boss. Do you want me to spread the news among the heads of houses that the wedding was sanctioned by Bert?"

"Of course," Aurora retorted with a huff.

I nodded my confirmation at him. "Get the pilot to change the flight plan. We'll be heading to New York, not Aspen."

"You're going too?" Brunu queried.

"I am."

"Is that wise?"

"Stan is family. The *Cosa Nostra* are allies. The Vitales, now mutual enemies, crossed onto our turf to kidnap him. What do you think?"

Very little made Brunu uneasy, and I didn't think he still possessed the capacity to blush, but at my words, his cheeks tinged the faintest pink. "Of course, boss. Sorry. Wasn't thinking."

"It's been a crazy morning," Aurora drawled.

Brunu shot her a grateful look. "It has. The guy who…" He swallowed. "The guy who…"

"Bert hired to kill him?" I prompted, my tone gruff, grim.

My Capo cleared his throat. "We sure about that?"

Aurora had keyed him into the situation before the ceremony.

"Positive," she rasped. "But that isn't to say you shouldn't investigate further."

I shot my Capo a glance. "Can I leave that in your hands, Brunu?"

"Of course. Should I inform the council of the news of Bert's passing?" At my nod, he raked a hand through his hair, clearly agitated, and not a lot agitated a man like Brunu. "The guy's got bad head injuries. They put him in a coma until the swelling on his brain goes down."

"Shame. Keep a guard on him. I don't want him disappearing before we can question him."

Brunu nodded. "Will do."

"He's an assassin," Aurora stated calmly. "You'll need better guards than the likes of Tweedle Dum and Tweedle Dee that you set on me this morning."

Adrianu coughed. "I'll see to it personally."

I shot them narrow-eyed glances. "Make sure you do." For the first time in history, both men shuffled on their feet as if they knew to be scared of me too.

I wasn't sure if it was because of how Bert had died, if it was because of the branding of the *Reyes'* coyote, or what, but it was evident they knew my words were as locked and loaded as a gun.

Before they turned to leave, Aurora stated, "You might want to keep this situation with Bert off the radar of that guy, Paulu."

I cupped her shoulder, frowning as she winced a touch. Distracted, I ordered, "You heard my wife. Keep it among yourselves."

The pair nodded and drifted out.

As the door closed behind them, I asked, "What made you say that?"

"He was lying last night. About the pictures and when they were received. I don't understand *why* he'd lie about something as simple as when a package was dropped off, but it was shady. We have enough of that going on without adding to it."

"Agreed."

I pondered the events of the council meeting, but I couldn't really recall Paulu's input.

The second I'd flipped through those pictures, the moment it had registered what others had seen of Aurora, a red mist had overtaken my vision.

The need to pluck out the eyeballs of any fucker who'd looked at us like that was an ache in my fucking soul, then she'd let out a sob and she'd taken off running. I'd been dead sure that she was trying to get away from me. That was one of the reasons I'd ducked in and swept her off her feet. Then, I'd recognized she needed the restroom.

So, no, Paulu hadn't been at the forefront of my mind.

He was now, though.

"If Paulu had anything to do with those pictures—" My hand tightened around her shoulder as she winced again.

"You'll make him pay for it," was her calm retort.

"Why do you keep wincing when I touch your shoulder?"

She tugged at her neckline and dragged it out of the way. Her grimace told me this was the first time she was seeing the bruises too. "I pulled some fancy moves to get away from that jerk in my car."

I stared at the red marks on her golden skin, my temper surging as realization struck. "Seat belt?" At her nod, I dragged up the hem of her shirt and found more mottling on her hip. "I'll kill him," I seethed.

"Not yet." She patted my chest. "We might need him."

Nostrils flared, I demanded, "Are you hurt anywhere else?"

"No. Just my shoulder and hip."

"I'll kill the guards then."

"I wouldn't say no to that—"

"Consider it done," I ground out.

"—but, they wouldn't have been able to help. He was waiting for me in the backseat in the parking lot. They couldn't have helped me when they had to stay away from the prison compound."

"Stop being rational," I complained.

"That's my job. Speaking of which, Alberto told me there were contracts to seal our deal, as it were. He'd already signed them, but I need to."

I dismissed that. "You can sign them when we come back to Vegas."

"Not sure that's how prenup contracts are supposed to work," she mocked. "I'm doing this for you—"

I didn't let her finish that sentence.

My hand snapped out and I cupped her cheek, slipping my fingers down to grab her by the neck as I hauled her into me. I was gentler than I ordinarily would have been in case her neck was tender, too, but I didn't stop until her head was tilted back so the only place she could look was at me.

Once our eyes were linked, I rasped, "There'll be no divorce between you and me, Aurora. So, worrying about prenups is unnecessary, isn't it?"

Her throat bobbed, and deep in her eyes, one of the many masks she wore disappeared. I vowed to free her from each and every single one.

I wanted nothing between us.

Ever.

"Worrying is unnecessary," she confirmed, and the tone of her voice did something to me, made the words worm a path deep in my soul.

I knew she was being careful with me and, to be fair, she was right to be. I *was* on edge. Grief and sorrow weren't emotions to be repressed, but at this moment, they weren't a priority. They couldn't be.

Just like Aurora with her strategies, Bert had planned this.

If he was dead, then what he wanted had come to fruition and I just had to roll along with it because Bert, in all the time I'd known him, had never let me down.

If he was ten steps ahead, then I needed to follow the path he'd laid for me because he'd instigated this for a reason.

Pressing a kiss to her temple, I loosened my grip on her and slid my arms around her waist instead. With zero hesitation, she returned the hug.

She was mine.

For better or worse.

In sickness and in health.

Thank fuck.

"Bert wanted me to be your Consigliere," she muttered against my chest.

Wily fucker.

"Consider it done."

A soft laugh escaped her. "Just like that?"

"Just like that. Brunu will uncover whatever he can about Paulu, we'll get him out either by death or demotion, and then we can install you."

"The *Cosa Nostra* is as much mine as it is Luc's and Stan's, Hunter."

"So? If anyone's smart enough to act as Consigliere for two factions, it's you. Don't pretend like you've enjoyed having more time on your hands since you quit the DA's office."

She pulled back to stare up at me. "You make me sound like a workaholic."

"If the Louboutin fits…"

"Look at you knowing ladies' footwear." When I just smirked at her, she grouched, "I'll need help."

"Stan was saying you need *stiddaris* of your own in New York. That's how it works here. Not just the Capo has his own crew, the Consigliere and Don do too."

"That's how the Irish do it."

"You get yourself a crew here and there, you'll be able to manage it. Whatever you need for this to happen, we'll make it work."

She blinked up at me. "Why go to so much trouble?"

"I know my grandfather's men. Not well, but I know them. I know who they are, what they're capable of, and what they can do. I know that he trusted them enough to keep them on his council, but he didn't trust them enough to not keep an eye on them—"

"Wait," she interrupted. "You think he kept Paulu close to monitor him?"

"No. The rest, yes. Brunu and Paulu knew about the shadow council but no one else did. There's a reason for that.

"Even with all the years apart, with the distance we've had between us, I've only ever trusted six people, Aurora. *Six.* You, Luc, and Stan. Your mom. Used to be your dad, and I can still trust him because the dead don't betray you. Then Rach came along, and finally, Bert.

"Why wouldn't I want you as my right-hand *woman*? When I trust you and when Bert sanctioned the move too?"

She pursed her lips, but I could sense her excitement in the way her hands tugged on my shirt at the small of my back. "I told Luc that we should invest in the Vallara."

I snorted as I recognized the name of a casino I knew was for sale. "Vegas is a Camorra-only town. Investing is one thing…"

"Closer ties," she dismissed. "I'll look into businesses in our territory that would make good investments for the Camorra. It's a smart move—diversifies funds."

"If you say so."

She reached up and cupped my chin. "You need to figure out what kind of Don you want to be, Hunter."

The words were gently uttered, and the lack of pressure in them had me tipping forward so that I could rest my forehead against hers. "I want peace, Aurora."

"Peace comes with a price."

Her warning made the hairs at my nape stand on end. "I'll shed blood for it."

She nodded. "I'll get you peace."

I smoothed my hand up her back. "I want us to live for a very long time."

Her smile set my soul alight, but before she could answer, the intercom sounded and Brunu declared, "New flight plan has been logged. Car's out front. We're ready to rock when you are, boss."

Letting go of her and putting a halt to this conversation was definitely not what I wanted, but I did, just so that I could head to the master safe at the back of the office.

"I'll be two minutes," I informed her as I unlocked the safe, stored the marriage certificate in there, then found what might appear to be an afterthought but wasn't.

A half-hour later, we were on the road to the airfield. After another forty minutes, on the flight to New York, taking the same path as Stan had last night, I watched as Aurora made arrangements on the ground while I nursed a snifter of Cognac and monitored the CCTV cameras I'd hacked into before we'd taken off.

The Messinas and Puglisis, for all they believed themselves to be master criminals, were *not*. If they thought they were intelligent enough to take Aurora's place on the *Cosa Nostra* council, they were more stupid than I could imagine because the paper trail was as damning as the warehouse where they'd holed up in Buffalo.

I'd have preferred for Stan to be snoozing off a hangover in Manhattan, but there was no doubt that his abduction gave my mind something to focus on, something that wasn't my grandfather's passing. The numbness came in waves, and working helped prolong it.

Unfortunately, when a task was complete, my mind was free to think.

In one of those moments, unbidden, my hand tightened around the glass I was holding. One second, the amber liquor was swirling around the fragile bowl, the next, I was hissing as Cognac seeped into the wounds the broken crystal had made upon shattering.

Aurora jerked upright and moved over to me. She grabbed my hand, studied it with a scowl, then demanded from one of the stewards, "I need a first-aid kit."

As the mess was cleared up, she wasted the next ten minutes doctoring the cuts and bandaging my hand—unnecessary, but I let her do it, mostly because I liked her fussing over me. She wasn't a natural nurse, and I liked that she was acting out of the ordinary for me.

With my head tipped back against the rest, I studied her as she clucked her tongue and shot me impatient looks that told me she was angry at my carelessness. It encouraged me to reach up and toy with one long, wavy curl that bobbed around her face.

She scowled at me. "I'm trying to concentrate, Hunter."

I liked it when she was bossy. I also liked it when she was begging for my cum.

"I'm not getting in your way," I disregarded.

"You're playing with my hair."

"So?"

Her brow arched at me. "So."

It took me a couple seconds to figure out where she was going with this, then: "I won't only play with your hair during sex, Aurora."

"Yes, I figured that out last night when you were stroking me like I was a cat," she retorted. "But for the here and now, that's what I'm used to."

I stuck my tongue into my cheek. "Is it making you wet? Or are you too stressed to be wet?"

"You're playing with my hair and your voice is that low rumble you use when you're making me punish myself. What do you think?"

"I think that I'm making it a rule that you can't answer a question with a question."

"What's the punishment?"

It was on the tip of my tongue to say, 'no kisses,' but I didn't. That'd punish me as much as it did her. I'd only started that 'no kissing' rule because I was half fucking certain that once she left Vegas, I'd never see her again.

Kisses were intimate.

Kisses with her were what I'd dreamed about for decades.

So, she had to earn them.

It was one way of keeping control of things before I got in too deep.

Now, however, I didn't have to worry so much.

As my wife, wherever she went, I'd follow. She didn't know what she'd unleashed by saying those two little words—'I do.'

That didn't mean I was eradicating the rule though. I wanted to test her limits and see how far she'd go for a kiss…

So, I informed her, "Spankings." I tugged her onto my knee, almost smiling when she shot me a disgruntled look.

"Spankings," she repeated with a glower, shuffling on my lap. "For answering questions with questions?"

I could have chided her for that glower, made a thing out of it to get her to stay where I'd put her, but I didn't need to. She remained sitting on my knee and it meant even more because she was there of her own accord.

My answer was a hum.

"What about when I do something worse?"

"Then the punishment will fit the crime," I assured her, amused by her use of the word 'when.' Even more amused when she bit her lip at my statement.

The dynamic between us would remain in flux until we were more comfortable with one another in that setting, and for all that I knew Sunny had needed a Dom in more than name only, I also knew that Aurora was incapable of being tethered to a twenty-four/seven dynamic.

I wouldn't want that either.

Not only would we never be able to relax, there was shit about her nature that I appreciated and didn't want to suppress.

As her friend, I could enjoy it when she got snippety and bitchy. As her Dom, I'd have to punish her for acting out.

"We shouldn't talk about this now."

"We can't go anywhere and we can't do anything. We're alone at the back, and Brunu is at the front. When better to talk about this?"

She swallowed. "Stan is—"

"Going nowhere. When we land, we'll sort that mess out and bring him home. We can't do that until we're on terra firma."

"Alberto just passed away."

"And he somehow convinced you to be my wife." I grabbed her hand, tipped her knuckles forward, and pressed a kiss to them. "A smart man never gets in the way of Bert's plans. He probably has you contracted to three kids before you're forty. I'm glad you haven't signed the paperwork he arranged. I won't make you have children if you don't want them."

"I can't believe we're having this conversation. Stan—"

"Is going nowhere until we land in New York," I repeated, tone firm.

She returned to fussing with my hand. "I never said I don't want children."

Her words and actions didn't line up.

Studying her, I decided to take pity on her and change the subject when her discomfort didn't fade. "You know they were only small cuts, don't you?"

Rory glowered at me. "Small cuts can turn septic."

"Not with the amount of iodine you just used. Plus the Cognac cleaned them up," I teased, then my tone softened. "Later, I'll deal with losing Bert, Aurora. I'm just compartmentalizing. I meant it when I said that Stan is my family. I don't want to grieve two people."

She swallowed. "Do you think they'll hurt him... More than a beating, I mean?"

"I think they already have." I reached up and rubbed my thumb over her cheek. "I also think he's built like a bull and that it'll take a hell of a lot to bring him down.

"Talk to me. Tell me what you think their end game is."

Her doe-like eyes narrowed upon me. "You want me to talk strategy with you?"

"Like the good old days."

Licking her lips, she muttered, "We haven't done this since we were nineteen."

Since her marriage to Marcus Macmillan—that harsh truth went unspoken.

"I was always your best sounding board."

Uneasily, she stared down at the hand I still gripped in mine. "You were."

"I can be again."

"I don't like depending on people."

"I'm not people."

"Yesterday, you said you were my man."

I had.

When we were talking about Nutella pancakes for breakfast.

God, was that really less than twenty-four hours ago?

"I am. Speaking of..." I tugged my bandaged hand away and slipped it into my sports jacket. Pulling out the small box I'd retrieved from Bert's safe, I perched it on her lap then I reached up and tugged on her pendant. "Did you ever look at this?"

"Of course I did. Only you'd send me a *Sleeping Beauty* pendant that's worth thirty grand."

"It took me a while to find the pink diamond worthy of *Sleeping Beauty*."

She shook her head. "You only know so much about Disney movies because of me."

"Is that a complaint?"

"No." She slipped the pendant out of my hold. "What about it?"

"Twist it around."

She complied, revealing the smooth golden backside.

"If you put pressure on the back, it'll pop out."

Brow furrowed, she pressed her thumb to it. "I can feel the little notch."

Nodding, I watched as it was unlatched, then I reached for the ring box. "When this is all official, this ring will never leave your finger, Aurora."

Her eyes were locked onto the box as I opened it.

In itself, the case was old. The velvet that covered it was worn around the hinges, and there were dark marks on it from staining over the years.

I stared at the ring that was sitting on the silk bed which had turned yellow with time. "Bert didn't love my grandmother. I think he was glad when she died, not that he ever said that. But—"

"This is the ring his father gave to his mother?"

"You can tell from the age?"

"No. It was something he told me this morning. He said that the way you loved me would be embarrassing if it didn't remind him of how his father was with his mother."

"Only Bert could still dole out shade from beyond the veil." My lips curved into a sad smile. "I'm going to miss the old bastard."

"You can always talk about him with me," she said softly, retrieving the ring from the silk cushion and staring at it.

Once upon a time, the platinum had engravings on it. They were visible but deeply blurred from wear.

"Bert once said that his *matri* told him to take it off after she died and that it was for the next De Laurentiis bride who was loved."

"Your father loves your mom."

"Don't I know it." My father loved Mom to the point where I'd barely existed in our family.

She patted my chest as if she knew she'd stirred up old wounds. "So why didn't Bert give it to him?"

"Because he had no need for it. Bert insisted that this was a good luck charm."

Her lips twitched. "Sicilians."

I grunted my agreement. "Sicilians. But who am I to argue? I'd like it to be true." I plucked the ring from her fingers and tucked it into the small compartment at the back of the pendant. "You can't wear it yet, but you can have it on your person."

"Why was Bert sure it was a good luck charm?"

"My great-grandmother was around during the prohibition. Three times she almost got shot in some raid or other, and she lived until she was ninety-three."

She squinted at me. "It'd have been a better good luck charm if she didn't get shot at in the first place."

"You're too pragmatic to be a romantic," I teased.

"I am not," she argued.

"You are."

I winked at her as I closed up the pendant, turned it around, and settled it between her breasts so the pink diamond could peek out at me.

Now that the ring was on her person, call me as crazy as Bert, but I felt better. Especially considering what we were coming up against when we landed in New York.

I watched her watch me as I studied where the necklace was nestled in her cleavage. "I'm surprised."

"That I agreed to marry you?" She hummed. "Me too. These last few days have definitely been unexpected." Her fingers trailed over my chin, one of the tips brushing over the line that bisected my bottom lip. They moved again, trailing to run along the arc of my upper cheek-bone, just below my eye. "Do you remember in December when you asked Sunny if it was that time of the year when 'she' began pulling away?"

"It was around my birthday, wasn't it?"

She nodded. "I knew I was going to have to say goodbye to you at some point."

"I always felt like you had one foot out of the door."

"Good instincts. I used to push distance between us because I knew what I had to do, but when you asked me if I was ready to walk away, I couldn't say yes. I never could. Even if it was the smart move to make."

"Why?"

"Because splitting up with you wasn't…" Her brow puckered as if she couldn't finish the sentence. Instead, her heart in her eyes, she rasped, "I loved you, Hunter. I didn't want to say goodbye."

I read between the lines. "That's why you said yes today, isn't it?"

Her gaze tangled with mine. "Now I never have to say goodbye," she confirmed. "Even if you decide I disgust you, even if I do something that pushes you away, there'll always be something that binds you to me."

"If you haven't pushed me away yet, Aurora, I don't think there's a damn thing you could do to make me turn my back on you for good."

"You walked away from Sunny."

"I didn't turn my back on her, did I?"

"No," she conceded.

"You were the one who wasn't happy just being friends."

"True."

"I went nowhere, and I'm going nowhere. This situation with the *Reyes* is a headache waiting to happen. With the Vitales too.

"L.A. is about to become a battleground, and we can't lose the war. I wanted you to be mine so that, whatever choices I make that the council disagrees with, anything that I might decide to do to protect you or our family, they can't give me shit for.

"That being said," I murmured, reaching up to gently tug on her necklace, "*this* isn't enough of a tie, Aurora."

"What will be?"

I tangled my gaze with hers. "I don't know yet, but I'll figure it out."

5

AURORA

WHEN WE LANDED in the private airfield a few towns away from Buffalo, I wasn't surprised to see the Carusos and the Brunos waiting for us with a convoy of armored SUVs at their back.

Their presence was a silent declaration.

Demarcation lines of loyalty had been drawn.

The Messinas and the Puglisis on one side.

The Valentinis, Brunos, and Carusos on the other.

As I stepped off the private jet, a hum of adrenaline buzzing through my veins at what was about to go down, a message came through.

Martínez: *Is there anything I can do?*

With the risk of offending the ex-leader of *Los Lobos Rojos*, a man whose help I wanted, I'd shared why I'd had to reschedule our meeting in Aspen.

Not having heard from him until this moment, I released a soft, relieved breath.

We dealt well with the *Lobos* in New York, and I saw no reason why we wouldn't deal well with them if I could convince the one-time leader to make L.A. his new turf.

As someone who'd built up a faction from scratch, I knew it wasn't something that could easily be walked away from. Martínez had done exactly that for his wife, but it wasn't as if Eva Kingston was known for being a 'homemaker.'

Strategies and plans raced through my mind so quickly that I couldn't pluck out a single one to nourish into being.

First Stan, then the *Reyes.*

That was today's to-do list settled and it enabled me to text:

Me: *Thank you for the offer, but we have everything under control.*

A flurry of pictures bombarded my phone as if he'd been waiting for my rejection.

Frowning, I watched as Hunter, who'd stepped off the jet first, held out his hand to greet Caruso and Bruno and to introduce them to Brunu —damn, Brunu and Bruno, that wasn't going to get confusing. At all.

Once the introductions were made, Bruno and Caruso nodded at me, and I shoved my phone at Hunter, watching as he flipped through the pictures, whistling under his breath.

"Drone footage?"

I shrugged. "It's from Martínez."

"He's helping?"

"He offered."

"This is more than an offer," was Hunter's retort.

"It must be why he took a while to reply to my earlier messages."

"He wants you indebted."

My mouth tightened. "Perhaps."

"Who's Martínez?" Caruso asked, his gaze darting between Hunter and me.

"Camorra business," I informed him then, with a wince, corrected, "It doesn't have anything to do with Custanzu."

"Sounds like this Martínez is making Custanzu his business," Bruno drawled, but his eyes were narrowed, and I knew he wasn't going to let this drop.

Hunter, his focus still on the screen, mused aloud, "There's a pissant street gang causing trouble in L.A."

"The *Reyes Dorados?*" Bruno inquired.

Hunter lifted a brow. "You stay abreast of West Coast troubles?"

"Always wise to keep informed; particularly when a 'pissant street gang' runs off with the daughter of the leader of one of Mexico's biggest drug cartels."

I shot him an approving glance. "I suggested Martínez and Eva Kingston might be willing to put matters to bed."

Caruso chuckled. "Smart. Isn't he that girl's uncle?"

"He is."

Bruno folded his arms across his chest. "So, what's the game plan?"

"Annihilation," I told them sweetly, watching as they shared a glance. "You kept this among the family, didn't you?"

"We didn't tattle to Luciu, if that's what you're asking," Caruso retorted.

"Why not?" Hunter asked, arching a brow at them both even though I could tell what Martínez had sent me intrigued the hell out of him. "He's your leader. He's the Don."

I told myself I wasn't offended by that question. It was a fair point. Especially from the Don of another faction who was new to the role.

Caruso scratched his chin. "The men in the *Cosa Nostra* with brains know full well that our Consigliere is as powerful as our Don.

"We also know that getting on the wrong side of the Consigliere would lead to a worse fate than getting on the Don's bad side.

"The Don will slice up our cheeks and exile us. The Consigliere will let us think we're exiled, and then she'll have us killed when we think we're safe." Caruso flickered a glance at me. "The Don is a dangerous force. But there's a reason they say there's nothing like a woman scorned. I know who terrifies the fuck out of me, and I'm not afraid to say it."

Fully approving that message, I smiled at him which had him taking a step back from me.

Hunter shot me an amused look as Bruno cleared his throat. "The Messinas and Puglisis are too fucking blind to see how terrifying our Consigliere is. I, on the other hand, am not."

And to think, they didn't even know all the dirty little secrets I had on them.

"Good answer. So, Luciu isn't in the know."

"I want to keep it that way. He deserves a honeymoon, and we'll have Stan back home tonight. Let it be known among your ranks that this is *not* to get leaked to Luciu. Neither is it to leak to Giovi. He's a fucking snitch."

Caruso jerked at that. "He's a snitch for the cops?"

"No," I groused. "For my brother." I stared at the convoy. "Hunter showed me the plans of the warehouse where they're keeping Custanzu."

"This drone footage merely confirms what I could see on the security cameras—"

"You hacked into them?" Caruso interrupted.

Hunter nodded. "They're hiding the jet in the warehouse. Not sure how the operator got so close without being shot at because no drone is silent, but Stan's on there with at least six other guys. I recognize the Vitales in the mix."

Bruno scratched his nose. "I don't understand their end game in all this."

I shot him a look. "It's either a power grab—"

"Puglisi doesn't want to be in charge," Caruso disregarded. "He's an old fuck who wants money and hookers on tap."

"Then, it's because of the information I have on him."

Caruso coughed. "You've been blackmailing him?"

"No. I had no need to." I huffed. "I don't blackmail people." Leverage was *not* blackmail.

"He was whining about you at the wedding." Caruso shoved his hands in his pockets.

"Messina didn't like having Custanzu pull that gun on him at the council meeting," Bruno chimed in. "But, if anything, I'd have thought you'd be the one targeted, not Custanzu."

"Stan didn't tell anyone he was going to Vegas," Hunter pointed out. "I know for a fact he had business to attend to that night because he was on the phone a lot while he was helping me out. Maybe Puglisi thought the only Valentini using the jet was you, Aurora."

I lifted my chin. "It wouldn't surprise me. Neither family likes me.

Puglisi might not be eager to take over the *Cosa Nostra*, but that doesn't mean Messina feels the same.

"Plus, I'm pretty damn sure Puglisi would like his son in my seat. Maybe that's the plan—Messina as the new Don, Puglisi's spawn as Consigliere, and whichever of you two they can worm over to their side as the new Capo."

Caruso shot me an uneasy look. "The Carusos wouldn't—"

"You're here. I know you wouldn't."

Bruno cracked his knuckles. "In the interests of total disclosure, I'd like to let you know that Puglisi called me this morning."

Intrigued, I asked, "Did you answer?"

"No. I hate the fucker. He's a short-sighted moron who still thinks we're back in the seventies.

"The Brunos have made more money this year with you, Luciu, and Custanzu at the top of the tree than in the past ten years combined. I know which side my bread is buttered."

Satisfied with his reply, I studied him long enough to watch him shuffle on his feet. Only then did I state, "Good."

Hunter pressed his hand to the small of my back. "What information do you have on them?"

"Nothing too heinous where Puglisi is concerned, but it is for him."

He frowned. "What does that mean?"

"A man like Puglisi perceives weaknesses differently than I do, but that doesn't mean I'm not willing to use those perceptions as pressure points." I bit the inside of my cheek, knowing he'd judge me for the information I'd collected. "He had two children with Down's Syndrome and he put them in an institution rather than care for them himself and won't allow his wife to visit them. Ableist asswipe."

Hunter's confusion was so clear that I could have kissed him myself. "That's what you have on him?"

"As I said, he perceives that as a weakness."

"Enough for it to be blackm—" I glowered at him, and Caruso quickly corrected, "—leverage?"

"Yes. Leonardo—" To Hunter, I explained, "—his son—also has a gambling problem. To the tune of three million dollars. He owes the Russians."

Bruno pursed his lips. "Now *that* is a problem."

"It is. I think he might have been the one who's been leaking information to them, but I've got no proof of that. Yet," I bit off the word, though I knew I might never get any answers if the Puglisis were eradicated today. "As for Messina, he killed his last wife when they lived in Rhode Island. The asshole buried her in his backyard. She was pregnant at the time with his youngest son's baby so that's two murder charges."

"How the fuck do you know that?" Caruso muttered.

"I have my methods," was all I said.

Hunter chuckled. "So, what's the plan?"

"We lay siege on the warehouse. Stan is tucked up safe on the jet. I don't care who dies but, preferably, I'd like Messina, Puglisi, and the Vitales alive for interrogation."

"That's a lot of foot soldiers to take down—"

"No more than what my brothers and our men overpowered when we handled the Fieris." Angling my chin, I scowled at Caruso and Bruno, "I'm not expecting you to get your hands dirty like *they* did—" Immediately, they stiffened at the slight. "—but if you wish to remain on my good side, you know exactly how you'll be spending the rest of today."

6

———

HUNTER
KEHLANI - GANGSTA

IT WAS ALWAYS amusing watching Aurora at work.

For someone who refused to believe in gender stereotypes and the limitations that came from adhering to them, she had no problem using them to her advantage.

With delicate slights to her council's masculinity, slices to their ego that were smaller than even the cuts on the palm of my hand from the Cognac glass I'd broken earlier, she had them on the hook.

As they bounded into their rides, we followed them at the back where the limo that had been waiting for us upon our arrival joined the convoy.

During the journey, Martínez sent more pictures which we checked out.

His intel enabled us to accurately count how many men we'd be up against—eighteen guards and six 'leaders' with another guard on board —and to have a rough idea of their locations.

Aurora passed that information on to Caruso and Bruno, allowing them to disperse the intel as they wanted, and in no time at all, we were a ten-minute ride away from the warehouse.

Each of the *Cosa Nostra's* SUVs held four men, so, with six cars to the convoy, as well as our limo, our side was fairly matched.

That was when Martínez called Aurora.

"Consider this a gift. When you're ready to do business, I'm here."

A couple seconds later, dead air on the speaker now that he'd cut the call, she received an email with login details and a link to a privately hosted website.

With my laptop already on my knees so I could study the pictures he'd sent, it took a few seconds for me to get in, and, suddenly, I had control of the drone. A military-grade piece of kit at that. One, by the looks of it, that was a prototype of a future generation of weaponry because I'd never seen anything like this before.

"Jesus, they've packed a lot of punch into a very small package."

Eyes locked on my screen, Aurora immediately rang Bruno and Caruso. "Keep the lines open," she instructed briskly. "I have access to drone footage of the area so I can give you more precise intel."

"Was the original idea just to storm the barricades and take them out by force?" I asked in her ear.

"It's how Luc and Stan claimed the Fieri compound for us and, trust me, I've seen the Messina and Puglisi foot soldiers in action. They make Mr. Potato Head look competent." Though I chuckled, she drawled, "Your men weren't much better this morning."

I pulled a face, but there was no defending the indefensible. I didn't have the chance to anyway, because, with the warehouse peeping over the horizon, she requested, "Take one final look around the area." Into the phone, she ordered, "Hold up."

The cars in front came to a halt, engines idling as I maneuvered the drone around the once-industrial site the others had used as their private landing strip.

"There's the runway," I pointed out.

"What was this place?"

"The warehouse owners must have dealt with overseas imports and exports."

She peered at the footage and took in the different angles the drone provided. "Can every vehicle hear me? One man per SUV say, 'Aye.'"

She received six 'Ayes' from the driver of each vehicle.

"SUVs one, two, and three, you're going to barrel straight into the warehouse where the jet is being stored. You're in the most danger from being hit so the drivers need to make sure they take out guards like they're pins on a bowling lane.

"Only lower your windows enough to let the barrels of your SMGs out and you spray the fuck out of every man in sight. The windows are bulletproof so keeping on the move is imperative, that way they can't barrage you with bullets.

"Custanzu is on board the jet. The leaders of this little mutiny are as well, plus an extra guard. Try not to damage the plane because, if you do, it could ignite whatever fuel is left in the tanks.

"SUV four, you take the left of the perimeter. SUV five, you take the right. Be prepared to deal with anyone trying to escape. No one is to leave the warehouse compound. *Capisci*?

"SUV six, you drive around the back to pick up any stragglers. There's a cargo bay exit with a ramp so you can penetrate the interior from that location.

"There are eighteen guards on the ground. You should have received pictures of their positions. There's very little to barricade behind, very few defensive positions they can take.

"This is obviously a short-term solution but we have yet to receive any kidnapping demands so we've no idea what their end goal is here.

"We go in, grab Stan, then we get out. If you die, your dependents will receive two hundred thousand dollars apiece.

"If you live, you'll get a hundred K in your next pay packet and each of you will be on the shortlist for the new Stidda I'll be creating for myself.

"I want Messina, Puglisi, Vitale Sr., and Jr. alive for questioning. Do not let me down, gentlemen."

As she cut the line, I mused, "I don't know how well they were concentrating. You bossing them around like that probably gave them a boner."

She just stared at me, and for a moment, I didn't know if she was going to punch my lights out or spit fire my way, then she clapped a hand to her face. "Shut up, you."

I heard the laughter imbued in those words though.

Pleased that I could lighten the moment, I grinned to myself as the convoy started up again. She shuffled nearer to my side, her gaze on the laptop screen.

"You control that drone like you've been flying them for years," she mused.

"Maybe I have," I retorted. "Plus, you know I've been a gamer since I first felt the calling of *Super Mario Bros.* back in the day."

Her lips twitched. "Ah, the original Nintendo. God, I haven't played video games in years."

While it came as no surprise considering her background, I still gaped at her. "We need to fix that."

"It's not a sin."

"It fucking is. With how you just bossed those foot soldiers around, I'm thinking something like *Assassin's Creed* or *Halo* would be your bag."

"I have no idea what you just said." Her lips were back to twitching but a somber cast overtook her features with every yard our limo ate up in our approach to the warehouse.

"You'll get it one day." Opting for a calm tone rather than a domineering one, I stated, "You're not wading into the fray."

"Of course not. Generals stay a hundred miles away from any battle. But you couldn't stop me if I wanted to be onsite."

For a moment, our eyes clashed and held.

She was the first to break.

Her gaze dipped to the screen where the drone was idling.

"Hmm," was all I said; I had no desire to ram home my position in her life, no desire to take over or to stop her from doing what needed to be done, but I wasn't going to let her endanger herself.

Not even for Stan.

Her cheeks had turned rosy at my prolonged stare, then, when I set the drone into action again, I murmured, "This model is armed."

"Martínez handed over control of a weaponized drone to us?"

Was that a squeak? I smirked. "He wants to ally himself with you."

"With you," she retorted.

"Us," I corrected.

"The *Lobos* are the best arms suppliers on the East Coast. It comes as no surprise to me that they have drones that should be in the army's possession. Can you fire the drones' guns?"

I shrugged. "If I need to. I'd prefer not to with the jet. You're right about potentially triggering an explosion."

"Ah, yes. I want Stan back in one piece, not fried like the bacon he loves."

"He'll be home tonight. Exactly as you said, BLT in one hand and a Little Debbie's cupcake in the other."

Her hum spoke of her nerves.

"I don't know much about Martínez." I changed the subject to take her mind off things.

"No one does."

"What I do know is that family is everything to him."

"When Luciu met him earlier this year on business, his wife was pregnant. He wanted help bringing her back to the US after that little problem they were having with the NYPD."

"Does beheading really constitute a 'little' problem?"

"In our world? *Se.* I ran some meager background checks on him and came up with hardly anything. *Lobos'* territory in New York is undeniably well cared for."

"Meaning?"

"Meaning that he helped his community. No tags on his streets, gyms for kids to burn off their aggression, schools with protection from Lobos that do a better goddamn job than the so-called men in blue. He's made his territory safe."

My brow puckered. "I should do that."

"We all should. It's easier said than done."

"Why?"

"His men care about their community."

"Don't ours?"

"Ours care about the cash. About vendettas. The *Lobos* don't work that way. I'm not saying Martínez, when he was their leader, wasn't ruthless, because that's not the world we live in, but—"

"You admire him," I remarked.

"He's a man worthy of admiration."

"Why did Luc meet with him?"

She heaved a sigh. "Long story short, the Anjou rubies."

I clucked my tongue. "Ah." No further words were required.

I knew exactly how insane the Valentinis were for those fucking rubies. Including dealing with unknown enemies to get the set of jewels back in their hands.

For the first time, Brunu twisted around from the front passenger seat. His look was pointed and directed at me, but he stayed quiet.

Tipping my head to the side as I studied him, I watched his glance dart between Aurora and me. Nodding slightly, I watched him turn back to face the road and made a mental note to ask him later about the Anjou rubies.

Now that I thought about it, on the walk down to Luc's wedding reception in The Victoria, Brunu had mentioned something about the rubies, hadn't he?

Did he, via Bert, know where one of the pieces was?

I put *nothing* past my grandfather.

The thought stung.

Bert wouldn't be surprising me anymore with his psychopath toddler routine.

There'd be no bringing him back from the edge when he got mad at a slight.

There'd be no more explaining that computer viruses didn't work like the common cold…

Knowing he was dead and gone didn't make it real.

There was a gaping hole in the pit of my being—

"Hey."

I blinked. Refocused. Saw Aurora watching me, her fingers settling over my stomach as if she could sense where that gaping hole was.

I stared down at the manicured fingernails that touched me with such ease, the white tips a sharp contrast to the dark blue shirt I wore beneath the gray sports coat.

"I'm here, Hunter. I'm here."

Her voice was soft. So soft. Not just because she cared, but because of the guys up front.

Turning blind eyes her way, I read the concern in her expression, something she doubled down with: "You're not alone."

Unable to stop myself, I reached up and tugged on her necklace.

She shook her head. "You didn't need to do *that* to not be alone anymore."

"He's gone, Rory."

"I know, Hunt. I know. I'm so sorry."

Gritting my teeth, my head bobbed of its own volition. A normal person would probably cry but I didn't have it in me. I could just feel the ache.

Rory surprised me by settling her head against my arm. "I'm here," she repeated wistfully.

And she was.

Bert's final gift to me?

Or one that I'd given to myself because the last three years hadn't been orchestrated by the grand master that was my grandfather?

She was here because of the relationship we'd struck together. A relationship that was given foundations from a friendship that had spawned from Kindergarten.

Bert had made a marriage between us a business deal. Maybe I should be pissed about that, but I wasn't.

Aurora was too fucking smart, too much of a strategist not to appreciate a fellow genius at work.

He'd have offered her something—that was how deals worked. I didn't need to know the intimate details because as much of a wild card as Bert was, there was one solid truth that undercut everything he'd done since that first time I'd called him 'Grandfather'—he loved me.

Whatever he did, whatever the contracts he'd signed were, whatever the shooting was about, and whatever he'd promised her, it was founded in love. A fucked-up love for sure, but that was Sicilians for you—crazy.

They lived by one tenet—family was *all*.

I pressed a kiss to the crown of her head, silently thanking her for her support, but I didn't say another word because we were there and my grief needed to wait until after our brother was back with us and safe.

The warehouse was surrounded by a chain-link fence and a gate that looked like a strong wind would knock it over. Against an armored SUV, it went down like a house of cards, taking the fencing on either side with it. As the convoy rolled onto the warehouse's grounds, we stayed at the back, watching everything through the drone.

This was my first 'siege'—her words, not mine—but the noise reminded me of a game of *COD* being played on a full surround sound system.

Auditory heaven.

Two SUVs split up and patrolled the sides of the warehouse as ordered, one went around the back and burst in, knocking down a partition wall to make it inside. The first three SUVs rammed into the front siding and were met with submachine gunfire.

In silence, with the noise of the *hostile* take-over filling the back of the limo, we watched as the first SUV mowed down foot soldiers, not stopping, not even opening the windows to fire at the enemies. Behind them, the other two took out whoever the first had missed.

The eighteen guards on the ground were annihilated—exactly how she wanted—without a single bullet of our own being fired.

"The jet door is opening," Aurora called, jerking me away from the action to spy that she was correct.

Something was tossed out, and immediately, smoke filled the warehouse. A spark came next, and she hissed, "Those fucking morons are going to get themselves blown up too."

One of the side walls was overtaken by flames, prompting the pair of us to tense.

"Use the drone," she barked at me, but she didn't need to—I was already there. "SUV one, get that fire under control."

"Aye," the driver shouted, moving over to the wall so the foot soldiers could control the spread of the flames.

I maneuvered the piece of kit through the smoke toward the jet door.

"I'm waiting until they toss something else out," I explained when I didn't immediately open fire. Her grunt told me she agreed.

We waited, impatiently patient, for the slither of light from the jet to seep into the smoky atmosphere.

That was when I fired.

Blood spattered on one of the drone's cameras, and the door itself flopped open as whoever had tried to hurl something through the aperture toppled down the stairs instead. That alone told me luck was on our side because the deadweight could have easily pinned the door in place, barricading us out of the jet instead of offering an invitation to enter.

"Get ready for them to shoot at the drone," she warned, her nails digging into my abdomen where her hand still rested.

Nodding, I shifted forward, edging the drone with me, one finger on the keyboard in preparation for firing, while the other hand worked the controls. As it edged forward, immediately, a wide bullet almost hit our kit.

"In and out," she muttered, obviously expecting me to know what she was asking for.

Lucky for her, I did.

I darted in, immediately hit fire, and retreated.

A scream joined the action, followed by a, "No!"

"Who was that?"

"Puglisi Sr. You must have hit his son." She sighed. "I wanted answers out of him too. Never mind. The world's a better place without the fucker. Do it again."

This time, when I fired, the drone got caught and the camera doused with blood went dark.

"There was no visibility anyway," she disregarded.

"Who's firing?" someone snapped from the jet.

"Messina Sr.," Aurora said, providing me with a name.

"It's a drone," someone else replied.

"Vitale Jr."

"We need to take it out," someone argued.

"Messina Jr."

"Fuck knows what it's armed with," Vitale Jr. snarled. "It could have missiles on there."

"They won't blow the jet up. Not with Valentini on board," Puglisi sniped.

"You never fucking said anything about armored drones. Jesus," Vitale Sr. growled. "How many have they got out there? Look at the plane. We're surrounded. You said this would be easy.

"With Valentini out of the country, you said she'd roll over to get her brother back—"

At my side, Aurora stiffened, her outrage clear.

"She's got bigger balls than either of you," Vitale Jr. spat. "I'm not willing to die for this, *Patri*. We should have spoken with the new Camorran Don and got him on our side. Instead, we've gone to fucking war with the *Cosa Nostra*.

"How the hell are we going to stop them from asking the Camorra to tear us to pieces?"

"We shouldn't need them on our goddamn side. They're the ones who killed your brother."

"Because he was a dumbass who kept on pushing his fucking luck," Jr. seethed. "The *Reyes* are making moves, and we need the Camorra to have our back if we don't want to be sharing that grave of Tommy's.

"I guess it doesn't fucking matter now if we're going to die in a shootout in Buffalo. I told you this was a mistake. You never listen to me—"

As they fell into an argument, I turned to her and, softly, asked, "What do you want to do?"

With her attention split between me and the Vitales, she stayed looking at the laptop. "Does the drone have a microphone?"

"It does."

She held out three fingers in front of me, and as she counted down on them, she cleared her throat just before I hit the microphone button.

"The *Reyes Dorados* are mutual enemies. There was no need to come looking for trouble on the East Coast."

"Is that the Valentini bitch?" Vitale Sr. whispered.

"It is," Aurora concurred. "And this *bitch* has no problem tearing off your balls. You have five minutes to get off that motherfucking plane or my men will storm it and you will die. I'm being generous so don't test my patience."

"Don't listen to her," Messina Sr. argued. "She's bloodthirstier than her brothers."

She smiled. "Didn't I just overhear Signor Vitale claiming you told him I'd roll over to get Stan back? Make up your mind, Piero. Am I a bitch, a coward, or a doormat? You have five minutes to decide."

I cut the microphone once her declaration was complete, and for the next few minutes, there was arguing on board the plane.

When the Vitales stormed off, Senior behind his son, I wasn't altogether surprised when he fell flat on his face, nearly knocking Junior over as one of the *Cosa Nostra* shot him in the back.

Vitale Jr. screamed and dragged him toward the exit where our foot soldiers were waiting.

"Do not kill Junior," Aurora shouted at the men.

Of course, that was when shit hit the fan and I knew I was in the wrong place.

"Driver, take us nearer to the jet."

Brunu twisted around, approval gleaming in his eyes as he shot me a quick grin.

"What do you think you're doing?" Aurora grated out under her breath.

"Acting like a Don," I muttered. *Either that or a moron.* I dropped my head, pressed a kiss to her mouth, and shoved my laptop at her. "The drone's idling. Brunu, make sure Aurora stays in the limo."

The second I leaped out from the backseat, the doors locked behind me, and I moved toward the fender. Brunu's hand stuck out of the passenger window, and I collected the piece he passed me and unclicked the safety.

As I strolled into the warehouse, spying the chaos of the dozen-plus corpses on the ground, I studied the Vitales on the floor, the son trying to stem the blood flow from a fatal wound, the light in the father's eyes already gone.

Pity filled me for the kid who was barely in his twenties, and I moved over to him, kneeling beside him as he tried to work a miracle.

"He's gone."

The kid's head whipped to the side, then when it registered who I was, his eyes flared and the color drained from his face. "D-Don—"

I pursed my lips. "What was this about, Vitale? Were you trying to get my attention? Or were you trying to steal some of my territory?"

"The *Reyes* are encroaching on our boundaries, Don. Every fucking day, that's why—" He swallowed. "First Tomasso, now *Patri*. What the fuck am I supposed to tell my mother?"

I clapped a hand on his shoulder. "You tell her that you did more than your father could. You tell her that you're going to negotiate terms with the Camorra for protection against the *Reyes.*"

Mouth working, he rasped, "You're not going to kill me? We—"

"I know what you did. But I'm not my grandfather. And, after this, you owe me a life debt, Vitale. I take my debts seriously. *Capisci?*"

His Adam's apple bobbed. "*Capisci.* But our men won't—"

"I'll be negotiating terms with *you.* No one else. There's no denying that your turf is an area fraught with strife. It's been a problem for years, and until the *Reyes* showed up, the Vitales did a good job of maintaining the peace.

"I'll be dealing with the *Reyes*, and you and I can work together to keep gang warfare off our streets."

A part of me wondered if I should have approached the *Reyes* with a similar offer, but after the pictures they'd sent me of Aurora, I didn't think so.

Negotiating with the Vitales wasn't simply a 'better the Sicilian devil you know' kind of deal—Junior was young.

Malleable.

And from the sounds of their argument, he'd advised against this clusterfuck—I could work with that.

As if to confirm I was right, his nod came quickly. "I don't want to die, sir."

It was a strange moment, one that was reminiscent of Luciu's wedding day.

Hadn't I uttered similar words to Stan?

Peer to peer?

But this wasn't the same.

Vitale was baby-faced. That was a problem waiting to happen. I might be throwing him to the wolves by sending him back with this message, but at least I was giving him a fighting chance.

"Neither do I." We shared a glance. "No *Cosa Nostra* member on board that jet is going to survive this. Payback starts and ends here."

It was a warning, one he heeded with a guttural, "Understood, sir."

I nodded my approval. "What's going on on board the jet?"

"Valentini's in the bathroom," he confessed quickly. "Two of my cousins were guarding him, but he lost his shit and knocked them both out. I don't know how, not when he was hogtied, but somehow, they're still unconscious, and he's furious as fuck in the bathroom."

"What was the end game?"

"New leaders on the *Cosa Nostra* who promised they'd help us fight—"

At his hesitation, I provided, "Fight the Camorra."

"Yeah." He blew out a breath and his hands moved away from the bullet wound that had gone straight through his father's gut. Blood coated his fingers as he rasped, "*Patri* would never have tried to broker peace with you. Not after my brother—"

"We only went in to stop the fighting between you and the *Reyes*."

"*Patri* said Sicilians were supposed to stick together."

"I don't disagree, but you were the ones who started up the fighting that time, weren't you?"

The kid gulped. "We were."

"You think you're going to have a problem controlling your men?"

"M-My men?"

"They're yours now, aren't they?"

His eyes rounded, and I knew this was not a conversation to be having over his father's corpse, but there was no time like the present. "They are. And no, I won't."

"If you think that'll change… Give me your cell." He complied, staining his jacket with his father's lifeblood in the process, and I tapped in my number when he handed it to me. "You know how to reach me now."

I got to my feet, leaving him behind as I headed over to the staircase that would allow me to board the plane.

When I approached the door, I (pretty dramatically and definitely in a manner worthy of an Academy Award) declared, "The Houses of Messina and Puglisi have brought war to New York. I declare you enemies of the Camorra."

I'd have laughed if these fuckers weren't armed up to their eyeballs and wouldn't hesitate to shoot me in the back like they had their *ally*.

"Enemies or not, we have Valentini. If you want him to stay in one piece, then…" There was a pause, then a blurted out, "You'll let us leave."

A thought occurred to me.

The cockpit was empty.

I'd seen that from the drone footage.

Where was the goddamn pilot?

"One of you can fly the plane?" I questioned, rolling with the thought process as I leaned against the doorjamb.

Curses flew around the jet like bullets.

"No," someone called out. *Messina Sr.* "But we'll give him back if you get us a pilot."

So they'd killed the pilot upon landing—talk about fucking morons.

"God spare me from idiots."

"Fuck you!" Messina barked. "Who are you, anyway? Is that bitch too chicken shit to face us?"

I cursed under my breath—that was a surefire way to make Aurora bristle and to encourage her to leave the limo.

Twisting back, I saw our ride was motionless and that she hadn't stormed out yet. Brunu was undoubtedly having a whale of a time keeping her locked inside.

"I'm the Camorran Don," I stated calmly, though my concern was definitely for Aurora. "You infiltrated *my* territory to kidnap Custanzu Valentini—an act that was not sanctioned by me or my council. You declared war on *me*. So I'd watch your fucking mouth if I were you, Messina."

Silence was his only retort.

"Yes, I know who you are. You need to ask yourselves what information you have on each other that'll make us take their lives first and not yours."

Hurried whispers were their initial response, then the jet shook slightly. But before I could even wonder what the hell was causing that, I heard the sound of fists smacking into flesh, heard the grunts and the groans of someone being beaten.

I took immediate advantage of the distraction.

Ducking through the opening, I rushed over to the other side where there was a curtain for the flight attendants to work behind.

Though I frowned at the sight of a fire extinguisher on one of the counters, a definite dent in the middle, I shoved the thought aside when I saw the corpses slumped there—I had my answer about where the pilot was.

He and the flight attendant had GSWs to the head.

Grimacing at the needless loss of life, I peered around the curtain to see what was going on.

Spying the men fighting in the small space, a brawl that was made even more awkward because of Puglisi Jr.'s corpse on the floor, I used their distraction to our advantage and beckoned a few foot soldiers on board.

Angling myself around the corner, I raised my gun then aimed and fired into the mass of humanity.

When someone yelped, I smirked upon realizing I'd gotten Messina Jr. in the ass.

The other foot soldiers were a better shot than I was because, in a matter of moments, each man on board had a bullet hole somewhere, and they were too busy moaning and whimpering like babies to give much of a fuck as Aurora's soldiers stormed the jet and began the process of 'forced' disembarkation.

Naturally, something had to go wrong.

Though they were patted down before they were dragged off the plane, the younger Messina managed to pull out a knife from only fuck knew where. The end result? One of ours got sliced.

On the way to the bathroom to free Stan from his bindings, I saw it go down and that instinct that I wished I didn't possess, that flight or fight response that always skewed toward fighting even though I was a goddamn lover, not a hater, had me dropping into a crouch, grabbing the blade with my bandaged hand, flicking it around, and thrusting it into Messina's shoulder.

As he screamed, I pulled it out, pressed it to his throat, and spat, "Are you concealing any other weapons?"

Messina's head wobbled from side to side as he blubbered. The knife's edge ran against his flesh, leaving a thin stream of blood behind.

"Are you okay?" I asked the guy who'd taken the blade to the arm as another soldier kicked Messina in the gut and hauled him off the plane like he was a sack of potatoes.

"Just a slice. I'll be fine."

"Make sure you get it looked at," I ordered.

Flushing, he nodded, more embarrassed at being taken unaware than hurting from the pain, I thought, so I let him go.

Finding two unconscious men toward the back of the jet, I called to the front, "There are two Vitales here. They're knocked out."

Stepping over them, I kicked both in the head for good measure, then I made it to a set of doors. One opened up onto a bedroom; there was another door in there as well which, I figured, led to a connecting bath.

To be on the safe side, I tried the second door first and hit paydirt— a trussed-up Stan, spitting fireworks from his eyes, was stuffed in the small washroom as promised.

Behind me, foot soldiers appeared and dragged the two Vitale cousins off the jet.

Ignoring them, I dropped into a squat in front of Stan. "We gotta stop meeting like this, bud." I tugged at the fabric they'd used to gag him and cut it with the knife I'd stolen from Messina. Careful not to injure him further, not when he already looked like he'd lost a fight with a meat grinder, I murmured, "Aurora's outside."

Stan's garbled retort became clearer when he spat out the gag. "What the hell is she doing here? I told her not to come."

I snorted. "I saw your video. *Para bellum*? That was practically a red carpet invitation for her. Anyway, she's safe."

"Stan!"

He scowled at me. "Yeah, she sounds really fucking safe to me."

Twisting back, I saw her rushing down the aisle and glowered at her. "I told you to stay in the limo."

She frowned. "The plane is clear."

"The plane could still be blown up, *soru*," Stan spat. "Would you fucking untie me, Hunter?"

Still glaring at Aurora, the promise of a punishment in my eyes for her disobedience, I watched as her head bowed before she tipped up her nose.

From sub to brat in less than sixty milliseconds.

If I wasn't worried, I'd have an erection.

Though my focus drifted to Stan as I cut through his bonds, I drawled, "How did they get the drop on you? Stop fucking wriggling, would you? You're making it take longer than it needs to!"

"I was boarding the damn jet and someone hit me over the head with only fuck knows what—"

I blinked. "In the flight attendant section, there's a fire extinguisher with a big dent in it."

"Only your skull would bend metal, Stan," Rory jeered.

"Don't start, Aurora. I'm pissed at you. What are you even doing here?"

"You told me to prepare for war so I did! What did you expect me to do? Go and get a manicure?"

"I don't know, but I didn't expect you to lay fucking siege to the jet. You could have blown our asses up!"

"Fuck. You. You and Luciu pulled exactly the same stunt when you overtook the Fieri compound. Don't make it sound like we reinvented the wheel today."

Before they could start arguing in earnest, I changed the subject, "You look like you went ten rounds with Mohammed Ali."

Stan pulled a face. "I remember being hit from behind and then falling face-first onto the jet stairs. The next thing I know, I'm waking up and am being guarded by two meatheads.

"When you're hogtied, your skull and feet are pretty much the only weapons you have so most of my injuries are from fighting," he admitted with a huff.

As I finally cut through the last bindings, he hissed as he wriggled his arms around then, when I hauled him onto his feet, cautiously took a step forward.

When he raised a hand to his head, I knew he must have a concussion. Not even Stan's head could take repeated blows without some adverse effects—carbs didn't exactly cushion the cranium.

"Where's your guard?" Aurora asked.

"I traveled alone," Stan said gruffly.

"Hypocrite," she hissed, clearly remembering yesterday's argument over pancakes about guards and how *she* shouldn't be traveling without one.

Wanting off the jet, I hauled his arm over my shoulder and carefully walked us down the aisle. The argument naturally died when Stan groaned with every staggering step we took.

Aurora scuttled beside one of the seats to get out of our way, and as I passed her, I warned her, "I'll deal with you later."

She scowled at me but broke it off with a sniff as we moved past.

Though she was following us, I noticed her snag something and saw that she'd grabbed a hold of the back of Stan's shirt as we descended the steps. It was a wise move because, halfway down, he started to wobble and she helped me stabilize him.

Caruso, driving one of the SUVs, rolled up beside us when we were on the ground. A foot soldier opened the door, and I boosted Stan into the passenger seat.

Caruso glanced at Aurora for directions, and she intoned, "Take him home. I'll arrange for the doctor to come and see him."

"Do you want me to stay with him?" Caruso asked.

"No. I'll get *Matri* to visit."

"Don't get her involved!" Stan whined.

"You're bound to have a concussion," I pointed out, trying not to laugh as he went from Capo to the baby of the family in the blink of an eye. "You'll need someone to make sure you wake up every hour."

"Traitor," he muttered under his breath, making me hide a smile.

As the car drove off, I saw Aurora was on her phone, and letting sleeping dogs lie for the moment as she called Lauren, I watched as her men cleared the area, dragging bodies onto tarps before picking up the bullet casings that had flown wild around the space.

Not for the first time, I wondered what they'd used this warehouse for.

"It belonged to Messina."

Assuming Lauren had been contacted, I turned to Aurora and read the mutiny in her expression. Ignoring it, I queried, "You looked into it?"

"I asked Martínez when you were dealing with Vitale," was her stiff reply.

"I saw from the paper trail that it belonged to Messina, but what did they use it for?"

"Importing car parts. The place got shut down when the Feds realized they were trafficking drugs from Mexico."

Though she'd fed my curiosity, her snippy tone had me fighting the need to grab her by the hair, haul her into me, and tongue fuck that rebellion away.

Instead of doing what I really wanted to do, I asked, "Where are the Vitales?"

"I had Brunu arrange for them and the unconscious guards to be taken away in one of our SUVs."

"Thank you." She waved a dismissive hand at that. "Who'll handle the bodies?"

"We have a clean-up crew incoming. ETA forty-five minutes." Her scrunched-up face was my initial warning before: "You didn't have to get involved with what went down here.

"You can't punish me for getting out of the car when the situation was under control after you waded into an active shooting."

"I told you to remain in the car, Aurora. That means you remain in the fucking car until I let you out."

"I'm not a dog."

"I never said you were. Messina Jr. sliced one of your men up at the very last minute. That could have been you."

"It could have been you too. I wasn't in danger. You waded into an active shooting!" she repeated, shrieking the words at me as her fear exploded.

"And you can't have missed Brunu's reaction when he saw me get involved. I can't always sit back—"

"But I can?"

"Yeah, you fucking can. I won't put myself in unnecessary danger. Most of the men were dealt with, and—"

"And nothing. You could have gotten your ass shot and I'd have been a widow before you had the chance to make me your fucking wife!"

Those last words were wailed, but we were fortunate that there was so much activity going down in the warehouse, no one overheard our argument.

Moving into her space, I loomed over her, watching her head fall back as her short ass struggled to maintain eye contact with me standing so close to her.

I didn't push it, because her soldiers could see and I had no desire to diminish her position in front of them, but it didn't stop me from whispering, "I'll make a wife out of you later, but don't you forget, Aurora De Laurentiis, that I know what kind of woman you are.

"A man who stays on the sidelines isn't the man for you—"

"Fuck. You. You put yourself in danger for me?"

"No. I did it because I had to. Men, and women, in our position are not allowed to show weakness—"

"And you don't think I'd have looked weak if I'd just stayed in the damn car?"

My jaw tightened. "My grandfather already taught me that I have to rule through strength or they'll tear me apart. *You* don't have to rule that way. I do.

"Wetwork doesn't come easy to me, but I know when to step in and when to step out."

She looked as if steam could blow through her ears and nose. "You're not a violent person, Hunter."

"That's where you're wrong, Aurora. I'm violent when I need to be. I don't seek out fights, but if they land on my doorstep, I have no problem in finishing what someone else starts." I grabbed her hand. "I won't drag you toward the limo because your foot soldiers could witness that, but I expect you to walk with me back to our ride, understood?"

Her jaw worked, but she gave me a brusque nod.

Together, we moved amid the blood trail where men had been mowed down then driven over and forged a path toward the exterior of the warehouse where we wouldn't be stepping in evidence.

"Where do you want to head to?" I questioned, my voice like silk so she could read how furious I was with her.

"*Russu.* That's where we'll be questioning Puglisi and the Messinas."

I graced her with a single nod as a reply.

When we were outside, the onset of twilight upon us, I guided her over to the limo. As she slipped into the backseat once I'd opened the door, I moved to sit beside her.

"Brunu, you failed to keep Aurora in the car."

It was a testament to the hard-won fight that Brunu's response was more of a whine than anything else: "Boss, how the hell could I keep her in here if she didn't want to stay?"

"I'll deal with you later," I snapped. "Put the radio on loud." I hit the button that raised the privacy screen then patted my knee as I cast Aurora a glance once the glass locked into place. "Time to prove that I keep my promises, *wife*. Jeans and panties around your ankles. Now."

7

AURORA

THREE DAYS GRACE - PAIN

THE PROBLEM WITH BEING A MASOCHIST?

Punishments weren't exactly punishments.

Hunter's threat that he kept his promises wasn't something for me to worry over.

To get pissed about? Well, that was something else entirely.

His acting like a he-man when I'd walked onto the plane after every single one of our enemies was under our control was a bit ridiculous, *but*, there was the rub.

Was I going to turn down a spanking?

I knew that I should.

Brunu and the driver, even over the radio and with the partition up, could potentially hear us. The windows were tinted. Enough that in the light of day, the cab was dark. But…

Nothing.

The temptation was there.

The words had been uttered.

The promise of pain was something I never wanted to avoid, and I was too hopped up on adrenaline to turn this into an argument.

I remained unmoving for no more than thirty seconds before I was straightening on the seat, unfastening my fly, and shucking my jeans down my legs. I took my panties with me at the same time and kept them hooked around my ankles as he'd specified.

My heart raced just as my pussy started throbbing in time to that heavy beat.

He'd promised me a punishment.

Not pleasure.

Fortunately for me, the two went hand in hand…

I shuffled over to his side and cupped the ball of his knee as I started to maneuver myself over his lap.

I knew this was inappropriate. The timing was all wrong, but God help me, I couldn't say no.

I just couldn't.

Shooting him a look, I whispered, "No one can see. Or hear."

His expression softened just a fraction. "I'll make sure no one can hear. The privacy screen is up and the windows are tinted."

I swallowed though he'd thrown my own logic back at me.

"Trust me, Aurora. I would never expose you like that. Not just because of last night, but ever. You're mine. No one gets to see you but me."

Seeing as he put it like that…

When I was positioned over his knee, the softness of my stomach resting on his thighs, I placed one hand on the floor to prop me up, and the other, I set on the cushion to his side. My chin rested against the cushion too.

As I settled down, he did something with his phone and the speakers started playing a song that barely registered with me.

When he was done, the music was loud enough that he couldn't talk quietly, and it was rock with a heavy bass that'd probably cover our misdeeds.

"How's your hip? Is it hurting in this position?"

It took me a minute to figure out what he was talking about. *Oh.* The bruises from the seat belt. God, that felt like it had happened a lifetime ago, not this morning.

"No. It doesn't hurt at all."

I didn't tell him that I didn't mind the pain. If he thought about it rationally, he probably knew that anyway.

One of his hands cupped the back of my thighs, making me jerk in response when his calluses dragged against the tender skin.

That felt so goddamn good.

So simple, yet so effective.

His hands were massive, and I decided that, once the day was over and we were able to go back to my place, I was going to study them and draw them. I'd never noticed how big they were before, and that was something I needed to fix.

I yelped when he pinched me. Tiny pinches on my sit spot, hard enough to sting. Sharp enough to make me squirm. His nails scraped down the sensitive flesh, then back up again, from ass to knee, before rotating his wrist so the inner muscles received the same treatment.

When he pinched one of my pussy lips, I jerked in surprise, especially when he dug the tips in deep. A few tugs on my labia rings had my abdomen rolling against him.

Every tug, every pinch, every time he scraped my flesh, I sucked in a sharp breath and released it.

Maybe it was my position because it was so long since I'd found myself over someone's lap, but it was harder than I'd like to inhale fully so, very quickly, I seemed out of breath.

He continued in the same vein. Small touches when I wanted a grand display. I wanted to scream, but instead, he was making me squirm with discomfort.

My face turned bright red when he started pinching my ass again, the soft flesh conceding to the harsh nip of his fingers. I knew I'd have bruises tomorrow, ones that matched those he'd given me yesterday—I shuddered at the thought.

Then, just when I started to roll with the pinches, his hand moved toward the fleshier part of my inner thigh where the scabs still lingered from my previous bout of self-punishment.

At first, I tensed, wondering what he was doing, then he angled my leg, splaying me apart.

Just as I released a shaky breath, he started—the flat of his hand straight to my pussy.

Over.

And over.

And over again.

At first, it was just a nice dull thud. I settled into that too. Humming with the sizzle that it sent showering through my clit.

Then, as he lifted his hand, he captured my clit ring between his fingers and dragged it up and back.

The first time he did that, I shrieked because it felt as if my skin, i.e. my clit, was what had to give.

Then, just when sweat beaded on my temples, he let go.

And he carried on.

Slap.

Drag.

Slap.

Drag.

It hurt.

Fuck, it hurt so good.

And the edge of panic was better than getting high on coke.

I'd started off—not a surprise—wet. Now, I could feel my slickness leaking onto his pants. It gave every spank a distinct noise until Hunter could have started up his own percussion band with how he played my cunt.

With the fingers of his other hand, he spread my pussy lips wide apart and this time, the spanks sometimes landed on my channel. Again, he'd catch one of my labia rings, pulling it back until my toes were scuttling against the limo's carpet to try to gain purchase.

Just as the panic set in, he let go.

Fuck, he was relentless.

It was strange. Not what I expected. But I wasn't disappointed. If anything, I was wary.

This wasn't predictable.

He had me on edge.

His finger traced a circle around my gate, and I shuddered as he murmured, "You like scaring me, Aurora?"

I tensed because the answer to that question could lead to a worse punishment than this—if he brought out those dried garbanzo beans and made me kneel on them, I'd probably fucking sob. (I bet he carried a small jar around just to torment me.)

"No, I don't like scaring you, Hunter," I said quickly.

"Then why did you put yourself in harm's way?"

Short answer, I hadn't.

He was being overprotective.

I got it.

I hadn't been ecstatic when he'd waded into the firefight when it wasn't over.

His grandfather had just died.

My jaw worked. "I'll try not to do it again."

I didn't expect it, that was why I choked on a scream as he slapped my ass. Hard. Heavy. It stung and left behind an ache.

Breathing heavily, I was surprised when his tie appeared in front of my face.

"Open your mouth."

Once I obeyed, he pressed the silk between my teeth and shoved it deep. Relying on my nose for air now made the odd breathlessness I was experiencing even worse.

"If you scream, I will cover your mouth to contain the sound. Do you understand?"

My eyes flared but I bobbed my head.

"Words, Aurora."

"I understandth," I garbled through the silk.

"You'll count and thank me for every spank."

"Yethh, Huntah," I rattled off, half certain he couldn't make out what I was saying anyway.

When the second spank came, I quickly gasped, "Twooo. Thwankk woo, Huntah." And then, he spanked the same spot for the third time. I shivered but doled out the words he required.

Another spank, and another, and another. Each one hard, each one on the same cheek. Just above my sit spot.

The burn started quickly because his fingers had a wide span. The spank licked toward my inner thigh, catching the outer edge of my labia.

The heat was already immense, and by the time I'd counted to fifteen, I was wriggling on his lap, half-surprised that he let me, half-relieved that he allowed me to move at all.

Over and over again, he hit that same fucking cheek and I sobbed my thanks as he did so.

When we reached twenty-five, the pain that juddered through my system was excruciating. It was beautiful. It hurt so fucking good but I couldn't stop myself from screaming.

Just like he'd promised, he covered my mouth for an extra sound barrier.

He maintained that coverage with one hand as he carried on spanking me with the other.

Oh, God, he carried on.

Over and fucking over, and as I struggled with air, I had to keep on counting and thanking him.

Some oxygen strained through the silk and I *could* breathe through my nose, but with every spank, and with every inhalation, it was as if the world narrowed down to just him and me.

It was beautiful.

Paradise.

No war, no enemies. No foot soldiers in need of orders, no council to boss us around.

It boiled down to his hand on my skin, my soul under his control.

As difficult as it was to breathe, it was as if each hit of air was pure oxygen when it did seep into my lungs.

When we reached forty, I slumped into him, and that was when he stopped covering my mouth. That was when the fingers that had been punishing that same goddamn butt cheek moved to my cunt.

I was ashamed of how wet I was. I knew, point blank, he'd have a wet spot down the side of his leg from how much I'd creamed myself, but I didn't have time to care.

His fingers were there, right there, exactly where I needed them.

Two slipped into my pussy, one curled down, and he didn't stop until he'd found that miracle spot he'd uncovered yesterday.

Already exhausted, the pressure had me jolting like I'd been zapped with a cattle prod. I yowled as I bolted upright on his lap when the sudden disconcerting urge to pee rammed into me as if I'd downed four gallons of water in one sitting.

"No, no, no, no," I whined through the silk as he carried on, rubbing that area and grinding the heel of his palm into my clit.

The noises he made with his fingers were obscene. I was already so fucking wet. Jesus—

I sobbed through the orgasm.

It hurt.

It hurt so bad and so good all at the same time.

It was painful. It was ecstasy.

It whittled me down to my core as he dragged the pleasure out, constantly bombarding that same spot.

Then, he fought dirty.

His one hand tormented my pussy, the other rubbed my sore ass cheek.

I rocked against him, yelping when his fingernails dug into the flesh that had to be glowing from his attentions. "Stay still, Aurora. It wouldn't be a punishment if you enjoyed it, would it?"

His words had me clenching my eyes closed as I came again.

That soft squirt had me turning my face into the cushion and shoving my forehead into it. I pressed down so much that I almost tumbled off his lap, but he kept me in place. Those fucking fingers tormented me time and time again until, by the fourth orgasm, a soft keening noise was all I was capable of.

I didn't even realize I was making it.

And that was when he stopped.

His fingers pulled away from my pussy. The others drew the silk necktie from between my lips.

At first, I thought he'd move me off his lap, but he didn't. He just petted me. One hand on my hair, the other on my ass, sometimes stroking over the outer folds of my pussy.

I relaxed into the position, especially when he massaged the back of my neck.

A couple moments later, he shuffled me around, gently turning me so that my sore ass cheek didn't have as much pressure on it and so that I was leaning against him. I pushed my face into his throat and sucked in breaths that were scented with him.

"When I tell you to stay in the car, what will you do in the future?"

My lips against his Adam's apple, I mumbled, "I'll stay in the car."

"Good girl."

I stilled against him, finally realizing what had felt so weird during that punishment—he hadn't spoken. No praise. No 'Well done's. No nothing.

Marcus had done that. He'd never said anything. Had just expected me to take, to accept, to endure. And I had. I'd probably have been okay with it if Hunter hadn't always been so vocal as D.

Before I could whisper how I'd missed hearing that, he rumbled, "You were such a good girl. So perfect for me, Aurora. Taking every spank and never missing a number. Always thanking me. So polite. You took each hit so beautifully too. Such a good girl for me, accepting your punishment and earning my forgiveness so prettily."

I nuzzled into him, suddenly content, but…

"Hunter?" I whispered his name in his ear.

He hummed.

"Can I take my jeans off?"

He didn't answer, just slipped his hand down my legs, unhooked my Vans from my feet, then removed my jeans. A couple minutes later, my jacket, top, and bra were also on the floor of the limo.

When I was bare, I wriggled on his lap, and knowing this was after a scene, and knowing he wouldn't stop me, I straddled him.

The movement made my sore butt ache, but I carried on regardless. He knew what I was doing, too, because he shuffled so he wasn't leaning against the backrest fully, meaning that I could slip my legs alongside his.

Once I was comfortable, I settled into him again, wrapping myself around him like a living stuffie.

His hand went back to my hair, and he stroked me there until I was half asleep and slumped in his hold.

It was… perfect.

So perfect.

I never wanted it to end, but, of course, that wasn't how life worked.

8

HUNTER

IT WENT without saying that I wasn't the kind of guy who enjoyed listening to people get tortured—it wasn't my thing. Not unless it involved Aurora and a pair of cuffs…

Regardless, I could tell 'regular' torture wasn't Aurora's thing either (thankfully), but she dealt with it better than I did.

She had Caruso and Bruno doing most of the heavy lifting, but she didn't shy away from being in the rooms as her enemies were interrogated.

Amid the screams as both men went from using their one-time fellow council members as punching bags to slipping cigar butts into the myriad bullet wounds each fucker was laced with, she peppered them with questions, tearing their stories apart, making sure she had the right of it.

Torture wasn't a turn-on.

Watching her work *was*.

My erection and the uncomfortable circumstances in which it 'arose' had me shuffling out of the back rooms and into the main office where I dealt with some work of my own.

It was there, at the desk she used, that Martínez called my private line.

How he'd gotten my number, I had no idea, and I wasn't pleased about it either.

"I heard the day ended successfully."

"If you mean the *Cosa Nostra's* enemies have been dealt with, then yes, you're correct."

"And the Camorra's foes have slinked back to L.A. with a coffin, no?"

Martínez was accent-less, though I knew for a fact he'd been raised in the Bronx. He'd managed to eradicate it better than J-Lo had.

"Some enemies should never have been foes in the first place," was my only retort.

"Interesting. Your grandfather wouldn't agree."

"My grandfather's dead." I almost choked on the words.

Fuck, how was Bert dead?

"I heard."

I dug my fingers into my eyes where that raw pain settled again. It was like I wanted to cry but couldn't.

"I thought you might have," I muttered wearily. "For a man who's supposedly retired, you keep yourself well-informed."

Not that that came as a surprise after what Aurora had told me about him. Safe streets necessitated a high level of intel to encourage a 'proactive style' of leadership.

"You said it yourself—I'm retired," Martínez stated, unaware of my musings. "What else am I supposed to do with my days?"

"Aurora Valentini told me your wife was pregnant the last time you met with her brother."

"Is that a threat?"

I huffed out a laugh. "No. It's merely a statement."

He grunted.

"Why *are* you willing to get involved with us? You're out of this life."

I'd Googled the man. He'd once been seated on the board of directors for the New York City Health and Hospitals Corporation, for fuck's sake. He'd donated only God knew how much to a new wing in the state library that was named after 'Juana Lopez Martínez' who, I assumed, was his mother. Now, he'd established himself in Colorado, so returning to this world seemed nonsensical to me.

"My niece is a good girl, De Laurentiis. But society is full of people who'll see something good and who want to tarnish that. Use it for their own gain.

"The moment Aurora Valentini contacted me and scheduled flight plans from Vegas, I knew what was happening.

"You were holding out your hand and offering me the annihilation of the fucker who stole *mi sobrina* away from her family. Was I supposed to stay out of this? I think not."

Apparently, Martínez and Aurora subscribed to the same 'word of the day' dictionary.

Both liked annihilating people.

Now that I thought about it, that was one of Bert's favorite words too.

I really knew how to surround myself with the same kind of person.

Aloud, I mused, "I guess the corruption of a niece makes a man think about revenge."

Martínez clucked his tongue. "I didn't anticipate Ms. Valentini reaching out, but when she did, I was looking forward to this afternoon's meeting.

"I'm annoyed that it had to be rescheduled until things have settled down in New York."

"She was acting on my behalf. We don't need to meet in person."

"You misunderstand. I prefer to meet." I heard the sound of fingers drumming against a table. "I'm in the city."

"You are eager, aren't you?"

"I love my family," he said flatly. "I will do anything for them."

I scrubbed my chin. "Have you heard of a club called *Russu*?"

"Of course." He was quiet for a second. "Why was a Valentini acting on your behalf?"

The *Cosa Nostra* might not have made her role official, but I had no compunction in doing so. "She's my Consigliere."

"That's not true. Paulu Ribaldi is the Camorran Consigliere."

"He is for the moment."

"Interesting. You believe he's unreliable?"

After Aurora's take on yesterday's council meeting, I had adjusted my opinion. That had me admitting, "I believe he's a rat. Whether he's peddling information to the cops or the *Reyes Dorados,* I don't know. Valentini—" I shouldn't choke on the name, but I did. *De Laurentiis.* My Neanderthal brain wanted to label her as mine. "—hasn't been sworn in yet but that's only because we had this situation to handle here."

He hummed. "Would you be willing to meet?"

"Naturally."

"On *Cosa Nostra* territory?"

"If you managed to find out my phone number, I'm sure you managed to uncover the fact that I was pretty much raised with the Valentinis in Sicily. But if it makes you uneasy, I can head to The Victoria."

There was a slight pause, then I heard a soft laugh. "I'm not scared to enter Valentini territory, but my wife has her concerns."

My brows lifted at the admission. "Aren't wives always concerned?"

"They are," Martínez confirmed. "However, Eva is also my self-professed bodyguard."

"Interesting."

"What is?"

I heard the stirrings of annoyance in his tone and immediately understood its source. I had no need to appease him with a lie, not when I believed every word I said: "Few men in our world understand a woman's power and strengths."

"Those few are very intelligent," he agreed. "If Aurora Valentini is also your Consigliere, then I think we're in the same boat, are we not?"

I slouched back in my seat. "My grandfather adopted a similar stance in his later years."

"I've heard about his shadow council."

"That's a miracle, seeing as his primary council doesn't know about it."

Martínez chuckled. "I make it my mission to understand the politics of the factions around me."

Around him?

He lived in Aspen.

The Camorra didn't have dealings in the Mountain States.

Apparently, he was as paranoid as his wife. Not surprising, I supposed. Getting out of the life didn't break the habit of being in it and of trying to protect everyone who mattered to you.

"How do you feel about a meeting in the morning?"

"At The Victoria?"

"Yes."

"Sure. Ten AM?"

"Perfect. See you then."

Once he'd cut the call, I rocked in my seat as I stared at the screens on the desk. I grimaced when I saw Caruso do something that had a puddle forming under Puglisi's right foot.

With his back to me, I didn't know Caruso's game but Aurora, spotting said puddle, shuffled a few feet away, a moue of distaste on her lips before her mouth started moving a mile a minute.

Staring at my wife wouldn't reduce my workload, so I switched focus to the night's to-do list.

Of the pictures that had been sent to me, I now knew the photographer's location for each of them.

The intimate ones, taken in my bedroom, pissed me off the most as the guy had been a couple floors below us, a feat that was only possible because of the Gallinaro's L-shape.

The *Reyes'* audacity didn't come as a surprise. What did was the potential murder scene they'd come across.

Reilly Green.

I was glad I'd killed Aurora's rapist—but I didn't feel like serving time for it.

The pictures spanned the last couple months but most of them were of people coming and going into my house because I hadn't been able to leave the damn place thanks to Dead To Me and her death threats.

But that the *Reyes* had followed me from the house to the Gallinaro was a concern.

They hadn't, however, included pictures of my grandfather's men bringing Green in or disposing of his corpse. Instead, they'd included those pictures of Aurora and me in my bedroom in Suite No. 1.

Why?

To threaten her?

Were they holding out on the pictures of Green in the hope of springing a surprise on me?

Or did they not see anything at all and showing us having sex was about as much as they'd uncovered?

I didn't exactly lead an exciting life…

The thought had me rubbing my eyes because, apparently, that had changed.

In the span of seventy-two hours, my world had gotten a whole helluva lot more interesting. Yet for the gains I'd made with Rory, I'd also lost Bert.

Life had a habit of giving with one hand and taking away with the other, and I didn't think there was a more shining example of that shitty reality.

I knew I was borrowing time with my grief. I could feel it welling into being. Lodging in my chest and obstructing the airflow to my lungs. So I was relieved when the door opened, bringing with it the reason for the sudden surge of excitement in my life and a delicious distraction from Bert's passing: my wife.

I had to give the old bastard kudos—he'd achieved more in one meeting than I had in fifteen fucking years.

Utterly unaware of my thoughts, she strolled in, a scowl on her brow, as she stormed over to the desk, pulled out the bottom drawer, and withdrew what looked to be a very old, very vintage Castarede Armagnac.

When she swilled it straight from the bottle, I chided, "That's sacrilegious."

"Could be moonshine for all I care. Goddammit, they never tell you how bad torture stinks."

My lips twitched. "You could always spray Febreze around the place."

"Stop making me laugh," she complained, a chuckle dying on her lips. "You're going to be bad for my street cred."

Unable to stop myself (and unwilling too), I slipped my arm around her waist. My hand settled right in the curve there—that nook was made for my hold.

With bated breath, I waited for her to shrug away from me, but she didn't.

Instead, she wiggled the bottle in my face. "Want some?"

I grinned. "Nah."

She stuck her tongue in her cheek. "Prefer some milk?"

"I would actually."

Though she rolled her eyes, she moved closer to me. "Can I sit?"

"Sure."

I made to stand, but she put her hand on my shoulder.

"I meant on you," she drawled, another laugh in her voice.

"Oh." My grin turned sheepish, but it swiftly morphed as she settled on my lap, twisting around so that she was facing me, her legs dangling on either side of mine again.

I loved it.

Her pussy was on top of my dick and her tits were smashed up against my chest, and those were the initial advantages of this position.

More than that, I loved how we were eye to eye with one another. I loved that I could put my hands on her hips and that I could rock back in my seat and she'd rock with me.

It was perfect.

And we were only sitting with one another.

In her office.

In a goddamn nightclub that was so fucking loud, I could hear the music through the sound-proofed windows.

With a tired sigh, she propped the bottle up and took another sip.

"You fixing to get drunk?"

Rory shook her head then pulled back slightly so she could put the lid on the bottle. "That's enough. I hate the stuff. Luc started storing it there for some ungodly reason."

"Maybe because you drink it and he thinks you like it?" was my dry retort.

She blinked at me. "Huh."

"You three, I swear. You don't have a clue what you mean to one another."

"When it matters, we know."

"Like today."

"Like today," she confirmed. "Any news from *Matri*?"

"She's still emailing instead of texting," I said with a wry smile.

"Can't get her to quit that habit."

I hummed. "She said he's got a major concussion."

"Shit."

"That's what happens when you use your head as a weapon." Though I was concerned, I was also amused. It was such a Stan thing to do.

"We need all the brain cells he's got if he wants to go ahead with this stupid plan of his."

"What stupid plan?"

"He's using the funds from Red, and eventually Agatha, to start his own..." She hitched a shoulder. "I guess it's an unofficial research lab."

"Legit?"

"Legit." She twisted back and put the bottle on the desk. As she did, I smoothed one hand up her waist—just because I could. When she turned to face me again, I half-expected her to comment on my touching her, but she didn't. Instead, she grumbled, "I'm sore."

I arched a brow. "Did you get involved with the interrogation? Or do you mean from the almost-collision?"

"It wasn't an almost collision. It was a controlled stop. What I meant was...I'm *sore*." A few bobs of her brows and waggles of her head informed me her pussy was out of action.

"Does ibuprofen work on a pussy that's been banged to within an inch of its life?"

Her gaze turned studious. "I imagine it does but if it doesn't, maybe that's what Stan should really be working on. Not the female version of Viagra."

Chuckling, I gently rubbed her side. "How's your ass?"

"Hurts more than my pussy. And trust me, that's aching like a son of a bitch."

I definitely wasn't mistaking the satisfied purr in her voice.

Aurora was *not* complaining.

My fingers trailed down from her waist, along her jeans' fly, and down her crotch.

Where I could reach, I ghosted the tips over her pussy.

It wasn't to tease, more like a stamp of ownership.

I petted her because I could.

Because she wanted me.

Because I'd never expected to have the right to do that.

Because she was mine.

"Martínez is in New York. He called. Wants to meet with me tomorrow at ten at The Victoria."

She squirmed against me. "I'm coming."

"Thought you were sore," I teased, laughing when she growled under her breath. "Don't be stealing my moves."

"So, you *are* aware of what you're doing with all the grunting and snarling."

"Huh?"

Her tongue peeped out at the corner. "Never mind."

Frowning, I retorted, "No, not 'never mind.'"

"You growl. A lot. It's… I wasn't sure if you knew…"

"If I knew what?"

"That you did it. If it was intentional. I always thought 'D' was a Primal."

I eyed her air quotes askance. "What the hell's one of those?"

"Someone like you." Her lips curled at the corners. "Primal is… you know… *primitive.*"

"That's not very informative."

"The clue's in the title!"

Wow. That took me back.

Sheepishly, I reached up and rubbed my jaw. "Last time I said that," I mused, "was when I was talking to someone about soft Doms and pleasure Doms."

Her eyes widened, and the faintest tension appeared in her shoulders. So slight, another person would have missed it. Not me. I saw everything related to her.

"Who did you talk about that kind of stuff with?"

"A mentor."

"A mentor," she repeated, tone bland.

"I had to learn from somewhere. I'd like you to meet her actually. Sara was very helpful in making me realize I wasn't as vanilla as ice cream." Her lips pursed, but before she could say a word, utter even a sound, I reached up and pressed my finger to her lips. "Hush. You can't get jealous when I've spent the last couple decades wanting you without you wanting me back."

Her shoulders sagged. "Sorry," she mumbled around my finger.

"It's fine." And it was. I'd dealt with her jealousy as Sunny before, but it was ridiculous for her to be feeling that way when she was the only woman I'd ever wanted. "I like that you're possessive but you don't need to be jealous. Everything I've ever wanted is sitting on my knees right this moment." I held her gaze. "Don't forget that. Every woman was a stepping stone to me reaching this point, just like every guy was the same for you."

"You were jealous of my exes," she pointed out.

"Sara wasn't an ex. Plus, I didn't let you see my jealousy," I retorted. "I let you see that I thought you had shit taste in men, and to be fair, I was fucking right."

Her nose crinkled. "I can't argue with that."

"No, you can't." I chuckled at her pout then reached up and dragged that sulky bottom lip down with my thumb. "Are you needed here, or can we go crash? It's been a hell of a day."

"We can go. Both Juniors are dead. The Seniors are still alive."

"Why?"

She shrugged. "For Stan. They were the masterminds behind this entire fuck fest. He deserves to dole out their punishment."

I sniffed. "Oh."

"A Don with a moral compass," she jeered, then she made my heart sing by leaning into me and nuzzling her nose down the side of my cheek before she pressed a kiss to the corner of my mouth.

Right in the corner.

Obeying my rules, but still kissing me.

I loved that she was sneaky.

I slipped my arms around her waist, hauling her tighter into me.

Once our foreheads were touching, she whispered, "How are you doing?"

There was no point in lying. "I'm sad, but I'm happy I'm with you too."

"Bert wanted that for you."

Nodding, I rocked back in the chair. "I know he did. I just wish—"

She kissed the corner of my mouth again. "It's weird, isn't it? How he planned this to happen a couple days after he was sent up instead of, I don't know, just electing to die at home?"

Her words had me frowning but all I said was, "I don't doubt some plot will come out of the woodwork. Nothing surprises me with Bert, and I'm sad that he won't be able to surprise me again."

A soft smile graced her lips. "It's funny how you two talk about each other."

"What do you mean?"

"I mean he made it out like you were a rebel and that you got into mischief that he cleaned up behind your back. But, you're saying the exact same thing about him."

I had to grin. "We kept each other on the straight and narrow."

"I'll bet, especially if that straight and narrow was plenty crooked," she teased, her forehead settling against mine again. "Would you like to see my apartment? Or do you want to stay at The Victoria so we don't have to maneuver the traffic in the morning?"

"I want to see your apartment *and* stay at The Victoria."

"It's nearly midnight, so you need to pick your poison because I'm as exhausted as you are."

"The Victoria. But tomorrow, I'll have to go back to Vegas."

A shaky breath escaped her. "I know."

With those two words and that shaky sigh, she showed me it sucked as much for her as it did for me.

Dissatisfaction never tasted so sweet.

"Come on. Let's go and get some rest." I kissed her because I wanted to and sank into it because I needed to.

It was, and I knew it forever would be, like coming home.

9

AURORA

I HATED LETTING people into my apartment when I wasn't there, but Giovi showed up at our suite at the hotel at eight AM with three different power suits for me to choose from.

As I checked them out, I realized I was grateful that I was going to be meeting with Martínez in one of these outfits and not dressed down as had been my intention yesterday, but they presented a problem.

Yesterday was an aberration.

Yesterday, I'd needed my wits about me.

Today, I did as well, but I really liked where Hunter and I had been going, and with Hunter being an inexperienced Dom—IRL—I knew I needed to be extra clear about my position on certain aspects of our dynamic.

That meant I had a choice to make.

In the grand scheme of things, it wasn't a difficult decision.

I grabbed the three garment bags out of Giovi's hands, removed the clothes, then laid them on the bed. I tightened the sash of my robe around me and headed back into the suite, leaving Hunter to find them when he finished up in the bathroom.

From Giovi's surprised expression, I knew he'd expected me to return dressed, but picking my outfit was something Hunter had told me he wanted to do from now on, and I liked feeling those ties that bound me to him.

They might be small, but they were insidious, and I loved the hell out of that.

Plus, Giovi was gay. He had no interest in me whether I was dressed or in a robe and, as my assistant (our next conversation would likely determine whether he wished to continue in that role), I wasn't always going to be gussied up as the big, bad Consigliere around him.

On the coffee table, there was a tray of coffee and pastries. I sat down on the sofa then poured myself and Giovi a cup.

Taking a seat in one of the armchairs, he accepted a steaming hot espresso and a cheese Danish when I offered him one.

"Go on then. Hit me with the updates."

"Alexandra Garcia Eugenio declined to accept your personal donation for her election campaign. She returned the check and everything."

"Damn. I didn't even expect anything for it."

"I told you she wouldn't accept it," he said, sounding amused. "She's reached her position with a squeaky clean reputation and as DA, you were squeaky clean, but she's a justice system reformer and you definitely were not *that*."

"I'll have to donate through a PAC, I think. I didn't want to get involved but she's the underdog in that fight. She needs all the donations she can get when Charles Ingram is a bloodsucker for Big Pharma." I took a sip of coffee. "What else?"

"Klara's going to be picked up by her family tomorrow."

"We're covering the funeral?"

"I told her family that we would."

Thinking about Klara's throat and how she'd been strangled, I murmured, "Have the morgue insist that it needs to be a closed casket."

"Why?"

"Because we don't want the family to see the bruising around her throat, Giovi. Jesus Christ, isn't it obvious? The pathologist falsified the autopsy results, *se*?"

He nodded, but from his grimace, I knew he didn't approve.

With a weary sigh, I said, "Giovi, are we going to have a problem here?"

"I don't know what you mean," was his stiff retort.

I couldn't stop myself from mocking him: "'I don't know what you mean.' You know exactly what I mean.

"I get it—you were friends with her. I'm sorry that she died. I'm sorry that it was a waste of a life. I'm sorry that it happened how it did. What more do you want from me?"

"Her family should know—"

"Why should they? What good would it do for them to know she was murdered by a john? I'm going to assume she didn't advertise her career to them?"

"No..."

His unease had me snapping, "See? You were giving me attitude and you didn't even think it through." Fucking men. "I like you, Giovi. You're relatively smart." Sometimes. "You do as I ask, and you're a good worker. But if you don't stop giving me these sulky looks and the shitty attitude, then I'll throw you back to Luc. *Capisci?*"

"I understand," he said woodenly.

"Good. You should also understand that I get that you're grieving." I shot him a pointed look. "So, let that be the last thing we say on the matter, okay?"

He took a large bite of his Danish. "Okay."

I heaved another sigh when he still sounded about as grim as the Reaper.

Rubbing my eyes, I asked, "What else has happened since I've been gone?"

"Aside from the kidnapping and attempted overthrow of the Five Families?"

My lips almost curved as I peered over at Hunter when he stepped into the room. Giovi's clear lack of interest in me in a robe was made all the more obvious when his eyes flared as he took in Hunter. In. All. His. *Majesty.*

I didn't even have it in me to bitch at my assistant because Hunter was finer than the Nutella pancakes I'd had yesterday after no carbs for a month.

He had a towel wrapped around his waist, covering the good stuff, but his abs, his arms, and his shoulders were totally on show.

It was enough to reduce an intelligent woman like myself to a bag of hormones.

Giovi too, apparently.

For a second, both of us just stared at him, watching as he moved toward the coffee table, poured a cup of coffee, and snagged himself a Danish before retreating to the bedroom after giving us a treat that was better than the freshly baked croissant I was going to eat for breakfast.

Giovi cleared his throat. "That's Hunter Lachlan?"

"It is," I confirmed, hiding my smile at his dazed expression with my coffee cup.

He cleared his throat again. "You're intimate?"

"Nothing gets past you, Giovi," I drawled, watching his cheeks flush with heat. "So, any other updates?"

"Aside from the fact that the Messinas and Puglisis were so outraged with your dictate on Red that they triggered a mutiny? No, right now, we're up to date."

"Good. Just so we're clear, if you run and tattletale to Luc again while he's on honeymoon, I'll definitely be giving you back to him."

"Are you going to tell him what happened here?"

"I'm his Consigliere, Giovi. Me telling him and you telling him are two separate matters."

"If Luciu asks me a question, I have to answer. Yesterday, Puglisi Jr. called him, and he wanted to know if it was true that you'd banned Red in our brothels. What was I supposed to do? Lie to him?"

"No," I conceded. "But in the future, just give me a heads-up if he asks something you know will cause shit down the line."

I'd checked my messages during yesterday's flight, and my dipshit assistant hadn't said a word about sharing the news of my banning of Red with Luc.

"Okay. I'm sorry about that. I guess I panicked."

Thoughtfully, I stared at him. "Why did you panic?"

"Being stuck between a rock and a hard place is never comfortable."

"Am I the rock or the hard place?"

He coughed. "Take your pick." His gaze drifted over to the bedroom door. "Is that everything?"

"For the moment."

"Do you need me to wait—"

"No. You can go and collect Stan from the compound. Bring him to *Russu*."

"Puglisi and Messina are barely hanging on. They're old men, Aurora."

"Stan won't have to overwork himself to deliver them to their maker, then, will he?" I retorted unsympathetically. "Good thing considering the state of him." As he got to his feet, something occurred to me. "Jeffreys and Granger were killed yesterday. Make sure their families receive compensation and the funerals are covered."

It wasn't enough, but it was something.

"Who are they?"

"The pilot and flight attendant."

Gaze thoughtful, he bowed his head. "Of course. I'll make those arrangements immediately."

"Thank you."

Finally, he headed out of the room and I watched him go, leaning back against the sofa as I finished up my croissant.

When Hunter appeared in the doorway, I blew a wolf whistle.

"A three-piece suit? How very old-school," I teased him as I got to my feet. I reached him quickly because he moved toward me at the same time.

Laying my hands on his lapels, I straightened up his tie then patted the single solitaire pin that kept it neatly tucked in place.

He surprised me by pressing a kiss to my mouth and following it up with a swipe of his tongue against my bottom lip. "That's what you get for remembering I wanted to pick out your clothes."

Heat filled me. "You won't have time to come to my place today. How will I know what to wear for the rest of the week?"

"Pick out three outfits every morning, send me the pictures, and I'll choose that way."

Though I was surprised he could be bothered, I shrugged. "Fine."

His lips quirked up as if he knew what I was thinking.

Thoughts, however, couldn't be punished. That smile said he knew that.

My answering one told him that loopholes could be found everywhere.

He tapped me on the ass. "Go and get ready so we can enjoy a coffee together before the meeting."

With that promise, I hustled and made it back to him in under ten minutes. Not bothering with makeup drastically reduced the time it took for me to get ready, so I mostly just blow-dried my hair to give it a bit of bounce.

I returned to the living room in a sharp black pantsuit that was tailored to my curves. Beneath the jacket, I wore a simple black camisole so the only splash of color was a pair of red heels that were my favorites. Giovi apparently had an eye for shoes if he noticed that I wore these often.

Studying Hunter who was staring out of the window, one arm raised against the glass as he peered onto the city, I strode over to him and settled at his side.

"Rachel said the next time the three of us are in New York, she wants to get together."

"I'd like that."

"I won't tell her you're here or she'll want to catch up today."

"Maybe next week? I think we should go to her though."

I thought about the last time I'd headed to West Orange. "Are you really ready to go to the Sinners' MC compound?"

He grinned. "Do you think I'm scared?"

"You should be. Rachel's got her own little niche there now. They call themselves the Posse. All the bikers' Old Ladies are insane. One of them, when she got pregnant, learned to vomit on command."

"Is that even possible?" he asked doubtfully.

"Rachel said so."

"Why would you even *want* to be able to vomit on command?"

I hid a laugh. "So that you can use it as a weapon."

His eyes rounded. "Jesus."

"Yeah." That one word said it all. "Plus, you know how Rach is, well, for lack of a better word, ladylike?" He answered with a wide-eyed nod. "I watched her get into an actual catfight with this bitch. It was fascinating. I've never seen her like that."

"Makes sense she'd be different around them. It's where she grew up."

"I guess." I shot him a quick grin. "I'll tell her next week then. She'll be happy. Fly into Newark if you want and I'll pick you up there. We could stay over? Rachel has plenty of room in that big house of hers."

"Hers and Rex's," he corrected, a gleam in his eye.

I turned to look down at Central Park in the distance. "Everything's changing, isn't it?"

"Is that such a bad thing?"

"No. But four days ago, I'd have said yes."

His chuckle warmed my heart, but what warmed it even more was when he slipped his arm around my waist and tugged me into his side.

I wasn't a tactile person by nature, but before *everything*, I'd always been more permissive with Hunter. It was a part of who he was. Much like with Stan and Luc.

I'd always thought it was ironic that of the four of us, the girl in the group was the least touchy-feely. Luc and Hunter were affectionate, but Stan was a teddy bear—he never could do anything half-assed.

For Hunter, though, I'd always 'permitted' his affectionate ways, never realizing that at some point in the future, I'd love that side of him. Because I, I could admit to myself, wasn't altogether comfortable with reaching out, it made it easier that he did it for me.

"Lauren emailed."

"What did she say?"

"That Stan told her we'd hooked up."

My mouth rounded. "I'll kill him."

"You just saved him," he remarked.

"Yeah, so that means he owes me." I gritted my teeth. "I don't believe that jackass! It's not like he can even blame it on pain meds if he has a concussion!"

"I think he was woozy. I'm not sure if he'll be up to your master plan of letting him end Messina and Puglisi. Amid outing us, he's got a crippling headache."

"They can suffer in the back rooms until he's ready."

"Is that practical?"

"It was impractical to plan an idiotic siege; if they could do that, they can deal with the aftermath. Anyway, you decided to ram a message home by branding an enemy. Stan has his ways too.

"Giovi is going to collect him now. If he can't make it, he can't make it. They can wait." Reaching up, I worried my bottom lip. "*Matri* will never let me hear the end of this now."

"The end of what?"

"'*He's such a good boy,*'" I said mockingly, in a low falsetto. "'*So kind and so compassionate. He'll make some lucky woman a wonderful husband one day.*'"

His low chuckle had me glowering at him. "*You're* the lucky woman, aren't you?"

"She doesn't know that though, does she? And we're not telling anyone for a while so that's no help." My gaze locked on his mouth.

How had I never noticed how fucking kissable it was before?

My tongue wanted *in* that slight line on the bottom one.

Someday, when he let me kiss him whenever I wanted, I was just going to explore those goddamn lips that were starting to drive me insane.

I must have stared longer than I thought I did because his head tilted to the side in question. "Something caught your eye?"

Twisting so I could lean against the glass, I agreed, "Something."

His curiosity was a tangible entity between us, and of course, my brother had to go and wreck things.

"*Luciu Valentini (brother) is calling.*"

Hunter blinked at Siri's intrusion. "You have him under his full name on your cell?"

"Better than having him down as 'Dipshit.'" I dug my cell out of my pocket and put it on speaker. "What do you want? Are you incapable of enjoying your honeymoon?"

"Are you fucking kidding me?" he shouted, loud enough that I was grateful I didn't have him in my ear. "What the fuck are you fucking playing at, Aurora? I go away for three fucking days and you—"

"For a supposedly learned man, you just overused the word 'fuck.'"

"Aurora," he snarled.

I put my brother on silent. "Your snarl is so much better."

Hunter snorted.

I untapped the 'mute' button. "What, Luciu? You do know that I am eminently capable of handling whatever these morons can throw at us, so what's the problem here? *Se*, I know you're a control freak, but I make you look relaxed."

"She has a point."

Luciu's indrawn breath was audible. "Hunter? Is that you?"

"Yup. Hey, Luc."

"What the fuck is going on?"

"My grandfather just died."

"What?! I— He— What?"

"In prison," I tacked on, enjoying discombobulating my twin.

Yes, I was a bitch.

Especially when he believed his own headlines far too much for my liking.

Italian Darcy, my ass.

"He— You—"

If the topic wasn't sad, I'd have smiled.

"Tell Hunter you're sorry for his loss, Luciu," was my prim retort.

"*Cristo*. Of course. I'm really sorry, Hunter."

"Thanks, Luc. I'm going to miss the old bastard," Hunter said gruffly.

"Time is the one thing we can't protect the people we love from."

"Poignant words," I mused.

"I'm feeling poignant right now. My wife's pregnant, my sister's lying to me, my brother won't answer my calls, one of my closest friends just lost his grandfather, and my mother, after I asked her what the hell was going on in the city, started talking about the likelihood of there being woodworm in the old Valentini crib!"

My lips twitched. "She wants you to enjoy your honeymoon."

"She thinks I'll enjoy myself by traipsing through the goddamn attics?"

I sniffed. "I'm sure Jennifer would have a whale of a time looking through the family antiques."

"Aurora," Luciu warned.

Hunter elbowed me gently in the side and shot me a pointed look.

Gaze darting from his, I glared at an innocent jogger in the park. "What? There is centuries' worth of family history in there. She's about to add to that, isn't she?"

"Oh."

Luc had been right on the money with my sass, so it wasn't like I could chide him for thinking badly of me.

"Anyway, I have work to do. Not all of us can vacation for two months."

"Don't start. You know I'm working here—"

My lips curved. "Then get on with it and stop bugging me."

"Aurora! Goddammit. I know something's going on. Puglisi called last night—"

"Tell him, Rory," Hunter said, his voice low despite having tapped the 'mute' button again. "He needs to know. *I'd* want to know."

"I'm giving him shit, but I really do want him to enjoy his honeymoon. I might hate Jennifer, but Luciu loves her for some reason. Plus, at some point, I'm going to want a two-month break for our honeymoon as well."

I divulged that to the universe, even though nerves had me wondering what his response would be.

His grin was electric; inadvertently, he gave me exactly what I needed. "I think that can be arranged."

"Did you put me on fucking mute?"

Smirking at Hunter, ignoring Luc for a moment, I just reveled in the sparks that collided at our prolonged stare. Then, I heaved a sigh when Luc threatened to cut the line and call Giovi.

Untapping the 'mute' button, I snapped, "Do you want him to lighten my workload, or do you want to use him as a spy, Luc?"

"Is it any wonder I need a fucking spy when you keep me in the dark? You should have told me about banning Red, Aurora."

"If you'd made that decision, would you have told me first?"

"Of course. We're a team."

"Oh."

"Oh?"

"You surprised her," Hunter tacked on. "She's doing a great impression of a goldfish."

"Why wouldn't you think I'd tell you that? We're supposed to discuss things as a unit. It's us against the world, isn't it?"

Guilt hit me like a ton of bricks.

Had I been acting as if the weight of the *Cosa Nostra* was solely on my shoulders?

While Luc had diversified his schedule so that he could spend more time with his fiancée, his workload hadn't grown lighter over the last couple months.

We all worked long hours, and it was unfair of me to think otherwise.

"I'm sorry, Luc." I knew I sounded wooden, but I couldn't help it. I—

Jesus, it didn't happen often but I was speechless.

"Hunter, you'll have to tell me if she's having a stroke. My sister rarely apologizes."

"Don't push your luck, Luc. I'd say she's having a 'come to Jesus' moment."

"You don't trust me." They weren't the words I'd meant to say, but they came out anyway.

Luc sighed. "I *do* trust you. But this past year, you've been worse than usual. So fucking secretive, playing your cards close to your chest. Maneuvering without sharing the whys with Stan or me."

He wasn't wrong. But that didn't make him right, either.

"I had a lot to prove."

"Not to us." His answer was immediate.

"I did to the council. You know they gave me a rough time. I had to establish myself. Do you think that's easy? I have to be twice as smart, as calculating, and as lethal as you, Luc, simply because I'm a woman. I've had to establish the means to enable that.

"You shouldn't punish me by not trusting me. Not when I've been pivotal to us holding the power we do. Not when everything I do is for this family.

"Hell, I've gone above and beyond for us, and I've shown you that time and time again."

"She has a point, Luciu."

"*Grazii,* Hunter. What would I do without your insights?" Luc groused. "I know she has a point."

"You threatening to keep coming back here only makes things worse." I knew, this time, I sounded hurt. "You're the one who's spent the past eight or so months endangering everything we strove to build.

"I understand she's your wife and the future mother of your child, but you've cleaned away bodies that are tied to allies, you've triggered fights with gangs that could lead to turf wars—"

"Like you haven't been as reckless," Luciu argued. "You had me arrested, Aurora!"

"It was about time people knew who you were in the city and it was a means of proving an inherent lack of favoritism without getting you sent up."

"You could have warned me."

"It had to be a surprise. It wasn't like I intended for you to go to jail," I derided.

"You pretended to be my wife to scare off Jennifer."

I sniffed. "Whether you persist in believing she's Snow White or not, she's said it herself that she's a gold digger. I was right to try to scare her away. I was protecting *YOU.* Like you wouldn't do the same with me in similar circumstances?"

At that, a loaded silence fell between us.

Until Hunter mused, "It's enough to make me proud. You two actually talking instead of arguing all the damn time."

I shot him a dour look.

"Shut up, Hunter." Luc blew out a breath as if he were seeking patience. "Since when are you with my sister at this time in the morning anyway? Hell, since when are you with her period?"

"If you have a question, ask it, Luc. Don't trawl for information."

"I'm sure *Matri* would love—"

"Don't you dare," I spat. "This is between Hunter and me. Stan's already shared too much, so don't ruin this for me, Luciu. I'll never forgive you if you do."

His silence was, I thought, telling. I half-expected for him to rib me, but he didn't. Instead, he asked, "Can we both agree that we haven't approached this year in the best way, Rory?"

Relief hit me that he was willing to change the subject. That meant he wouldn't say anything to *Matri* about Hunter and me hanging out more. That was the last thing I needed—her getting suspicious or, *worse*, hopeful. Well-intended or not, her invasions of privacy could aggravate me like nothing else.

Whatever Stan had shared, I'd downplay because of his concussion until we were ready to be outed. If Luc got in on this, she'd never believe me.

Hunter nudged me again, making me realize I'd gone quiet. I thought about what Luc had said then mumbled, "We can agree on that, yes."

"We did things we regret."

"I didn—" At Hunter's second nudge, I grumbled, "We did things we regret."

Luc clucked his tongue. "If you want me to stay here, then we need to communicate more."

"Sometimes, communicating isn't possible. Action is needed."

"I know. But that doesn't mean we can't discuss a situation after the fact. You've had days to come to me about banning Red, Aurora, and you didn't say dick."

My shoulders hunched until Hunter tucked me against him. He

surprised me by tugging on the lapels of my jacket so that he could nuzzle his face against my neck. As he kissed the bruise on my shoulder from yesterday's incident in the car, I told my brother, "In the future, I'll keep you informed."

"I'll stop being reckless and won't threaten to return to New York before my honeymoon is over."

"Good," I ground out.

"So… update me."

I cast a look at the watch and, unfortunately for me, there *was* enough time to update him before our meeting with Martínez.

Grimacing, I began…

10

HUNTER

IT INTRIGUED ME THAT, after she shared the events of the last twenty-four hours with Luc, she didn't say anything about her visit with my grandfather, her new role in the Camorra, the *Reyes*, or the upcoming meeting with Martínez.

I'd half-expected her to share the fact that we were married now, but after listening to her concise summary of the attempted mutiny by the Five Families' council, I recognized that she'd compartmentalized recent events.

With her dual roles in the past, her ease in doing so wasn't surprising. Impressive, yes, surprising, no.

As we walked toward the elevator, our destination the meeting with Martínez, Brunu appeared in the hallway as if he'd been peering through the peephole of the door to his hotel room, lying in wait for us.

He appeared less ebullient than usual. That was probably because yesterday evening, I'd still been pissed with him for not keeping Aurora out of the line of fire, and I'd shown my displeasure by making him stand outside the office door in *Russu* for most of the evening.

While he'd proven that he didn't mind the position of sentinel, it was a menial job for a man of his standing.

"Morning, boss." He blinked at Aurora, evidently unsure about how to label her.

"Aurora," she said wryly at his hesitation. "You're Brunu, and I'm Aurora."

Brunu graced her with a grateful grin that flashed his gold teeth. "Morning, Aurora."

"Good morning, Brunu."

I cut my Capo a look. "Anything I need to know before we head into the meeting?"

"I had Adrianu, Matteo, and Luca check out the locations where you said the photographer was positioned and correlated them with the dates and times on the pictures—we got ourselves a name."

"Just one?"

"The same guy was booked into each room at the time according to the date stamps."

I pursed my lips. "He's in our custody?"

"Soon. They're hunting him down."

"If he's following you around, maybe he followed you to New York," Aurora pointed out.

"What's the guy's name? After the meeting with Martínez, I'll check recent passenger lists on flight logs."

"Ernesto Albarez."

I dipped my chin. "Good work."

That added some bounce to his step. "I arranged with the management for us to have our own suite on the floor below. I told them to have reception keep an eye out for our man and to let him know which room we're using. They don't want us having this kind of conversation in a public area, anyway."

"Good thinking," Aurora said approvingly.

We boarded the elevator, and fifteen seconds later, we were on the floor below, being guided by Brunu to the suite in question.

Upon entering, Brunu set off, peering around corners, looking in closets, even going so far as to check under the bed. For a man who could only be described as beefy, he was flexible as fuck.

When he was done, his face was a bit red, but he told me, "All clear, boss."

I took a moment to check out the area. Smaller than the suite we'd been using last night, it was, nevertheless, large enough for a table to have been brought in here with several chairs without impacting on the space and making it feel claustrophobic.

Aurora moved over to one end of the table, peered around it, then moved over to the other side. She stared around the room some more then declared, "You should sit here." She patted the chair at the head, the one in front of the window.

"Why?" It was easy enough to figure out for myself, but she had a skewed logic that was always intriguing.

"The sun will be in this room soon and it will be at your back and in his eyes."

See? Skewed.

She wanted me to sit there not because I'd be showing Martínez my back upon his entering the room if I took the other seat, but because of the position of the sun.

Fuck, I'd missed her deductive reasoning.

"This is a friendly meeting," I pointed out. "We want him to do us a favor."

"You don't let him know that. This is a mutual offering. He'll eradicate those fuckers for you; you'll let him own a slice of L.A.—"

"That he might not want," I interrupted.

"Perhaps he won't, but he'll want to get his niece back. *That* is your leverage, Hunter. Don't let him think he's in a position of power.

"If you're unsure, let me do the talking; you know I want what's best for everyone here."

Anyone else, that would have gotten my back up, but Aurora's strategies were like Bert's, and it was best to butt out. Still, I appreciated the deferential tone. Not because I needed it, but because Brunu was watching us with as much interest as if Sampras and Agassi were playing the US Open in front of him.

Though I shot him a warning look, to her, I merely said, "I'll let you lead the discussions."

"Fine. How do we know this place isn't bugged?"

"The Victoria doesn't work that way!" Brunu sounded so scandalized that it was almost humorous. "There's an honor system at play."

Before Aurora could reply—she looked unimpressed by his assertion—a knock sounded at the door.

"Answer that, Brunu," Aurora ordered.

Brunu, still huffing, did as bade. "Who's there?"

"Martínez and Kingston here for a meeting with De Laurentiis and Valentini."

It was a woman's voice: abrupt, arrogant, *authoritative.*

I already knew Aurora was either going to hate Eva Kingston *or* she was going to have a girl crush on someone who had as much attitude as she did.

My Capo warily opened the door, peered through the gap, then tugged it wider. "Who was the captain of the 14th Precinct seven years ago?"

Though I frowned, Kingston ground out, "Captain Lewis Mankiewicz, and what an asswipe he was too."

I could see Brunu's gold incisors gleaming from over here. "Kingston, how you doing?"

"I'm well. You, Brunu? Still as bent as the Brooklyn Bridge?"

"You didn't get me to cop to any of those charges. Innocent until proven guilty…" he finished slyly.

Kingston grunted. "We both know you did it. I just don't know *how* you did—"

"Pleasant times, I'm sure," a smooth baritone drawled. "Can we actually enter the suite, or do you intend for us to conduct business out in the hallway?"

Brunu stepped back with a debonair wave of his arm, allowing the two strangers into the room.

"You know Eva Kingston?"

My 'Why the hell didn't you tell me earlier?' went unspoken.

Brunu shrugged. "She arrested me for the Charles St. heist. We ain't best friends, boss."

"The Charles St. heist?" Aurora mused out loud. "That was a

Camorra job? Thirty million in gold bullion gone like that, right?" She snapped her fingers.

"It wasn't anything, Aurora," Brunu demurred. "I was an innocent man."

Kingston made a scoffing noise, but Martínez, a man as well-dressed as myself in a tailored suit that screamed Savile Row, placed a hand on her arm.

They made a study in contrasts.

Where Aurora embraced her femininity and, together, we looked smart, Kingston looked like a bodyguard. The meager differences were that her suit was cut to her shape, not boxy, and the fabric was expensive. Unlike Aurora, who was elegant and dressed to impress in a pantsuit that screamed designer chic, Kingston didn't give a fuck.

I liked her already.

I'd bet my left nut that she was a secret gamer. She probably fangirled over *Fortnite*.

My lips curved as I strode forward, hand outstretched to take Martínez's.

He stared at it, then me, and clasped his in mine. "It's nice to put a face to the name, De Laurentiis."

"Same goes, Martínez." I turned to Brunu. "Let me make the introductions. This is Brunu Borlesconi, my Capo. Aurora Valentini is my Consigliere."

If the news shocked Brunu, he didn't show it. Knowing Bert, he'd have let Brunu in on his plans before his final appearance in court.

For a man who trusted few people, Brunu had held a strong position in my grandfather's life.

To Aurora and me, Martínez stated, "I'm pleased to meet all of you. This is my wife, Eva Kingston. Excuse her manners. She's part feral."

Kingston just smirked at that.

"You brought no other men with you?" Brunu asked.

"We saw no need. This is a friendly chat, isn't it? We both want to help each other out."

That he showed his hand so easily, when, after Aurora's warning, I'd been sure he'd be close-mouthed, took me aback.

Then, deciding that I didn't want Aurora to hold my fucking hand throughout this, I mused, "I'm surprised Torres is still alive. I'm not sure I'd allow a man to live if he'd kidnapped my underage niece."

Martínez's smile was more of a grimace than anything else. "She claims to love him."

Kingston snorted her opinion on *that*.

"Love is like a cucumber. It starts off sweet and ends up bitter."

Brunu snickered at Aurora's declaration, and I hid a smile.

"I didn't mean to be rude by speaking Sicilian," she apologized. "It's just a saying from our homeland."

Martínez arched a brow as he folded his arms across his chest. "And it means?" At her explanation, he huffed out a laugh. "That sounds about right. My niece isn't only underage, she's naive."

"Teresa is a fool."

Martínez shot his wife a look. "Be kind."

"Be kind? She ran off with some two-bit moron who's in self-destruct mode. She could have married the President of Mexico with the connections you and Carlos have. Instead, she ties us to a war."

"She's not as naive as you think, and you do none of us any favors by underestimating her."

Kingston shot a look at Aurora. It was almost uncanny when both of them, simultaneously, grouched, "Men."

"Whatever she is, she's currently fucking that two-bit moron, and I don't relish the idea of it. I've had people watching the place where she's living. It's unsafe."

Knowing the *Reyes* as I did after listening to Bert bitch about them for the entirety of the gang's existence, I understood where he was coming from.

He shoved his hands in his jacket pockets. "I'm not interested in starting a new branch of *Los Lobos Rojos* in L.A. I want you to understand that." He directed the words to both Aurora and me. "But that doesn't mean I won't take it if it means bringing my family home."

"Will you keep it?"

That'd be a massive blow to Aurora's plans if he didn't want to.

Martínez shrugged but merely said, "It's bound to be more interesting than Aspen."

While the rest of her face remained expressionless, Kingston's lips twitched.

"If you've had eyes on Torres's place, you'll know it's not exactly millionaire's row," I commented.

"I'm aware that it's a fixer-upper."

"Fixer-upper?" I pshawed. "It's in one of the deadliest neighborhoods in the city."

"Kingston will whip it into shape, and once I establish loyalty and links, business will resume and the area will prosper," Martínez said easily, then something leached into his eyes. Something that revealed the *laissez-faire* attitude was but one facet of the man's nature. "The territory, once I take it, will be mine."

Before I could answer, Aurora stepped in. "It bows to Camorran dominion."

Kingston narrowed her eyes. "Meaning?"

"Meaning that we have no desire to govern the land, but you answer to us if we come calling."

"In what situation would you come calling?" Martínez queried.

"We rarely do. *But,* for example, the territory rubs up against another piece of land that we've, shall we call it, sublet."

"The Vitales run the neighboring territory," Martínez stated, letting me know he'd more than just had 'eyes' on Torres's main residence. He'd clearly done extensive research on the gang and its enemies and allies.

I cast a look at Aurora, wondering what she made of Martínez's easy admission.

"They do," Brunu concurred, "but they get into stupid fights and we wade in and break them apart before it brings the LAPD down on everyone's heads."

"That won't be an issue when we're in charge," Kingston dismissed.

Their verbiage was absolute. Definite. It was clear they didn't have a doubt in their minds that they'd take over the *Reyes* and own their asses.

It made me wonder if Aurora reaching out to them worked in their favor. Had they been intending to lay waste to the *Reyes* without consulting the Camorra?

Studying the couple, I could easily imagine that being the case, and our wading into the fray had merely given them approval to something they'd intended to do all along…

Deciding to test the waters, I inquired, "How do you plan on containing the situation?"

Martínez tilted his head slightly, his gaze glancing over me before it seemed to pin me in place.

I just mirrored the move, unintimidated by him.

My wife was a ball-busting shark. I was friends with Luc and Stan, was the grandson of Bert, and, in my own right, had as much, if not more, power than Martínez.

At that moment, I was the Don.

He was nothing but the ties he had to a gang on the East Coast and a cartel in Mexico, ties he was trying to bury.

He might have come here with a proposal in mind, one that my sanction would facilitate, but this was down to me.

If their plan didn't go through me, I had the right to end them. Nothing went down on the West Coast without my approval.

I didn't know it, but my shoulders straightened just a touch, and a blankness overset my expression.

Later, Aurora would tell me that my eyes turned cold and calm, totally unlike the Hunter she was used to.

That was, I supposed, because I *was* unlike the Hunter she'd known.

I had to be.

"Guerrilla tactics at first," Martínez eventually said, recognizing that I wasn't about to bow down to his stare.

"Meaning?"

"Dirty meth. The *Reyes* have problems with their source and it's the leadership's favorite drug."

"What if your niece takes the drug?"

"She would never—" Martínez started to snarl, for the first time, his composure breaking.

Kingston placed a hand on her husband's shoulder and, in a tone that was completely unlike her dictatorial one, drawled something in Spanish. She didn't glower at me, just said, "Teresa *is* a good girl. I think she's a fool, but she's good too. Far too trusting. You weren't wrong to ask the question, but my husband is highly concerned about her, as you can see.

"Family means everything to him."

"Not to both of you?" Aurora queried, hitching her hip so that she was leaning against the table.

Kingston's mouth tautened. "Martínez is my family, so yes."

She tipped up her chin. "If there's anything I understand, it's family loyalty. The poisoned meth isn't guaranteed to work and, in the process, you could wipe out a lot of innocents."

"The *Reyes'* personal meth is harvested in one particular lab in Boyle Heights," Kingston said calmly. "It's unlikely that the product will affect anyone other than *Reyes'* leadership."

"You want to eradicate the whole gang?"

Martínez growled under his breath. "He stole *mi sobrina*. She's a fucking child and he's a goddamn grown-ass man. I want to eradicate the fuckers who backed up that decision and to make matters worse, I know they're using her to get to *Las Alphas*—"

At the mention of the Mexican cartel, Aurora, Brunu, and I shared uneasy looks.

Kingston hummed something under her breath and surprised the hell out of me by pushing her forehead against Martínez's. Whatever she was saying, her Spanish so quiet it was barely a whisper, it had a calming effect on her husband.

I guessed, without particularly meaning to, that I'd found Martínez's Achilles' heel.

But I could respect that.

Wasn't Aurora my weakness?

Wasn't that how it should be?

He had no means of knowing that *that* was the reason I began to trust him.

When he'd calmed down, Kingston grabbed his hand and moved aside, leaving Martínez to grind out, "Most of the *Reyes* are kids. I've no desire to hurt them. They're just pawns in a game they don't understand. A game that's much bigger than they realize, especially if they're talking business with *Las Alphas*."

We shared a glance, and he further cemented my trust in him. We had, it seemed, similar management styles.

"How is she being used to get to *Las Alphas*?" Brunu piped up. "Is she being whored out?"

"Brunu," Aurora hissed.

"What?" he retorted. "I'm concerned for the girl!"

"Is that what's happening, Martínez? Are they using her in that way?" Aurora asked, quieter, *kinder* than usual.

"No. *Las Alphas* and the Sonora Cartel, Teresa's father's cartel, are enemies." Kingston shot a measured glance at Aurora as Martínez pushed away from her and strolled over to the table where there were several bottles of water. Kingston watched him as he opened one, but to Aurora, she explained, "As much as Teresa thinks Torres loves her, enough for her to run away from home, there's not a doubt in any of our minds that *she's* the reason why *Las Alphas* are suddenly interested in the *Reyes*. So the keyword to whether or not she's being whored out is *yet*."

Any irritation I might have felt at being managed by this pair was phased out entirely. I didn't need to consult with Aurora to know that she'd be on board with this. I just said, "Take out the leaders of the *Reyes*. You can have them all apart from one piece of shit who's *mine*. Do with them what you will.

"And, in the aftermath, accept Camorran dominion over the territory. We're not interested in your patch; it's yours to do with as you will so long as your business doesn't conflict with ours and you maintain the peace with your neighbors so the authorities don't darken our doors." I thought about what Bert had told me so many times over the years. "The Camorra keeps the peace on the West Coast, Martínez.

"We keep the situation with the gangs from combusting in L.A., and we make sure that civilians don't get caught in the fray because if they do, that's when the LAPD and the Feds sweep in. Nobody wants that."

"You'd be our allies," Aurora tacked on smoothly. "Don't act as if you're our enemies and you won't need to worry about what Camorran dominion looks like."

I had no means of knowing which of my statements convinced him, or whether it was what Aurora had said, but Martínez placed his bottle down on the table, strode over to me, and held out his hand again. "Allies."

It was a statement.

I accepted his hand and shook it. "Allies."

11

AURORA

JAX JONES - I MISS YOU (WITH AU/RA)

A SINGLE KISS.

It wasn't enough.

His lips on mine.

His nose nestled in my cheek and mine in his.

The scent of him filled the space between us.

I wanted to crawl into him. I wanted to be a part of him.

I didn't want him to go.

But we were at the airfield and the jet was idling, waiting for him to leave the limo and to board.

The morning had passed so fast. Too fast. One minute we'd been finishing up with Martínez and Kingston, and the next, we were here.

He pulled back first, and how that stung, enough that I clenched my eyes closed to dispel the ridiculous surge of tears. He stroked a thumb over my cheek, letting his fingers drift through my hair as he cupped the back of my head.

"Look at me, Aurora." His tone sent sparks through my exhausted body.

I did as he asked.

"One week, that's all it is. I'll speak with you tonight, okay?"

I swallowed. "Yes, Hunter."

His eyes were somber, the gray overtaking the blue, silently letting me know that he was just as unhappy as I was about having to part.

The fifteen years I'd pushed between us suddenly felt like a lifetime. A wasted lifetime. It didn't matter that unique circumstances had brought us back together again; it was time that would never be returned to us.

"I'm going to miss you," I whispered.

He stared down at me, and the blue broke through the gray in his irises, reminding me of an overcast sky where the sun eventually peeped through the clouds.

"I'll miss you too." He reached between us and tugged on the pendant, silently reminding me of what it contained. "I'm on the other end of a phone."

"I guess I just thought you'd be leaving later tonight."

I hadn't expected us to head out of The Victoria and suddenly be on the goddamn road to the airfield.

He heaved a sigh. "It's probably for the best." My scowl must have conveyed how unimpressed I was with that statement. "What?" he teased. "I'd end up spending the night if I stayed any longer."

"And what about that sounds as if it's a bad idea?"

His grin was like quicksilver. Fast and beautiful *but* what I loved more than anything was how expressive it was. It was happiness and need and desire and want and affection all rolled into a single curve of his mouth.

Unable to stop myself, I reached up and traced my thumb over his bottom lip. "Can I taste this, please, Hunter?"

His eyes narrowed into slits, but he nodded. "Because you asked so nicely…"

Angling upward, I pressed my mouth onto his and I dove right into that kiss like he was the Great Barrier Reef and I was a seasoned pro at scuba diving.

I never wanted to come up for air because *these* bends would be a thousand times worse than anything oceanic pressure could ever do to me.

My arms slid around him to hold him close, hands clinging, nails digging into his shoulders. His fingers shaped my cheek before they cupped my nape and he held me against him there.

His touch was light; mine wasn't.

It was desperate.

Needy.

The whirlwind of emotions that was spiraling through me was disconcerting, but his gentle hold stopped me from flying away.

He grounded me.

It was interesting that he achieved that while we were kissing, because Hunter had always done that. I'd once likened myself to being the forest fire and he was the water that'd put out the flames…

In this, he remained true to form. Except, the flames weren't from my temper, and he didn't exactly extinguish the fire, more like he put it on hold for next week.

He was the one who pulled away. He was the one who dotted small kisses around my mouth, who pressed our foreheads together before he put a small amount of space between us.

My hands curled up, nails digging into my palms to stop myself from reaching for him. "Hunter?"

"What, moonlight?"

I bit my lip at the endearment. "I'm feeling weird."

"What kind of weird?" He straightened up, suddenly alert. "No self-punishments, Aurora—"

Scowling at him, I groused, "I didn't mean that."

But my body felt flushed because that ever-present need wasn't there.

My ass was *killing* me. Just sitting on it was sweet torture from how hard he'd paddled me with those goddamn hands of his. Then there was my pussy which had been fingered and fucked to within an inch of its life.

No, if anything, my body was sore and tired and deliciously aching.

"Oh. What kind of weird?" he queried, his tone calmer now that he knew I wasn't about to make a date with my vampire paddle. Like he knew where my mind had gone, he rumbled, "I'm not happy about not seeing your apartment. I wanted to throw some of your shit away."

"I won't use it. You told me not to."

His hand snapped out, his thumb sinking into the soft flesh of my chin. "You'll regret it if you *do* use anything without my permission, Aurora."

I shuddered at the warning, and my very sore cunt fluttered at the timbre.

God, what he could do with his voice alone was more powerful than a bottle of vodka in my bloodstream.

"I won't use it, and if I feel the need to, I'll tell you," I said calmly, not particularly wanting to piss him off before he left.

He grunted. "Good. Now, what are you thinking? Why is it weird?"

"I'm feeling…" I cleared my throat. "Clingy."

Hunter surprised me by giving me a goofy grin. "You are, huh?"

That grin was so dopey that I had to laugh.

Shoving my hand against his abs, I faux-grouched, "Hush, you."

He winked at me. "You can cling to me anytime you want. I'm not going anywhere, Aurora. I think the past fifteen years have proven that, haven't they?"

He was right. They had. They'd also proven that I was a fucking idiot.

"I don't want to freak you out," I admitted softly.

"You won't. I've waited years to be the one you feel safe with, Aurora. I can take you at your best, your worst, and anything in between." His words had me choking up. He knew it, too. "No tears. I'll see you tonight."

I nodded then uttered my promise, "Tonight."

HUNTER

FKA TWIGS - MEASURE OF A MAN

A FEW DAYS LATER

I CLIMBED out of the SUV and stared around the patch of land where the Vitale's very pleasant mini-mansion was situated.

Most of the council had advised against it, but I'd chosen to attend Vitale Sr.'s funeral when his son had extended an invitation to me.

Perhaps there was a potential Trojan horse situation about to go down, but I'd prefer to foster peace than the alternative.

The council hadn't crouched beside Vitale as his father bled out. They hadn't seen the grief in his eyes and hadn't extended a hand of friendship to him.

Maybe if I ended up in Cedar Sinai tonight, they could tell me, 'I told you so,' but I didn't think that would be happening.

Not for me, anyway…

Brunu drifted over to my side, eyes darting about our glowering audience, muttering, "If looks could kill—"

"You'd be dead, not me," I interrupted, amused when he grumbled nonsense under his breath. It was a mixture of Sicilian and English that made no sense, even to someone who spoke both languages. "You're the face of the Camorra to them, not Bert. Not me," I pointed out. "You're the one who brought Camorran edicts to their door."

"You trying to cheer me up or something, boss?"

I hid a grin, making sure my expression was appropriate for the circumstances.

Brunu, I was finding, could be surprisingly humorous when he was in a dour frame of mind.

Since our return, there hadn't been any cause for him to tip away from that dourness—Bert was dead and the investigation into his passing was moving as slowly as evolution.

Everyone on the council was in a mood, and so were our Stidda as we allayed our annoyances on them, and with the tensions in L.A. at an all-time high, it was small wonder that the general level of 'cheer' was low.

On my other side, Matteo appeared, bolstering me so that I was going in protected. I felt as if I were a dick and they were my condom. Matteo gave me the kind of vibes of a man who'd poke a hole in said prophylactic so my trust in him was dubious.

Seriously, what they thought could happen at a funeral that wasn't taking place in an episode of *Game of Thrones* was beyond me.

A family like the Vitales respected the dead. They honored and cherished them.

Plus, I'd already checked to make sure that the funeral hadn't been held earlier and had investigated when the church had been reserved and which priest too.

I wasn't an idiot—I knew to cross-reference things as well.

The mini-mansion was only mini by comparison to Bert's *palazzo*. Otherwise, it was a monster. All gleaming marble Doric columns which gave off a weird White House vibe considering who it belonged to. The original owner of said property was obviously overcompensating for something.

Unlike the *palazzo's* interior, which Bert had once confided to me had been modeled on a bordello he'd visited as a young man in Rome, it was all clean lines, plenty of blues and greens, lots of light, and references to boats.

In fact, it looked like it belonged on the page of an Instagram influencer who'd sailed for the US in the Olympics.

The entryway housed several off-shooting doors that'd lead to other rooms, but a grand staircase was the major focal point of the space.

A woman old enough to be Vitale Sr.'s wife was standing on the bottom step. My major take from her expression was one of stoicism.

Having lost her eldest son and now her husband, with the Camorra having had a hand in both deaths, I figured stoic was about right for her.

Her son, however, was standing at her side, just off the steps, and the moment he saw me, he rushed forward, hand outstretched. "Thank you for coming, Don."

The posturing was mortifying but I'd seen Bert do it too many times to be unaware of what I had to do.

Cringing internally, I let him take my hand and kiss my signet ring.

"I appreciate the invitation. How are people accepting your new role?"

His Adam's apple bobbed—he needed to learn how to hide that reaction. "My brother was next-in-line, but *Patri* taught me the same lessons because he was a younger son who had to lead the family when his older brother died.

"I-I don't think there'll be any challenges, not for a while anyway. And not overt." His unease suddenly faded. "If I wind up dead in the Porciúncula tonight, then you'll know I spoke bullshit when you see my face on the news."

The graveyard humor had my lips twitching, especially because my mind had gone there only a couple minutes before. "Let's see if we can't keep you alive for longer than tonight, hmm?"

A soft gasp made itself known to me, and I darted a glance at his mother who was suddenly as white as a sheet because of our conversation.

"*Mama*," Vitale murmured. "I was only joking. I'm sorry. It was in poor taste."

Her bottom lip trembled. "Excuse me, please?"

Without waiting for a reply, she twisted around and stormed up the stairs.

As Vitale watched her go, he sighed heavily. "I'll never understand love."

Brunu shot me a disbelieving glance. "What the fuck is going on?" he muttered under his breath.

I elbowed him in the side but, to Vitale, I asked, "Your parents had a love match?"

"No. It was an arranged marriage, but they grew to care for each other very deeply. By the time I was born anyway." He turned back to me. "My mother is one of the most gentle women you'll ever meet. My father was a fucking brute and a headcase.

"She should be glad he's dead. Instead, she's on more tranquilizers than an injured racehorse. It's a wonder she's standing." He pursed his lips at me. "You meant it when you said you'd help with the transition?"

I hadn't specifically said that but… "That's why I'm here."

He dipped his chin. "Come with me."

Brunu and Matteo tensed up immediately, but I didn't. I saw no suspicious signs, just proof that the Vitales had been a family forged on love. That was probably why Vitale had to act excessively aggressive in front of his men.

In this world, love was a weakness. One that enemies took advantage of and so-called allies used in their strategies to gain more power.

As we stepped into a drawing room, I glanced around, immediately on edge at what I found.

I figured this was a scene that might feature in Brunu's and Matteo's worst nightmares, but I forced myself to remain calm.

What was done was done, after all. Appearing anxious would be like getting a nosebleed in a tank of piranhas.

The space was full of foot soldiers. The women who'd attended the church service were either in another drawing room or they'd returned home—to a safe place.

Smart women.

I narrowed my eyes, calculating the likelihood of Vitale displaying a show of strength by butchering my men and me, but before I could come up with any odds, he moved toward an armchair. It was leather and old, very vintage with wingbacks, and didn't fit in this nautical-themed house at all. If anything, it was a throne fit for a librarian.

As he peered around the room, one of his hands settled on the wingback, and I ambled behind it, instinctively knowing that he wasn't offering me the seat and that, by not inviting me to sit down anywhere, he wanted me to stand with him.

Brunu's and Matteo's tension was so palpable that I could almost smell it, but I refused to lose my cool. My research into Vitale indicated an educated man, not a fool like his father.

"*Patri* should be sitting in this armchair today." The words had rumblings of agreement filtering from the men, and a couple angry looks were aimed at my small group. "My brother should be standing on his right side. Instead, I'm the only one remaining.

"Luckily for you, I'm a lot saner than either of them were. Plus, I'm the only one with a business degree from Yale.

"We're all aware of the fact that money has been tight recently. Product hasn't been flowing in as smoothly as it should because of the *Reyes Dorados*—" The flash of rage on every man's face was immediate. "—and our beef with the Camorra has meant that we're isolated in our feud with them." His mention of the Camorra didn't trigger the same expression of rage in the men, but they each glanced at me, eyeing me dubiously, with none of the anger of before. "My father died because he involved us in something that was none of our business.

"Each of us here knows that the Camorra is not interested in us unless we bring attention to ourselves. That was something my father, God bless his soul, frequently did.

"After my brother died, that exacerbated his ridiculous strife with a faction who have only ever left us alone unless our beef with the *Reyes* started appearing in the newspapers.

"We're New Yorkers by blood, and thanks to Camorran generosity, L.A. became our home after the Fieris took power, but this year, my father was invited back to the Five Families' council in New York. Because his judgment was questionable, he rejected the offer from the new Valentini Don, preferring instead to court mischief because Valentini wouldn't help us fight the Camorra." For a moment, Vitale shook his head. "He was stubborn, pigheaded, a fool, but he was my father. I loved him, yet I will not reign like him.

"Your money will increase, as will your security. None of your wives will have to stand beside a grave under my leadership. Your children will know their fathers. But more importantly than any of that, you'll be able to hold your head up high and be proud to be one of us.

"With my father at the head, that wasn't always possible. He involved us in a mutiny in New York. I advised against it. I explicitly told him that to join forces with others on the Five Families council in the way that he did was the height of idiocy, but, as always, he didn't listen." Mouth tight, he spat, "He never listened.

"The time for joining leagues with the Valentinis has gone, but the Camorra has extended a hand of friendship to us.

"Even in the face of my father's betrayal, of the potential war that could have brewed between the Camorra and the *Cosa Nostra* over our actions, even with my complicity, the new Don has seen fit to show us that we are not the rats the Camorra want to stomp on. We are men worthy of our land."

"And what about the *Reyes Dorados*?" someone hollered from the back.

It wasn't my place to speak, but I did so anyway: "They won't survive the year."

While the room had been quiet, it hadn't been silent as men rumbled their agreement or disagreement with whatever Vitale was saying at any given moment. At my declaration, however, a dead silence filtered through the space.

Vitale turned to me. "How do you know that? And why would you eradicate them?"

Someone called out, "Does that mean we're not safe?"

It was a valid question and I raised a hand to stem the tide of words. "The *Reyes Dorados* saw fit to challenge me. They're bringing war to L.A. with their new ties to *Las Alphas*—" The sudden tension in the air told me the Vitales had known about this development and were worried about it. "The Camorra reign over the West Coast. We keep the peace. We want our tithes and for that, we make sure that the Alphabets don't come down on all of us." I looked around the room, making sure to catch the eye of every man in here, and as I did, I stated firmly, calmly, *quietly,* "Upset the balance and *I* will right it."

13

———————————

TEXT CHAT

AURORA: *How did it go at the funeral?*

Hunter: *Well. I don't think Vitale will have many issues leading them. He spoke eloquently.*

Hunter: *I think after dealing with his father, they'll appreciate a man who knows what he's talking about even if he lacks the proper experience.*

Aurora: *He majored in business at Yale.*

Hunter: *I know. I didn't think you would. You've looked into him?*

Aurora: *Of course. I'm your Consigliere.*

Hunter: *I didn't forget lol. I just thought you might have been too busy.*

Aurora: *I make time for the things that matter.*

Hunter: *Speaking of, did you receive my picture?*

Aurora: *I did. Sorry, I didn't have a chance to reply until now. It's been busy. Messina almost died. I had to get a doctor in.*

Hunter: *Why not just let him die?*

Aurora: *Stan's still not ready to deal with him.*

Hunter: *He wants to?*

Aurora: *He says so.*

Hunter: *Seems inefficient to keep a man going only so you can end him.*

Aurora: *Vendettas aren't always practical, Hunter. Jeez.*

Hunter: *:P I thought you were imminently practical.*

Aurora: *I am. But yes, I saw your photo and I'll set out the clothes you picked for me this week when I'm home. It's remarkably freeing, actually—not having to worry about what to wear lol.*

Hunter: *It's a different kind of worry, isn't it? Now, you're worrying about pleasing me…*

Aurora: *Ugh. Don't say that.*

Hunter: *(˘ᴗ˘)ۯ̂ Where are you?*

Aurora: *In my office at Russu.*

Hunter: *Alone?*

Aurora: *Yes. Are you?*

Hunter: *No. I'm with Brunu and Adrianu. We're discussing the situation with the Reyes Dorados.*

Hunter: *I know you're wearing a skirt, so lift it and show me what's underneath.*

Aurora: *You also know I'm not wearing panties…*

Hunter: *The only appropriate answer is, 'Yes, Hunter,' and a photo.*

Aurora sends photo

Hunter: *Already so wet for me. Take a close-up.*

Aurora sends photo

Hunter: *I want you to slide a finger through your folds, and I want you to tell me what you taste like.*

Aurora: *A little salty. Mostly of soap, I guess. Can I touch my clit?*

Hunter: *How's your ass?*

Aurora: *Still bruised.*

Hunter: *Still sore?*

Aurora: *No.*

Hunter: *Hmm. I want you to rub your clit and I want you to tell me before you come.*

Three minutes later

Aurora: *Hunter, I'm close.*

Hunter: *Stop touching your clit.*

****Aurora sends photo****

Hunter: *Did I ask you to send me a photo?*

Aurora: *No, Hunter.*

Hunter: *Did you just want me to see how needy your pussy is? How wet it is for me?*

Aurora: *Yes, Hunter. Please, may I come?*

Hunter: *Please... You're getting politer, pet. This I like to see. How wet are you? Could you take my dick?*

Hunter: *Be honest, Aurora...*

Aurora: *No. I'm not wet enough for your dick.*

Hunter: *Then you can't come.*

Aurora: *Fuck.*

Hunter: *Tell me how you'd earn an orgasm from me if I were there.*

Aurora: *God, Hunter, I can't write this down!*

Hunter: *Why not? You could tell D, couldn't you?*

Aurora: *Yeah*

Aurora: *Damn.*

Hunter: *So tell me, Aurora. Tell ME how you'd earn an orgasm from me. Not D. ME.*

Aurora: *I'd ask you what a fantasy of yours is, and I'd fulfill it.*

Hunter: *Interesting technique. Is that your way of trying to get me to tell you what one of my fantasies is?*

Aurora: *Yes, Hunter.*

Hunter: *I'll tell you two. In return, when you come, you send me an audio file. I want to hear you moan my name, moonlight.*

Aurora: *You won't listen to it when Adrianu and Brunu are there, will you?*

Hunter: *For that, I shouldn't let you come at all. I sure as fuck shouldn't tell you one of my fantasies!*

Aurora: *I'm sorry, Hunter. I'm just nervous.*

Hunter: *That's understandable, Aurora. It makes sense for you to be nervous, but not around me. Do you think I want ANYONE to see your pleasure? It's mine.*

Hunter: *You think I'm not discussing with my men where the fuck that bastard photographer is right now because I want to scoop out his eyeballs for seeing you in that position?*

Hunter: *You. Are. Mine. Have you forgotten that already?*

Aurora: *No! No, Hunter, I swear I haven't. I swear.*

Hunter: *Who do you belong to?*

Aurora: *YOU.*

Aurora: *I'm sorry, Hunter. So sorry.*

Hunter: *You don't have to be. You just have to remember to whom you belong and what I'm willing to do for you.*

Aurora: *I won't forget again. I promise.*

Hunter: *You will, but I'll keep on reminding you. And punishing you for infractions. Is there a ruler nearby?*

Aurora: *There is?*

Hunter: *Tap your pussy thirteen times.*

Aurora: *Yes, Hunter.*

Hunter: *Don't you want to know why it's thirteen times?*

Aurora: *'You won't listen to it when Adrianu and Brunu are there, will you?' Thirteen words.*

Hunter: *Exactly.*

Aurora: *Do you want a picture afterward?*

Hunter: *Of course. And I want you to hit hard enough to make you howl, Aurora. I want a sound file of that, seeing as you're not allowed to orgasm now.*

Aurora: *Yes, D.*

Hunter: *Add an extra tap. I'm not D. Who am I?*

Aurora: *You're Hunter. I'm sorry... I'm getting confused.*

Hunter: *Hmm. Go on. Get on with your punishment. I'm waiting.*

Ten minutes later

****Aurora sends audio file****

Fifteen minutes later

Hunter: *Did that hurt, pet?*

Aurora: *It did, Hunter.*

Hunter: *Do you feel less confused?*

Aurora: *Yes, thank you.*

Hunter: *That was very smart of you to say sorry each time, Aurora. I like that word on your lips.*

Aurora: *I'm glad, Hunter.*

Hunter: *For that, because you pleased me, I'll tell you one of my fantasies.*

Aurora: *<3*

Hunter: *Does that mean you're excited?*

Aurora: *Yes. Very. Thank you, Hunter.*

Hunter: *One day, my dove, I want there to be ultimate trust between us. I want you to believe in me so deeply that when you're asleep, you'll let me touch you. I want to slide my dick across your lips and coat them in pre-cum so that when you wake up, the first thing you taste is my need for you.*

Hunter: *I want to slide my fingers between your legs as you sleep. I want to spread your thighs and rub my fingers over your clit before I eat you out. And I want you to wake up with my dick sliding into you.*

Aurora: *I didn't think you'd be into somnophilia.*

Hunter: *Are you disturbed that I am?*

Aurora: *No.*

Hunter: *Are you turned on?*

Aurora: *Yes, Hunter.*

Hunter: *Good.*

Aurora: *We're not there yet, though, are we?*

Hunter: *That's a very clever way of phrasing it lol. No, we're not. It'll take time, but we have plenty of that, don't we?*

Aurora: *Yes. Yes, we do.*

Aurora: *Thank you for sharing that with me, Hunter.*

Hunter: *My pleasure. I have to go. I have a call with a contact in Dubai.*

Aurora: *Dubai?*

Hunter: *Sheikh Hashim. Have you heard of him?*

Aurora: *Of course, but he was also discussed at your last council meeting. I didn't think he had dealings in the US.*

Hunter: *He doesn't. Only with the Camorra.*

Aurora: *Interesting.*

Aurora: *I spoke with Rachel, Hunter. She can't meet up with us this weekend. But next weekend, we can stay with her.*

Hunter: *Great. I'll switch the flight path.*

Aurora: *Awesome. TTYL <3*

Hunter: *TTYL. I want a voice message when you're about to get into bed.*

Aurora: *Okay. <3*

14

EMAIL CONVERSATIONS

From: 'Lauren Valentini': valentiniforever@email.com

Subject: Hunter

A little bird told me you've been seeing Hunter?

Is that why you won't answer your damn phone?

I'm thinking about visiting Jennifer and Luciu in Sicily. She doesn't have her mother around to help her, and Luc sounded really worried last night. I'm sure it's nothing, but I've had three of you so I know more than they do.

What do you think?

Love,

Matri

From: 'Aurora Fitzwilliam': r0ryfitz@gmail.com

Subject: Re: Hunter

Matri, little birds are *not* reliable sources of information. Especially if they're concussed.

I think that if you want to go, you should. But I don't want it to set you back with your drinking. I know returning there will be difficult for you.

Jennifer would probably appreciate your advice.

I love you, *Matri.*

Rory

From: 'Lauren Valentini'
Subject: Re: Hunter

If we all went together, then it could be a reunion of sorts.

What do you think?

Love you too xo

Matri

From: 'Aurora Fitzwilliam'
Subject: Re: Hunter

If I could visit, I would. It'd hurt too much just to visit for a couple days and that's all I'd be able to swing. It's always been my home, and I've always known that I'll never be able to live there again.

You have to accept that, sometimes, I know what's best for me, *Matri.*

As for Stan, I doubt it. He's barely leaving his lab as it is.
Love,
Rory

From: 'Lauren Valentini'
Subject: Re: Hunter

Does Hunter make you happy?
Matri

From: 'Aurora Fitzwilliam'
Subject: Re: Hunter

I don't want to talk about it.
Rory

From: 'Lauren Valentini'
Subject: Re: Hunter

I think I *will* go to Sicily. Could you help make the arrangements, please, darling?
xoxo

. . .

From: 'Aurora Fitzwilliam'
Subject: Re: Hunter

Leave it with me.
xo

15

AURORA

A FEW DAYS LATER

"IN THE INTEREST of this new sharing thing we have going on—"

Luc snorted in my ear. "You mean trust?"

"I trusted you before," I disregarded. Why was trust the subject on everyone's lips?

"That's debatable."

"It isn't. I always trusted you." When Giovi sniffed, I glowered at him then turned my face to the traffic. "*Anyway, Matri* is coming to visit."

"She is?"

"A surprise. I think she's more concerned about you not getting that Valentini crib than we realized." I pursed my lips. "Or, she's ripping off the Band-Aid and going home while her family is there."

Trust. Ugh.

Did I tell him about her alcohol dependency issues?

"*Cristo,* of course. She hasn't been back to Sicily in years."

I sighed. "Almost as long as me."

"It's good to be home," Luc admitted in my ear, and the deep contentment in his voice had the stirrings of envy rumbling to being inside me.

The craving for Sicily wasn't something that had died over the years.

I knew my country had its flaws, but it was a gem that few recognized. Those blessed to see its glitter were forever changed.

Ever since I'd seen that sketch *Matri* had sent into a magazine of Hunter, my siblings, and me around the kitchen table at our estate, ever since Luc had begun talking about his honeymoon, and ever since I'd learned Hunter was D, the cravings for home had grown stronger.

I missed it. More than I could easily verbalize.

"I'll bet." I'd meant to sound bored. Instead, I sounded wistful. "I just wanted to give you a heads-up. She's sworn Stan and me to secrecy but I'd want to know if she was about to photo bomb my honeymoon and figured you would too."

"I appreciate that, Aurora." He was silent a second. "It'll be good to have her here. I know she and Jen get along, and Jen's struggling right now."

I grimaced at his words. "Why?" There, that didn't sound at all forced, did it?

"She has high blood pressure."

The words had me straightening in my seat. "What are the doctors doing about it? Is the baby okay?"

"They're monitoring her."

"I'll arrange for her OB/GYN in the city to come and stay at the estate—"

"I have a resident doctor here—"

"They're not the best," I dismissed.

"Her OB/GYN will have other patients," he retorted. "She's popular—"

"As if that matters," I interrupted with a sniff. "I'm sure they need a vacation."

"It'll be a working vacation."

"One they're heavily compensated for. Leave it with me."

"If you're sure, *soru*…"

I knew from his tone that he was grateful. "You should have said something. I'd have dealt with it sooner."

"It's only recently become an issue."

"How is she doing?" I asked carefully.

"She sleeps a lot and she isn't hungry."

"I'll deal with the OB/GYN—" was my immediate reply until I paused to look at my watch. One AM. Even *I* knew that wasn't the best moment to handle this particular variety of business. "I'll manage the situation with the doctor later today. I'll have them on the same plane as *Matri*."

"If you want something done right, get Aurora on the case," Luc drawled in my ears, but as amused as he was, I knew he meant it and it felt good to be recognized. "I didn't realize how much I missed you until I went to Sicily, *soru*."

"You miss me?" I quipped. "We've spoken nearly every day this week, *frate*."

"I know, but I don't just mean *now*. I mean while you were DA and I was undercutting the *Famiglia* at every step. We've grown apart and that saddens me. We're not... We weren't supposed to have so much distance between us."

I allowed his words to percolate in my head. I knew my silence went on too long because he cleared his throat, undoubtedly embarrassed by sharing his feelings when I hadn't replied.

Before he could be dismissive of what he'd just told me, I murmured, "I think I've been putting distance between myself and everyone who matters to me. I think I've been doing it for a lot longer than anyone really knows. I-I think that it's time for that to change."

Luc sighed in my ear. "I'd like that, *soru*. I'd like for us to become confidantes again, like we used to be."

My free hand balled into a fist. The urge to share my secret with him, that Hunter was now my husband, was strong, *but...* I didn't. Not only because it was something Hunter and I should discuss, but because I wanted it to be a secret.

I liked that it was my secret.

For over a decade, my double life had been complex.

This was amazingly simple.

It warmed my soul.

It filled me with excitement.

It gave me hope.

So, no, I didn't want to break that yet. I just wanted the realization to have time to settle in. I wanted to enjoy it without the farce of a wedding and the politics getting in the way.

"I'd like that as well," I concurred, swallowing down my secret as I tugged on the pendant Hunter had given me, the one that housed his ring.

"How are things going with the council?"

"We spoke after yesterday's council meeting," I countered, knowing he was changing the subject because we'd gotten too touchy-feely.

"A lot can happen overnight."

He had a point.

"Not today. The Carusos and Brunos have never tried to supersede my rule. They respect me. They're not even questioning my lack of a wedding ring—"

"They're good men."

I thought about how they'd tortured the traitors and just hummed.

"Are Puglisi and Messina still alive?"

"Barely. I brought in a doctor to give them a transfusion."

"How kind of you."

"I know. Stan's still under the weather."

"Fuck, he must be if he hasn't dealt with them yet."

Worry rippled through me. "*Se*. He's more exhausted than he lets on. He's working in his lab at all hours. He should be resting."

"Maybe he's feeling his mortality."

I pondered that just as the private airfield appeared in the near distance. "Could be," I agreed. "Have you spoken with him?"

"He still isn't picking up his phone."

"That's weird in itself," I remarked, knowing how close they were.

Coming up through the ranks, taking over New York as a pair had forged a bond between them that I'd become jealous of since I'd quit my role as DA.

While I was isolated, they'd had each other.

I tugged on my pendant—I wasn't alone anymore though. And Luc clearly wanted to break through the barriers that our dual roles had constructed.

Maybe we could have a bond of our own now that we were in charge of the city.

Maybe I could have my family back.

"It *is* weird," Luc said gruffly, his concern throbbing down the line. I knew it must have killed him to be in Sicily. All of this going down the moment he was overseas was unfortunate. "He always answers."

"I'll check in with him today as well. I spoke with him yesterday, but I'll go to the compound."

"You have quite the to-do list, Rory," Luc teased.

"*Se,*" I retorted cattily. "A woman's work is never done. With that in mind, I'll go."

"Before you do, when's *Matri* coming?"

"She hinted at some time this week, but it might be as early as tomorrow once I convince Jennifer's OB/GYN to go with her."

Luciu's laughter sounded in my ear, but for all that it sounded vivacious, his tone was like gravel as he stated, "Spend whatever it takes."

"I will, *frate*," I soothed. "I will."

We ended the call, and I darted a look at Giovi who was staring out of the window, pretending he hadn't heard that whole conversation.

He'd been with us long enough that I didn't worry about him having overheard something that had mostly been personal. Instead, I took advantage of our ties and let him know, "Jennifer is ill."

He frowned. "What's wrong with her?"

"High blood pressure. Who's her OB/GYN? Where do they live?"

"I'll find out from Lorenzo."

I nodded at him as he withdrew his phone and started piecing together the information I needed.

As he worked on that, I stared out of the window and spied the private jet in the distance. I watched as it started its descent and cruised toward the airfield where we were headed.

A thrill of excitement whirred through me.

This week had been very productive, but it had been impossible with Hunter. We'd only managed text chats because we were both so busy with work. I'd called him that first night and had fallen asleep partway through the damn call.

I'd missed him.

Really, truly missed him.

And it wasn't only about the sex either.

Though I wanted that too.

Just thinking about some of our texts this week made my temperature surge.

I'd never, not in a million years, have imagined that Hunter would be into somnophilia, but there he was, showing me that the boy I'd known was definitely not the man standing here today. He had facets of his nature that, until he revealed them to me, were outside of my awareness.

I liked that.

I appreciated that he could surprise me.

Biting my lip as we pulled up outside the main entrance, I waited for Hunter's arrival.

I hadn't intended on meeting him with Giovi in the goddamn town car, but we'd left one of our brothels in Queens and this airfield was in this district, too, so I figured dropping him off at home was the least I could do, seeing as it was one AM now.

Never let it be said that I wasn't a fair boss…

Heart leaping faster than before, I saw my husband through the outer doors of the small private terminal. My palms started sweating and my cheeks flushed. The visceral response to him being here was like electricity slamming through my veins.

But there was a problem.

Consiglieres didn't greet Dons by kissing their face off.

They didn't run to embrace someone.

They didn't hug in public.

They didn't display affection and, fuck, *love* to the world.

They were cold and calm and collected and everything I normally was but didn't feel right this second.

Though I was definitely a fair boss, and fair bosses didn't get their employees to grab a cab at this time of the morning, I rasped, "Giovi, I know you're busy but I'd very much appreciate it if you stepped outside the car for five minutes."

I felt his eyes on me, but I kept mine glued to my husband, then he asked, "Do you want me to get a cab home?"

"No." *Yes, please*, I thought inwardly. "It's fine. I just need five minutes."

"Sure."

One thing I liked about Giovi was he knew when not to ask questions.

As he alighted from the car, the doors to the terminal opened and Hunter finally strolled out. I saw him look at Giovi, noted his surprise, then I saw the moment the cocky smirk appeared on his lips as he walked over.

God, he was *everything*.

Everything I'd always needed and hadn't realized because I was an idiot.

For the first time in my life, I would label myself as that because I should never, ever, *ever* have let this man out of my sights when I was a teenager.

I shouldn't have wasted a fucking minute with the Giovanni Kammlers of this world. I should have snapped him up the moment I recognized his crush was developing.

Sucking in a shaky breath, I dragged my butt across the backseat so that he could climb in easily. But I angled myself so that the moment the door opened and he slipped inside, I was able to crawl onto his lap. My thighs straddled him and my arms slid around his waist as I burrowed my face into his throat.

He released a soft, surprised chuckle—one that spoke of happiness and relief—and his arms tunneled around me too, holding me close. So close.

It felt right.

Perfect.

Like everything I'd always been missing and hadn't even realized.

God, I'd been so alone before. That truth, after the conversation with Luc and now *this*, had never felt more monumental.

I released a shuddery breath. "Hi."

That soft chuckle made another appearance. "Hello." His mouth brushed over my temple and I sagged into him at the tender gesture. "This is unexpected."

"What is?"

"The welcome," he teased. "I thought you'd still be mad about this morning."

My nose crinkled against his jaw. "I am. You shouldn't have called Martínez to ask if he was intending on mobilizing his plan sometime this century... But, your impatience aside, I can still be glad to see you."

His laughter filled the barren places in my soul.

God, how hadn't I known how empty I was inside?

Had I actually been dying from isolation and it hadn't registered amid the major crises that my days were peppered with?

He hummed as he dotted kisses down my jawline. "It's good to see you."

"I missed you," I whispered.

His head rocked as he nodded his agreement. "I missed you too."

"This..." I choked. "...distance is going to be impossible."

Hunter blew out a breath. "I'm glad."

Pulling back, I blinked at him. "What?!"

He shrugged. "I'm glad." His smile turned sheepish as he reached up and tucked a couple strands of hair that had fallen onto my cheek behind my ear. I trembled as his thumb brushed over my earlobe. "I don't want you to be unhappy, but there's a joy to be found in being wanted by you. I'm not going to get bored by that for a while."

Again, I blinked at him, but this time, my surprise was replaced with the need to apologize which combined with the need to sob and the need to have him hug me and never let me go so I couldn't be a moron again and ruin what had the potential of being the best thing that had ever happened to me.

Thoughts racing, I could only get five words out: "May I kiss you, Hunter?" Shit! It needed a sixth. "Please?"

His top lip quirked up, but his grin was so satisfied that it made me melt. "You may, Aurora." His low tenor sent shivers down my spine.

I tipped forward and pressed my mouth against his and I just appreciated the moment.

It was a chaste kiss. Nothing dirtier than what a ten-year-old girl would give to her class crush at a school dance.

It was a gentle welcome.

Exactly what we needed after a week apart.

He pulled back and nipped my bottom lip. God, that sting hurt so good. "You can always kiss me 'hello' like that."

Excitement raced through me. "Really?"

He nodded. "Really."

I took that for the good sign it was. More kisses. More permissiveness with them. More trust.

Reaching up, Hunter traced my cheek with his thumb. "Where are we staying?"

I had no idea why, but the answer made me shy. "My place."

He nodded. "I'm very curious about this apartment of yours."

"I don't let many people in."

"In more ways than one." He winked at me. "Okay, let's get your guy back in the car so we can ride home."

God, that sounded good.

Perfect.

Home.

"How long do I have you?"

"Until Monday morning."

Not long enough.

Not so perfect.

But we'd make the best of it.

"Okay," I mumbled, pressing a kiss to his forehead before I scuttled onto the backseat and opened the door. "Come on, Giovi, let's get you back to your apartment."

16

HUNTER
JOHN NEWMAN - FEELINGS

AURORA'S PLACE was like nothing I imagined and everything I expected.

Which made no sense and made complete sense at the same time.

It was more spartan than I anticipated. Very elegant but warm. Neutral tones that didn't make the place feel as if it were chilled through. But then, there were the personal touches that were fitting as what I knew about 'Sunny' and Aurora was represented here.

There was a wall of wine bottles in her hallway; most of them were the Riesling she preferred, but there were some that had peeling labels on the fronts that spoke of a very old, very vintage bouquet.

She had another wall of decorations in her kitchen, this time filled with terrariums. Small globes with succulents in them that dripped greenery into the white space. The kitchen had no character apart from those plants, and that gave it the personality it needed.

Then, naturally, there was the greenhouse Sunny had mentioned to me once or twice. The Yuzu plant I'd sent her was there, looking barren because, from memory, I knew they tended to ripen in December and January. As for the rest of the space, it was filled with different fruit trees.

It amused the hell out of me, in all honesty.

This woman who claimed to have no hobbies *did* have them. And that was without the sketches. There were none on the walls, which was a shame because I knew a talent like hers deserved the spotlight, but there were small signs dotted here and there too.

She had an old-fashioned phone stand in the hallway with a vintage cream and gold rotary phone perched on top of it. Beside a notepad, there was a pot of pencils as if the urge to sketch often hit her as soon as she entered her apartment.

These pots of pencils were everywhere, pads ranging from letter-sized to tiny ones that were smaller than the palm of my hands nearby.

It was a fascinating insight into my complicated woman, but more than that, as I walked around, it felt restful. After the week I'd had, that was a bonus. It had been busy, but we'd gotten nowhere. In my opinion, that was the worst kind of work because it meant we were chasing our own asses and not the fuckers I wanted to skewer.

Earlier today, Aurora and I had argued when I'd insisted on contacting Martínez. I wanted to know when the fuck he was getting his contacts to distribute dirty meth to the *Reyes,* and she'd argued that plans like that took time to kickstart.

What I hadn't told her was that fucking photographer had sent more pictures. This time of her here in the city.

Knowing I was coming tonight, I'd intended on telling her when we were together. I didn't want her freaking out when she was alone. It definitely marred our first weekend as a married couple, but I wouldn't allow it to for long.

Especially when Martínez had given me an update—the dirty meth would be in the *Reyes'* bloodstreams within the month.

I wasn't sure what was taking the man so goddamn long, not when this was evidently an ongoing plan, but I had a deadline to work with now so I felt like *something,* at least, was happening.

Once Giovi was on his way into his walk-up, we'd ordered takeout, and upon arriving at her place, she'd told me to take a look around as we waited for it to show up. So, when I heard the doorbell, heard her get the food, and even heard her setting out dishes in the kitchen, I stopped poking around, despite not having seen her bedroom or Sunny's playroom yet.

I wandered over there, passing a particularly aggressive houseplant that had taken over a bookshelf and half a wall as I entered one of the few spaces I knew she spent barely any time in. That was obvious from the fact there was no drawing pad or pencil pot in the kitchen, just the terrariums which, I thought, wouldn't require that much upkeep.

She was standing there, looking oddly domesticated. Odd because Aurora wasn't that type of woman, but that didn't stop me from enjoying this side of her.

I did notice that she was jittery from nerves which was sweet. I knew she'd expected me to jump on her the second we made it out of the elevator, but I'd been too curious for my own good—I'd wanted to see her home. Had wanted to see the sides of Sunny that I'd never been able to access before.

In this apartment, the two halves of her nature merged more than ever before. What Sunny had shared, Aurora allowed me to uncover by letting me wander around her safe space.

Aurora liked flowers, that hadn't changed since childhood, but I didn't think it was to this extent, with the greenhouse and the jungle-like vine plants she had around the apartment.

I knew she sketched, but I didn't realize how often inspiration hit her until I'd seen the clues for myself.

I'd also learned from Stan a couple years ago that she had a fondness for wine, but again, I hadn't realized how vast her collection was.

Her home was a reflection of the woman, I thought. On the surface, elegant, under the surface, teeming with an energy she didn't quite know how to control.

Luckily for her, I did.

When she caught me studying her, her bottom lip was sucked into her mouth and drawn between her teeth. I didn't chide her for it as I strode toward her, just watched as she tensed up with every move I made.

Settling behind her, I ran my hands up and down her arms, feeling her relax some at my touch, then I pressed my chin against her shoulder. "I have a gift for you."

She tensed again. "You didn't need to do that."

I clucked my tongue, but my voice was a low growl, "Do you want to talk yourself out of getting it?"

"No, Hunter," she said thickly.

"Put your hand in my jacket pocket. Left one."

She twisted slightly, her hand settling outside the pocket before awkwardly digging in deep. I kept my chin on her shoulder so her movements were constrained, and I felt her tremble when she accidentally brushed my erection as she retrieved the gift.

From this angle, I saw exactly how she was responding—her tits were shaking like we were in the middle of an earthquake.

"Calm down, Aurora," I chided her. "Take a deep breath." As she complied, I breathed with her, not entirely sure where these nerves were coming from, but knowing her, it was down to her feeling vulnerable because I was in her sanctuary. When she'd quietened down, I ordered, "Open it."

The box was long and thin. She pulled the wrapping off then sucked in a breath as it revealed a small, innocuous strip of carbon rod.

A soft moan whispered from her—obviously, she knew what it was.

"Give it to me."

She held it out for me. "Thank you for the gift, Hunter."

My dick ached at her gratitude.

"Bend over," I whispered, watching as she immediately complied, her elbows settling on the table, forearms flattening against it.

I let my hand drift down her spine, loving the immediacy of her response to my present.

I grabbed the length of her skirt I'd chosen for her to wear today and tucked it into the waistband to reveal a set of pert cheeks that were free from proof of any of last week's punishments.

Pursing my lips, I told her, "Spread your legs."

I crouched down behind her and stared at her inner thighs—healing. She hadn't self-punished. She'd told me as much, but what kind of Dom would I be if I didn't confirm what I'd been told?

Unable to stop myself, I let my fingers settle on her knee and I trailed it up and up and up, coasting over the tensed line of her inner thigh until I reached her slit.

Though I tutted, I rumbled, "Who's this wetness for?"

A groan escaped her. "You, Hunter. You."

It was always there—I heard it. On the tip of her tongue. *Sir*. A part of me wanted to hear that as well. But I also liked my name on her lips...

Dismissing the thought, I asked, "When was the last time you touched your pussy?"

"When you had me edge last night, Hunter."

My lips twisted.

Yes, this week I'd been particularly cruel to her.

Frustrated at my inability to call her, the fucking time zones always screwing us over, I'd decided that she couldn't come. Not once. Until we were back together. But I'd allowed her to edge so that when I got here, I'd be greeted with the drenched mess that was her greedy cunt. Which was exactly what had come to pass.

Mouth watering with the need to taste her, to savor her, to fucking *feast,* instead, I watched as a single bead of her juices began to trail down her inner thigh. Moving closer to her, I let the flat of my tongue swipe it up, then I pulled back just as she arched onto tiptoe, a guttural moan drifting from her.

God, her scent lit me up. So fucking heady, so fucking *mine*.

Straightening, I flicked the toy a few times. I'd never used one before, but I knew what I wanted to do. To look at, it was a simple stick. But nothing about it was simple.

Made of carbon, it had a give to it that would enable me to flick the tip. I'd seen the pictures of the aftermath online and knew this would leave marks behind until we were together again.

I dragged the tip back with my pointer finger then let it fly forward against her ass. Immediately, a line appeared on her flesh. A second later, as if her pain receptors were processing it, she howled.

I smiled.

I shifted an inch away and graced her with another stripe.

She yowled as she bucked against the table. Legs tensing, feet drawing her up and down as she wailed through the pain.

"The reviews said it packed a punch," I drawled around her screeches.

Watching her ass sway from side to side had me hiding a smirk.

I let her dance off the pain, mostly because I liked how her butt jiggled, but only when her hand moved back to rub the marks did I grab her wrist and snap, "Did I tell you I'd finished?"

"N-No, Hunter," she whimpered.

"Now, stay still," I commanded.

"Yes, Hunter."

Sir...

My throat bobbed with the bizarre need to hear that from her.

I was the one who'd stopped that, who'd told her to call me Hunter, dammit.

Sucking in a breath, I pivoted my hand to the side and graced her with another stripe, one that settled horizontally between the two vertical lines I'd already made.

H

I grinned to myself at the ludicrously infantile method of marking her, but it got even better when she shrieked and started up with the dancing again—the stripe had snapped the other two tender lines, doubling down, I assumed, on the sharp sting.

While she was still wriggling around, I moved onto her other cheek.

"Only two here," I informed her, ignoring her whine. "If you move, I won't touch your pussy all night."

She gasped but froze in place.

I graced her other ass cheek with a vertical and a horizontal line.

H L

Both were on the lower curve, just where her sit spot was.

With her butt appropriately branded with my initials, I asked, "Red, amber, or green, Aurora?"

Her words were slurred. "W-Whaa?"

"Are you red, amber, or green?"

She swallowed. "G-green."

"Good," I crooned. "Straighten up, baby girl."

She did, but her movements were wooden. Settling myself behind her again, I absorbed some of her weight.

"You took that so well, my pet," I praised, nuzzling my nose against her throat as she sagged deeper into me. "And now, when you look in the mirror, you'll see who you belong to."

She gulped. "Thank you, Hunter."

"Such a good girl," I whispered, my lips tracing over her throbbing pulse. "*Who* do you belong to, Aurora?"

Her words were almost inaudible. "You, Hunter. You."

Because I liked her answer, I offered, "Would you like some stripes on your inner thighs, pet? You've been good, very good, so I'm going to give you a choice. You know you won't get those often."

Silence followed my question but her breathing deepened.

"Talk to me, Aurora," I demanded, voice sterner now at her lack of response.

"I-I might come if you do, Hunter," she mewled.

"Ah, honesty is the best policy. For that, my beautiful baby girl, I won't make you hold back if you *can* come."

She whimpered, which made my heart leap in my chest but allowed me to twist her around and prop her up on top of the table.

I parted her legs, looking at her slick folds with a hunger that had nothing to do with the swanky food on the placemats a few feet away and everything to do with the need to devour her.

As she sat back, she winced, and I knew my aim had been true for the initials—right on her sit spot. She'd feel that every time she sat down for the rest of the week.

Pleased, I trailed my free hand along the older wounds, the deeper ones still lingering from her final self-punishment, and hummed to myself.

Her head flopped back as she released a guttural groan at my touch, allowing me to study the delicious sight of her.

"You'd win a restaurant five Michelin stars if they served you on their table." Her eyes flared at that but they caught mine as I raised my hand to my lips to grace her with a chef's kiss. "The presentation is perfection."

She let loose a soft giggle, the sound light and young and carefree.

I knew this week had been hard on her.

I knew it, not only because it had been hard on me, but because I sensed she was wavering between the masks she wore. The role of Consigliere necessitated a certain level of dominance from her, an ability to command, but deep inside, all she wanted was to submit. To me.

God, I was a lucky bastard.

"No restaurant has five stars," she teased, her pupils like pinpricks, as if she were high on what I was making her feel.

"This is a unique establishment and it has only one patron."

She nodded but breathily told me, "Yes, Hunter. Only you."

I hummed. "Now, stay nice and still for me like a good girl."

Her eagerness was in her second nod, and I angled my hand against her thigh and graced her with the first flick.

The carbon rod was a cruel mistress. The stripe it left behind was bright red, almost purple in hue, and the stark lines of it were sharp and mean. The skin immediately rose in a bump that I couldn't stop myself from tracing with the tip of my index finger.

Her cries would have broken me a couple years ago, but now, I was starting to understand them. They were a good sound. I knew it seemed strange—how could cries of pain be a *good* thing? But I recognized her need. She *needed* to hurt. It was as delicious for her as an orgasm was.

She remained still throughout my ministrations, and only when the tension in her body released some did I give her the second stripe on the opposite leg so that each one would have the letters H and L on them.

I worked quickly, sensing that she needed me to do that, needed the avalanche of pain to get off without any other stimulation.

When both legs were graced with my initials, I literally saw her pussy pulse and she screamed, back arching, butt rocking in a way that had to rub against the other marks, head flying from side to side on the table.

Her hands flew up, one over her head as she writhed against the surface, the other covering her eyes as she sobbed through it.

It was the most erotic thing I'd ever seen.

While it was something she needed... I knew *I* could get addicted to seeing her like that as well. To seeing her fly through the pain she craved, that only I could give her without her burning herself or fucking scarring herself.

No, as much as this was about her, as much as I didn't approve of her self-punishments, her cravings belonged to me too, and like any good Dom, I'd give my good girl exactly what she needed...

Me.

For a moment, I let the joy of being allowed *this*, her, *access to Aurora*, flood me. I took that for myself, savoring the truth, staring at the ring that was tucked away in her locket, and then other desires hit me.

Love was pure, but it was faceted. It came with needs and desires, and mine aligned with hers in more ways than she'd yet to realize.

"Uncover your eyes, my beautiful girl."

With a shaky sigh, she complied.

Wanting more from her, I bowed my head to press a kiss to the top of her pussy, enjoying her shudder as I unfastened my pants and worked my dick out of my fly. Straightening up once it was free, I placed it against her folds, rocking my hips so that she'd get some friction against her clit.

If Aurora's brain ever permitted her a moment of peace, I figured that she'd found it there. *Then*. I'd never seen her features so free from any expression. I wanted her to have that. Again, and again, and again.

I wanted to be her peace.

Until I didn't.

Until I wanted to drive her crazy with want.

For me.

Her eyes popped open as a second shudder wracked her in response to my rubbing her clit with my cock. Those cocoa-brown orbs were dazed. Foggy, almost. I placed my thumb on the glans, making sure that our piercings kissed before the metal ran over her sensitive flesh.

Her keening wail was going to be the star in the upcoming week's spank bank material.

Swallowing, she asked, "Hunter?"

"Yes, moonlight."

"Can I have your cock, please?"

"When you ask so prettily," I purred, "how could I refuse?"

Letting the tip sink into her, our piercings shining silver from her slickness before mine disappeared from view, I watched as her pussy swallowed me whole.

Admiring the blush of her labia, the piercings that provided a pleasant contrast to the intense pink of her sex, I ordered, "You can come but you have to do all the work. I want to watch."

She blinked at me then started to wriggle, arching her hips, her cunt clamping down on me like a vise, as if she were trying to suck the cum straight out of me. Each time she rocked back against the ungiving surface of the table, she grimaced because I knew her 'stripes' were hurting her.

Of course, that was when she started releasing soft puffs of breath.

Those little gasps let me know how close the line between pleasure and pain was for her.

I got it—I was fucking inches away from coming.

Having broken the seal last week, I'd been ready to be back inside her the moment I'd last fucking left her cunt.

As much as I wanted to watch her, I rocked my head back on my neck as I savored what she gave me, what only *Aurora* could give me. It was too good. So good.

I couldn't stop myself from rasping, "Your pussy is fucking perfect, Aurora." Her inner muscles showed her appreciation of my praise. "I swear this is my home." I tipped my head forward to simultaneously grace her with words and eye contact. "You're my fucking home, Aurora. Not my place in Vegas. You."

Her throat bobbed and, out of nowhere, tears budded in her eyes. She straightened up, her arms sliding around my waist as she clung to me. I angled my head down so that she could reach my mouth, but she surprised me by whispering in my ear, "You're my home too, Hunter. I missed you."

My whole body clenched at her admission. At her softly spoken, brokenly uttered confession.

"You mean that?"

She pressed her forehead against my chest, nodding as she whispered, "I don't know how I lived without you."

"You never have to find out now." If ever there were words that deserved a kiss, it was those. "My beautiful, beautiful baby girl," I told her as I urged our mouths to meet.

Her hips started rocking as we gripped one another so tightly, like the other could disappear in the blink of an eye. My fingers met her hips and I started to thrust back, needing to come, needing to seal our words with the promise of pleasure.

When it came, the explosion started behind my eyes, and as everything blacked out, I heard her cries of ecstasy and they fed the fires of my release.

17

—————

AURORA

HOW CAN *something that feels so good be so wrong?*

It was a question I'd asked myself at least a dozen times a month for the last decade when the craving for pain hit me.

As I dealt with the aftermath of a self-punishment that, more often than not, went awry and as I tended to inadvertent wounds.

But tonight, while sitting at the table eating a very pleasant chicken arrabbiata (I didn't mind that it wasn't as hot as it should be) with no clothes on, Hunter's cum making a bewilderingly pleasing puddle between my thighs on the dining chair (the best use it had *ever* had in my opinion), opposite the man himself as we discussed the latest happenings in our mutual 'businesses,' I had to accept that it was bizarre how natural this felt with my one-time childhood best friend.

That wasn't a complaint, more of an observation.

I was, I recognized, comfortable in my skin with him. Figuratively, literally, and every other adverb going.

It made it easier to start a conversation on a topic that was more personal than business. One neither of us had brought up, making it very much the elephant in the room. Which was saying something with my current creampie situation going on.

"When's Alberto's funeral, Hunter?"

His mouth tightened as he took a sip of one of my favorite Merlots. (He wasn't to know I only shared that particular vintage with people I considered my favorites too.) "When the LVPD releases his body back to us."

I narrowed my eyes at him—he'd managed to surprise me. "You aren't demanding the…" I hesitated. "…*his* return?"

He shook his head. "Bert played the long game. He didn't do anything by halves. I won't fuck up his final plan by being over-emotional. His funeral can wait until his end goal comes to fruition. Even if that means waiting for the slow wheels of bureaucracy to turn. I have to have faith in him."

"And how will we know if his plan *does* 'come to fruition?'" I asked, including the air quotes because his reply had morphed from surprising me to worrying me.

"Oh, I'm sure he'll figure out how to tell me 'I told you so' from heaven." His lips thinned. "Or hell. Whichever the case may be."

Reassurance was not a part of my husband's skill set.

Gently, I prodded, "Do you have any idea what his intentions might have been?"

The drink in his hand sloshed unsteadily as he placed it down on the table with a care more befitting a newborn than a piece of glassware. The sight had me hesitating again, but I knew he was repressing his grief, and this was my moronic way of trying to touch upon a difficult subject.

Hunter and grief never went well together.

He was the kind of man who felt things too much.

Once upon a time, I'd seen that as a weakness. Now, I was just grateful he did because no one else would have shown as much goddamn patience with me as Hunter.

When we were growing up, our family had multiple pets. Hunter had a single cat. When Nauru passed away when he was eight after being run over, Hunter refused to get another animal. Nauru, he'd said, was his friend and, to Hunter, friends couldn't be replaced. Nauru had *never* been replaced. That was how deeply my husband loved.

I knew marriage was making me soft because the thought was enough to bring tears to my eyes.

It wasn't good for someone in my position to feel so much for him. My only relief came in the fact that I'd watched Messina being patched up this morning to keep him chugging along until my brother decided to end him and hadn't felt a morsel of pity.

Evidently, my emotions were selective. That was something I could deal with.

"I miss him," he confessed, his voice raw, triggering an ache so stark in my soul because this was something I *couldn't* fix.

He didn't look at me either, which felt like another failure. Instead, his gaze had locked onto the focaccia pizza hybrid that made my Sicilian heart weep with distress at the bastardized dish.

Neither of our meals, Michelin stars aside, was reminiscent of what we'd eat back home on the island.

But, beggars couldn't be choosers. And right now, what we were eating—*fuel for the next round,* my inner pain slut crooned—was utterly unimportant.

"I'm sorry," I whispered, reaching out to touch his hand. "I know that's what people say when you lose someone, and I know it's trite, but I wish—" I sighed, feeling helpless again. "I guess I just wish I'd been able to do something." It couldn't have been more spectacularly out of my hands, but that didn't mean I didn't resent being useless when it had never mattered more to be use*ful*.

"We've not discussed what happened that day. Before or after..." His fingers tucked around mine as if he knew it was the last thing I wanted to talk about.

Unfortunately for me, I'd raised this topic, so now I had to play fair.

I squeezed his fingers back and, though I wasn't particularly hungry, returned to my meal.

Taking a bite of pasta, I chewed, swallowed, then started at the beginning. "I arrived at the facility and after I got out of the car, someone bumped into me in the parking lot. It was a woman—"

"Lodestar," Hunter prompted. No question mark required.

"Yeah. But I didn't know that at the time. I just knew there was something fishy about her."

His smile was grim. "That about sums her up."

"You know her well?" I studied him. "I know you recommended her to Stan."

"I did. I regret that now, seeing as she's up to her neck in this bullshit."

"How did you meet?" I asked curiously.

"I was in Lebanon about nine or so years ago. I'd gotten it into my head to hike through the Qadisha Valley and, out of nowhere, this half-naked woman stumbles into my path.

"She was limping and bleeding and had been beaten. She was also practically feral. I thought she was going to kill me. She only didn't because I was American, had zinc oxide on my nose, and a rucksack that was packed with camping gear."

"You couldn't have looked more like a tourist."

He nodded. "That was what saved my ass."

"Who knew zinc oxide could prevent melanoma *and* murder?" I teased.

His lips twitched before his smile began to fade. "I offered to help clean up her wounds but she was frantic. I thought she'd escaped… *someone*," he said carefully, "and thought they were coming after her."

"Do you know who?"

"No. But I came to learn that she's ex-CIA, so it doesn't surprise me that she has enemies."

"That was when you became friends?"

"Not exactly. I woke up at the campsite we'd made and she was gone."

"Did she steal your stuff?"

"No. I found out later that whoever 'had' her, came back for her."

"You're lucky they didn't injure you."

"They did. I had a concussion and had to camp until I was better. Those fuckers left me to die."

"Are you kidding me?" I screeched.

"No. Star told me later that she'd distracted them."

"How kind of her," I sniped, reeling at the fact that I'd almost lost him before I ever had the chance to have him.

"It *was* actually. A couple kicks to the head are better than a bullet. She said I'd offered her a helping hand and she couldn't let me be punished for it."

"Who took her?" I queried, keeping my tone bland by willpower alone.

"I found out it was her 'owner.'"

"'Owner?'" I gaped at him.

He rubbed a finger down his nose. "She was a sex slave."

I pieced the puzzle together. "The New World Sparrows?"

"Yes. She realized that her boss was pulling shady moves during Operation Enduring Freedom. Before she could blow the whistle, she found herself in the slave market."

"Jesus."

"Yeah. It makes it tough to be close to her. A part of me knows that what happened to her couldn't have been more damaging and that it will have royally fucked her up, but that doesn't take away from me being pissed.

"We're fucking friends, we've worked together on so much shit over the years, and yet she pulls this stunt behind my back with Bert? That's not okay."

I could empathize with his anger, but I still tried to reason, "Lodestar told me Bert called in a favor."

He grunted. "I'll bet. Anyway, we got waylaid. Tell me what happened that day?"

"Wait, how did you reconnect?"

"She found me." He hitched a shoulder. "I was willing to help after she told me a little of what she'd gone through."

There was Hunter—ever the helper.

"I bumped into her," I continued once he'd answered, "and I didn't know it at the time, but she planted a couple notes on me. One was her new telephone number and the other an address. Bert said I should go there to sign the contracts for our marriage."

Hunter narrowed his eyes at me. "She'd met with him before you?"

"Yes. When I got into the visiting room, the cameras were turned away and faced the walls. We were completely alone—no guards or other prisoners in sight."

The fist he pressed to the table clenched. "I wonder what they discussed."

"I don't know. He never said. We talked, mostly about the fact that you're naughty—" At his snort, I grinned. "No, I mean it. He was all, 'Aurora Valentini, you need to watch over him because without me there, he'll get himself into trouble.'"

"Ha. He was more trouble than I am."

My lips curved. "I'll bet."

"Did he call you by your full name too?" He didn't sound surprised by the prospect.

"He did. Anyway, he shared his truths with me, told me how he'd helped my family over the years, and then *he* left.

"I was flustered because I hadn't expected him to marry you off like you were a virgin bride—" He snorted again. "—and I got out of there.

"My first instinct was to call Lodestar, but she didn't pick up. Then I saw I had a text from Luc, demanding to know where the plane was because he'd just found out about my ban of Red in the brothels and he intended to fly back to the States, and that was when I realized I'd received a video of Stan. It wouldn't load so I called Lodestar. She picked up that time."

"What did she have to say?"

"That she would help us when required but that she had a preference for *interesting* projects only.

"We don't use her services that much anyway so I wasn't that concerned, but she said that Bert had called in a favor. That was when the alarms went off and all hell broke loose.

"I-I heard on one of the guards' radios that there was a prisoner down." I sucked in a breath. "I got in the car, the video started playing, and this idiot shoved me in the back with a gun."

"I've seen how you smashed up his face." He tilted his head to the side. "And here was me believing you when you said you don't get your hands dirty."

I sniffed. "I don't. I just went fast and then braked. It wasn't my fault he wasn't wearing a seat belt."

Shaking his head, he chuckled. "'Never give up until they buckle up.'"

"You watch too much TV."

"Agreed. What happened after?"

"I drove to the guards. When I met up with them, Lodestar called me and I realized that Alberto *was* the prisoner who was down and that it was a plan Lodestar had cooked up with your grandfather. She was friends with the killer and she was pissed that I'd put him out of action. Is he dead?"

"No. He's in one of our warehouses."

"Good. Are you going to question him?"

"Brunu has. I'm staying away for obvious reasons." His fists clenched. "We're keeping him around until the cops decide to act on Bert's case." He shoved his plate away. "Where was Star by this time? Do you know?"

"She was on a plane. That was all she said." I frowned. "Oh. I'm lying. She said that her flight had been delayed and she was heading out of the country, but she had contacts in the States who'd help if we needed them. She said she was part of the three-person Valentini fan club."

"Who were the other two?"

"Your grandfather and," I hesitated, "Dead To Me."

"She mentioned her name?"

"No. I just know it was her... You asked me about her once, didn't you?"

"I did."

"Why did you?"

"Because I've spent the past year being her personal search engine in exchange for her not killing me."

My mouth rounded. "You were a target?"

"Past tense is correct."

"Thank fuck for that."

"So, she's working with Dead To Me," he snapped, more to himself than at me. "I should have fucking known. That bitch." As he rubbed his forehead, I could sense that he was trying to make sense of what he'd learned. "Why do you think Dead To Me is in the Valentini fan club?"

"Our grandfather had some jewelry that Fieri stole. He was buried with it. She unburied it before Stan and Luc could do the honors."

"Good timing on her part. You owe her now."

"I know. But it was worth it. I managed to spread the word about Luciu and the *Famigghia* being under new leadership."

"That's what Luc meant by you getting him arrested?"

Cautiously, I nodded. "I'm surprised you didn't read about it in the news."

"It's been a busy year. What were his charges?"

My nose crinkled. "Desecrating a coffin."

Though he snickered, his fingers drummed against the table, making me think he was more agitated than he wanted me to know. "Do you intend on getting me arrested?"

"No. You can't use private jets in prison, and while I'll drop my standards for you, I'm not the kind of woman who's into conjugal visits in a trailer."

A gleam of humor at my joke drifted in and out of his eyes before he let loose a sigh. "Wonder who he's pinned his murder on."

"Your grandfather?"

"Hmm."

I knew it was very inappropriate, but I wanted to take that sadness out of his eyes again, wanted to replace it with that gleam that had flashed way too briefly and, because I knew him too well to recognize he'd never be able to resist… "Want to make a bet on it?"

"For cash?"

I stuck my tongue in my cheek. "A thousand?"

He straightened up in his seat. "You're on. Who?"

"I'm thinking…" I warned, "It's a long shot but Robert Macmillan."

Hunter groaned. "Your ex-brother-in-law? Good call."

Winking at him, I agreed, "I know. What about you?"

"I'm thinking Paulu Ribaldi."

I held out my hand and we shook on it.

18

———————

TEXT CHAT

TEXT CHAT

A FEW DAYS LATER

Hunter: *Lauren take off okay?*

Aurora: *Yeah. They landed about an hour ago. The OB/GYN and her family are settling in to their quarters on the estate as well. Luc messaged to let me know.*

Hunter: *Did he say if she'll need antidepressants for the rest of her life?*

Aurora: *I didn't scare her that badly.*

Hunter: *It's cute that you believe that.*

Hunter: *Let me know how Jennifer gets on.*

Aurora: *Will do. Any news from the cops?*

Hunter: *No.*

Aurora: *God, could they be working any slower? How aren't you prodding them? I'd be up their asses until they got me some results… I still can. Nudge nudge.*

Hunter: *No. I trust in Bert.*

Aurora: *You're more patient than I am.*

Hunter: *Lol. That shouldn't come as a surprise.*

Hunter: *Did you start looking around for that peep show prick?*

Aurora: *I have my people on the hunt for Albarez. The second I know where he is, I'll loop you in.*

Hunter: *Using the homeless as your information hit squad... I don't think I've ever heard of anything more 'Aurora Valentini' in my life.*

Aurora: *:P*

Aurora: *Society treats people like trash. Everyone deserves the chance to earn an honest buck. If that's earned by watching and snooping, it's not my fault my enemies don't look homeless people in the eye so they don't see where their gazes are trained.*

Hunter: *Did it sound like I was judging you?*

Aurora: *No. Sorry. I'm just getting fucking sick of how the mayor isn't doing anything about our homeless problem. I swear we need to get Rachel into office. She'd achieve more in a year than these fuckwits achieve in a term. But I can't see her giving up her retainers.*

Hunter: *Plus, she can't hide her teeth.*

Aurora: *She could get braces.*

Hunter: *LOL. I didn't mean that. There's nothing wrong with her teeth.*

Aurora: *Then why bring them up?*

Hunter: *I was referencing the fact that she's a shark. *sigh* Anyway, you like Alexandra Garcia Eugenio, don't you? She'll make effective policy changes.*

Aurora: *She will if miracles happen and she gets into office. With that whore for Big Pharma on the ballot against her, it'll be a tough race.*

Hunter: *Still bristling about her returning your donation, I see.*

Aurora: *She needs all the help she can get.*

Hunter: *She needs LEGITIMATE help. Surely you've got a front that's squeaky clean? You want her in, help her how you can.*

Aurora: *It's strange... As annoyed as I am, I also want to respect her integrity. Even though I know it's foolish.*

Aurora: *Naive.*

Aurora: *Hopeless.*

Hunter: *My God, are you sick or something?*

Aurora: *You can't see what I'm doing with my fingers.*

Hunter: *No, but I can imagine. Do you need reminding of who owns them?*

Aurora: *Tonight, please, Hunter.*

Hunter: *Hmm. Gladly.*

Aurora: *Anyway, that IS for tonight. As much as I wish it were now, I still have a couple hours of work left here.*

Aurora: *How are you holding up?*

Hunter: *You only ever ask me that when we're texting.*

Aurora: *I know that I have more chance of getting the truth out of you when we're not on the phone…*

Hunter: *I miss him. That answer's not going to change for a long while.*

Aurora: *I won't stop asking.*

Hunter: *I don't want you to.*

Aurora: *I wish you could have closure.*

Hunter: *We'll get answers soon.*

Aurora: *I miss you.*

Hunter: *I'll SEE you tomorrow.*

Aurora: *Can't wait.*

Hunter: *I have another present for you…*

Aurora: *I like your presents. But I'm feeling bad about never having anything for you.*

Hunter: *You're my present.*

Aurora: *Oh, Hunter. Don't say things like that.*

Hunter: *Why shouldn't I?*

Aurora: *Because you're too far away for me to do anything about it.*

Hunter: *:P Duly noted. Call me when you're home and wearing my jersey. Nothing else, understood?*

Aurora: *Not even the belt?*

Hunter: *I'll watch you remove the plugs. I like seeing you squirm.*

Now, go. The sooner you finish your work, the sooner I get to see your cunt.

Aurora: *Jesus.*

Hunter: *I'll never get tired of the sight of it, Rory. Never get tired of the sight of YOU wanting ME. I should make you wait until we're together, but I want to see you come undone. I'm the only one who can truly do that to you, aren't I, moonlight?*

Aurora: *Yes, Hunter. <3 You are. <3*

Hunter: *Until tonight. Xo*

19

AURORA

I WAS PRETTY pissed when I made it to Vegas the following evening and Hunter wasn't sitting in a town car waiting for me when I landed.

Last night had been an exquisite exercise in torture, after all. Call me greedy, but one orgasm, self-inflicted, was no longer scratching any of my itches.

I needed him.

His dick, his fingers, his tongue, hell, I'd even take his *teeth*…

His words got me there, but I was the one who let my body down.

As usual.

At least this time there were no inadvertent bruises or accidental scars like when I'd gotten my nipple clamp stuck in my blouse and had felt sure I'd ripped off a part of my areole. (Spoiler: I had, but the skin had grown back without even a bump.)

Unfortunately, Hunter's dick, fingers, tongue, and teeth were elsewhere, much to my dismay.

Brunu did not make an adequate replacement, and he suffered for it with a glower that was known to make Giovi gulp. A man of his experience was accustomed to worse, however, and he simply arched a brow at my glower, raising his hands in surrender, declaring, "Not his idea or mine."

Frowning at that, I demanded, "What are you talking about?"

"Mia Raleigh wants to speak with you."

"Is that name supposed to mean something to me?"

"It will after this meeting. You gotta sign those contracts Bert created for you, and Mia is our queen of contracts. Hunter says he'll be waiting for you once you're done."

"Waiting for me where?"

"The Milazzo."

Another casino.

The Milazzo wasn't like the Gallinaro, though, which had been featured in so many movies thanks to the water displays with their fountains that it was a household name.

The Gallinaro was for tourists.

The Milazzo was for heavy hitters—the whales who thought nothing of dropping ten million on a poker game.

Every casino had a place for whales, but the Milazzo (i.e. the Camorra) had doubled down on their investment to create a six-star luxury hotspot in Vegas.

I knew from the market research I'd been doing on the casino industry, thanks to my interest in purchasing the Vallara, that an executive suite in the Milazzo—the cheapest in their brochure—cost upward of twenty thousand a night and came with a butler service as standard. (Probably a cockwarming service, too, if you were friendly with the concierge.)

"Why the Milazzo?" I asked.

He shrugged. "Bert always had his command center there."

Curious, when the square footage that the 'command center' took up would probably be better served as another suite or three.

Brunu held open the car door for me and I slipped into the backseat. He closed it, then rounded the trunk, and took a seat at my side.

As the town car set off, he turned to me. "You need to get the boy to open up about Bert."

Here was me thinking Brunu was all business.

"He's not a boy."

"Always was to Bert."

"You're not Alberto. He's your Don."

"I know he's my boss, and even if I didn't like him, I'd serve him and keep his ass safe because Bert was like a father to me and he adored Hunter, but you need to do something."

"I *am* doing something. Plenty of 'somethings,' in fact. I'm coordinating with Martínez—the dirty meth has begun weeding its way out of the lab in Boyle Heights and I've spoken with the new Vitale leader to ensure a smooth transition as he tries to stabilize their fluctuating income streams—"

"I'm not talking about that stuff."

"I am. Has Hunter dealt with Paulu Ribaldi yet?"

"He hasn't."

"Why not?" I scowled at him. "My position isn't official until he's out of the picture. You and I need to start communicating more."

"We do. It's going to be awkward, you being in New York for most of the week."

"Only while my brother is waiting for his kid to be born. When he's back, I can switch up my time better."

Brunu studied me. "You as clever as Bert thought you were?"

"I don't know," I admitted. "But he seemed to think I could handle two roles."

"And you have faith in a man you only met once?"

"I have faith in a man who loved Hunter, and who Hunter loved in return."

"Good answer. Hunter's got his eye on Paulu. He's waiting for him to trip up. No resignations/firing at this level."

"Only death?"

"And demotions. But if he's a rat, then he's dying and he doesn't know it yet." Brunu squinted at me. "We need to get you a Stidda."

"I need a lot of things. On both coasts. Mostly, I've just been dealing with crisis management, but regular business will resume shortly. It's been two weeks—"

"Did you wipe out the families who betrayed you?"

"No. Luc says killing the sixty men who are loyal to them wouldn't be a smart move."

"Sixty?" Brunu wiggled his head. "I can see why he'd say that. You don't agree?"

"I don't disagree. But I'm keeping them monitored."

"Can you do that?"

I hesitated. "How honest should we be with each other, Brunu?"

"As I told you, I don't want Hunter to die... and I think he'll be great for the Camorra.

"Bert was very set in his ways. I loved the man but he was quick to shoot first and didn't ask as many questions later as he should have. Hunter will temper that. And you'll temper him. So, it's all good for the West Coast.

"I've lived through a lot of turf wars, Aurora. I don't want to live through another. Brothers going to jail for shit they did to defend themselves—" He thinned his lips. "Nah. Bert started to calm down when he hit his sixties, sure, but it was only when Hunter came along that he changed. I have your man to thank for that, so I won't betray him and I won't betray you."

I studied him, read between his lines, sought out the micro expressions that would inform me of a lie before his words could even be uttered, and the end result was... *I believed him.*

"Then you're on my team. I can keep an eye on the men but not around the clock, and I can't get into their homes. I can only monitor their behavior but not accurately. There are places they can go that I can't get into."

"You can't bug their phones?"

"Not so many of them. We don't have a Hunter in the *Cosa Nostra.* That kind of thing needs someone working on it full-time. We don't have that capacity yet."

Brunu tapped his fingers against the leather seat. "Might be time to look for one?"

I nodded. "I agree. I'll see what can be done, but it requires a hell of a lot of trust, and that's something that takes time to be earned."

The problem was, of course, finding someone. It wasn't like we could post an ad for an unethical hacker. Of course, I knew one, so maybe Hunter could point me in another direction. Not that his last reference—Lodestar—had turned out to be a good fit.

"True. But if you don't start, then you don't get anywhere."

"I know." Pursing my lips, I asked, "I need to build a Stidda here. Should I take Paulu's men?"

"No, he picked dipshits. *Stiddaris* are traditionally selected from each of the families. Sometimes, depending on the size, we look to the lower ranks. I tend to do that."

"Why?"

"Fresh meat. Hunter took Bert's Stidda, but I only really like Adrianu and Matteo."

I knew *of* them. Adrianu reminded me of Matt Bomer with dark eyes instead of blue, and Matteo made Adrianu look ugly. Seemingly impossible, nonetheless true.

"Why do you only like those two?"

"They're not just good with their hands. They have brains. Luca's okay, too, but he's hot-headed." He pondered the situation. "We can share *stiddaris* until you come to know the men."

"That could take years."

"It probably will, but I'll expand mine, and they can work for us both. We'll just have to stay in close contact about who we need to do what and on which tasks we've set them. But that won't be a problem seeing as we'll be keeping in closer communication, no?"

"Hunter's been tight with the information about you. I don't even have your phone number."

I coughed out a laugh. "He didn't give it to you?"

"No. To be fair, the boy's got a lot on his plate. Which is why I wanted to speak to you about him. He's barely talking about Bert. Acting like he ain't dead. It's not healthy."

If we weren't talking about Hunter, I'd think this conversation was hilarious; I was discussing emotions and grief with a gold-toothed Sicilian Peter Griffin. I half-expected to hear Lois' voice in the background singing the theme song to *Family Guy*.

Still, it wasn't like I could disagree with him. "I know. It's what he does though. It's normal for him."

My reply didn't ease his concern. "It's not healthy."

"It's how Hunter copes. I promise I've discussed it with him. Just last night, in fact."

"As long as you do." He scratched his chin. "He's spoken with Sheikh Hashim a couple times."

I thought back to the council meeting I'd eavesdropped on. "*Does the Sheikh have more than one client in the US?*"

"He won't say. He wants to meet with Hunter on his home turf."

"That's not possible right now."

Brunu shrugged. "I know. Think he'll compromise though. Europe is halfway between if my geography isn't altogether rusty."

"Europe isn't ideal either." I blew out a breath. "It might be a good thing it's just you and me heading to the Milazzo. We need to figure out a way to coordinate better."

The remainder of the journey was spent doing exactly that.

Consiglieres were advisors, so it was a desk job. I didn't need to be in Vegas to work, but I did need to make sure that I had good links with the people who were on the ground.

Brunu and I getting along would make my position a lot easier, so while I didn't bend over backward to accommodate him, I certainly pulled some yoga moves out that I hadn't practiced in far too long.

We eventually drew to a halt beside the Milazzo, and when my door opened for me, I noticed Brunu didn't budge but one of my guards did.

"You're not coming with me?"

He snorted. "Nah. Mia's a pain in my ass. I don't put myself in her line of fire if I don't have to."

Though I smirked at him, intrigue hit me.

Alberto's shadow council… All women. No testosterone. Was that what heaven sounded like?

Well, on a professional front.

I enjoyed Hunter's dick too much to sacrifice that now. (As we'd already established, his fingers, tongue, and teeth too.) Maybe testosterone was something to be appreciated in my husband.

Upon heading into the hotel, a little like my automated vacuum bot, a guy in a discreet uniform drifted out of a nook and approached us. I just eyed him as he shot me a blank smile.

"Ms. Valentini, would you step this way, please?"

I followed him as he led me down a marble hall away from the reception desk. It didn't hum with activity here. There was a relaxed atmosphere, as if everyone who stayed at the Milazzo was too rich to be rushed.

They likely were.

I was wealthy. My family was wealthy. But dropping ten million on a card game was above my pay grade.

A thought occurred to me…

Was Hunter that rich?

I didn't covet wealth. Not by any stretch of the imagination. I had plenty in my bank accounts, after all. But if Hunter owned *this*, then ten-million-dollar buy-ins were a walk in the park for him, which *was* impressive.

That being said, his grandfather didn't trust him not to fuck up the new job position—less impressive—but this was different.

It was clear to me that Alberto believed the illegal side of things would get Hunter killed, not the legal.

A shiver brushed a path along my spine.

I'd cut him out for so long that, in a sense, he'd been dead to me, but I'd always known that somewhere, he was safe. Well. *Alive.*

The prospect of walking this earth without him being on it hit me like a hammer to the temple.

I even paused.

The pain triggered the expulsion of a sharp breath that was loud enough to have my guide pausing and shooting me a wary look.

Biting the inside of my cheek, I forged onward, aware I'd made a fool out of myself when my guard hovered at my side instead of a few steps behind me, but even so, the ghostly fingers clawed at my heart, wrenching at the veins and arteries that kept it in place.

Alberto thought Hunter would die without my help…

Was he right? Or just being overprotective?

The concierge, my guard, and I made it to an elevator shaft that read 'Private' above the buttons.

At his touch, the doors opened and we stepped inside. Only, we didn't go up, as I'd anticipated, but down.

Even more curious.

The doors opened again a few moments later onto a larger lobby that was far more chaotic than the one upstairs.

People shuffled around, heads burrowed as they flipped through case files on sleek desks that belonged in an office on Wall Street.

Some workers were armed, but most weren't.

A guy in a suit pushed one of those trolleys that bellboys used but it wasn't transporting suitcases, just cellophane-wrapped stacks of cash.

My brows rose at the sight until I realized Brunu's choice of words was correct—it *was* a command center.

Excusing my slow reaction time to jet lag and exhaustion, I took in as much of the scene as I could while we stepped down a long corridor.

It was like a barbell in shape. Two round lobbies at either end were joined by a pathway. One access point by the elevator was a fire hazard that the fire chief must have been bribed to overlook.

The decorations weren't as swank as upstairs, but I noted two very nice paintings in each lobby that looked to be genuine Jackson Pollocks.

When my guide stopped outside a door and then tapped once, a light flicked green above us, a light I hadn't even spotted until now, and he opened it then stepped aside so I could enter.

Turning to my guard, I told him, "Wait out here."

Once he nodded his understanding, I pulled my shoulders back and straightened my spine as I mentally declared, 'Para bellum,' then proceeded to step into an office.

When the desk chair spun around, I came face to face with a woman about my age, dressed in a sharp Prada suit that I knew was *not* off the rack. This was pure couture, and she rocked it.

I almost whistled my appreciation as she straightened to her feet, her hands coming to the buttons on her jacket as she fastened them back together again.

The move was one I'd made in the past.

Men unfastened the buttons of their jackets when they took a seat, then buttoned them up again when they stood—the masculine energy set the tone in a meeting.

I tipped up my chin, feeling grateful that I hadn't changed out of my Ferragamo pantsuit after I'd finished up at *Russu* and had headed to the jet in my work clothes.

"Aurora Valentini, we meet at long last."

The greeting was unexpected, as much as the suit was. Even I didn't tend to wear couture for business casual meetings and I'd been handed manuals on 'how to be a lady' since I was a small child.

"I'm afraid you have me at a disadvantage," was my cool retort as I stepped over toward the desk where I uncovered the most fascinating of sights.

This place was a hub.

The wall she'd been facing when I entered was full of monitors. *Full* of them.

I almost shook my head when I saw the camera feeds came from hotel suites.

One man was getting dressed; he stood in front of the camera without knowing it in an unbuttoned shirt, some socks, and a set of sock garters. *Sock garters.* (What was this? 1980?)

There was a woman who was getting eaten out by one of the bell boys on a dresser. (The bell boy had missed his vocation in life if her facial expressions were anything to go by.)

Another woman was devouring a table full of room service. (Definitely mourning a break-up. Too much dessert and not enough protein.)

Fascinating.

I dragged my attention from it and took a look around the space now that I'd set eyes on both the occupant of the office and what she was wearing.

The desk was as grand as Luciu's Barbary pirate one, and the first editions that lined the bookshelves around the rest of the room were equally as impressive. Their green leather spines gave a demure cast to the space. Overhead, there was a fresco. Vegas hadn't existed in the times of Rafael, but it sure as hell looked authentic to me, so that was pretty damn clever.

While I was studying, she rounded the desk and held out her hand for me to shake.

It was only then that I realized she wasn't as young as I first thought. Maybe late forties? Tiny lines had appeared between her brows and at the corners of her eyes, but those were the only signs of smile lines. Her mouth was set in a stern moue, and she wore the most pristine bronze-tinted lipstick that looked as if it didn't dare bleed into her skin.

With every step, her hair bobbed and swayed, the curls both a declaration of intent and a warning, because they were the only free things about her. Everything else was locked up tight in a way that reminded me of myself.

"Who are you?" I questioned as I slipped my hand away and took a seat in front of her desk where she motioned.

As I did, the hardwood collided with my sit spot where Hunter's initials remained. Heavily faded, but still there. Just.

Until tonight, when he'd mark me again.

Now is not the time to get turned on, Aurora.

Mia surprised me by taking a seat next to me, not retreating to her side of the desk. Her gaze drifted over me as she did. It was an inspection, but I refused to show any affront. Not when I'd just treated her to the same appraisal. Instead, I angled my chin up and let her take her fill as both our egos settled in for the ride.

"My name is Mia Raleigh." She angled her head, revealing small golden sapphires that sparkled in her ears. "I was Bert's right-hand woman."

"Did you know about his plans at High Desert?"

Her hesitation told me she hadn't. Huh. Not so 'right-hand.'

"Sometimes Bert played his cards close to his chest. One of those plays was that he has contracts he wanted you to sign, but also, he wanted you to meet me."

"You're not a face of the Camorra I recognize," I pointed out, and it wasn't a lie—I'd never seen this woman before in my life.

The West Coast was something I'd monitored in the past, but I had my hands full with the East Coast and, until this year, the DA's office. That meant I had a rudimentary idea of the top players over on this side of the country, and she wasn't in my memory banks.

"I wouldn't be. None of the women in the Camorra are." She stalled my next words by sniping, "Not because the Camorra are ashamed of us, but because it's smart to keep your best players under wraps.

"Notice I said 'under wraps.' Not shoved in the kitchen and forced to spawn the next generation and make ziti by hand."

My jaw tensed at that, but I couldn't argue with her.

She was right.

"The *Cosa Nostra* hasn't moved with the times," I conceded, "but I'm bringing them into the 21st century.

"I understand that you're the head of Alberto's shadow council. Is that why you wished to speak with me?"

"Yes, and no. We won't interact as much as I will with Hunter. I brought you here to sign the contracts Bert left with me. Other than that, our roles are divergent."

That didn't surprise me, not when Hunter had told me that only he and Alberto ever dealt with the shadow council.

I didn't care.

I already had enough of a workload for four people; I wasn't about to get possessive over this.

If anything, just being here, seeing the scope of what was clearly an information trawl on the Milazzo's ultra-rich clientele, provided me with a sense of relief.

Since I'd handed over one of our prime sources of blackmail material to the Attorney General to buy *Prozio* out of prison, I'd been missing the steady flow of information.

As she retrieved something from a desk drawer, my gaze scattered to the multiple screens behind her. A couple was fucking in the elevator, and another pair looked as if they were trying to entice a house-keeper into a threesome in a fancy suite.

"Are staff allowed to fraternize with guests?" I queried, pointing to the screen in question.

She peered behind her. "That one is."

Huh.

Deciding not to ask because she wasn't particularly forthcoming, I stared at the papers she'd placed on the table in front of her. There weren't as many as I'd imagined and there was a jewelry box, an old one, perched beside them.

Interested by the box, by its antiquity, I reached for the papers once she pushed them over to me. A pen was proffered next but I ignored it as I picked up the top sheet.

As I read, a shiver rushed down my spine.

Aurora Valentini,

At this point, I've yet to meet you but I'm excited about our initial meeting, even though it will also be our last.

I'm certain you'll live up to the panache I've come to expect after watching you turn from a shrewish hellion into a Consigliere who would have made her grandfather proud.

These contracts are simply a formality.

Brief outline:

<u>Business</u>

You will act as Hunter's Consigliere for as long as you both consider yourself able to hold the position.

You will receive two million dollars a year for this role.

In case of his murder by allies or enemies alike, you *will* seek retribution and will help appoint a worthy successor OUTSIDE of the council.

<u>Personal</u>

Any children will have the De Laurentiis surname. De Laurentiis-Valentini is acceptable.

In case of a divorce, (unlikely, but I'm a pragmatist) each of you will retain your wealth. You bring nothing to the table and you will leave with nothing.

Any children will be raised on the West Coast primarily in case of a divorce. The eldest child, whether male or female, will be educated appropriately to ensure they are adequately able to hold the role of Don.

Sorry to get formal on you, Aurora, but I'm sure you understand.

Once you've signed these papers, I have a gift for you.

When you present Hunter with his first heir, naturally born or adopted, you'll receive a second gift.

I wish I had the chance to know you better, but make him happy. That's all I ask. Well, that, and keep him alive. I'm sure I'll have warned you about his propensity to cause trouble.

Wishing you a long life with my grandson,

Alberto De Laurentiis

MY THROAT FELT ODDLY thick by the time I was done reading—that part about my grandfather didn't help.

Some of the stipulations pissed me off, but mostly, it was just strange knowing he was dead and that he'd thought so far ahead.

Because I was capable of such forward thinking and planning, it wasn't alien to me, but Bert had dotted so many Is and crossed so many Ts that I thought we'd be feeling his spirit for years to come.

For Hunter's sake, I almost hoped we did, even if it meant there were unknown variables to account for down the road.

A glance through the contracts revealed nothing more than what he'd spelled out for me. I signed without compunction, curious about the jeweler's case when Mia handed it to me.

As I opened it, the rubies inside gleamed in the bright lights from the screen.

For a moment, I nipped the inner flesh of my bottom lip between my teeth to withhold an excited gasp.

The settings to the earbobs were ancient, the rubies were like blood, and the gold gleamed in a manner that spoke of antiquity—as if years of being worn, of the oils from its owners' flesh had changed it on an elemental level. Impossible, I knew, breathtaking nonetheless.

The desire to put them on was intrinsic. They weren't, however, mine. They were Jennifer's. She was the Valentini Queen, not me. I'd never wanted to be either, and today was no different, but that didn't diminish my temptation.

My fingers traced over the cool gems as I glanced over at Mia. "The second gift he promised me upon delivering an heir…"

"Also one of your Anjou rubies," was the dismissive retort.

It was like being punched in the stomach. But in a good way. No pain, but I was winded.

Three of the rubies were in our possession, and a child would give us the fourth.

A child.

Hunter's child.

A daughter. Or a son.

My child.

He'd make a great father. I'd be a terrible mother.

I nipped my bottom lip again.

The truth hurt.

Straightening up, I got to my feet and stared her down. "Is that all?"

"It is."

I nodded at her in farewell, and she reciprocated.

Palming the box, I tucked it into my pocket and strolled out of the office.

Dazed, it didn't even register with me that my guard joined me as I walked along the hall and returned to the elevator that had delivered us to this subterranean floor.

When I was back in the reception area, I saw the town car waiting.

Hunter was seated inside. I spotted him immediately. His head angled away from the door, a phone tucked against his ear.

The need that crawled through me at the sight of him was new and oh, so precious.

I'd never anticipated this, had never expected to be married to him, had never thought about having children, especially not his. Yet that was my future.

Somehow, that was my tomorrow.

Unbidden, I looked up at the ceiling and, under my breath, whispered, "*Grazii*, Alberto."

20

TEXT CHAT

RORY: *Don't ask me how, but… I got my hands on an Anjou piece.*

Luc: *Are you fucking kidding me?!*

Stan: *No way!*

Rory: *Yeah.*

Rory sends photo

Luc: *Holy shit.*

Stan: *The earrings!*

Rory: *They're even more beautiful IRL.*

Luc: *How did you find them?*

Rory: *Which part of 'don't ask me how' didn't you understand?*

Luc: *I see they didn't put you in a good mood.*

Stan: *LOL.*

Rory: *You can't see me but I'm sending you two birds.*

Luc: *Pigeons?*

Rory: *Feel free to shove them up your ass.*

Stan: *He's an ass guy, Rory. Don't think that would be a punishment.*

Rory: *Didn't need to know that.*

Stan: *You did. How could you punish him with something he'd like?*

Luc: *I'm an ass guy when I'm giving, not receiving, Stan. Jesus Christ. How do you know that anyway?*

Stan: *I've tripped over way too many bottles of lube in your room in my time.*

Luc: *What were you doing in my room?*

Stan: *Usually checking for hidden cameras and bugs.*

Rory: *How is this our life? Lol. FML.*

Stan: *Which part freaks you out?*

Stan: *The bugs and hidden cameras or that Luc is into anal play?*

Luc: *I'll pay you to stop this conversation right now.*

Stan: *How much?*

Luc: *How much do you want?*

Stan: *Pretty sure you wouldn't be able to afford my price. :P*

Luc: *I'm biting my thumb at you.*

Stan: *Little Debbie cupcakes taste better. Just FYI.*

Rory: *If we're finished derailing this conversation… I have to go. I wanted you to see these rubies though.*

Luc: *Good catch, soru. I won't ask, seeing as you won't tell, but well fucking done.*

Stan: *Seriously, Rory. Great catch.*

Rory: *Should be able to get another piece, too, in a while.*

Luc: *Why a while?*

Stan: *How long's a while?*

Rory: *Leave it with me.*

Luc: *You and your fucking secrets, Rory.*

Stan: *Don't we always 'leave it with you?'*

Luc: *Fair point.*

Rory: *Don't I know it lol. But I will tell you this… I think I know where another piece is.*

Luc: *Where?!!*

Rory: *Rachel Laker told me that the Prez of the Satan's Sinners' Ohio Chapter had heard a rumor about a necklace that the ex-Prez had hidden somewhere in their clubhouse. He's on the hunt for it. Rachel will tell me if they find it.*

Stan: *And what about this other one?*

Rory: *It comes at a price we can't afford yet.*

Stan: *We'll pay whatever it costs to get it back.*

Rory: *The price is time.*

Stan: *Huh?*

Rory: *It's difficult to explain. I'm trying not to be so secretive. It's not an easy habit to break though...*

Stan: *You're asking us to trust you?*

Rory: *Yes.*

Stan: *That's easy then.*

Luc: *Se. You'll tell us what you know and when. We have faith in you, soru.*

Rory: *Grazii, frates.*

21

HUNTER

"WE DIDN'T DO ANYTHING!"

Aurora arched a brow at the whine. "That's a lie. You went for fucking hot dogs—*that* is exactly what you did."

"You were gone for almost an hour!"

Brunu shook his head, his embarrassment clear. "Since when do you decide when you can and can't leave your post? You fucking morons. You earned this beating."

I wasn't a violent man but the urge to wade in was strong. Adrianu and Matteo were the ones doling out the punishment when the disrespect was handed down to *my* woman. But I knew Bert never got his hands dirty.

That was how he stayed out of jail his whole life.

It was even why he'd died in prison—because he'd *chosen* to be there. On his terms.

Yet he'd been the one to encourage me to kill Reilly Green. Violence had a place in our hierarchy. Few people knew who Aurora was to me, *what* she was, but they were here. In this room. And they were the ones doling out the punishment.

Maybe she could see me getting riled up because, from across the way, I watched as Aurora strode over to me, coming to stand at my side. She didn't touch me. Just stood there. Watching.

"We didn't know she was important," Ricardu sobbed around a split lip.

That had me jerking to my feet. "When Brunu sets you on a task, a task that comes from *me*, it isn't your place to determine whether the person you're supposed to protect is important or not."

Aurora's hand tugged on the back of my jacket, but I ignored that soft clasp and I strode toward the men who cringed as Adrianu and Matteo backed off when Brunu cleared his throat.

A glance at my Capo showed me the twisted gleam in his eyes as he settled in for the show.

"Please, Don, please, we didn't mean any harm," Nino cried. "We were just hungry!"

"Need a baseball bat, Don?" Brunu questioned dryly, and Ricardu's eyes widened.

"You're not going to die today," I informed the hapless pair. "But that doesn't mean this won't hurt."

With a care I wasn't feeling, I shrugged out of my jacket and tossed it at Brunu. After cracking my knuckles, I pulled my arm back and slammed my fist into Nino's gut.

As he yowled, twisting in his bondage, Matteo and Adrianu drifted to either side of him and held him in place for me.

"When I tell you to do something, what do you do, Ricardu?"

"We listen, Don," he yelled over Nino's groans.

I hit the man again.

And again.

"When an order comes from me, do you ignore what I specifically request, even if *you* don't view it as important?"

"No, Don!"

Another punch to the gut.

And another.

"What is my word?"

"Law," Ricardu shouted as I dropped a flurry of jabs that had Nino coughing up blood.

That final time, with an uppercut to the jaw, I slammed the prick's head backward and knocked him out.

The silence in the warehouse simmered. Loud enough that it was a soundtrack in itself.

A towel landed in my arms. Casting a look at Brunu, his approval registered as I swiped the terry cloth over my face where sweat from the impromptu workout had gathered.

My knuckles ached like a son of a bitch, but I pushed aside the discomfort, stepped over to Ricardu, looked him in the eye, and drawled, "Are you ready for your punishment?"

His throat bobbed. "I'm sorry, Don. Forgive me—"

He choked on the word as I punched him in the stomach.

By the time both men were unconscious, some of my temper had drained away. I turned back to Aurora, saw her disapproval was in perfect contrast to Brunu's approval, then told my men, "Dump them back at their places. Dock them a week's pay and make sure I don't see them for at least a month."

As Brunu, Matteo, and Adrianu scurried around to do my bidding, I waggled my fingers as I approached my wife.

"You didn't have to do that," she told me coolly, her gaze on our men, not on me.

"They disrespected you. That means they disrespected me," I informed her, equally as coolly.

Not liking being ignored, I stepped in front of her, not moving until she looked at me.

As our gazes collided, the shitty warehouse faded into dust, the grunts of the men as they lifted dead weights off hooks disappeared, and the scent of blood and sweat drifted on a non-existent breeze.

"You're mine, Aurora De Laurentiis. No one disrespects what's mine."

Her pupils dilated.

That was the response from her I needed.

22

AURORA

THE FOLLOWING WEEK

"HUNTER," I whined.

No response.

God, I hated when he did this.

And yes, it made me feel like I was five.

I did *not* need constant attention. Certainly not his. But need and want were two different problems, neither of which I was able to resolve at the moment.

"Didn't I tell you no complaining?" he murmured a couple moments later.

"You did," I grouched.

"Didn't I tell you that every complaint would lead to a punishment?"

"You did."

"Isn't it already bad enough that you earned this punishment by being a brat?"

I bit my lip. "I didn't mean to."

My whispered response didn't gain me a reply.

I swallowed as I stared blindly up at the ceiling of the library in my mother's home in Brooklyn.

Technically, it was the family home in the city, and technically, we were only here because the majority of said family was in Sicily right now and Stan didn't come here unless *Matri* was cooking.

I rocked my head from side to side against the coffee table, feeling utterly exposed in a way that was both liberating and terrifying.

I'd fucked up.

I knew that I had.

The second he'd asked and I'd blurted out the words, I'd known I'd fucked up, but there was no going back.

The gentle noise of a page turning rustled in my ear, making me shift toward it. I thought he was sitting in the armchair to my left, but he'd blindfolded me so I didn't know for sure.

I wanted to reach out for him, my hands ached to connect with his, but he'd cuffed my ankle to my wrist on each side, spreading me wide and pinning me on my back like a defenseless turtle that couldn't roll onto its front.

Exposed wasn't the word.

It was warm in here too. The fire licked at the hearth, and one side of my body was hotter than the other as a result.

The exposure, the lack of sight, the binding… Each was a punishment but it was the silence, the inattention, that was crippling.

My hands balled into fists as the stupid emotions I was fighting began to resonate hard. His splaying me out like a frog about to be dissected in biology was a physical punishment, but it was triggering something I knew he wanted—an emotional outburst.

"You told me you'd never put me in this position again," I rasped.

"What position is that exactly?" He sounded bored. He even, goddamn him, turned another page in his book. How the fuck could he read at a time like this? "You're in a house you own, in a room that has curtains on the window—curtains that are closed. The books sound-proof the walls if your mother's live-in housekeeper *could* hear you orgasm, but she won't because her place is annexed.

"The only exposure is in your head."

"Tell that to my pussy," I snapped. "I've got a draught tsunamiing it."

"Would you prefer me to turn you toward the fire?"

"So it can burn?"

"So the draught will be warm."

I heard his amusement. "This isn't funny!"

"I never said it was. I told you back at *Russu* to bend over the desk. You chose not to. Did you, or did you not, earn a spanking?"

Finally, there was passion in his voice.

"My office in *Russu* is—"

"A soundproofed room where no one could see in through the windows even if we could see out of them? With doors that lock and entry is limited because no one apart from Stan would dare open a door without knocking and he's still acting like the nutty professor in his lab?"

"It doesn't matter! It's the—"

"We've established this, Aurora. I am just as pissed as you are about the photos. That I let you down, that I let some bastards take pictures of you in that state, a state that belongs to *me*, that is *for* me and me alone, is not as bad as how you're feeling but it's pretty damn close.

"Do you think that I would do anything to put you in a position where you could be captured like that again?"

So, his boredom was a mask.

His anger razed over me, hotter than the fire in the hearth.

Give me that over apathy.

"No."

"Do you think that I hadn't already checked the office for bugs and external recording equipment?"

My brows rose. "You did?"

"I did." The breath rattled out of him. "I understand this is a trust issue. This is something that scares you. This is something that is outside of your control. That's why we're here. Somewhere that isn't your home where you feel safe, but somewhere that's still a space where you can feel protected."

My throat felt thick. "I don't like this."

"Did you, or did you not, use one of my toys to punish yourself this past week?"

"No, I didn't," I whispered, eyes prickling with tears. "I bought my own."

"Did you call me before it happened?"

"No, Hunter."

"Why didn't you? Wasn't that the one thing I asked of you when you found yourself in those situations?"

"It was, Hunter. I'm sorry." *I really was.*

Two nights ago, one of *Russu's* guards had broken up a fight between a couple of patrons. The way the woman's boyfriend had lit into her made me cringe at the memory. Something in my brain switched off. A bizarre kind of shame filtered into being.

What was the difference between her being punched and me having my ass spanked so hard that I couldn't sit down for a few days?

My consent?

Was that it?

It had spiraled into a bunch of self-deprecating thoughts. I knew Hunter would never hit a woman. Ever. He wasn't that kind of man.

But that niggle in my head had triggered a spate of bad behavior that I couldn't talk to him about.

So I'd bought another vampire paddle. Not to punish myself but as a test. I'd even stopped after a couple licks because it didn't feel as good as when Hunter used just his hand on me. By that point, the damage was done. The small wounds were back and the healing had to recommence.

"I want to know why you did it."

Another page turned.

God, if I were standing, I'd hurl that fucking book against the wall.

I didn't care if he was using that as a shield for his control. I wanted his attention on me even if it was in the form of a punishment.

"I don't like that my grandparents can see this."

I sensed his confusion. "Your grandparents are dead, Aurora. I can't stop ghosts from watching us from beyond the veil."

My lips *would* have twitched but I was in a mood now. "Their portrait. Above the hearth."

He heaved a sigh. Rather than tell me I was ridiculous, that I was being a brat, I heard him get to his feet.

A few seconds later, there was a scraping noise and a soft grunt, then more footsteps.

"Their back is to you now." A slight tension in my shoulders lessened. "Now talk, Aurora. No more distractions."

"I went to a therapist once. She was like you. She said it wasn't a pain kink, that it was self-harm."

The down cushions on the sofa depressed as air escaped upon his weight sinking onto them.

He was behind me, not to my left in the leather armchair.

"I *used* to think it was self-harm."

I rolled my head toward him. "Why the past tense?"

"Because I never saw your face when you were doling out your punishments. Because I didn't feel how your body reacted, didn't see it in person. It's more difficult long distance.

"I could see the way your tits would shake from panting, but you had the damn space so dark that I couldn't see sweat or if your muscles were quivering from strain.

"I couldn't see your expression or look deep into your eyes to read the situation as it needed to be read. I'm sorry your therapist wasn't understanding. I'm sorry I judged you incorrectly too."

I swallowed. "Thank you." He had no idea what that meant to me.

"You don't need to thank me. D let you down, but *I* will not."

That had me licking my lips. "D didn't let me down. Like you said, how could he when he wasn't able to see the full picture? I never blamed him for that."

"No, you just…" He sighed. "You reverted to old, *bad* behaviors."

"Yes." My admission was loaded with my personal shame.

"Why?"

I wriggled on the coffee table. "A couple got into a fight in *Russu* the night before last. He punched her before security got to her. Over and over—"

"You drew parallels between that and our dynamic?"

His words were toneless, and it helped me whisper out loud, "Some subs like being punched. Some like being forced."

"And some will probably go to any length a Dom or Domme demands of them," he concurred. "Are you questioning your inclinations?"

"No," I muttered. "It just put me on edge."

"Which is why you not only didn't tell me about your self-punishment but why you didn't answer my call and sent a text instead?"

That was probably the reason I was lying here exposed. Not the four licks with the vampire paddle to each inner thigh. But *that*.

It seemed neither of us liked being ignored—how similar we were in some things.

"I'm sorry."

He grunted. "'Sorry' is just a word, Aurora. Do you feel safe?"

"Yes, Hunter."

"Thank you for telling me where your mind's at."

"Thank you for caring."

"This is us. This is how it's meant to be. *We* are perfect, Aurora. Never doubt that." I didn't have an answer for that, but it didn't seem like he needed one either. He fell silent after he ordered, "Now, be quiet. I'm reading."

The pages of that damn book continued turning, and the faintest shift of fabric against fabric was audible as he moved on the sofa.

It had been an unseasonably cold night, but the fire wasn't necessary unless you were naked. I almost wished he'd strip off, too, to combat the heat, then at least, I'd know where he was going with this.

My back ached from the contact with the coffee table, and the strain in my inner thighs felt good from how I was positioned, but my shoulders were starting to feel pinched. I was so aware of how my tits were pushed together, of how my pussy lips, already parted by the piercings, were separated farther by my position—if I relaxed, my legs fell wider apart. If I tensed my thighs, it eased things.

I knew he could see straight down my torso, from the tunnel of my cleavage to the pooch of my belly.

His languor told me we could sit here all night like this. He was in no rush. Not to move, not to punish. *This* was my punishment.

Yet, though my sight was isolated, I wasn't alone. He was here. I could *smell* him. I was safe—no one could see me or get to me, not with him standing guard.

My breathing started to quicken. I just didn't know why.

Was it panic?

Was it need?

Was it exertion from holding the position?

God.

It was something.

There was a pile of work at *Russu* that I needed to attend to, but it didn't cross my mind a single time. I was focused on me. On him. Us.

Only us.

My head rolled from side to side and I couldn't stop myself from whispering, "I always hated it when you made me stand in the corner, Hunter."

He hummed. "I know."

This was a similar punishment, but at least he was here. Not on the other side of the country. Not watching me sob through a screen—

My mouth rounded at the thought.

Was that what he was waiting for?

My tears?

It made sense.

Release had more than one flavor.

Could I cry though?

Did I need to?

There was a definite shakiness to my emotions. A vulnerability. It had been there since I'd rolled back the tapes to watch that couple argue. When I'd ignored his call and texted him that I couldn't talk. When I'd bought the goddamn paddle.

What the fuck was wrong with me?

He was a part of my life now. I could speak with him about *anything* and he didn't judge me. He trusted me—not just with this, but with his life because, as his Consigliere, I had the power to destroy that. He'd made me his wife. But here I was, pulling mental gymnastics. Wasting time. Energy.

Here I was, not being held by him, because I'd made the wrong choice.

Why did I do that with him? Why did I continually make the wrong choice?

The only right one was when I'd said, "I do."

I sniffled.

I didn't mean to.

The inelegant noise was beyond my power to contain, however. My chin trembled and my lips quivered. Behind the blindfold, my eyes burned as tears started to form.

"I'm sorry, Hunter," I whispered.

"Do you think I'd punch you?" he asked quietly.

The words gave me pause. "I-If I needed you to, maybe?"

"I wouldn't," he disagreed. "I understand your pain kink. I understand that you treat it as pleasure. But for all that I learned about this dynamic for you, Aurora, I have my own preferences and my own boundaries. I will only go so far for you, but I will never demean you. It's not in me. I won't debase you or degrade you. That's *him*."

"Is that why you punished yourself? Did you miss him?"

Him—*Marcus*.

My ex-husband.

Now, the burning at the backs of my eyes had morphed into a full-on fire.

I sobbed, "NO!" It was more of a scream than anything else. *I'd made him doubt himself.* "No! No! No! Never. Ever. I never miss him. Degradation isn't my thing, I promise! You're perfect for me. So perfect."

His tone was a touch less wooden. "Then what happened?"

"I didn't question *you*. I questioned me," I cried.

"Why?"

It was a bark. A demand for an answer.

Deep inside, I cringed. "Because it's weird. Because sometimes *I* wonder if it is self-harm."

"And is it?"

I thought about how it hadn't felt all that good. How it had just hurt. "No. I like your hands on me. T-The paddle didn't—wouldn't… *couldn't—*"

He spoke over my stammering, "I still can't believe you bought another of those goddamn toys. I know I threw that out."

He had. As well as a bunch of other items from my closet.

"I'm sorry."

His sigh was heartfelt. "Are you ready to be punished?"

I blinked behind the blindfold. *There was more?*

Like he heard my thoughts, he drawled, "Yes, Aurora, there's more. Now, answer the question. Are you ready to be punished?"

I swallowed. "Yes, Hunter. I am."

HUNTER

BEHIND ME, the fire burned, making me understand how bacon felt in a pan. I didn't complain though, not when my mouth had other things to do.

Better things.

"Fuck, you taste like honey, moonlight. So goddamn sweet. So fucking perfect."

"Hunter," she cried. "Yes, please! More. More."

Her pleas got to me as nothing else could. With my name on her lips, her begging couldn't be mistaken—she wanted me.

My mouth. My tongue. My lips.

My cock already ached like a motherfucker but hearing that had me reaching down and unfastening my fly. I didn't think I'd ever take for granted that she wanted *me*.

"Remember, use your words," I reminded her before I got to work.

I sucked on her clit, hard enough for her to shriek before I tugged on her piercing and flipped it back and forth with my teeth. Her hips bucked up, pushing my chin and nose against her cunt. Uncaring, I moved down, letting her ride my face as I thrust my tongue into her slit.

"Oh, fuck. Please, please, Hunter," she whimpered, wriggling as she ground into me again. "I'm so close, so close."

The litany set up in my head as I trailed my tongue along the channel her piercings exposed for me. When I reached her clit, I fluttered the tip around it, fast, before I wiggled it from side to side.

"I'm going to come," she sobbed. "Hunter!"

I immediately pulled back. "Do *not* come."

Her chest heaved, making her tits jiggle as she strove to hold off her release. Around the mask, she was flushed and sweaty. Her body was a taut line as she fought the pleasure I was making her feel.

"How many more times?" she whined, making me smile to myself as I pulled up and back.

I didn't answer her, just moved over to the dresser where there was a small drink tray. Along the way, I almost knocked over the damn portrait she'd had me take down.

Only Aurora would think a painting had eyes.

Smiling at the thought as I poured myself a small brandy, I reminded her, "How many times did you spank yourself without my permission?"

She sobbed at my answer, which hadn't changed since I'd started.

Six times I'd edged her this far. Each lick of the vampire paddle earned her twice the torture.

It was no wonder she was a sopping, drenched, starving mess.

I twisted back and around and took in the state of her.

Beneath her ass, juices had puddled on the coffee table. Her cunt was bright pink, as was the rest of her body.

She was sweating, muscles straining in a manner that spoke of fatigue but also with an edge that came from adrenaline.

She wasn't the only one suffering here—my dick needed inside her yesterday, and my lips were starting to buzz with numbness. I'd just have to punish her for that too.

"Hunter," she cried. "Where are you?"

I didn't answer her, just made my way back to her.

With each step I took, she shuffled, twitching as she angled herself toward the noise. It was a minute movement, but one I registered because I noticed everything about her when I was in Domspace. I knew at that moment I'd never seen anything more goddamn beautiful in my life than her responding to my presence in such a simple manner.

When I moved around her, I commanded, "Open your mouth."

Her lips popped open with an eagerness that told me she was hoping she'd be tasting my dick soon.

"Only good girls get cock," I informed her as I carefully poured a couple drops of liquor onto her tongue. She sputtered some but kept her mouth open without prompt. After a few more drops, I placed the crystal tumbler of brandy on her stomach. "Don't spill any," I warned her, watching as she tensed her muscles in silent obeisance.

It was hot in the room, something the small shot of alcohol had exacerbated, and with her nearing the end of her punishment, I felt like I could finally strip off. She wasn't the only one sweating. Even with the fire banked, it was still overheated. Worth it though, considering how long she'd been splayed out on the coffee table naked—it had taken longer than I'd thought to break her.

Too long.

Something else we had to work on.

She twitched her head as I stripped off, letting me know she'd figured out what I was doing.

"I wanted nothing more than to sink inside you tonight. You denied us both that, Aurora."

Her mouth opened, lips quivering as she tried and, ultimately, failed to restrain herself: "No, Hunter, please—"

I ignored her, just folded back to the floor and worked to edge her.

Maybe it was the fact she knew I was naked, or maybe it was that I'd just told her I wouldn't be fucking her and she feared being denied entirely, or perhaps it was that she couldn't move without the glass falling from her stomach, but she got there faster than expected.

As I tongued her clit, I kept an eye on the brandy that, somehow, she managed to keep from spilling over.

A shrieked, "Stop!" was all she was capable of saying, and it came amid a garbled flutter of sounds that could have been words but failed in the execution.

"Stop? Red?"

She froze. "No! Not red!"

I wiggled my jaw which was aching from how long I'd been going down on her, then I grabbed my cock and let it drop against her slit. Another moan escaped her, long and low. Her breathing increased, and her stomach started to tremble under the duress of holding her muscles for such an extended period of time.

"Aurora, do you need to use your safe word?" I prompted.

She sucked in a breath. "N-No."

I heard her confusion.

"I wanted to check in with you, baby girl. That's all," I soothed, watching her suck in a shaky breath that I sensed was coated in her relief.

"H-Hunter," she moaned thickly, "I'm sorry. I'm so sorry."

I ignored her apology. "Will you do it again? Or would you say anything to get my dick? To earn my cum?"

I monitored her as her body locked with tension, wanting to know what she'd say next. We wouldn't be fucking tonight, but only one of us would be climaxing if she talked herself out of earning an orgasm.

I distracted her by running the tip of my shaft along the tender channel that connected her clit to her slit. I never let it connect with the small nub, just ran my cock piercing around the sensitive area and let her feel the shape of me before ghosting her with pressure as if I were going to slide into her… Only, I never did.

God damn her need to self-punish.

This was torture for me too.

As D, I'd never had the promise of her cunt anyway. Now, that was all I wanted. To end every night buried balls deep inside her.

That was probably why I'd been harder on her tonight.

Denying *her* was satisfying

Denying myself, not so much.

"Answer me, Aurora," I reminded her, aware my voice was almost a taunt.

She whimpered, "I-I want to promise that I won't do it again, but I don't know if I can." She didn't know that my eyes narrowed at her in response. "I-I can promise that if the need strikes, I *will* contact you. I'm not alone in this anymore.

"You're here for me. I should have answered your call. I shouldn't have just texted you and—"

Texting me was more than she'd have done as Sunny. I had to concede that.

"—I should have behaved better," she ended on a wail.

"You're right. You should have."

But she'd given me the words I'd needed to hear.

I let my cock collide with her clit. I rubbed along the little nubbin of nerves and I rounded it with my flesh and with the warm-to-the-touch metal. She groaned, hard and deep, as I ran back down to her slit, popping the head inside her, just enough to let her feel the stretch before I repeated the move over and over again.

"So fucking wet for me, baby girl," I ground out. "You're denying us this. I can't say you're my good girl tonight." My words had her crying. "But you're so beautiful. So fucking perfect for me even when you make mistakes, even when you're bad."

She started sobbing at that, the mixture of hormones and endorphins in her body giving her pleasure and release at the same time without even needing to orgasm.

Forgiveness went a hell of a way with a sub.

"I'm so fucking close, baby," I warned her. "I'm going to cover your cunt in my cum. You're going to feel me all night, getting sticky with my seed.

"It won't be inside you because you didn't earn it, but you'll feel the mess I leave behind and you'll deal with knowing the consequences of your actions."

"Can I have it, Hunter? Please? I'm so sorry. I-I don't deserve it, but please, I want your pleasure. *You* deserve it. You need it. Please," she whimpered, her begging easing my snit with her as little else could.

I groaned at her words and moved faster. "Do. Not. Come," I seethed as I ground my dick into her soft, slick folds and let myself find the release I'd been needing all goddamn week.

As cum spurted onto her sex, she shuddered in response but I could see that it wasn't in orgasm, just need.

As I coated her pussy, loading her up in my seed, I pursed my lips as I saw she'd managed to keep the brandy on her stomach.

It was expensive stuff, but as I let my spent cock flop onto her, I grabbed the glass and poured it on one of her inner thighs, making sure that it didn't touch her cunt. As the alcohol seeped into the myriad cuts on her flesh, she screamed, and amid those screams, I permitted, "*Now, you can come.*"

Her body went ramrod straight like I'd jolted her with a cattle prod and the keening wail she released hurt my ears until it cut out abruptly. So abruptly that it was jarring.

The climax hit her hard, to the point where I knew it was probably painful. Her abdomen muscles crunched, her limbs tensed, and she jittered with the force of her release.

I was watching her fly.

She stayed locked in that orgasm for an impressive amount of time, long enough that I started to worry until, finally, soft, soughing breaths escaped her lips as she returned to me.

As she came down from it, I finally let her free from her restraints, unsurprised when, now liberated, her hands and feet tunneled around me, drawing me into her as she dragged me with surprising strength into a hug that made my lips curve.

For someone who, I knew, aftercare had always been a necessary evil, not something she thought she craved, Aurora had definitely changed her tune…

24

___

HUNTER

A FEW WEEKS LATER

"HAVE you seen this morning's headline?"

I peered at her over my tablet and tried not to get turned on at the sight of her tits sporting the weights I'd placed on them after a shower this morning.

They were screwed on, which seemed antiquated and medieval, but her eyes had lit up when I'd showed her and her pupils had dilated with every turn of the screw.

"My eyes are up here, Hunter," she teased, and for all that she sounded jovial and was wearing no clothes, I knew Aurora, the businesswoman, was sitting at the head of the table, not Aurora, my sub.

That I got to see both sides of her was an honor, but I didn't mention that, just locked my eyes on hers. "No. I haven't checked the news. I'm working on my AI program that will identify card counters more accurately."

"For fun?"

"Yeah." I grinned at her, amused when she grinned back. I liked that. The businesswoman might be sitting opposite me but she was changing. Slowly. Surely. But they were steps in the right direction.

Whether those steps were a foot long or four inches, I'd take each and every one. "Okay, so what's the headline?"

She lifted her own tablet in a silent prompt and I frowned at the screen. "That's in Mandarin."

"Cantonese, actually."

"Since when do you read Cantonese? And since when do you check out Cantonese headlines?"

"I read a lot of different papers, and the Chinese government doesn't tend to censor Cantonese," she admitted.

"What's interesting about this one?"

"One of the Vice Chairmen of the Chinese Community Party's National Security Commission was found dead in his apartment. Overdose. 'Ke Jintao was discovered in a girlfriend's apartment,'" she quoted from the article. "And when I say girlfriend, I mean mistress."

"So?"

Her nose crinkled. "You don't think that's odd?"

"I don't know enough about the PRC to say."

"Someone so high-ranking wouldn't just be 'found' like that. It would be covered up. Not with drugs in his veins and beneath the roof of a property not belonging to him, his wife, or someone in his family."

"Wouldn't they have buried the story if it's suspicious?"

"This is a paper based in Hong Kong. Some of the truth filters out of China and through these articles. It's why I subscribe to it."

"Does the *Cosa Nostra* have business in China?" I queried, still uncertain why this interested her so much.

"We helped the Triads earlier this year," she said dismissively. "Gained back some territory as a result. I keep an eye on my enemies. Especially ones who are still ordered around by the base back home."

I pondered that. "Meaning you keep an eye on Russia too?"

She nodded, her lips pursing.

I wanted to kiss her.

Did she know that?

I always wanted her mouth on mine. This goddamn rule was starting to inhibit how often I could taste her.

You have to earn my kisses?

What had I been thinking?

The tight look had me forcing myself to concentrate. "Any news from Moscow?"

"The new Pakhan in New York isn't as popular at home as he is over here."

"Upstart, right?"

She chuckled. "Maxim Lyanov is the dictionary definition of upstart, but depending on who you talk to, the Valentinis are also upstarts."

"Do the people who dare label you as that have 'V's sliced into their cheeks?" I joked.

Aurora tapped her nose.

"Say no more," I teased. "So, what about this story has you thinking it's unusual? A politician with a drug problem *and* a girlfriend? Sounds like your standard congressman."

Her shoulder hitched. "This isn't the US we're talking about. It's odd. I don't like oddities."

"That's a lie. You like me."

"You're not an oddity."

"A Don who doesn't like to kill?" I winked at her. "It's fine. You won't hurt my feelings if you say it out loud."

Rory huffed and raised her tablet back up so she was hiding behind her screen. "If you're odd," she mumbled a second later, "then I like odd."

I tried, and failed, not to preen at that.

25

TEXT CHAT
THE FOLLOWING WEEK

AURORA: *You'll be glad to know that Messina and Puglisi are dead.*

Hunter: *'Glad' is overstating my interest lol. I'd prefer to know if your period is over.*

Aurora: *It will be in time for your visit.*

Hunter: *That's DEFINITELY nice to know, but mostly I was wondering if you were still feeling like shit.*

Aurora: *(₀●‿●₀) Do we have to talk about this?*

Hunter: *You don't have to be embarrassed with me.*

Aurora: *I'm not. I just don't like talking about them.*

Hunter: *I want to try something with you next time if it aligns with a visit.*

Aurora: *I don't want to have sex while I have my period.*

Hunter: *Not even an orgasm?*

Aurora: *No, not even an orgasm lol. Unless... ugh. Sorry. I mean, if you want to, then, of course...*

Hunter: *You're allowed to not want to do something, Aurora. Nothing is mandatory.*

Aurora: *I feel bad.*

Hunter: *You don't have to.*

Aurora: *You were trying to help. I just forgot myself.*

Hunter: *I'm glad to hear that. We're not always 'on.' You can just be yourself around me too.*

Aurora: *You'd be surprised how difficult it is to remember who I am sometimes.*

Hunter: *No. I know you too well for that to surprise me. Anyway, how did Stan deal with those pricks?*

Aurora: *You sure you're not mad?*

Hunter: *I'm sure. I told you I can handle bad behavior, Aurora, but this isn't bad behavior. It's called bodily autonomy. :**

Aurora: *Thank you. <3*

Aurora: *Stan poisoned them.*

Hunter: *He WHAT?*

Aurora: *Lol, right? I was surprised too. He walked in, punched them, pinched their noses until their mouths opened, then forced them to swallow a pill.*

Hunter: *What happened?*

Aurora: *It looked painful. He promised them the antidote and started asking them questions. Messina died quickly but Stan got out of Puglisi that his spawn WAS the guy talking to the Russians.*

Hunter: *The one who knew Jennifer had killed her mother's pimp?*

Aurora: *Yup.*

Hunter: *Prick.*

Aurora: *Definitely.*

Hunter: *Think Stan was cooking up that poison in his lab?*

Aurora: *Yeah. I think his research is a lot more focused than he's letting on.*

Hunter: *What do you mean?*

Aurora: *I went to see him in his lab to remind him he has a job outside of there. It's been a long time since I took chemistry, and I never studied anything as in-depth as him, but I remember him talking about something at the wedding. I dismissed it because I thought he was bullshitting me. Now, I don't think he is.*

Hunter: *What was he talking about?*

Aurora: *How the compound in Viagra is good for heart patients, but its one use in erectile dysfunction is what Big Pharma focused on.*

Hunter: *You think he's trying to create a heart medication?*

Aurora: *Yes. I just don't know why.*

Hunter: *Does Lauren have heart issues?*

Aurora: *No. Liver problems, yes. Thank you, red wine. But no issues with her heart.*

Aurora: *Although that might be down to the red wine too. FML.*

Hunter: *How is she?*

Aurora: *Loving Sicily. Loving Jennifer.*

Hunter: *Not long until she pops, right?*

Aurora: *Luciu's beside himself. It would be humorous if he weren't so terrified.*

Hunter: *Why's he scared?*

Aurora: *Jennifer's best friend had a miscarriage earlier this year. She ended up in the hospital. I think he's scared something will happen to Jennifer now.*

Hunter: *Understandable. I once read that making babies is the most dangerous thing a woman can do to her body.*

Aurora: *Yes, the things we sacrifice for our ungrateful spawn.*

Hunter: *Lol.*

Aurora: *Do you ever think about kids?*

Hunter: *Sometimes. They always have curls and big cocoa-brown eyes that make me melt.*

Aurora: *You'd be a pushover.*

Hunter: *You'd be the disciplinarian.*

Aurora: *Irony...*

Hunter: *Yes. :P You're not pregnant, are you?*

Aurora: *No. I got my period, remember? Lol. Bert's contracts just made me think, that's all.*

Hunter: *Do you want children? If you don't, fuck his contracts. I'll pry the final Anjou out of Mia Raleigh's cold, dead hands. It wasn't right for him to try to blackmail you into getting pregnant.*

Aurora: *Calm down. :* He added adoption to the mix so he was forward thinking. But tbh, kids haven't been on my radar because of what I do. Plus, I couldn't find a man who I wouldn't loathe marrying, never mind procreating with. Things are different now.*

Hunter: *They are.*

Aurora: *I'm not ready for them. Don't get me wrong. But... in time. With you. Yes.*

Hunter: *Really?!*

Aurora: *Really. Lol. It's still very early days though, se?*

Hunter: *Yeah. Definitely. But you just put the biggest smile on my face. And you can take that bottom lip from between your teeth. You bite it in front of me, and I'm going to demand an orgasm from you in the future.*

Aurora: *Fuck. Is that supposed to be a punishment?*

Hunter: *Orgasms don't always have to feel good...*

Aurora: **gulps**

Hunter: :*

26

AURORA
BILLIE EILISH - MY FUTURE

"LUCIU (BROTHER) IS CALLING."

Hunter stopped mid-thrust at the sound of my phone's declaration.

"NO! Oh, fuck, please, Hunter, please. I need it. Please!"

He'd been teasing me all goddamn day. I thought I was going to lose my shit if he stopped fucking me. His dick slid back in, making me cry with how good he felt. My head sagged on my neck, my face almost smothered by the pillows, but did I care? Nope. So long as he never stopped.

Ever.

Never, ever, ever, ever.

A deep sob of relief escaped me when my phone stopped buzzing and his pace sped up. I twisted my hands against the restraints that held them behind my back, feeling his command settle in my bones to come as many times as I could and 'I'll reward you for each one later.'

I wanted those rewards.

I'd seen that new whip he'd brought with him. It tied around his wrist like a small bracelet. Innocuous. Innocent. But also obscenely evident that any time, any place, if he wanted to punish me, he could.

And would.

Fuck.

FUCK.

The orgasm was there, within reach. So close. A fingertip's distance away. Oh, God. "Oh, God!" I screamed as he pounded my pussy with a hunger that spoke of our time apart…

Then:

"*Luciu (brother) is calling.*"

"Goddammit," he growled.

"FUCK," I sobbed when Hunter pulled out for real.

Stalking off, snarling with each step, he answered the call on my behalf, seeing as my hands were bound, and placed the cell beside me on the bed.

I hissed, "Luc, I swear to God, if this isn't important—"

"Rory." A sniff echoed in my ear. "She's fucking beautiful."

I stilled. "What? Who is?"

Was he crying?

No, Luc didn't cry.

My brain whirred, trying to understand what was happening as, mostly, it mourned, *Where the fuck is my fucking orgasm?*

"She's beautiful."

I cast Hunter a look but he shrugged at me, as in the dark as I was.

"Jennifer?" I mean, I didn't like her but I could see she was pretty. "You only just figured that out?" Jeez, maybe he *did* love her? "Did you really need to call me though?" The orgasm was slipping away, confusion taking its place.

Was he drunk?

"No," he choked. "Saverina."

Who the hell was Saverina?

I huffed out a breath that let my hair flow away from my sweaty forehead and twisted into a sitting position. It pulled on my shoulders in a way that wasn't a 'good' pain, not the kind I liked, but as I struggled to sit up, I groused, "Luc, I get that we're sharing more with each other, I do, but you don't want me to share what you're interrupting me from doing—"

"I have a daughter, Aurora," Luciu said, his tone dazed.

It was clear he hadn't listened to a word I'd uttered.

My eyes rounded. "Jennifer gave birth? And you called her Saverina?"

"Her idea. I have a daughter, Aurora. A daughter. If she's anything like you, she's going to give me a heart attack."

My smile made a swift appearance. "I'll make sure of it."

"Nah, you won't," he dismissed. "You never wanted to be the Don. You like being Consigliere."

Hunter snorted. "Congratulations, Luc."

"Hunter?"

"Yeah."

"You two are spending more time together, huh? Stan said you'd started fucking. Didn't know if he was winding me up or not." He still sounded utterly jacked on adrenaline. "Remind me to give you the talk when we catch up?"

It was difficult to take him seriously when he was talking like he'd been smoking a joint, and I knew Hunter agreed with me because his lips twitched into a smirk. "Yeah, *frate*. You can give me the talk when we're back together. Seriously, congratulations, Luc. You're going to make a great dad. You had the best example."

Luciu sucked in a sharp breath. "We did."

We really had.

Hunter's hands went to the cuffs at the small of my back and I was grateful instead of resentful when he started to unfasten them. Sure, I wanted my orgasm, but I had a niece.

The next generation had been born.

It was a bizarre moment.

Somehow encompassing everything I'd been building toward without even realizing it.

The future wasn't just ours now… It was her. Saverina. Living proof.

She was why we'd strived for so long to take back what belonged to us.

For her.

"We'll make her the first female Dona in history, Luc," I rasped. "She'll never have to fight like I did."

"She can be whatever she chooses to be," Hunter affirmed, his hand coming to clasp my shoulder once he'd tossed the cuffs on the bed.

I cast him a look, saw his gentle smile, and decided not to be offended.

"Yeah, Hunt, you're right. She'll be whatever she chooses to be," Luc said dreamily before his tone turned wistful: "I wish you were here. You, Hunter, and Stan."

"Next time, don't let Jen give birth in Sicily, but I get it. It's perfect. A new line. A new dawn." We had a reason for 'tomorrow' now. Everything we did would be for her. "How's *Matri*?"

"In love?"

"Kiss my niece for me."

"I will. I need to tell Stan—"

My lips rounded. "You told me first?"

"*Se. T'amu, soru.*"

He cut the call before I could do more than choke at his admission. Hunter gripped my chin and turned my face so we were looking at one another. A soft kiss on my lips made me shiver and nuzzle into him.

I had a niece and Luc had told *me* first.

Hunter's arms slipped around me as if he knew how shaken I was. Something he confirmed by asking, "You thought he'd tell Stan before you?"

My throat was annoyingly thick. "Yeah. They've had the last ten years together, and I couldn't associate with them because of, you know, everything."

He squeezed me as he tugged me into his arms for a hug. "You're his twin. Souls split at birth."

I pressed my face into his side, but all I could think was that he was wrong…

My soul had been waiting for yours.

I didn't say that though.

We weren't ready for 'I love you's. Not yet. I didn't know when, but I knew it was coming. Knew it like I knew I was now an aunt…

Maybe it'd be tomorrow.

Or the next day.

Or the next.

"You changed his name on your Caller ID."

I blinked at him. "Huh?"

"It used to be his full name. Now it's Luciu."

My nose crinkled. "You're too observant."

He chuckled and pressed his mouth to mine. As I lost myself in his kiss, in his hold, I sighed.

Saverina.

'The new house.'

We had a lot of things coming up in the future and, for the first time in too long, I was actually looking forward to what it might bring instead of bracing myself for the fallout.

27

———————

TEXT CHAT

HUNTER: *Rory says you're being weirder than usual.*

Stan: *So she sent you in to make me normal again?*

Hunter: *I don't think 'normal' was the word she used.*

Stan: *Ahhh, siblings. They always know how to make you feel better. There's nothing wrong with me.*

Hunter: *No?*

Stan: *Nothing that I can't fix.*

Hunter: *Explain?*

Stan: *What would you do if Aurora were sick?*

Hunter: *I'd fix her.*

Hunter: *Well, I'd pay people to fix her.*

Stan: *That's what I'm doing.*

Hunter: *What?*

Stan: *I'm fixing someone I love.*

Hunter: *Currau? I haven't met him yet.*

Stan: *You're in for a treat. He's a miserable bastard. Only Rory would put up with him.*

Hunter: *What do you mean? And don't think I didn't notice how you skipped my question.*

Stan: *She visits him, I think it's every week, and he ignores her.*

Stan: *I don't have the patience for that shit.*

Hunter: *No. I don't think I would either. Why does he ignore her?*

Stan: *It's a traumatic response to being forced to leave prison. Aurora's worked her whole life to get him out of that fucking pit, and she didn't take into account the fact that the old man has spent more time in the system than out of it.*

Hunter: *He'd have preferred to die in a cell?!*

Stan: *Technically, it'd have been a prison hospital. But yes.*

Hunter: *She's never talked about it.*

Stan: *She wouldn't. She's hardheaded like that.*

Hunter: *What was with the poison?*

Stan: *For Messina and Puglisi? Lol. That was fun. Gave them blood septicemia.*

Hunter: *Jesus. You turned their blood against them.*

Stan: *:P Tell me that's not fitting.*

Hunter: *You're as much of a headcase as your siblings.*

Stan: *But you still wuv us. Ha. What does that say about you?*

Hunter: *Who do you love that needs fixing?*

Stan: *That's for me to know, and for you not to find out.*

Hunter: *Mature, Stan. Real mature.*

Stan: *I'm the baby of the family. Whatcha gonna do?*

28

HUNTER

"PRINCE LUDWIG, who died childless and was a lifelong inhabitant of Liechtenstein, was the last son of the House of Ferdinand, a pretender to the Greek throne—"

Aurora switched the channel on the TV before the news reporter could finish the sentence and set *Sleeping Beauty* to play on low.

I knew she wasn't watching it because her nails tapped against the armrest of the sofa where she was splayed out, a cellphone on her stomach, a tablet plunked on her chest, a kindle on the cushions, a newspaper tossed at her feet, and two computers at her side on the floor.

With any more tech around her, she'd start glowing.

"Hunter?"

Sitting at Bert's desk in his office at the *palazzo*, I swiveled my seat around to give her my full attention.

It was late at night but we both had some work to do, so, as we multi-tasked, my cum was leaking out of her cunt and gracing the antique sofa and her ass was plugged with a tail that had taken me a while to find as it matched her hair color perfectly.

A quick glimpse had me ignoring an erection I didn't have time for at the moment. Her tits bore my initials, her ass was a bright purple, and I'd left her pretty much purring after I'd helped her come down from the high.

I would have been next to her but the Camorra called. She'd only just arrived but her work day was complete; mine was halfway through. Matteo and I had finally caught Paulu Ribaldi in an act of treachery. I was torn between ending him now so I could plant Aurora on the council *or* trying to figure out what his end game was.

"You're still running the Ledger, right?"

My mind had drifted back to work so it took me a couple seconds to answer her. "Yeah. For what it's worth. There aren't many jobs right now."

"Why not?"

"Sniper witch hunt."

"What?" she sputtered.

"Someone's targeting snipers," I explained. "Ones with a long-distance skill set."

"Why?"

"I don't know. They just are. Of course, there are more ways than a gun to kill people. But it's all quiet on the paid-to-murder front at the moment.

"What made you ask? I'm surprised you even know about that."

"Alberto," she said succinctly. "He was very proud."

"He would be."

She cleared her throat. "So, the Ledger…"

"Yes?" I prompted her when she dragged out the sentence. Did she know that she looked kissable when she was deep in thought?

How could I work a command into this conversation so that I could kiss her?

And why the fuck hadn't I just stopped with this bullshit already?

"Is it for US-only jobs?"

I blinked at her—our minds were definitely not on the same topic. "Mostly. Sometimes, overseas. But those are fewer. They have their version of it over in Europe."

"They do? Run by who?"

"A hacker group. BDSec."

When my lips curved, she arched a brow at me. "What's so funny?"

"The name always makes me laugh. They're renowned for being run by women, but the BD stands for Big Dick."

"Leave it to women to get the biggest E penis going."

"I'm surprised you know what an E penis is."

Aurora preened. "I might have been reading up on this stuff for you."

The warmth that filled me at that admission was disproportionate to the act, but it had me praising, "Such a good girl for me."

Her throat bobbed in surprise at the 'D' tone. "So, BDSec runs a Ledger of their own?"

"Yes." I shot her a knowing look. "They manage the kills of some of Europe's most skilled shooters."

Rory tipped her head to the side. "Do you know someone in this group?"

"I do." I flicked a glance at the TV that, before *Sleeping Beauty*, had been showing the news. "Do you want me to ask if Prince Ludwig was on the books?"

She nodded. "Please."

"Wasn't he in his eighties? A heart attack doesn't come as much of a surprise at that age," I pointed out.

"Would you mind asking?"

I shrugged. "Sure. You can make it up to me later…"

She chuckled. "Make *what* up to you later?"

"BDSec always has a price for sharing information."

I watched as she bit her lip, and, more importantly, her eyes darkened. "Whatever you need, Hunter."

Fuck, that tone. I loved it when she went all breathless on me. Like that, thoughts of work disappeared in a flash.

I curled my finger at her, pleased when she got to her feet. Then I pointed at the ground. Her throat bobbed but she complied and then,

Aurora Valentini-De Laurentiis, Consigliere of two factions of the Sicilian mafia, crawled on her hands and knees over to me, that tail of hers swinging with each move she made.

"How can I earn your kiss today, Hunter?" she breathed once she was in front of me.

Could life get any better?

AURORA

THE FOLLOWING WEEK

"WHAT THE HELL DO YOU MEAN?"

My hand paused, hovering in midair as Hunter snarled at someone on the phone. He glowered at me which had me sighing and replacing my knife and fork on the table—I wasn't in the mood for pancakes anymore.

Leaning back in my seat, I waited for him to finish the call. If I distracted him with my tits then so be it.

When he'd finished, I knew what had gotten him so angry so I went on the defense. "I had guards with me at every point of the journey apart from on the private jet."

His nostrils flared. "What about going without your security detail seemed like a smart decision?"

"I was without a detail *on board*. No one can get to me in the air," I sniped. "I was safe."

"You were planning something."

"I wasn't."

"You forget I know you, Aurora. You forget that I can see when you've got something in mind. What was the plan? Were you trying to draw out Albarez or something?" I strived to keep my expression blank but to no avail. He clicked his fingers at me. "You let your men find the fucker. You don't put yourself in the goddamn crosshairs!"

"I am letting them find the asswipe, but they're failing! The bastard's been living in New York for weeks now, sending us both pictures as reminders of his presence. I wanted to draw him out—"

"What was your plan?" he bit off.

I narrowed my eyes at him. "Don't talk to me like I'm an idiot, Hunter. At no point did I disobey you. The flight attendants and the pilots have been a part of our team for years." I faltered at that, knowing Jeffreys and Granger had recently lost their lives in the Messina-Puglisi siege. "I was in no danger."

The way his top lip curled told me he recognized *why* I'd hesitated. "So what was the end game?"

"He's been quiet for a few days now. I'm sick of this. I want to weed him out. I want this situation over with. It's frightening, Hunter, dammit."

His expression softened. "Did this nonsensical experiment work at least?"

"It wasn't nonsensical. He doesn't take pictures of me at the airfield that often. Each time, it's in one of three places. I had people monitoring those locations."

"And?"

"He wasn't at any of them. So this argument is for nothing."

"No, it isn't. Because you were trying to draw him out. Planes can be hijacked, as we've recently learned," he growled. "You don't put yourself in danger. You don't act like bait. What the fuck were you thinking?" He slammed his hand against the table, making the cutlery and dishes jump. "What the fuck would I do, Aurora, if anything had happened to you?"

When his voice choked, I closed my eyes. "I'm sorry, Hunter. I didn't mean to frighten you. I was safe—"

"You underestimate your worth. You always have." His gaze darkened. "It's why you traveled that first time here without a guard. You have more to lose than anyone because of the roles you've played in the past. Only God knows what that ex-brother-in-law of yours is up to right now.

"It's about time you recognized that there are people who will die for you. That there are people who will suffer if anyone hurts you."

My shoulders straightened. "I don't—"

But he didn't let me finish. "Get on your knees and crawl under the table toward me."

For a moment, I just stared at him. My heart was racing, and my skin felt flushed. There was no mistaking what his intention was, and like Pavlov's dogs, my entire being reacted to that promise.

Though I was angry, I *could* see it from his point of view. Only, it hadn't been a dumb test. I hadn't put myself in danger. My guards had checked the plane before I boarded, and when I'd landed, Brunu and his Stidda had been waiting to deliver me to the *palazzo* that had become Hunter's HQ.

He was mad at me because he cared.

We hadn't said the words.

But they were there.

In his eyes.

In the twist of his lips.

In the way his hand balled into a fist against the table at my procrastination.

He was wrong—I hadn't put myself in needless danger. My squad of watchers had been in position, waiting for a visual, ready to track the bastard down to his accommodations. If he had deigned to show up, we'd know where he was staying.

"I wasn't a sitting duck."

I needed to tell him that.

Needed him to know *that*.

"I would never have put myself in danger because I would never want you to lose me when we've just found each other."

As I uttered the words, I didn't see the effect they had on him because I slipped from the chair and crawled beneath the table.

When I was in front of him, and not a second more, he snapped, "In those moments where you were climbing up the steps, if Torres's demands had switched up from him simply asking to stalk you around the city and take pictures of you to a kill order, a guard would have taken the shot on your behalf.

"We don't know what's likely or not. We don't know how the dirty meth is affecting Torres's judgment. What we do know is that you came up with a plan to draw Albarez out without telling me. You could have put yourself in danger because you calculated the variables and you put a plan in place.

"Where *our* safety is concerned, Aurora, we don't act ham-handed. We plan and we plot. *Together.* How would you react if I put myself in such a position without telling you about it?"

My jaw worked. "I'd be annoyed."

"Exactly." His mouth tightened as he sank back in his seat, rolling his shoulders, then he patted his thigh. "Put your head there."

I didn't argue, just shuffled nearer and rested my cheek against his leg where he'd requested.

His fingers settled on my head, and they stroked through my hair before he slouched slightly. That was the moment when his focus shifted. It was no longer on me. I heard some taps as he did something on his tablet, then I heard the click of his keyboard as he started to work on his laptop.

As he concentrated on that, I just sat there.

He did this a lot—left me to think about my actions. I preferred *this* to that time in the library though. At least here I was touching him and he was touching me.

Had I really acted out?

I *should* have told him. He was right that I'd have been pissed, too, if the roles were reversed, but he'd never have let me act. I hadn't even done that damn much in the grand scheme of things.

Yes, a guard could have taken a shot for me if Torres had decided to use Albarez to end me.

Yes, planes could be hijacked and the staff on board could be used as pawns in a bigger game.

Had I acted as bait, I'd let him rail me to hell and back, but I didn't think I had.

In fact, I *knew* I hadn't.

He was always going to be protective of me. That was what Hunter did. I liked that, too, usually.

But who'd told him?

I'd kill Brunu if he was the one who—

He appeared to sense my growing agitation. "I wanted to speak with one of your guards so I had Adrianu go collect him. He wasn't there because you didn't bring any men with you, did you?"

Why did he want to speak with a guard of mine?

My lips thinned. "I was safe."

"You acted rashly. I thought we'd already goddamn settled this when you got out of the car after Stan was secured in Buffalo."

Keyword = secured.

"I didn't do anything wrong."

"We're married, and this is a *partnership.* You didn't confer with me on this. This is so, in the future, you remember to talk to me *first.*"

"I'm well aware that you can decide to do whatever the fuck you want with your body, *but* you need to communicate with me about this shit before you put yourself in danger. Just as you'd expect *me* to do if the roles were reversed."

I turned my face into his thigh, shifting my expression away from him so he couldn't see the mutinous cast on my features. "I wouldn't get to spank you though, if the roles *were* reversed."

He chuckled. "Never say never. A Dom shouldn't put his sub through something he himself wouldn't be willing to endure."

My eyes rounded, but when he didn't continue, silence fell between us again and I decided not to push my luck.

When my knees started to ache, I shuffled around, and he let me. He also permitted me to lean deeper into him to ease the strain on my legs. The move tugged on my piercings, making me hyperaware of my sex as my inner thighs rubbed together. A quick look at his dick told me my position at his feet was having an effect on him too.

Good.

At least we were both suffering here.

"Stop pouting, Aurora."

I gritted my teeth but stayed silent.

"If you die, I hurt. If I die, you hurt. That's our truth now."

I tensed up at that then let out a choked sigh when his fingers tangled in my hair again. This time, however, he dragged my head back with his hold on my soft curls, making the roots sting.

"Isn't it?"

I swallowed. "Yes. That's our truth."

"I've spent decades wishing I could be with you, Aurora." Pain shifted into his expression. "Don't do anything to jeopardize the future we can have. Do you understand me? You'll be dealing with more than a punishment if you do."

That was the moment his words penetrated my shields.

When I got where he was coming from.

To be wanted so much was an honor. Especially by him. This man who could have anyone, who was beautiful, who was sexy, yet who'd spent a lifetime wanting *me*.

"I understand you, Hunter," I whispered, the truth infused into each syllable.

"Good."

His fingers returned to petting my hair, but it was different this time. Softer. Gentle. I reacted to it, my body responding as I recognized the shift in his mood.

"I didn't mean to scare you, Hunter. I'm sorry that I did."

Another stroke of his fingers. "Just don't do it again."

There'd be plenty of stunts I'd pull over the years that he wouldn't approve of, but I understood that he was hyper-concerned about me. Understood and accepted that he wanted to wrap me up in cotton.

At some point, he'd have to accept that I *never* acted rashly. That my moves weren't sloppy and that I had no desire to die. My kinks were many and varied but I didn't have a death wish.

That'd take time for him to recognize.

Time we hadn't had together yet.

But we would.

Accepting that, I zoned out.

My mind shifted off business, which was boring, and shuffled onto the topic of his scent. How could his legs smell good too? His bare feet were right there as well. They should stink, shouldn't they?

Instead, I could smell the soap he used and which I associated with aftercare. There was his aftershave too. Laundry detergent. Him— something intangible. Something that was just Hunter.

Need began its slow crawl through my system as my body took over.

A shiver whispered through me as I peeped up at him and the first thing I saw was his erection straining against his fly. When I looked at his face, I found him watching me. The heat in his eyes made me want to burn forever in that fire.

"Are you full from breakfast, baby girl? Or are you hungry for something else?"

Baby girl.

Inside, I melted.

I wasn't Aurora. I was his baby girl.

Another flash of heat whipped me as I gave him the truth. "I'm always hungry for you, Hunter."

"That's what I like to hear." His gaze tripped over me. Settling on my shoulders, down to my tits, to the way I'd shuffled my legs together to get more comfortable from the sustained position. He licked his lips as he studied me before murmuring, "Spread your legs, baby. Let me see that pretty pussy." I did as he asked, wincing as my muscles protested the move. "Those labia rings, do you like that I can see how wet you are?"

"They tug sometimes but yes. I want you to see how wet you make me."

He let loose a soft rumble that was part laugh, part groan. "My moonlight's clever."

Oh, Christ, it was getting warm down here. His mind was not on our argument anymore either. Thank fuck.

"Take my cock out."

I shuddered at the order. "May I move my head?"

"Good girl for asking." There went my pussy. From wet to drenched in zero to five seconds. "You may."

Drifting back, I wriggled my neck to ease the strain then carefully unbuttoned his fly and unfastened his zipper. As I pulled it down, I saw his erection pushing against the fabric. Saw the slight markings from the tines that pressure had imprinted onto his skin.

With the constraints gone, his dick popped out.

The head was wet.

God.

If his pants weren't black, I'd bet there'd be a spot from where pre-cum had been gathering.

Need crawled through my veins, replacing the blood that usually resided there.

"Ask me for a lick."

Moaning, I closed my eyes.

"Look at me, Aurora," was his next order.

My lashes fluttered, and as our gazes collided, I whispered, "May I lick your cock, please, Hunter?"

He made a fist around his shaft and started to stroke himself. "Ask me again. Nicer."

Lust puddled in my core. The urge to touch my clit was strong, to slide my fingers into my cunt, but it wasn't him. Nothing felt the same anymore. Doing it myself wasn't enough.

Staring at him, I whimpered, "Pretty please, Hunter? I want your cum in my belly."

His hips rocked and his fist tightened. His jaw clenched and his eyes turned stormy. I knew, point blank, I'd never seen a more beautiful man in my entire life.

"You have to earn my cum," he chided. "Especially today. Open your mouth."

I did as he asked.

"Move closer."

I complied.

"Don't lick your lips." He pressed the tip to the Cupid's bow then drifted it around my mouth like it was gloss. "Show me some spit."

It was awkward with my lips parted but I let it bubble under my tongue.

He hummed. "I still have some work to do, Aurora. I'm going to give you my dick, and you're not going to do anything with it. Do you understand?"

I blinked. *What?* "No, Hunter."

He smirked. "You will. If you suck or if you tease me, you'll regret it."

There was a gleam in his eyes that I didn't trust. At all.

"That's right," Hunter mused, seeming to pick up on where my mind had taken me. "You did wrong, baby girl. Punishments aren't pretty. Do you want chastity? Or do you want this?" He stroked that big dick again and my pussy pulsed.

"No chastity," I pleaded. Since we'd gotten together, chastity was the *last* thing I craved.

"Then behave. I'll let you get it wet, but I'll tell you when to stop."

His pre-cum made my lips sticky as I whispered, "What if it gets dry when it's in my mouth?"

"I'll tell you when you can lubricate it if it's necessary. But I think the opposite happens—you should produce a lot of saliva."

"Am I allowed to touch myself?" I made my eyes plenty big. "Please?"

He laughed. "No, baby girl. Your pleasure belongs to me now. Remember? Not you."

As if I could forget.

The sound that escaped me was both hungry and desire-filled. It encompassed everything and nothing. How empty my pussy was, how badly I wanted his cum.

"This is a teaching moment. Are you ready to learn, Aurora?" he asked me quietly.

I wasn't, but I didn't want him to fill me with sex toys. Didn't want him to deny me, well, *him*.

Nodding, I opened my mouth wider than before.

"Words."

"Yes, Sir. I'm ready. Please, may I have your cock?"

"Clean the tip first." He held his dick as I licked the glans, tonguing the piercing and flipping it between my teeth before using spit to lubricate him. Only then did he pull back. "Beg me for it."

The burn in my core hurt as I pleaded, "Please, Sir. I need your cock. *Please*, I want your cum. I can't… I don't want to…" Speech failed me. "I need you. *You*. Only you. Please. *Please*."

As inelegant as my begging was, it must have stirred him. His eyes became heavy-lidded and his tip was placed against my tongue. I parted my lips to accept him inside. That in itself presented a problem, however. He was thick and I hadn't managed to lube the rest of his length up with saliva yet either.

A panicked sound drifted from me as he continued feeding me his shaft, but he stroked my hair and uttered soft, soothing noises, rumbling, "You can do it, baby."

I whimpered.

"You take me so well."

I winced at how wide my jaw was spread.

"Look how beautiful you are now."

I knew he meant it, and that helped me settle nearer to him. His attention soon shifted to his tablet, but I didn't mind. It felt like a Herculean task not to lick or suck because I really wanted to move my tongue. My head wasn't at the right angle, and my knees started to ache again. My back hurt too, and as for my neck—ouch. Breathing was difficult and, every now and then, pre-cum would drip into my mouth and I'd nearly choke on it.

It was uncomfortable, irritating, and an absolute nightmare.

I fucking loved it.

I'd never been more aware of my body. All I could think about was his dick and not moving, and every time I squirmed, the position with my spread thighs meant that my heel kind of dug underneath my pussy which provided me with some friction. I could feel juices sliding down my parted lips, and I wanted nothing more than to rub my clit, to get off, but this wasn't about that.

This was about obedience.

About punishment.

About his dominion over me.

I could do this.

I really could.

Slowly, I figured out what he'd allow because if he disapproved, he'd tug on my hair, and if he approved, he stroked it. That meant fidgeting wasn't permitted unless I was slipping on the floor, but it meant that resting my head on his lap was.

Saliva gathered in my mouth and it seeped from my lips. It made me uncertain what to do because while it trickled down his length, it kept making me gag. When I had no choice but to swallow or to choke, I swallowed.

Instantly, his hand was in my hair, and he dragged it by the roots. "Are you trying to tease me, you bad girl?"

His retort had me mewling words that were garbled around his shaft, "No, Hunter. No!"

"You are. You want to get out of your punishment," he hissed.

I started to shake my head but he kept me in place with his hold on my hair. His hips jerked up, and his dick slid impossibly farther down my throat. Panic settled in me, cumbersome and unwieldy, particularly when the saliva issue presented itself for inspection again.

Breathing through my nose, I tried to keep myself calm but I had to swallow. He had to know. He just had to. I waited as long as I could, hoping he'd give me an out, but he didn't.

I swallowed.

His hand tightened on my hair and I yelped around him, the pain slaloming around my veins as he pushed my face deeper onto his shaft so my nose was buried against his pubis.

"Bad girls who top from the bottom get punished."

I whined around his cock as he kept me there for endless moments.

"Swallow," he ordered.

With relief, I did. My throat caressed a large chunk of his entire length.

"You can be such a good girl when you obey me."

The words almost had my eyes crossing. But the tone? The tone of his voice was everything. I'd do *anything* to have him talk to me like that. *Anything.*

His gaze locked on mine, he asked, "Red?"

I shook my head.

"Amber?"

I shook my head again.

"Green?"

I nodded with my mouth full of cock.

"Good girl. You can suck on it now," he said after five minutes, an hour, *a day*, but he didn't let me move my head. The angle was awkward, so I just stroked my tongue beneath his shaft and swallowed often.

I wanted his cum.

It was my reward.

His fingers continued stroking through my hair while, with the other, I heard him type something one-handed. That he was my whole focus and I wasn't his pissed me off. I nipped where I could, and that had his gaze flashing down to catch mine.

His temper—oh, fuck. I'd thrown a Molotov cocktail at him and it had doubled back on me.

I'd forgotten *why* I was down here. That was how much I'd spaced out.

One second, I was on my knees with his dick in my mouth. The next, I was yelping as his tablet and some dishes and a fork flew onto the carpet, his shaft was pulled out from between my lips, and his hands were under my armpits.

With brute strength, I was manhandled onto the table. A soft, rumbling growl escaped him as he arranged me on the surface, head over the edge, his dick back in my mouth, tunneling down my throat.

My legs curled up to shield my pussy and my arms did the same with my tits until he snarled, "Enough."

I froze.

"Spread your legs."

I spread them.

"Hands on the table."

I laid them on the table.

His fingers went to my throat and he squeezed.

Gently.

I sucked in air through my nose and tried not to panic, but the adrenaline that whizzed through my system was enough to make me feel light-headed. I groaned around his shaft and slowly, he began to thrust into me.

Softly, at first.

My earlier panic had been unnecessary. This was Hunter. My Hunter. He'd only give me what he knew I could handle.

As if he wanted to challenge that, he spanked my cunt with the flat of his hand again.

Around his cock, I howled as he crooned, "So fucking wet, moonlight. So wet. You fucking love this, don't you?"

Tears poured down my face as he went deeper. Deeper. Timing each thrust into my mouth with another spank.

My clit throbbed. The labia rings bared the soft channel to my slit to his signet ring. It hurt. But good God, it hurt so beautifully.

"You gonna leave a puddle of cum on the table for me, baby girl?" He gave me another slap. "Answer me!"

I released a garbled, "Yes, yes, Hunter. Yes."

"Good," he snarled though I knew he couldn't have understood what I said.

His hips started to pump. Faster. Deeper. And his other fingers shaped my throat again. Not hard enough to cut off my breathing, just—

Fuck.

He was touching himself there.

Another slap to my cunt.

"You do not bite me."

Slap.

"You do not act like a brat to get what you want."

Slap.

"Do you understand?"

"Yes, yes, yes, Hunter," I mumbled around him.

His hand sped up in time with his hips. My mouth felt sore from how wide my lips were spread, and my throat would be tender later, but I didn't care.

Short, stuttered thrusts were my first clue to how close he was to release. Then, he barked, "You'd better climax, Aurora. If you don't, I won't give you my cum. Do you hear me?"

I groaned and focused on my clit. Focused on that rather than him. Each time his ring glanced off my tenderness, it stung in the best possible way.

I—

Could I?

No.

Yes.

Fuck.

This was punishment but it was pleasure. It hurt so good. Too good. A single stinging slap had more power than my fingers rubbing my clit as I tried to get off.

Another slap.

And another.

It happened so fast that it was in a blur.

Another slap.

I screamed as darkness pooled around the edges of my vision. He came. His seed poured down my throat as I choked on it. I could feel saliva and cum start to seep past the edges of my mouth and I knew I'd look like a mess, but I didn't give a damn.

All I could think about was the ecstasy whittling around my system and the taste of him on my tongue.

I sobbed, I choked, I cried, and I moaned. It was too good, much too good. A person should die from this much pleasure, but for the first time in a long while, I had something to live for.

It was beautiful. It hurt. It was like dying. It was like living. It was a study of contrasts. Impossible yet possible. I'd never felt so intrinsically *his* and I loved it.

Loved him.

I had no idea how much time had passed when, eventually, he

pulled his shaft out of my mouth, and he proceeded to help straighten me up.

Blood had rushed to my head, but as I wavered there, trembling and exhausted and overdosing on endorphins, he cleaned my face with a napkin.

He wore a stern expression as he did so and I felt suitably chastened when he informed me, "Once you clean up the mess you made, the bite is forgiven, moonlight. Your actions yesterday are too so long as you understand that I won't allow you to endanger yourself again." His gaze narrowed. "And when you make these types of calls, you're to use my measure as judgment, not your own, understood?"

Dazed, I nodded. My mind was gone. Literally gone. I didn't know what he was talking about. He could have been speaking Klingon for all my brain knew. Then, his hand moved, and I followed his finger as he pointed at the cum on the mahogany table.

My release.

That's what he meant by 'cleaning up the mess you made.'

Settling onto my knees, I crawled, shakily, over to the small puddle and once I made it there, I grabbed my hair and held it from my face with one hand, and I stared at him as my tongue popped out and I cleaned up my spilled juices.

His gaze darkened, his softened cock started twitching, and everything in me preened that I had the full attention of this, the man I loved.

Then, he made me moan without even touching me. He curled his fingers at me in a beckoning motion as I crawled back to him once my task was complete. I knew he loved seeing me on my knees like this, and I loved giving this to him in return.

His fingers cupped my chin, tilting my head up and back. For what felt like a lifetime, he studied my mouth. It was painful—the need for his kiss. It hurt how badly I wanted it. How deep the craving went. Like the roots of a thousand-year-old tree—I needed him, his kiss, his love.

His thumb swiped along my bottom lip. I could feel the slickness from my juices ease the journey and registered his visceral response in the flared nostrils that spoke of a man who was *not* grossed out by what coated my mouth.

"No more earning kisses."

Hope stirred. "What?"

"I'm denying myself more than you."

I stared at him, feeling lost from the abruptness of the scene to his silken words. His hand cupped my chin as he tilted my face to the left and then to the right, and before I knew it, he was hauling me into his arms.

I didn't fight, didn't argue.

I felt oddly limp.

As if my emotions were about to riot, but I didn't know why.

A weird blankness overtook my brain. It was powerful. Overwhelming.

I blinked and realized he'd taken us into the bathroom. I'd been so dazed that it hadn't even registered that he'd filled the bath a quarter-full already.

When we stepped into the tub, I felt the heat of the water hit my skin and I sighed in response. His hands stroked up and down my arms, trailing down the small of my back, then he cupped my nape and pulled me into him, angling his face in a way that meant he could tuck me into the nook of his throat.

My thoughts started to return to me in slow trickles.

"Aurora," he murmured. "Tell me what you smell."

The smell of the soap—*him.*

"Words, baby girl. Words," he requested as if he knew I'd answered, just not verbally.

"You. Soap."

"What do you see?"

The lights were dimmed—comforting to my eyes.

"Nothing. Too dark. Nice."

"Such a good girl for me, such good answers," he crooned, making my heartbeat settle down—I hadn't even realized it was still racing.

"Thank you, Hunter," was my meek response.

My tone was off.

Was that really me talking?

"What about what you can feel, hmm?"

It took me too long to recognize that he was grounding me through my five senses.

What *did* I feel? I bit my lip as I pondered the answer.

The water was a touch too hot—it made my face sweaty, *but* it glued my skin to his and only that was close enough.

"The water. Silky. Too hot. But nice."

He hummed. "And what about what you can hear?"

The softness of his breathing in my ear—calm, just like this moment.

"Your breathing." I held mine and then slowly followed his pace, making our breaths sync up.

"What about taste, hmm?"

That was the only missing sense.

It felt like a gnawing empty hole so I stuck my tongue out and tasted his skin.

Salty from sweat. Musky. *Him.*

I sighed. "You."

His hand moved over my hair—petting me. So different than his roughness of earlier. "How are you feeling?"

"Tired." Sad? No. I *had* felt… down? No. "Tired," I repeated, tone firmer.

His fingers rubbed a knot he found in my shoulder. "We can sleep afterward."

Nodding, I closed my eyes, then it registered what he'd said before. What he'd said and what I *hadn't* reacted to.

I could kiss him.

I didn't have to earn kisses anymore.

"Hunter?"

"Yes, baby girl."

I tested, "May I have a kiss, please?"

"You don't have to ask anymore, do you?"

I didn't have to ask. That meant more than he could know.

Ignoring how our skin didn't want to let go of the other, I tipped my head back as I looked at him.

He was watching me.

His heart in his eyes.

His need for me as prevalent as I knew mine would be for him.

I reached up and settled my lips atop his.

I had no idea why, but a soft laugh bubbled inside me. When he didn't pull away, when he didn't tell me I was a bad girl for breaking rules, I let my arms crawl around his neck. When he didn't chide me for that either, I held him closer and let my tongue prod the seam of his mouth for entrance.

He let me in.

It was messy and dirty and nasty and *beautiful*.

Perfect.

Just like him.

Just like us.

I'd never tire of this.

Never.

30

AURORA

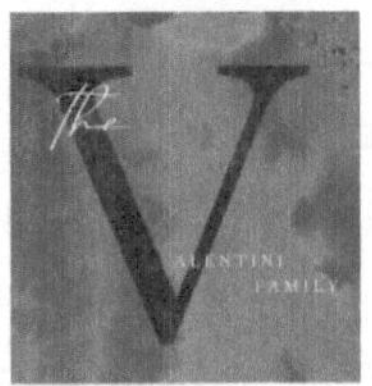

"ANYTHING?"

"Nothing, Ms. Rory."

"He sent more pictures to my—" I nearly choked on the word *husband.* "—boyfriend. Albarez is somewhere. The squad just isn't focused enough."

The pictures Ernesto Albarez had sent were of me getting onto the plane alone.

God damn that man.

He'd pinpointed another location from where to shoot the photos. My whole plan had been for nothing… Well, the punishment had been epic.

"We're spread thin," Chadwick commented, his tone serene in contrast to mine.

"Recruit more people then."

"Takes time to train them."

"Get help." This situation was starting to drive me crazy. My life was perilous enough without this fucker stalking my every move. "He isn't a ghost. Someone must have seen him."

"Maybe he's hiding out in an apartment and getting supplies

brought to him then sneaking out undercover," he suggested, scratching his jaw which had recently been shaved.

He had pink spots from his first shave in two years.

Chad was one of my projects, and I meant that in the kindest possible way.

He'd lived on the streets for eighteen months. I'd given him responsibilities, had asked for his help, had given him a place to stay, had him checked out by a doctor, and had put food in his belly.

Shaving had been his idea, but it was a relief he'd gotten rid of the beard because I was sure things were living in it and, more importantly, I knew it was a step in the right direction for him.

"He isn't hunkering down in an apartment because the pictures aren't all of me in my building." Trying to find Albarez in New York City was like trying to find a needle in a haystack. I pondered the situation. "Maybe check out the buildings around *Russu* and cast a wider net?"

"What do you want me to do with him if we find him?"

There was something in his question that had me narrowing my eyes. "Chad, what did you do before… everything went down?"

I'd kept things impersonal thus far, not wanting to trigger any paranoia in him. But he'd gotten used to my temper by now so I figured this was as good a time as any to get him to open up to me.

"I was a soldier, ma'am. Served with some of the finest in the Green Berets—the Chaos Platoon."

That fit.

I knew he had PTSD—there were complaints from the other residents of the dorms where he lived that he woke them up screaming at night. But his posture, his response to orders, how he commanded the men around him even though I wasn't running an army here—Stan teased me that it was, but I always told him to fuck off—his previous employment made sense.

"If you catch Albarez, follow him," I said eventually. "Don't lose him. Call Giovi. Make sure he has accurate coordinates. We'll deal with things afterward."

Chad nodded at me. "Yes, ma'am."

After he'd gone, I stared at the door he'd left through until Siri announced Hunter's name.

The moment she did, I felt the ache in my pussy and ass from the chastity device I was wearing.

Snatching my phone, I grimaced when another ache made itself known to me—on my tits, I had more H and L letters dotted on the sides so they rubbed against my bra every time I moved my torso or arms.

It hurt.

Better than the spikes ever had.

It was bliss.

"Hey, Rory," he rumbled in my ear, sounding like he'd just woken up.

A soft thrill rushed through me, a dumb one—I liked thinking that I was the first thing on his mind.

I swore, around him, I was reverting to my teenage self. Except I was no longer just content with my hair being pulled…

"Good morning," I greeted him, aware my voice was soft and not even caring.

Keeping my walls up was impossible with him.

I heard rustling, which was confirmation he was still in bed, then he yawned. "I have news."

"About?"

"Martínez's war of terror on the leaders of the *Reyes*," he drawled, amused.

"And?"

"Vitale contacted me, said Martínez's niece had run away and had come to them for refuge. The dirty meth is making the leaders more aggressive.

"I thought the goal was to annihilate them with the drugs, but maybe it's so they'll kill each other? It'd make sense," he mused. "Looks less suspicious that way. Would explain why it's taking a while too."

I reached up and pinched the bridge of my nose. "Is she safe there?"

"I think so. Vitale sounded furious at the state of her."

Another victim of misogynistic abuse on my watch.

Someone else I'd fucking failed.

"Christ." I let my mind race to burn off some of my nerves. "You're due to come up here, but I'll fly down. We'll need to conference with Martínez."

"He doesn't know about his niece," Hunter agreed. "He'd have contacted me otherwise. I told Vitale to keep it on the down low."

"Good. I won't use her as leverage—"

He heard my warning and interrupted, "As if I'd ask you to."

I smiled. "But we need to make sure she's okay first."

"Why?"

"Because I like how Martínez is handling this. It keeps the aggression focused on the *Reyes'* leaders and means it won't spill outside of the epicenter.

"If Martínez realizes his niece has been abused, then there'll be overspill.

"I also like his plan to just deal with the leadership. He's right about the rest of the *Reyes*—they're mostly kids."

Hunter hesitated. "You want to keep her hidden away if she's bruised?"

When he put it like that… "Perhaps."

"Torres won't let her go that easily. He'll be searching for her. The violence will spill onto the Vitales whether you want to keep it contained to the *Reyes* or not."

I pulled a face, hating that he was right. "Not if we bring her to Vegas."

"True."

"And if we brand any *Rey* who is spotted on Camorran territory, then it'll register that we mean business."

Hunter hummed. "Did I ever tell you I like it when I can hear the cogs turning in your brain?"

"Shut up," I said around a laugh.

"What? I do!"

I didn't bother hiding a grin when he couldn't see it anyway.

Instead, I informed him, "I asked Brunu to ride into *Reyes'* territory yesterday."

"Why?"

"I had a feeling."

"About?"

"Something Martínez said when we met." I paused. "Remember I told you how the *Lobos* look after their turf?"

"I do. I also remember saying I wanted to be a leader like that. All this murdering business, it's not good for the soul."

"Eat some chicken soup then."

"Yeah, yeah."

"Anyway, I was curious about what was taking Martínez so long to act. I thought the dirty meth would just poison them too. Brunu's visit plus investigating local records confirmed my initial suspicion—he's already started his campaign in the neighborhood.

"They had a baseball field that was going to rack and ruin in the center of their turf—guess what's just been cleaned up?"

"I assume that's a rhetorical question."

"It is." Absentmindedly, I picked up my pen and started scratching out a doodle. "The land that borders the Vitale's is littered with burned-out cars. A group of moms was fighting to get them taken away— someone listened."

"He's cleaning the place."

"He is. There were empty lots in one of their commercial districts; they've been bought up. Plans have been set with the council for a non-profit kid's nursery that'll be running on 'donations' and what appears to be some kind of community center."

"Interesting," he mused. "He said it was a fixer-upper."

"He has a child now," I pointed out carefully. "He created a conspiracy theory so his wife could safely return to the US."

A conspiracy I knew Jennifer had been pivotal in as she'd convinced the journalist and wife of the heir of the Irish Mob, Savannah O'Donnelly, (also her best friend), to publish that theory. One that simultaneously vilified the New World Sparrows further and made it less of a theory and more of a reality in the public eye.

Legally speaking, Eva Kingston was on shaky ground, but it was something that could be battled in the court for years.

I'd looked into the case with my DA hat on and wouldn't have touched it with a hundred-foot barge pole. Too much likelihood of bad press for the NYPD whose rep was only getting worse in the face of wave after wave of exposés on police corruption, and not enough certainty that a jury would convict her when the New World Sparrows were involved.

In the new United States where every aspect of government had been infiltrated by a secret society more invasive than black mold, conspiracies had become truths and truths were becoming conspiracies.

It was an interesting time to be alive, that was for sure.

Hunter mused, "You think Martínez just wants to clean the place up and raise his kid and have a family in peace?"

"You don't sound like you blame him," I said carefully.

"How can I? I didn't ask for this life. I'd prefer to live in a safe neighborhood where my kids can grow up without a target on their back too."

Those words rattled me more than I could say.

Saverina.

Our tomorrow.

He wasn't wrong—her security was going to be a massive headache. I'd need to confer with Luciu and Stan about that.

And it wasn't like NYC was a 'nice' suburban neighborhood where kids played in their yards and only got scared if they thought they were going to miss out on a popsicle when the ice cream truck drove down their street.

Hunter, unaware where my mind had taken me, muttered, "To be honest, it'll be nice to deal with someone who means what they say."

"As opposed to me." I couldn't help myself from teasing him.

"You're much easier now that I can spank you for speaking mistruths." Another hum sounded in my ear. His words and that hum combined to craft my downfall in regards to him—*lust*. And I needed it or I'd freak out about Saverina's security. Then, he had to go and kill my buzz. "Speaking of... Do you still like Robbie Williams?"

What kind of segue was that?

My cheeks immediately burned bright red. "Shut up, Hunter."

He chuckled. "I'm going to take that as a yes. Remember that time you spent the summer in the UK, and you came back home, and he was all you could talk about?"

I huffed. "What's made you turn reminiscent on me?"

"I heard one of his songs in the casino yesterday."

"That's random."

"I know. But it made me think of you. Anyway, I'll arrange for the jet to pick you up tomorrow—"

"No, it's fine. I'll use ours." I reached for my phone and, as I made the arrangements, reasoned, "Luc isn't here and Stan's still doing the bare minimum so no one will know."

"Would it matter if they did?"

"Not particularly, but I figured we're still keeping things under wraps."

"The 'you're my wife' thing or the 'you're my Consigliere' thing?"

My lips curved. "Both? Mostly, right now, the Consigliere thing seeing as you haven't fired Ribaldi yet. I'm stretched pretty thin anyway. I don't need anyone, even my well-meaning brother, knowing that."

"When is he returning to the States?"

"As soon as Saverina can fly. She had some sort of baby ailment that went wrong and she can't travel until it's gone."

"What kind of baby ailment?" He snorted. "Only *you* would call it that."

He wasn't wrong. I wasn't aware of most things to do with pregnancy. "I don't know. Something undoubtedly gross and involving bodily fluids."

"Have you seen her?"

"Of course. Luc video-called me to introduce her. She's very…" I pulled a face. "Pink."

His laughter was judgment-free and it settled something in me, some hidden concern that he'd dislike how it seemed I wasn't comfortable around children. But how could anyone think I'd be comfortable around them? Whereabouts in a boardroom did a kid fit in?

To the outside world, I should hate kids. The world would never think I'd like crotch goblins, and who was I to change the world's opinion?

That he maybe saw behind that mask made me feel better.

Children were a future thing. An ethereal dream. One he allowed me to have…

"Luc called and showed her to me too. I told Brunu she was bright pink with fluff on her head."

"He asked?"

"Brunu loves kids. Has about forty grandchildren."

"Are you being serious?" I screeched.

"Nope. He had eight of his own, adopted two of his nieces when his brother died on a job, and they've all had anything from two to six kids a piece."

My mouth rounded. "I couldn't cope."

"Me either. I can see Luc having a big family though. Can't you?"

"Stan will. I think Luc will settle with two or three. Jennifer…" I cleared my throat. "I think she'd like a family. She didn't have much of one as far as I can tell."

"You know, we've never talked about her."

"About her, what? That we dislike each other?" I countered dismissively, already bored by the topic.

"I'm not sure you dislike her. She just represents..." He sighed. "You've strived for years to reach this position and all she needed to do was charm your brother and look beautiful to be the queen of the Valentinis.

"Throw in the fact that she's everything you never wanted for your grand plans for the family, and it's small wonder she grates on you."

"It's annoying how well you can read me sometimes."

His knowing chuckle didn't chafe my temper. Not when, for the first time since Jennifer had waltzed into my sphere, I felt seen. *Understood.*

Validated.

"I'd like to think that if the roles were reversed, Luc would have stopped any self-professed gold digger from targeting you…"

"Luc would have sliced and diced him before he managed to kiss the back of my hand," I agreed grouchily. "When I do it with him, it's as if I'm the Wicked Witch of the West!"

Hunter grumbled, "You're lucky you said 'kiss the back of your hand.'"

A quick, wry grin creased my lips. "Hunter, there's no need for jealousy."

"There's every need," he said briskly. "I have one of the most gorgeous women on the East Coast wearing my ring around her neck, *not* on her finger."

My brow furrowed. "Hunter, you don't need to be jealous. I'm being serious. I don't want anyone else. Surely you've learned by now how bad my tunnel vision is."

Another guy, I might have courted their jealousy, but I didn't want him hurting. Not over something so ridiculous.

He grunted. "True. Anyway, I was talking about the fact that Jennifer was recorded while she was date-raped."

I immediately grimaced. "Yes. I don't want either of them to find out."

"Understandable. It would wreck her and break his heart."

"Plus, the guy's already dead. So it's not like he'd have the satisfaction of killing him."

"It wouldn't."

I frowned. "It wouldn't what?"

"Killing the rapist doesn't make it better."

I thought about what he'd done for Rachel. "No, I don't suppose it would for you. You're not that kind of guy."

"What kind of guy am I?"

I heard the aggrieved snipe and dismissed that too. "You're rational and reasonable. You don't snap unless goaded. I appreciate that about you.

"A man like Luciu would drive me insane. When I listened to you explain why you didn't want to kill that coyote the morning after Luc's wedding, why it didn't make sense, why branding him *would* be sensible, I think I already knew how perfect you were for me."

"You suggested killing the coyote too," he pointed out, but I heard the smugness in his voice at my compliment overtake his earlier irritation.

"I did. Because that's what's expected. That doesn't mean there aren't smarter ways to go about things."

"True. It is a 'kill first, ask questions later' kind of world we inhabit." He sighed. "I need to tell you something. You forgot about it, and I keep putting it off."

"Okay." I braced myself. "About Jennifer?"

"No. I checked her out weeks ago. There's no footage of her online. Not on any porn sites, or any dark web repositories, and I'll keep crawlers on it just in case."

"How do you know for certain?"

"Used an AI program to hunt down her face."

I blinked. "You can do that?"

"I just did," he teased. "My software's advanced, enough that I'm comfortable her secret is safe with us."

A niggle that had been between my shoulders, right at the back of my brain, suddenly unraveled.

God, I hadn't recognized how stressed I'd been about this.

"You know," I choked out, my voice raw with relief, "I didn't realize how attractive intelligence was until recently."

"You'll have to remind me of that when you get here."

"Oh," I purred. "I will."

"Fuck."

"What's wrong?"

"I still need to tell you something and I'd prefer the conversation not be diverted—"

My cheeks flushed again. "That bad?" I'd definitely been veering us toward phone sex.

"Depends."

"On?"

"Do you remember a guy, Reilly Green, from college?"

I recognized the name from Alberto's prompt to ask Hunter about him. "We knew him at Brown?"

"He was on the football team with me."

"Oh. That explains it. I was only interested in you back then. The rest of the team were piles of shit."

His chuckle was soft. "You're good for my ego."

"Not really. It's true. You had it in you to go further than just college ball."

"Fucked up my rotator cuff," he said, tone blasé. "But that doesn't matter. Bert had me handle Reilly Green."

"Handle?" I repeated. "To the death?"

"Yes."

Huh. "Why? Because he was crap at football?"

"Because his DNA was uncovered at the scene of your date rape."

My eyes narrowed. "What position did he play on the team?"

"Linebacker."

I let the news sink in as I tried to recall the starting lineup back when Hunter had played ball at Brown. I couldn't see his face though. I guessed that could have been a good thing.

Considering.

A strange blankness filled me. It was neither positive nor negative. Just... nothing.

Maybe it made sense seeing as my rapist had been faceless and nameless for so long.

"Did you make him hurt?" I asked quietly when I could feel his anxiety throb down the line.

"Pretended he was a piñata."

I pictured that in my head. "Baseball bat?"

"Yes."

"Remind me to thank you when I get there?"

"It doesn't make it better. You don't have to thank me."

I thought about those lost hours, the pain I'd been in, the indignity of it all, of the tests and the nurses who'd tried to be kind but who'd been asking me questions I couldn't possibly answer.

I thought of the nightmares and the fear and the solid truth that I'd been unable to live alone, without Hunter (that was why we'd moved out of the dorms early and had rented someplace together), until Marcus had come along… An unwise relationship that was undoubtedly founded on the trauma from my attack.

Carefully, I said, "I think you'll find I owe you more than a 'thank you.'"

31

HUNTER

AURORA WAS PRICKLY. There was no other word to describe her that wasn't also derogatory. Prickly like a cactus, not a porcupine. Those prickles were constantly engaged, not just a defense mechanism.

It was, therefore, unsurprising when she saw Martínez's niece that those prickles turned into hackles. Especially after our conversation about Reilly Green.

Her hands balled into fists as if she were trying to contain the urge to punch something before she unfurled one and tucked the girl's fingers in her own.

"My name's Aurora."

The girl peeped at her. "I'm Teresa. I know who you are." Her accent was there in a soft sibilance, but her English was perfect too.

"Who am I?" Aurora queried.

She bit her bottom lip then peeped at Cesare Vitale, whose smile was kind. "You can trust them, Teresa. These guys mean you no harm."

Though my brows arched at how she'd looked at Vitale for reassurance, I shifted focus onto the girl again when she explained, "Torres has one of his men photographing you. That's how I know your face."

Aurora's jaw clenched. "We're trying to find him."

"Ernesto is…" Her nose crinkled. "…like a snake. He slithers here and there, too fast to be caught."

"We'll find him," I said grimly.

Teresa hitched a shoulder. "Torres gave him good money to keep you scared and guessing."

Rage slalomed through my veins faster than vodka ever could. But her voice had been small, scared like she anticipated she'd be the one paying for the intel. It took everything in me to dampen down my fury, and instead, I demanded, "Why set a photographer on us in the first place?"

"To keep you distracted."

Aurora, having invited her to take a seat on the sofa, planted herself on the coffee table in front of Teresa. She was dressed in a pantsuit that was tailored to her curves which lent a softness to her image, but the sharp cut spoke of her position in the mafia.

With her elbows on her knees, she looked more approachable as she muttered, "They should worry about themselves. Your uncle is giving them the runaround."

Teresa's eyes flared. "*Tío* Martínez? He knows—"

"He knows everything, and he's willing to wage a war to bring you back home."

Her mouth rounded. "The baseball pitch."

I studied her. "What about it?"

"Torres went crazy when it got cleaned up. That was *Tío*, wasn't it?"

Aurora nodded. "We believe so."

Tears flooded the teenager's eyes. "I've made such a mess of things. Antonio, I mean, Torres, he was so kind until… he wasn't. I thought he was like my father. Like my uncle." She swallowed. "They're good men."

When her words waned, I asked gently, "What happened to…make you run away to the Vitales?" My hesitation was formed by the bruises she was covered in.

Teresa gingerly rubbed her eyes and patted her cheeks. "The *Reyes* were furious when the Don—" She fluttered a glance at me. "—

attended old man Vitale's funeral. They knew that meant they had Camorran approval. I realized if I got to the Vitales, then they'd get me to you, and the Camorra is safer than the *Reyes*."

"You had no way of knowing that," Aurora pointed out, her tone soothing.

"Trust me, I did. They were always aggressive, like hyped-up frat boys, but recently—" She swallowed. "I knew that I could get hurt. I had to get out of there. I had to." Her hand wafted in front of her face. "Too late."

"You're safe now. We'll get you back to your uncle."

Teresa squeezed her hand. "I know it's an imposition, but would you mind waiting until the bruises have faded?"

I didn't have to see Rory's expression to sense her relief. "Of course."

"*Tío* will be angry, and I can't handle that right now. I know he's…" She fidgeted. "…but I don't want him to… Have you met him, Aurora?" she settled on finally.

"I have."

Her shoulders sagged. "Then you'll have met Kingston."

"Yes," Aurora concurred.

"She probably thinks I'm a fool." Irritation slithered into her expression, making her frown. "She'd be right." Somehow, I thought Teresa was more distressed at the idea of Kingston seeing her bruises than her uncle. "I don't need her to *see* how stupid I was—"

"Teresa, I'm sure Kingston would never judge you for what you've gone through. Nor would she rub it in that you've been beaten, and so badly. Not with her past." Aurora patted her hand. "I was going to ask you if you wouldn't mind waiting before we contacted your family anyway."

"You were? Why?"

"Because your uncle intends on eradicating the leaders of the *Reyes*. Not only do I not want him to stop, and now that you're here, technically, he *could*...

"On the other hand, if he saw your injuries, it might trigger more violence, which I would like to keep contained to the bare minimum."

Pleating her fingers together on her lap, Teresa questioned, "Why?"

"Why..." Aurora frowned. "What do you mean?"

"I mean why do you want to keep the violence contained to the bare minimum?"

"Because I believe in looking after my people. I don't want anyone to be unnecessarily harmed.

"I've lost a lot of family in my life, and if someone had been smart enough to keep a situation contained, maybe they wouldn't have died."

"That's very noble of you."

"I believed your uncle when he said he wanted to target the leadership, and I wouldn't want that to change because of, well, everything.

"I'm truly hoping your uncle's plan to destroy the *Reyes'* top men with dirty meth will work and..." Her gaze darted around Teresa's beat-up face. "...will be quite painful."

Teresa's eyes rounded. "He's poisoned their supply?"

"Yes. I have to assume that's why..." She waved a hand, but didn't say, 'That's probably why you were beaten.'

Teresa surprised us both by chuckling. "*Tío* can fight nasty." She sounded quite proud about that.

"He does. You can stay in one of our hotels on the Strip if you'd like. When the bruises fade, if you want to contact your uncle, then you can, but we keep this between ourselves?"

"I'll just say that I ran away because I was scared?" Teresa peppered.

"That's a perfect cover," she approved.

As Adrianu eventually led Vitale and Teresa Martínez away, leaving Rory and me alone, I watched as she stayed in her position on the coffee table, elbows on her knees, head bowed in thought.

I didn't disrupt her, just headed to the small bar in the corner. While I knew she'd prefer a glass of Riesling, I pulled out some orange juice for her and some water for me. With both tumblers in hand, I slipped into the seat Teresa had used and waited to gain her attention.

It didn't take long, but longer than I expected. Long enough that I let my mind wander to what we'd learned from that brief conversation.

The photographer had been encouraged to scare Aurora, according to Teresa.

That would explain a lot.

It also explained why I wanted to garrot him and string him up by his intestines.

I wasn't a fan of bloodshed, but for Aurora's safety, I'd paint the fucking country red.

"I have my men looking for Albarez," she murmured like she knew where my thoughts had immediately gone, hand reaching for the glass. As she accepted it, her other popped out and she slipped her fingers against mine.

The touch was simple.

Uncomplicated.

Everything Aurora wasn't.

"How are you doing?"

She glanced at the orange juice in her glass. "I'm on edge but I have a team of guards watching my back. They'd have to get through them to get to me. Rationally, I know that."

I knew she was trying to convince herself and that pissed me off more than anything. She was too good at hiding her fear.

I tugged on her fingers. "I'm glad you're finally aware of the importance of security."

She nodded but startled me by changing the subject. "It's a shitty world we live in, isn't it?"

This time, I squeezed her fingers. "Not so shitty from this angle."

Her smile, when it came, packed the power of the rising sun and I had no alternative but to taste it. To taste her. To taste what belonged to me.

To taste what I'd kill to keep safe.

32

HUNTER
TWENTY ONE PILOTS - HEATHENS

I GRINNED when I saw Rachel hovering on the stoop of her house, dressed down and relaxed in a pair of jeans and an oversized tee.

I hadn't seen her in years, and aside from the baby bump, she hadn't changed much.

Aurora shot me a look as her fingers tightened around mine. "She'll be so happy to see you."

"It's been too long," I agreed, sitting forward as we passed through the gates and finally came to a stop.

Rather than let her leave via her door, I dragged Aurora across the backseat, which had her both chuckling and grouching about her arm being attached to a socket, but I ignored that and hauled us over to Rachel.

It was awkward but also great how we hugged at the same time. She slid one of her arms around each of our waists as we embraced, and in my ear, she muttered, "Only for you would I be complicit in a hug."

"Same," Aurora groused, making my lips curve.

"You're more affectionate than either of you realize," I chided, uncaring about their complaints, just reveling in being back together again.

Being back together again, however, was a thousand times better than I'd expected because one of Aurora's hands was pressed low on my butt, her thumb dipping under the waistband of my jeans. It was a possessive hold, an absentminded one—that made it all the more powerful.

"Affectionate? Us? Ms. Ice and Ms. Stone?"

Rory started laughing in earnest. "My God, it's been years since I've heard those utterly unoriginal nicknames."

"Do you remember Harry Kalowski? He came up with that. Said I was the Ice Age and you were the Stone Age."

"I'd prefer to be the Ice Age," Aurora complained. "The Stone Age was just a bunch of cavemen running around—"

"Are we talking about this right now?" I retorted. "We're here. Together. The Three Musketeers!"

"Four now," Rory added. "She's cooking one as we speak."

"Talking of my favorite subject in the world… I've got some food waiting for us." She pulled back to look at me, and her hand came up to grip my chin. She twisted it left and right, forcing my head to move as she studied me. "You've lost weight." It was uncannily similar to what I'd done to Aurora at the Gallinaro the day after Luc's wedding.

"I haven't. I bulked up," I argued.

A gleam appeared in her eyes. "Must be all the sex. You're wearing him out, Rory." Rachel grinned at me. "I always knew you had it in you, slugger."

I snorted, too used to her bullshit to be offended, especially when I saw how genuinely happy she was for me. *For us.* Christ, it was almost beaming out of her.

Throw in the 'glow' from being pregnant, I figured they'd be able to see her from the International Space Station.

Not that I said any of that out loud… I was a smart man. "Where's the food?"

"Kitchen." She grabbed a hand from each of us and dragged us into the house.

A glance around told me Rachel still liked her place to be minimally decorated—whether she was a poor student or a rich lawyer—

but there were things dotted here and there that marred what had once been an undoubtedly barren space.

A scarf on a console table that housed a vase—guess which one didn't belong there. A pair of sneakers in front of the coat rack near the door. On the staircase, there was a coat hanging on the post.

Nonsense items that were signs of life.

"Is Wynter here?" Aurora asked.

"No, but she'll be back tonight. I want her to meet Hunter. She went off with Rain and Priest though."

"Do I want to know why?"

The voice was one I recognized. *Rex.* I barely knew the man, but he'd helped me get rid of Marcus Macmillan's body. When you did shit like that together, it left a mark.

Rex eyed me up and down and held out a hand as he stood up from his seat at the table.

As I shook his hand, Rachel hustled over to his side, her arm immediately sliding around his waist. "When did you get back?"

"Couple minutes ago. I came in through the kitchen door." He kissed her temple. "Where did Wynter go with Rain and Priest?"

Rachel's lips twisted. "I don't get why you're so worried about them. Rain is her freaking uncle and Wynter's more of a threat to Priest's vow of celibacy than he is to hers."

My brows rose. "Why's he called Priest?"

"He quit the seminary before he took his vows." Rach shrugged. "MC road names are predictable sometimes."

"Nyx isn't," Rory mused as she took a seat at the table where there was a large fruit pie.

She served herself a slice then arched a brow at me in question. When I nodded, she gave me her plate then doled out some more for her.

"Who's Nyx again?" I asked while keeping my eyes on Rory.

Rex picked up the sandwich he'd made from fixings on the table. "My VP."

There were several loaves of bread, a charcuterie board, a couple small wheels of cheese, a bowl of fruit, several pies, and a cake. It wasn't the type of food I'd imagined a Prez eating, but he seemed at ease with Rachel's bougie indoor picnic.

"Nyx is the female personification of night," Rory reminded us as she tucked into the pie I swiftly learned was cherry.

"Rach, I love you for remembering this is my fave." She winked at me. "So why is your VP called Nyx? Or, wait, Nyx is a woman? Is this an equal opportunity MC?"

Rachel chuckled. "No. He got his road name because he had this dog growing up called Nyx. She was a mean motherfucker. Awesome though." Her lips twisted. "Even I was sad when she died, despite the fact that she bit me twice."

Rex chuckled. "I forgot about that. She hated you."

"She hated *all* girls. Indy—she's Nyx's sister, Hunter—got nipped all the time. Not that she cared. Nyx was super aggressive but loyal."

"Are we talking about the man or the dog here?" Aurora asked, tone dry.

"I *think* they're talking about the man," I teased, making Rach snicker.

Rex turned pensive. "Maybe we should think about taking Amara up on her offer. It'd be good for the kids—"

"What offer?" To me, Aurora said, "Amara is one of the nuttier Old Ladies. Lily, she's nice, told me at Rachel's baby shower that she spread the gossip around town that her guys have STIs."

Guys? Huh. Okay. "Why did she do that?"

"Keeps other women away from her men. Quite inspired, really," Rachel mused. "She's got her own way of doing things."

Aurora rolled her eyes. "Just a little."

"She wants us to take in a dog or a cat," Rex added.

"Why? Out of the kindness of her heart?" I questioned, bewildered at the connection.

Rachel crinkled her nose. "It's a long story, but one of her Old Men tends to collect sick animals. They come to him. I know it sounds crazy but it's true. They just follow Quin around. Amara's decided that it's her role in life to house them after they're healed."

"I don't want a pet," Rex admitted. "But Nyx was fucking awesome. Why shouldn't our kids have that?"

"If we get one and they bite the baby like Nyx bit me, then we're getting rid of it," Rachel warned.

Rex snagged her hand. "You don't even have to say that."

"But I'm not against the idea."

"Only because Amara won't leave you the hell alone about it." This time, the voice was one I didn't recognize.

"This is Parker. She's my executive assistant." Rach's eyes gleamed with malevolent mischief. "How's Sweet Lips, Parker?"

The woman's cheeks burned red. "Would you stop talking about him? Jesus."

"I'm not the one messaging him all day, every day," she sniped in return.

Rory's lips twitched when she saw me watching the interplay with the zeal of a fan binge-watching every *Lord of the Rings* movie back to back. (I might have done that more than once in my lifetime.)

Seeing Rachel like this, in her natural sharky habitat, came as a shock. A good one. Hell, a great one. I was used to her being manically busy while existing in a state of low-level depression. Here, she was zen. She'd found her place in the world, and it showed in how at peace she was.

Intellectually, I'd known that she was doing okay. Busy with work before she and Rex had gotten back together, isolated, but fine.

I'd always hoped for more for her, though, and seeing that for myself made me feel a damn sight better about the still-raw wound that was me letting her down in regard to Marcus Macmillan.

While Rachel *teased* Parker about a guy called Sweet Lips—apparently MCs were more inclusive than I'd realized—Parker just shoved pie in her mouth as Rex switched his time between reading something on his phone and studying Rory and me.

"Are you two together then?"

Though Rach and Parker were still arguing, they fell silent at Rex's question.

"We are," I said easily.

Rex angled his head to the side. "Huh."

"What's that supposed to mean?" Rach demanded as she snagged a piece of ham and ate it.

"Nothing. Just… huh. I never did get the chance to thank you for what you did for Rachel," he mused out loud. "Back then, there never really seemed to be the right opportunity for a talk like that."

"I only wish I'd gotten there sooner." It would be a regret I'd die with.

Rach cleared her throat. "Do we have to talk about this?"

"Better to dismiss the elephant in the room than to pretend it's not there." He gently squeezed her fingers again. "You're spending the night?"

She answered for us, "They are. Good timing too. The next time we get together, this kid will probably be six."

Aurora chuckled. "We're not that bad."

"You so are!"

She rubbed her nose with her middle finger, the gesture enough to make me bark out a surprised laugh.

I'd forgotten how playful the two were around each other.

"When do you pop?"

"Not long now."

"Next time," Rex started, "you'll have to come to a party—"

Rachel hooted. "No way. I don't need Aurora getting into an argument with Giulia and them fighting about antipasti at the clubhouse."

"We got along fine at the baby shower," Aurora dismissed, spooning some pie into her mouth.

"You started arguing about pasta," Rachel retorted.

She huffed. "*Al dente* is overcooked."

Rex reached for his coffee. "I thought Rachel was joking when she said you were arguing about overcooking pasta."

I grinned to myself as Rory argued, "Food is nothing to joke about. I'm *Sicilian*. My blood is half-carbs."

We spent the next few hours hanging out around the kitchen table. Parker left, but others came and went in that time. A guy called Steel popped up, and I met the 'Queen of Night' himself, followed by a Tiffany and an Alessa.

I also met Amara, who eyed me up and down. "You like cat?"

Aware of her proclivities in foisting animals off on people, I just blinked at her. "I have one."

She wasn't to know mine had two legs and was sitting beside me. Rory did though—she snorted.

"Two cat better than one only," she argued in her heavily accented English.

"No, it damn well isn't," was Rory's answer.

"Leave my guests alone, Amara. What do you want?" Rachel had sniped, but Wynter appeared so I never heard what she *did* want.

Knowing that the last time I'd seen her was when she was a baby was weird as fuck. Seeming to sense that I was 'bewildered,' Aurora introduced me.

Wynter was pleasant and kind and more interested in ice cream until this guy, Priest, showed up again and she disappeared with a wave.

My head pivoted to follow her out of the room. "That was intense."

"It's more of a gift than I ever expected having her live with us," Rach confessed.

Silently, Rex kissed the backs of her knuckles.

"Does Priest have good intentions?"

Aurora cackled as she peered at me. "What are you? Her dad?"

Rex chuckled. "If he has bad intentions, trust me, I'll make him pay."

Rachel complained, "We've already had this conversation."

As they bickered about respecting their daughter's boundaries, I thought about the girl who looked uncannily like her mom had back at nineteen. Except without the shields.

I knew from what Rach herself had shared, as well as Aurora, that Wynter had had a good childhood and things had only derailed toward the end. Unlike her mom, whose family life had sucked from an early age.

Was it any wonder I felt protective?

Aurora, seeming to sense my unease, tipped her head to the side as she looked at me. "What is it?"

"I don't know," I admitted, aware I was making a dick out of myself but not really able to stop it. "I guess I'm just realizing how fucking hard it was with both of you so fragile back then and I still goddamn failed you both."

Their eyes rounded, but Rex was the one who said, "You did better than I could, Hunter."

I had the blood of both their attackers on my hands, but it wasn't guilt over their deaths that kept me awake at night. "Maybe."

Aurora soothed, "It wasn't your job to be our guardian."

"She's right, Hunter," Rachel said. "And you, more than anyone, know I hate admitting Aurora's right about anything."

Though I forced a laugh, I let the topic go because I hadn't intended for things to get maudlin.

When I pressed a kiss to Rory's temple, I saw the gleam in Rachel's eye, and I knew what the source of her joy was—the three of us were with the people we were meant to be with.

Letting my arm cup her shoulders, I squeezed Aurora gently as I maneuvered my hand around so that I could play with the locket. That she let me, in front of people, was telling. One day, that ring would be on her finger and she'd wear my coll—

No. Not yet. I didn't want to push things. Push her. I didn't need to get ahead of myself.

"I was down there recently. Burbank."

Rex's segue had me blinking at him. "Disciples' territory."

Rory cut me a look. "You know that?"

"Of course I do. It's my turf," I drawled, amused that she thought I wouldn't know which factions resided where on Camorran land—whether those factions accepted our dominion or not was another matter entirely.

I might not have wanted the position of Don, but that didn't mean Bert hadn't prepared me for it.

"Been hearing whispers about the *Reyes Dorados* and *Las Alphas*. Are they true?" Rex queried.

"They're true." I frowned. "Why do you hear whispers about territory that isn't yours?"

"Wynter lived down there. I had my eyes and ears on the place for years. People still talk to me even if my interest is muted.

"It's not good if *Las Alphas* gain any territory in the US," he continued, for the first time sounding uneasy. "Better the Sonorans than the *Alphas*."

"We're dealing with them," Rory answered.

He picked up his beer, took a deep sip, then asked, "How? I know we're on different coasts, we have different allegiances, but we're tied by family." His gaze drifted to Rachel.

In complete agreement, I dipped my chin. "We are. What do you know of *Los Lobos Rojos*?"

"Street gang in the city. They stay on the down low. Best private army in the States. Their men are mercs by any other name and their weapon stores are beyond impressive. Though I *have* heard the Hell's Rebels in Texas is starting to expand their ghost gun operation and they've built up some nice stores of their own."

Interest pricked, I queried, "I hadn't heard that."

Rex shrugged. "As I said, people talk to me even if I'm not interested. What about the *Lobos*?"

I explained the situation, how the *Reyes* had gained *Las Alphas'* interest when Martínez's niece had run off with the leader, and how we were currently working *with* Martínez to eradicate the gang's leadership and install him in a position of power. A position we'd since learned he didn't particularly want.

"Sounds like you have a lot on your plate," was all Rex said when story time was over.

"We do. Now we've got this goddamn photographer following Aurora around in the city because of the *Reyes,* which is a bigger concern."

Rachel frowned. "That's disturbing."

Aurora shot her a glance, and somehow, within that glance, she managed to convey *something* because Rachel gasped in horror.

"No!"

Aurora ducked her gaze to the table, her discomfort evident. "Yes."

Rex shot me a meaningful look, but it wasn't my place to say anything.

"I'm so sorry, Rory," Rachel breathed, her misery clear.

"You don't have to be, Rach. It was rough at first, but Hunter made it better."

Rex glanced worriedly at Aurora. "Did the photographer hurt you?"

"No, but he sent us pictures of Hunter and me in a compromising position, pictures that his council saw."

His jaw clenched in understanding.

Later on, when Rory and Rach disappeared into her office to talk about some business that had cropped up, he rumbled, "You're going to make that photographer pay, aren't you?"

"Going to scoop out his eyeballs with a teaspoon."

Rex shook his head. "Trust me, if you want him squealing like a little bitch, use your thumb and push deep."

Tipping my bottle of beer at him, I nodded. "Thanks for the tip."

"My pleasure. It's more satisfying than you realize. These fuckers believe that being in love is a weakness. They think they can use a guy's woman as target practice." He clinked his bottle with mine. "We have to show them otherwise."

We were practically strangers, but at that moment, I knew we were about to become damn close friends. Not just because of Rach, either.

Before I could comment, someone came wandering into the kitchen, a young kid, hair disheveled, his phone blaring out what appeared to be a random news headline.

"What you listening to, Drew?" Rex asked as Rach and Rory made their return, chatting about the Vallara—the casino I knew Rory wanted the *Cosa Nostra* to invest in.

Picking up a piece of ham from the charcuterie board, he turned his phone around so we could see the livestream. "My mom was a real lover of the royals." His cheeks turned pink as he admitted, "I set up notifications so I could tell her the news, and I forgot to turn them off."

Had she died?

Though Rory and I shared a look, we remained quiet as the newscaster announced:

"Prince Edward of Midlothian was found dead in his castle on the outskirts of Edinburgh. Police say it appears accidental and have assured the King that there was no foul play."

Aurora and I shared *another* look.

Rach, knowing us too well, demanded, "What's that about?" She pointed her finger between the two of us. "That look. What's going on?"

"I know Lodestar has been living with you," I started slowly. "Where is she?"

Rex shrugged. "She's been AWOL for a few weeks now. Her kid says she's fine though. Been keeping in touch with her, just no one else."

Three random, allegedly accidental deaths, three random dignitaries, three random nations… Nothing was *that* random.

I had a feeling Lodestar had been in China, Lichtenstein, and Scotland recently.

The question was…

Why?

33

HUNTER

JUNGLE - BUSY EARNIN'

AS MATTEO SNAPPED the neck of one of the *Reyes'* foot soldiers, I stepped out of my ride.

With a sigh, I shot Brunu a dour look. "Really?!"

He shrugged at me, unsurprised by what had gone down. I, on the other hand, was beyond surprised.

Nothing about this had gone to plan. Not that the *Reyes* realized I had a fucking psychopath as a henchman.

Until today, I hadn't either, to be fair.

Matteo had gone through the five-strong team of gangbangers like a Tasmanian devil, snapping bones as if he had a personal grievance against them.

Maybe he did.

Who the fuck knew?

I'd stayed on the outskirts of the Camorra ever since I'd moved to Vegas, learning whatever Bert insisted I learn, paying my way through my skills rather than getting my hands dirty. That meant I didn't know many of the men, and I sure as hell didn't know about their grudges and what made them tick.

What I *did* know was that Matteo belonged in a Tarantino movie, and no, that wasn't a compliment.

Moving around the fender of the town car, I pressed my hands into my pockets as I waded through the corpses on the road toward the guy Matteo had on his knees.

"The fuck are you doing, man?" the guy cried.

"You sure he's in the SUV?" I questioned Brunu who'd watched Matteo like he was the star of his very own personal action movie.

"I'm sure," Adrianu called out as he started dragging corpses toward the *Reyes'* ride. "This fucker is the guard of Torres's underboss, Hernandez."

I waited until Matteo had snapped the guard's neck, who crumpled onto the ground in a whirl of dust, then followed him toward the SUV.

Matteo motioned at me, muttering, "Stay behind the car door. They're bulletproof. Don't forget—the leaders are using that dirty meth so they're more aggressive than normal."

Because I didn't feel like getting shot today, I complied, keeping back as Matteo slammed his hand on the window and hollered, "You can get out of your ride or we can wait you out. In this heat, I think you'll be cooking in around twenty minutes."

My lips twitched at his idea of negotiating. "Or," I continued, "Hernandez, you can pay the price of being on Camorran territory, take it like a man, and can live to see another day by giving up Paulu Ribaldi."

Matteo scowled at me. "You going to let him go, boss?"

I didn't mind being questioned, but I didn't think it was particularly prudent to be asked the damn question right beside the guy I was trying to coerce out of the SUV.

When I arched a brow at him, Matteo shot me a sheepish grin. "Sorry, Don. Adrenaline makes me dumb."

It wasn't as if I could blame him for that. Not really. Not with the brutal efficiency he'd shown as he went through men like a human semi-automatic.

Snapping my fingers at Adrianu, and over the roof of the car, I pointed at the other door. He nodded and moved into position just as it opened and Hernandez stepped out, hands raised.

"I don't want no trouble, man."

Even from this distance, I could see he was high.

Liability, my mind screeched, so I sliced my finger across my throat.

Adrianu popped his gun against Hernandez's temple and blew his brains out.

With him on the ground, blood spatter every-fucking-where, Adrianu nearly got his head blown off too when Paulu started trying to fire his way out of the SUV.

"And you call yourself my Consigliere," I shouted over the racket. "Think, man. How the fuck are you going to get out of here alive? You're not only outnumbered, but you're a treacherous fucker. If you kill one of my *stiddaris*, that's going to piss me off even more."

"You've seen him when he's angry, Paulu." Brunu waded into the fray now. "I've got a baseball bat in my trunk if you feel like reminiscing."

Though I rolled my eyes at that, Paulu called out, "You're going to have to shoot me."

"That can be arranged. But the question is, do you want your family to pay for your treachery? Today's the day you're going to die, old man, *but* the question is whether you want your wife and two daughters to join you."

"You wouldn't kill them. You're not a goddamn monster. They're innocent!"

I heard the tremble in his pitch and I doubled down on the threats.

"You betrayed my grandfather, you betrayed me, and you've put Aurora Valentini in danger… Why would I give a damn about any traitorous scum you've spawned?"

"They didn't know anything," he shrieked.

Unhappy with how slow our progress was, Adrianu started waggling his head at Matteo in some bizarre form of communication.

I hissed, "Stand down."

"He's pointing the gun at himself, Don," Adrianu argued.

"Leave this to me."

"You heard the boss," Brunu warned.

Both *stiddaris* hunched their shoulders but did as I requested.

"How can I believe they're in the dark if you don't tell me what the *Reyes* know?" I countered. "This is your one chance to spare them, Paulu, because, trust me, I won't if you don't bother defending them."

A gun came flying out of the open doorway. It skidded on the asphalt, glinting in the dying rays of the sun.

"That the only weapon you're carrying?"

Two knives came next.

"Come out slowly. Hands raised," I ordered, watching as the old fuck complied. Once he was standing beside the SUV, I told him, "Now, put them behind your head."

Again, he did as I asked but turned to look at me with a plea buried in his eyes. "You mean it when you say you'll leave them alone? My kids are good girls," he rasped.

"Should have thought about that before you made them scum," Adrianu spat.

Paulu tensed. "They ain't fucking scum. Your grandfather wanted them for his shadow council. Andrea's going to Columbia to study law and Ignazia's halfway through her MBA—"

His words made this entire situation more bewildering.

I knew Bert hadn't trusted his council entirely. I, myself, had believed there was a leak. Information had a way of filtering out that I didn't think was purely accidental.

Aurora was the one who'd said he'd sounded shifty when he'd tossed me the pictures the night of my first council meeting as Don. After hunting in his bank account, I'd found a paper trail leading from one Luis Hernandez to Paulu, and Matteo had found them 'chatting' together in a booth in a bar off the Strip.

I just didn't know why he'd betrayed Bert.

"Were you so strapped for cash that you had to sell out your people to the *Reyes*?"

I wasn't the one who snapped that—Brunu did. And he was pissed. How did I know that? I'd come to learn his tells over the last month or so.

Like a pissed-off barnyard mutt, he tended to reveal one of his gold teeth when he was snarling at someone.

"Do you know how much it costs when both of your kids are attending Ivy League schools?" Paulu spat.

For a moment, I was speechless. Truly fucking speechless. Then: "Why the hell didn't you just ask Bert for help?"

Brunu snorted. "Paulu knows he'd never have gotten a loan from your grandfather."

"Why not?"

"The man's on a couple million a year, he ain't exactly paying Uncle Sam his dues, and he can't afford to send his kids to Ivy League colleges?" Brunu sniffed. "Why do you think that is?"

Drugs? I tipped my head as I studied the old bastard. Nah. "Gambling?"

"Got it in one. Thought you had it under control, Paulu, especially after that last time when Bert paid for you to go to rehab." Brunu's disappointment was apparent. "Just never imagined you'd sell us out for a bet."

Paulu swallowed. "The *Reyes* wouldn't take installments. It was a sure thing!"

"Why would they when they wanted you beholden to them, asswipe?" Matteo jeered. "You practically begged them to target you. *Sure thing*, my ass."

Paulu sneered at him, but the sneer quickly faded as his expression crumpled. "I owed too much, and Bert said if I got hooked again, he'd toss me out. He left me no alternative."

"You leave *me* no alternative."

"I-I can help!" Paulu argued. "They still got that photographer following your girl. I can help you track him down!"

"It's a little late for that," I retorted, shooting a glance at Adrianu who pistol-whipped him. "Get the bodies to the graveyards the *Reyes* have been using in our territory, Matteo. Send Hernandez back to Torres with a brand on whatever's left of his face, Adrianu. Brunu, I want you to call a council meeting and to take Paulu back to the *palazzo*—"

"What? Why?"

Grimly, I informed them, "Because the council needs to see what happens to traitors and it's time they learned who my Consigliere is."

A sparkle glittered in his eye. "Come on, boys. You heard the Don. Let's get this show on the road."

34

HUNTER

"GENTLEMEN, I'd like to introduce you to Aurora Valentini."

The men around the table frowned as they peered at my wife as she passed through the arch into the council room.

That they'd seen her naked before they'd even gotten the chance to meet her aggravated the living hell out of me, but there was nothing to be done about that.

Nothing that wouldn't undermine her at the same time.

She strolled in with the confidence of a catwalk model. Shoulders back, the tailored bloodred suit I'd selected for her as pristine as could be, eyes glittering, the Anjou earbobs dancing in her earlobes, and a cutthroat smile that should have had anyone in the vicinity shaking in their Oxfords.

She was mesmerizing.

There was no other way to describe her.

A living, breathing flame that would burn this *palazzo* down if the council didn't watch themselves.

Nothing about her expression revealed she'd had a hectic twenty-four hours thanks to working a full day in New York and then flying here for this meeting.

Lombardo was the first to react: "It's a pleasure to meet you, Ms.

Valentini. Is there a reason you're attending a Camorran council session?"

I could have answered on her behalf, but why would I castrate her like that? She had a voice of her own and I knew she wasn't afraid to use it.

"Because Alberto and I came to an arrangement before he died."

"Alberto?" Marina queried. "We're aware of your marriage, but being a De Laurentiis wife doesn't allow you to sit on the council. Particularly with your ties to the *Cosa Nostra*."

She cut him a look. "Unfortunately for you, Alberto didn't agree with you. He arranged for Hunter and me to wed *and* it was his idea that I sit at Hunter's side as his Consigliere.

"This, of course, was before Paulu Ribaldi revealed his treachery. He fully intended for me to take his place."

Shifty looks were passed around the table before they peeked warily at Paulu's corpse—Matteo had dumped him on the floor earlier.

"Ribaldi's disloyalty has come as a surprise to all of us," La Rosa muttered.

Abellardo nodded. "Knew he had a gambling problem but didn't think he'd sink that low."

Amato sniffed. "Fucking disgrace."

"It would seem that your judgment was clouded when it came to Ribaldi," she slipped in, as easily as a knife through butter on a hot summer's day.

"None of this is your business," Papparlardo stated, his hand slapping the table. "We've never had a woman on the council, and Alberto had no right to change—"

"I beg your damn pardon," I growled. "Alberto had no right to change, what, exactly? The Camorra runs at the De Laurentiis' *pleasure*.

"*You* answer to me, not the other goddamn way around."

Papparlardo countered, "You're new to the role of Don, Hunter. You need strong advisors, not women who think with their emotions."

Aurora's brows lifted. "You're thinking with your emotions right now. Instead of looking at my background logically, *rationally*, instead of seeing what I've accomplished over the years, you're throwing a tantrum like a petulant two-year-old."

Papparlardo glowered at her. "Are you calling me an idiot?"

"If the shoe fits… But I didn't say that. I said you were acting like a child. Look, my position was sanctioned by both Alberto and Hunter —that's all that you need to take from this meeting."

"This is an introduction," I stated, casting a glance around the council table before Papparlardo could wade in. "Aurora has already proven her capabilities with the Valentini's ascension on the East Coast. She's a catch, gentlemen, and we're lucky that she's agreed to Bert's terms and is on *our* side.

"I expect you to facilitate the transition between Ribaldi and her so that the men don't register any sign of weakness among our leadership.

"Understood?" The grunts I received were lackluster, so I barked, "Understood?"

This time, I got the 'ayes' I wanted but I knew the interrogation wasn't over yet.

La Rosa squinted at her. "Why you?"

"Excuse me?"

"Why you?" he repeated. "Why did Alberto want *you* to be Hunter's Consigliere?"

"You were a DA," Papparlardo agreed with a sneer. "Your identity has to be under wraps—"

"Is that a threat?" I interrupted, tone seething.

"No! I'm merely pointing out that no one can know who she is or her position and her faction are compromised."

"I work behind the scenes," was Aurora's calm response. "And have no intention of ever changing that. As for why Alberto wanted me to be Hunter's Consigliere, it's probably because I'm as invested as he was in keeping Hunter alive."

La Rosa frowned, but deep in his eyes, I saw the stirrings of panic. "You think our enemies want him dead?"

Her gaze flickered over to me and I watched her make a judgment call, one I could read as easily as if she were a newspaper.

A common enemy created a united front.

"Some might believe Alberto's death left a power vacuum behind," she said smoothly. "It's down to us to ensure that not only can no one touch him, but that the Camorra comes out from the shadows of the last Don's passing stronger than ever."

When the councilors started arguing about who would have the audacity to want me dead, their loyalty to my family as strong as ever, I watched her sit back in her seat, satisfaction practically dripping out of her pores.

Silently, I applauded her.

Game.

Set.

Match.

35

AURORA

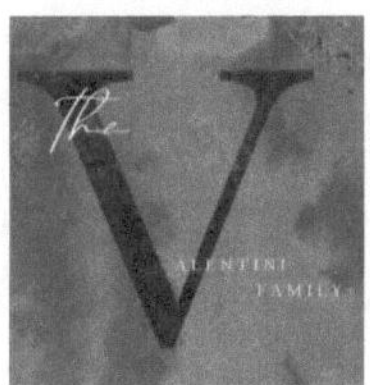

"*PROZIO,* I have someone here who'd love to meet you."

Unsurprisingly, the old man didn't leap for joy at my introduction or the greeting.

As usual, he kept his head turned to the corridor.

As usual, I ignored that he ignored me, and I started to putter around his bed. The nurses cleaned up for him so I didn't have to, but it was better than just staring at the man who repeatedly made it known that he didn't want anything to do with me.

Unaccustomed to this little charade we had going on, Hunter glanced back and forth between us, but as expected, he made the duty visit a thousand times better by being Hunter.

The nonsense conversation that I had with my *prozio* morphed into a discussion about an upcoming soccer match in the UK, then it twisted onto why hospital coffee tasted like crap despite costing a hundred dollars a cup in the VIP section. It veered into another debate about where the best coffee came from, and then we mused on *kopi luwak,* the coffee made from beans plucked from civets' feces.

Naturally, Hunter had sampled it in Indonesia and had it imported because he loved it so much.

"We'll find some in the city," he assured me, his gaze still drifting between my great-uncle and me as if waiting for Currau to leap into the conversation. "I promise you'll love it too."

"How do you get over where it came from?" I questioned. "You know I'm adventurous but… civet poop?"

"You do know that beef doesn't just appear in cellophane-covered wrappers in supermarket refrigerators, right?"

I knew he was teasing, but I still shot him a dour look. "It's different."

"Is it?"

"Those beans are picked out of poop!"

"And the puppet theatre doesn't freak you out?"

My nose crinkled. "They're creepy too."

Sicily was famous for wooden marionettes that were dressed in armor and that acted out the Norman conquest of the island.

"The best part of any country is its unusual customs," Hunter lectured, but he was laughing at me mid-lecture.

Currau, for maybe the first time since his release, turned his head away from the hallway. Okay, that was an exaggeration. Maybe it was by an inch. Whatever, I'd take it.

Hunter noticed, of course, but didn't let on that he had. If anything, he picked up his phone to find a place in the city where he could serve me cat poop coffee, but it rang in his hand before, I hoped, he found somewhere that served the 'delicacy.'

He was right that Sicilians had weird traditions, too, like *brioscia*—brioche—dipped in *granita* for breakfast, so I didn't judge, but I'd have to compartmentalize…

I'd probably have to compartmentalize the next time I saw 'cellophane-covered beef,' too.

Thankfully, I wasn't exactly the kind of woman who frequented grocery stores. Bodegas, sometimes, but even then, Giovi was there for those particular tasks.

"You're certain?"

Hunter's tone had lost its playfulness. It was the one he used when he was taking care of business. I'd first heard it at his inaugural council meeting. As time passed, I was hearing it more often.

Studying him, I watched his eyes close and the lids bleed white as he clenched them down hard. His free hand balled into a fist and he pushed the knuckles into the leather cladding the armrest.

I didn't have to know him to recognize that this wasn't just business—it was personal.

That meant either Ernesto Albarez, the photographer who'd become my second shadow, had been picked up by the cops—unlikely because, if he had, I'd have been the one getting the call from Commissioner Kingston—or this phone conversation was regarding Alberto.

As much as I wanted Albarez handled, I also wanted Hunter to get closure. That was impossible without a funeral.

I kept my focus on him as he eventually cut the call. He'd spoken few words, listening instead to whoever had contacted him.

When he'd finished, he tucked his phone back into his jacket pocket, but he stayed silent. I didn't push him, preferring for him to speak when he was ready.

It was difficult though.

"They're releasing the body within the week."

I reached out, tangling my fingers with his. "They've made an arrest?"

He stared at our joined hands and released a soft laugh. "Canny old bastard."

"Who?" I insisted.

Finally, he looked at me. "Robert Macmillan."

Now, I understood his amusement.

My lips twisted into a smile at the thought of my jerk ex-brother-in-law being arrested.

The Macmillans might be American royalty but they were scum, nonetheless.

"What proof?"

"Money trail of a payment to an offshore bank account. It belonged to the 'guard' behind the murder."

"Lodestar?"

"She must be behind the money trail, yeah."

"How concrete?"

"The Commissioner of the LVPD told Brunu that not even the Macmillan family fortune would get him out of this."

My lips twitched again. "I won the bet. Time to pay up."

He huffed. "Did the cops ever contact you?"

"About my presence at the prison that day?" At his nod, I answered, "No. I think Lodestar must have made that information disappear." Under my breath, and staring up at the ceiling where I hoped was Alberto's general location rather than down below, I said, "*Grazii*, Alberto." *For everything.*

Hunter's grandfather had rid us of a problem that was only going to fester. Robert's next target would undoubtedly have been Hunter.

"Alberto De Laurentiis?"

It was a testament to how often I'd visited my uncle without him uttering a word that I didn't recognize his voice. I even looked around the damn ward, wondering if someone had stepped inside without us knowing it.

"*Prozio!*" I called out, straightening up and rushing over to his bedside.

The tears that pricked my eyes were ridiculous but I'd waited so damn long for him to talk to me that the relief was instantaneous.

"Alberto De Laurentiis?" he repeated, his wizened gaze narrowed on me.

His voice was more of a croak than anything I'd ever heard before. The nurses told me he never spoke to them, so that made sense, but it didn't lessen my upset.

I nodded. "Hunter is Alberto's grandson."

My great-uncle frowned as he glanced between us, then, to Hunter, he rasped, "You're Camorra?"

"I'm the Don."

I bit my lip at my husband's admission. I wondered if he knew how assured he sounded as he uttered that title. How confident.

Not allowing either man to speak, I stated, "Hunter's grandfather helped *Nanna* escape to Sicily, *Prozio*. Alberto is the reason I'm standing here today."

Currau's mouth tightened. "He didn't stop the Fieris."

"Was it his job to?" I defended even though, until a couple months ago, I'd have argued that it was.

My great-uncle sniffed then turned his head to the side, dismissing us both.

Spying this dismissal, Hunter arched a brow at me.

I heaved a sigh. "We should go. I need an early night if I have to smile all day tomorrow."

"You have a great-great niece," Hunter stated, not getting to his feet, but remaining seated at Currau's bedside.

"Her name's Saverina. It's her christening tomorrow," I inserted softly, curious if he'd be interested.

I knew I shouldn't have been surprised when he didn't ask about her.

Disappointment had me reaching for Hunter's hand and clutching at his fingers. He squeezed back as he got to his feet at my silent urging.

I thought he'd leave the place without another word, but with one foot out of the door and one foot in, he drawled, "Your lack of gratitude for a family that strove to liberate you is appalling. My grandfather died in prison. You're lucky that you don't have to.

"The next time my wife visits you, you should show a damn sight more appreciation for the sacrifices she made to get you here."

I almost choked on his declaration of what I was to him, and a quickly darted look at the end of the corridor where our guards were stationed reassured me that no one would have overheard Hunter.

Tugging on his hand, I muttered, "Leave him."

"No. He's old and sick, but he's in a luxurious room instead of a prison hospital because of you." He raised my knuckles to his lips. "He doesn't need to thank you on bended goddamn knees. Just a 'hello' and a 'how old is my great-grandniece?' would be enough."

With a nip of my bottom lip, I hesitated to agree with him when I didn't disagree.

It was a tough stance.

He was right, but I also understood that Currau felt as though I'd robbed him of his home. As bizarre as it was to think that a cell could be home, what else would it be after so long inside?

Currau was institutionalized and the hospital ward wasn't the freedom I'd wanted to offer him.

I squeezed Hunter's fingers and, rather than commenting on that, just murmured, "Thank you for defending me."

My knuckles were returned to his lips, and a gentle kiss on them was the only answer either of us needed.

Because I was choked up, I had to switch my mind to business. "What will you do with Alberto's killer?"

"Crayon's a part of the investigation now. I should have him dumped outside a precinct and be done with him."

"I'm not sure that's wise."

"No," he commented gruffly.

"Is he fully healed from his injuries?"

"Yes. So, I'll give him an offer he can't refuse."

My lips quirked. "You're just missing the phony Italian accent to make that line perfect."

He startled me by winking as we stepped into the elevator.

"What's the offer?"

"Become one of us or die."

"Crayon could testify against Robert," I said thoughtfully. "We could get someone in the Vegas DA's office to cut him a deal.

"I doubt he made many friends among his colleagues. Someone in there will be willing to sell him out, and if it makes Robert's actions appear more authentic…"

"True." He cut me a look. "What would you do?"

"There's a reason you've kept Crayon alive this long," I remarked. "Let him work for his keep. Then, when he's done his job, bring him back into the fold.

"He's clearly a magician if he can escape a prison like he did. There's no reason for him to only be Lodestar's friend. You'd never seen him before, had you?"

"No. He's French."

"Well, he's got a talent for breaking out of jails. That's a good skill to have on our side." As we left the elevator and stepped into the foyer, I asked, "Heard from her recently?"

"Lodestar?" He pursed his lips. "No. And that's a problem just waiting to happen because she's the loudest person I've ever known even when she's in 'silent' mode."

I processed that, but simply said, "Just think about Crayon, hmm? His usefulness doesn't have to be over."

His nod told me he'd consider my advice, and once we were back in my town car, I left him to his thoughts while I started looking into funeral arrangements.

36

HUNTER

LIGHTS - ELLIE GOULDING

THE FOLLOWING DAY

I DIDN'T NEED Aurora to tell me that she was dreading Saverina's christening.

The fact that she hadn't even gone to visit her niece since Luc, Jennifer, Lauren, and the baby had arrived a few days ago was proof enough.

Plus, she was in a bad mood from the moment she woke up until the moment we were about to leave—that was when I hauled her over my knee and spanked her ass a couple dozen times before sending her on her way.

Orgasm-less.

She was growing greedy for orgasms. To the point where that was turning into her main focus and not her need for pain.

My dastardly plan was working, I thought wryly, as I watched her fix her dress. It was a tight fit so it was as awkward going down as it had been getting it over her hips.

I straightened, ironing out any creases on my pants and jacket with my hand, and mused, "You look like a princess."

Her white dress cupped her waist and thighs in a loose pencil skirt, but the neckline was high with a half-Mandarin collar that was slit down the middle. Her locket peeped at me from the cleavage it revealed.

She blinked at my compliment. "Don't think you can smooth talk me. You just spanked me when we're going to my niece's christening!"

I shot her a cocky grin. "Like you weren't *begging* for it."

Her nose tipped into the air. "I think I'd have known if I was begging for anything."

"What was the wriggling about then? All that squirming? Trying to get my hand where you really wanted it?"

Anyone else would have been wary about how she narrowed her eyes at me. I wasn't 'anyone else' though.

I smirked at her, amused when she huffed again and grouched, "We're going to be late if we don't hurry up."

Before she could head for the door, I grabbed her hand and hauled her back against me, not stopping until she was leaning into me.

I rested my chin on her shoulder and wrapped my arms around her. "Everything will be fine."

"You don't know that," she argued, but her tension lessened some as she cupped her hands over mine.

"I do know that. You're still her aunt whether or not you're her godmother." And that, I thought, was the crux of the matter. *She hadn't been asked*. To arrange the christening, sure. To be the godmother, no. "Maybe they thought you'd refuse?"

She sniffed.

I guess that told me what she thought about *that*.

This was definitely Jennifer's work. It wasn't like I could blame her. The pair of them weren't exactly friendly.

"Stan's the godfather, at least," I tried to appease. "Maybe when they have kid number two, you'll be the godmother."

"I doubt it. It's fine. As you said, I don't need to be Saverina's godmother. I'm her *only* aunt."

"You have to learn to get along with Jennifer."

"It's impossible to like everyone, Hunter."

"Are you telling me that specifically? Or just the world in general?"

"Both." She twisted around in my hold. "I don't need her to like me and I'm sure she feels the same way. We're family now. That's what matters more than anything."

"Just like that?"

She hitched a shoulder. "Just like that."

"I'm sure Luc would appreciate it if you made an effort."

"I'll make an effort not to be cutting. That's about as much as I expect from her in return as well."

"Stubborn *mugghieri.*"

Her lips curved into a smile at long last. "*Your* stubborn wife."

I dropped a kiss onto that smile, needing to taste it.

"You know attending together is a declaration in itself, don't you?"

Her worry wrapped around me—another source of her anxiety. "Is that a problem for you?" I asked carefully.

"No." She peeped at me from under her lashes. "I just… didn't…" She sighed. "Never mind."

I didn't make it easy on her. Not because I was a jackass but because I was waiting for the words. Today *was* a declaration, but we were still keeping our marriage a secret.

The deadline for that being over was when she finally told me what I knew she'd been feeling for a while: 'I love you.'

I deserved to hear the words before the world learned we were man and wife.

To stem her anxiety, I kissed her again. "Come on. Let's get this over with."

She chuckled at my faux excitement but didn't chide me for it because I knew she was about as thrilled as I was to spend the morning in church and then at a boring event with people I didn't really want to hang around with anyway.

I'd have much preferred to stay in her apartment and fuck her brains out, but like she'd said, family mattered more than anything.

New York traffic made Vegas traffic look like a walk in the park.

By the time we were pulling up to the church where a small crowd had gathered outside, I knew we weren't as early as she wanted because she had some last-minute things to check with the priest.

While ducking inside was more about ensuring all her plates were still spinning, I knew she was trying to keep a low profile too.

The last DA of New York City couldn't exactly be seen attending the christening of the *Cosa Nostra* Don's newborn, could she?

Letting her rush away once we arrived, I hovered around the edges of the gathering outside the church.

The sidewalk was pretty packed, but I was content not to circulate, preferring to check my phone for updates from Brunu and my Stidda who were somewhere in the vicinity.

I didn't have much of a chance to check anything, however, before someone shuffled next to me, remarking, "You're Actaeon."

My handle wasn't a state secret, but still: "I'm Hunter, actually. Lachlan De Laurentiis." I peered over my phone. "And you are?"

"aCooooig."

"What are you doing here?"

"Received an invitation."

"Really?"

"My family did. I decided to represent the O'Donnelly delegation along with my brother and sister-in-law."

"Why? You enjoy church services?"

"No, I wanted to meet with you and I knew you'd be here."

"How?"

He tapped his nose. "I'm sure you can figure it out."

Word on the street said he'd developed some kind of spyware that trawled conversations better than anything the NSA had come up with. Was that a confession?

"What do you want?"

"To know where Lodestar is."

"Why do you think *I* would know where she is?"

"You're friendly."

"How do you know that?" I scoffed, knowing that Star would never in a million years have labeled our relationship with that adjective.

"Eighteen or so months ago, she waded past my security. I was looking at the code she used and happened to notice another hacker's signature—"

"You just happened to be looking, hmm?"

He shrugged.

"Why do you think she's gone anywhere?"

"You can leave a room and still have a physical presence there."

"Are we about to get into a philosophical debate?"

"No. I'm sure you know what she's been through."

"I do." I saw no point in lying.

"So, you *are* friends?"

"Lodestar doesn't have friends." I thought about what I'd learned yesterday. "She calls in favors."

His head tilted to the side. "You're angry at her." When I didn't reply, he continued, "What did she do?" Again, I didn't answer. "I thought the headlines coming out of Vegas were interesting this morning. Wonder if your anger with her has anything to do with your grandfather's murder…"

"If you *had* read the papers, then I'm sure you'd know ADA Macmillan was behind his death. He's had a grudge against my family for years."

O'Donnelly pursed his lips as he looked over the gathering. "Funny that. You'd think life imprisonment would be enough to quench a grudge."

"Clearly not. The man was obsessed."

"Maybe your anger with Star is something to do with Aurora… Valentini?"

The slight hesitation after her name wasn't born from a lack of knowledge. It was the opposite.

I narrowed my eyes at him. "Exactly how deep have your investigations into me gone?"

"Deep enough. Lodestar's mine, Actaeon. I protect what's mine."

My brow furrowed. "I mean her no harm. And as we're staking claims here, you go anywhere fucking near Aurora Valentini, I'll reap whatever you can sow. Understood?"

He tipped his chin in agreement. "Understood."

"I *am* angry with Lodestar. She went behind my back—"

"That's what she does," O'Donnelly said grimly.

"Yes," was my simple retort. "But we've collaborated for a while now. I'm used to her insidious habits. I'll get over it. You either roll with it or drop her and…" I sighed. "I've never been able to do that."

"Why not?"

"Our initial meeting left a lasting impression."

He frowned. "Where did you meet?"

"Lebanon."

Nostrils flaring, he nodded his understanding.

"Seeing as it's likely we're the only people who know Lodestar well, we should probably start our own support group."

O'Donnelly let loose a soughing laugh. "You might be right about that."

The church doors opened and people began to wade inside. I didn't bother heading for the front, content to stay at the back. Much as he was.

"I'd appreciate it if you kept whatever you uncovered about Aurora Valentini to yourself."

He hitched a shoulder. "If you know anything about Lodestar, I'd appreciate being kept informed."

A fair exchange.

"I genuinely don't know where she is. I *assume* that she's in and out of the country."

He stilled. "Why?"

"Doubt she'd leave Kat for long. Though I do know she's keeping in contact with her. But I think Lodestar has been busy overseas."

"Meaning?"

"Meaning there have been some interesting deaths recently. But I have no proof it's her. I just know her MO. This crusade that she's on won't end well," I warned, ascending the steps with that and leaving him behind.

When I made it into the church, I saw Luc and Aurora talking to each other just to the side of the baptismal font, Stan hovering close, but he was on his phone. Luc appeared as if he were apologizing, Aurora seemed... stoic? I pondered her mood as I strode down the aisle and took a seat in the first pew where I knew she'd be sitting.

Lauren, sun-kissed and brighter than I'd seen in years, greeted me, "Hunter, sweetheart. It's good to see you!"

I grinned at her. "You too, Lauren. We need to catch up."

Lauren shot her daughter a knowing look. "I don't think Aurora would like that. She's keeping you under wraps. That girl is always so secretive."

I felt the need to defend her. "I think it's second nature for her now. Some habits are impossible to break."

Lauren's nose crinkled. "Maybe. She certainly dances to her own beat."

"How was Sicily?" I questioned, knowing that would get her off this topic.

As she told me all about the estate, I took note of Jennifer on the other side of the font. She was holding a fussing baby while a red-haired woman was cooing at Saverina to hush her.

I hated these types of ceremonies.

Church wasn't my thing. At all. Probably because my father had forced it down my throat for the entirety of my childhood.

I knew, at some point, Aurora and I would have to go the whole nine yards, but I much preferred the simple, no-bullshit service we'd had in my grandfather's office to anything that could go down with a priest in attendance.

My ruminating culminated in Aurora plunking herself at my side with a huff. I reached for her hand, squeezing her fingers in reassurance.

There were many facets of her nature that I knew I'd never understand. Pondering how stilted the conversation she'd had with Luc appeared from the outside looking in, I realized that one of those inexplicable facets was why she was so awkward around her siblings.

Hence the double squeeze of her fingers. Not enough, but it was better than nothing.

She shot me a quick, grateful glance then shifted her focus to her mother. "*Matri*, you look beautiful."

Lauren beamed at her and reached over for a quick one-armed hug. Her gaze locked on our joined hands but she didn't say anything. Didn't even shoot me a knowing smile. Just closed her eyes as she embraced her daughter.

Lauren wasn't going to prod—go figure. Maybe coming to church had reaped a miracle.

Before I could wonder about Lauren's silence when she'd never been silent in her life—nosy was one *kind* way to describe her—the service began.

After the priest greeted his congregation, he asked, "Are you willing and able to fulfill your duties to raise this child in the Catholic faith?" Luc and Jennifer answered, then Stan and Jen's friend did as well.

It was at that point that a loud, "*Kingston is calling*," sounded from Aurora's purse.

Her eyes widened in surprise as the priest glowered at her, and she swiftly opened her purse and cut the call. "Sorry," she whispered, rushing through her settings to turn on 'Do Not Disturb.'

Her cheeks were flushed as the ceremony continued, and as we were called to stand, I murmured in her ear, "Your cheeks are probably as pink as your ass was earlier."

She elbowed me in the side. "Not in church."

My lips quirked up as she angled herself into me.

One thing that could be said about Luc's not asking her to be Saverina's godmother? It made her seek me out more. No way in fuck was I going to complain about that even if common sense dictated that its source wasn't particularly *nice*.

I was already working on several of her insecurities, however, so I didn't feel too bad about her making up for the last twenty-plus years of zero affection.

As Saverina had the Oil of Catechumens gently anointed onto her neck, Aurora's cell buzzed again. This time, there was no declaration of *who* was calling, just a ringtone.

"For God's sake, just switch it off!" someone hissed behind us.

"Savannah," another chided.

"Honestly, is it so hard to turn on 'Do Not Disturb?'" the woman continued.

"She's right, Aurora. Turn off your phone!" Lauren complained.

Aurora whipped around to glower at the stranger. "I *did* put it on 'Do Not Disturb.'"

She jumped to her feet then shot an apologetic look at Luc. Jennifer glared at her, but Luc didn't. He tipped his head at her in understanding as she scuttled away.

I wanted to go with her because I knew, much as Luc did, that only someone she'd prioritized would get through to her, which meant it was business. And Jennifer might not get it, but Luc had only been able to spend the last couple months in Sicily, and was here, no business worries on his mind, because his sister had borne the brunt of managing the Valentini empire.

Annoyed on her behalf, I stayed put simply because it'd draw too much attention to what had just happened.

I was relieved when Saverina squalled as she was blessed with holy water and the service finally concluded.

As the front rows of the pews rushed around the family, I edged toward the back where I found my wife sitting in the last pew. Her cheek was sucked in as if she were gnawing on it while she stared at the cluster of people around the font.

Crouching down at her side, I told her, "I've never known anyone who loves their family as much as you so consistently be on the outside looking in."

Her gaze didn't even flicker away from them. "You never make me feel that way."

That had me arching a brow at her. "Did you think I would?"

She shrugged. "I don't just mean now."

"When we were kids?" Her nod had me sighing. "Honey, they were my pals, but *you* were my best friend."

I watched her throat move as she swallowed. "I don't know why."

"Because you're caring and loving? Because you go the extra mile for people you consider yours? Because you want everything to be perfect for them? Because you give so much of yourself that it's no wonder you don't have anything left for *you?*

"How about that you love soccer more than I do? That you can quote back more stats than I can? How about the fact that you could get me off a murder one charge with your hands tied behind your back and can burn water without even trying?"

"That last one wasn't a compliment," she complained.

I grinned at her. "Had to make sure you were listening."

The makings of a smile stirred as her gaze drifted to mine. "Thank you."

It was my turn to shrug. "Only speaking the truth. You okay?"

"I feel like a moron for not turning my phone off but the calls were important."

"They always are," I said. "Luc wasn't mad."

"No, but Jennifer was. Bet *Matri* was too. They probably think I did it to be spiteful."

I grunted. "Jennifer might because she doesn't know you. Lauren knows you don't spite family."

"Just the rest of the world?"

My grin made another appearance. "If the shoe fits…" When she snorted, I reached for her hand. "You're kind, Aurora. Just because it doesn't look like other people's kindnesses doesn't mean it isn't there." Because I knew she was in her feelings, and because I also knew she didn't like that, I distracted her, "Which Kingston called?"

"The commissioner. He's found Albarez."

My brows rose. "That's great. Thank God for that. But—" I frowned. "—the cops have him?"

"One of my guys was arrested beating him with his camera."

"That's funny. You're so spiteful that one of the men, whom you've fed and clothed and given a roof to, would defend and protect you."

Her lips pursed. "It's going to be difficult to get him off the charges."

"Good thing he knows you. Not that you can head to the precinct. Do you think Rachel will help?"

"I called her." She rubbed her eyes. "Chad shouldn't spend even a night in a cell but he might. She's crazy busy getting ready for the baby's arrival."

"What can we do? You're right; he shouldn't be in jail for helping you."

"Nothing. Not until Rachel gets there and gets him out on bail. She knows I'll pay." She sighed wearily. "I just hope he doesn't think I've forgotten him. Chad's been through enough."

"Chad's the guy from the Green Berets, isn't he?" At her nod, I squeezed her fingers again. "Who was the second call?"

"Brunu. We need to fly back to Vegas."

"Why?"

"Martínez burned down the *Reyes'* compound."

My mouth rounded. "That's unexpected. What the hell triggered that?"

"Teresa." She started massaging the back of her neck. "She called her mom. Brunu says she learned she was pregnant and freaked out."

I pulled a face. "Is Torres dead?"

"Yeah."

It wasn't the ending I wanted. Not for Teresa, not for Martínez. But I understood his actions, even if Aurora didn't.

A man protected what belonged to him. Even if it was retroactively.

"Is Albarez dead too?"

"He's in a coma."

I frowned at that. "I thought you said your guy, Chad, was picked up beating him."

"He was a Green Beret, Hunter," she said dryly. "They don't let their enemies get away. What a mess."

I couldn't argue. Instead, I straightened and tugged on her necklace. "Come on, Mrs. De Laurentiis. We got places to be."

"When don't we?" was her tired response, but she got up and slipped her arm around my waist. The look she shot at the font was wistful.

As we stepped out of the church, she mumbled, "On the flight to Vegas, can I draw you?"

It hadn't escaped my notice that she'd stopped using her art as a crutch for a while now…

Fuck.

This wasn't about relaxing.

It was about *hiding*.

I grimaced at the setback. "If it'll put a smile on your face, sure."

Her hand patted my abs. "Thank you."

37

HUNTER

"IT'S imperative you isolate the Sheikh's next moves."

I stared around the table where Bert's, now mine, shadow council was seated. Seven women, each terrifying in their own way. Each capable in their own right. Each with a skill my grandfather had exploited over the years.

This wasn't his first shadow council. Unlike the Camorran council, seats weren't inherited. Here, women earned their place by merit.

"If you didn't think I was aware of that already, Mia, then you mistake me for a fool. Of course, I need to isolate the Sheikh's next moves. We need to be his sole client or we won't have enough A-grade product. I might be new to the role, but I can do simple arithmetic."

From the other end of the boardroom table, she shot me a disapproving look. But she wasn't who answered me, Janet Porter did. "We never meant to imply that we couldn't trust in your intelligence, Hunter. We merely wished to ram home the importance of the upcoming meeting."

"It would be wise to bring one of us with you."

That came from Lindsay Newton, and I skewered her with a look in response. "As much as I appreciate having my hand held, I don't think that will be necessary."

"If this is about pride—"

"Mia, it isn't about pride. It's about optics. The Sheikh has tried to communicate with us for months now, and my grandfather dropped the ball on our biggest supplier of heroin. I have to make that dishonor up to him.

"Plus, I'll be leaving the city in Brunu's hands while Aurora and I are gone. I'll need all of you on red alert."

Mia shook her head. "If I attend, it won't skew the optics, nor will Vegas be left in dire peril."

I wasn't about to tell her that I intended for the meeting in Rome to be a short honeymoon. Mia looked as if she had the ability to suck the joy out of Santa. I didn't want her third-wheeling when Aurora and I would only have four days in the Eternal City.

"I will meet the Sheikh with my Consigliere alone." My tone was finite. "Now, is everything set for next week?"

Mia's disapproval was blatant, but she shrugged as if to silently say, 'Your funeral.'

No, actually, it was my fucking honeymoon.

"Yes, the permits are in order," Hilary Wharton assured me. "We had to grease some palms at city hall to allow the funeral procession to head down the Strip but we made it happen."

"Good. Bert would have wanted it that way."

"We have the RSVPs back. There'll be over eight hundred in attendance."

"He'd have liked that as well." My lips almost twitched into a smile. Instead, I rubbed my jaw. "Is security in line?"

"Of course. Your Consigliere is coordinating with Brunu on that matter."

The shade was subtle, but their consistent refusal to use Aurora's name told me they weren't happy about her taking the role of my counsel.

"Why do I sense you have a problem with the woman my grandfather hand-picked for the job?" The tension around the room soared, then doubled down when, silkily, I drawled, "It's almost as if you don't trust his judgment."

"It isn't that—"

Before Mia could finish, I snarled, "I should hope it isn't. Whether you like her or not isn't the issue. I dislike most of you and I'm sure you wouldn't hang out with me on a Saturday night, but we have to work together.

"You are my shadow council. You are there to advise me, yes, but you are not here to question me. *Or* Aurora. Understood?" When no response was forthcoming, I slammed my hand against the table.

A few of the councilors jolted in surprise, but Mia was the one to reply, "Understood, Don."

"Good." With that settled, I demanded, "Any news from the DA's office?"

"Yes. Macmillan is pleading his innocence and claiming he's been set up."

"It's obvious he would, seeing as he *was* a patsy. Is the DA making a deal with Crayon?"

"Oh, yes," she said with no small amount of satisfaction. "Macmillan's going to rot. We've made friends in the DA's office now, that's for sure."

The news had me grunting. "Any news on the autopsy results?"

"They came back earlier today," Mia admitted. "He had end-stage pancreatic cancer."

The news came as a shock. "Are you sure?" I choked.

"No question about it. He was terminal," she said softly, her own pain making an appearance.

She hadn't known either.

He'd kept this to himself.

I released a breath as I thought about my grandfather and his fatalistic approach to his diabetes and other medical issues.

Knowing this helped me understand why he'd done what he'd done. Why he'd pretty much allowed himself to be sent up. Why he'd arranged to bring down ADA Macmillan.

This was his gift to me.

His wedding gift as well as his swan song.

I gritted my teeth to hold back the wave of grief that hit me and, instead, changed the subject: "Is there anything else?"

"There's an issue with the *Cosa Nostra*," Porter stated.

"What about them?"

"They're showing interest in the Vallara."

"There's nothing wrong with other factions owning stakes in casinos so long as they don't maintain a presence here."

I'd wondered, to be honest, when this would become an issue.

"Surely you can see there's a question of where loyalties lie—"

I frowned at Mia. "No, I don't see that. Not at all. Aurora's role is to unite two powerful Sicilian factions. She's already earmarked a five-star hotel that's for sale in Manhattan as a potential investment for the Camorra in the city." Her lack of response had me complaining, "You forget *again* that it was Bert who gave her the role."

"Maybe he wasn't in his right mind," Wharton said hesitantly.

"You dare question his judgment? For the second time in my presence?" I slammed to my feet, both hands slapping against the glass table this time. "He single-handedly set up the asshole who's been working on Caponing him for years. That bastard is in jail now and that's down to the man whose sanity you're questioning?"

"He didn't consult us on this matter," was all Mia said, but her disapproval was apparent.

"He didn't need to. As far as I'm aware, both of the councils act in advisory capacities.

"That means when the ax falls, it's the Don's head on the line. No one else's. A good thing when it came down to my octogenarian grandparent being sent up, no?" I narrowed my eyes at all of them. "If the *Cosa Nostra* purchases the Vallara, be their stake one-hundred-percent or a smaller percentage, so long as it remains an investment, there's nothing wrong with that. It's business."

"How can it remain purely an investment when one of their own is the Camorra's Consigliere?" Mia complained.

"I know they've been interested in the Vallara for a while. Did Bert know too?"

Porter nodded. Once.

"Then you have your answer because he'd have put a stop to it by buying it himself if he foresaw a problem."

"There might be repercussions—"

I rounded the board table. "There are always repercussions. If you haven't figured that out yet, you're the fools, not me." As I walked toward the door, making it clear this meeting was over, I tossed back at them, "And I want to sue the state of Nevada under whatever guise you can think of. Wrongful death, mistreatment of the prisoner, *whatever*.

"Let's be the burr under their saddle like they were with Bert this past year and let's squeeze them for every fucking cent we can."

38

AURORA

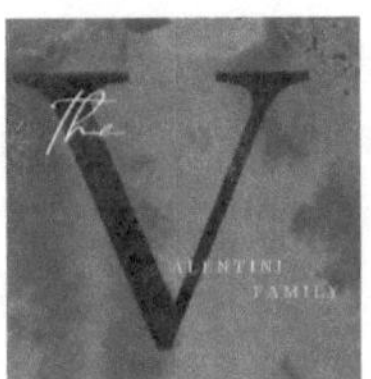

HUNTER WASN'T A VIOLENT MAN. Not really. I knew he had it in him. Much as every man did. But Luc jumped into violence with both feet. As did Stan. They waded into the fray, uncaring of who started it just as long as they ended it.

Hunter was more composed. More calculating.

I loved that about him.

So watching him press his thumb to a man's eye and push down was both the most non-violent way to kill someone I'd seen and also the most cringe-worthy.

Albarez was cuffed to the hospital bed. He had a dish towel in his mouth that Hunter had duct-taped into place.

Screams escaped through the gag, enough to draw security inside if we hadn't paid them to wear noise-canceling earphones for the rest of the hour. The staff on shift was also being paid to turn a blind eye as Albarez disappeared forever.

"You think you can follow *me mugghieri* around and take pictures like she's Linda Evangelista?" Hunter scoffed as bloody tears began to roll down Albarez's cheeks.

I watched, wincing with distaste at the sight.

I'd seen worse torture than this, but the eyes… *Matri* used to watch this show that featured live plastic surgeries. I could watch any of them with her, but never ones that took place in that area.

Just the thought made me shudder. *Ew.*

I had to admit, however, that hearing him call me *me mugghieri* was a definite turn-on. I loved those words on his lips, and I even understood why he was doing this, why we were here, *tonight*, when we were supposed to be heading to Rome in a couple hours for a meeting with the Sheikh and a micro-honeymoon.

We'd buried Alberto yesterday.

Hunter was compartmentalizing his grief via spankings and work. Not healthy. But at least he wasn't shutting me out.

If I asked him how he was doing, he'd say with a smile, "Badly." Then he'd kiss me and hold out his arms for me. I'd plunk myself on his lap, straddle him, then slide my arms around his shoulders and hold him close.

I didn't want him to hurt but it was one solid way in which my brain allowed me to be affectionate, *tender*. He needed me. He was hurting. Mourning. The side of me that had once viewed aftercare as 'more for him than for me' shut the hell up. It had been shutting the hell up for so long that I actually thought it was making me evolve into someone who'd be able to hug him when I wanted to.

A radical thought.

"The *Reyes* all burned in their beds, you fucker," Hunter was crowing to the now-shrieking man. "They suffered and you will too—"

The sounds emitting from him had me turning away and staring at a picture on the wall as I thought about the grand send-off that I'd arranged for Alberto.

It had been worthy of a Broadway show, with a Victorian-era black carriage pulled by horses that sported feathers atop their heads as his coffin rode down the Strip.

Cars had been blocked from the section in front of the Gallinaro for the procession before we'd ended up at one of the cemeteries where he had a plot.

Said plot was on a hill that overlooked the city.

Hunter had joked that Bert once told him, "It's there so I can watch over the Camorra in death too. You gotta keep people scared, Hunter. Fear does good things to people's brains, makes 'em behave."

Alberto was clearly a psychopath.

Anxiously, I scratched my nape when a shriek made my ears ring.

I knew that, technically, an eye couldn't be pushed back into the brain because the orbital socket was too small. *But* there were instances where it would and could happen. Albarez was either going to be blind or brain-damaged or both.

Not that it would be for long.

His death was imminent.

When the screams turned deafening—even with the gag—and then were abruptly muffled, I grimaced until there was silence.

Twisting back to see the man was sagging into the bed, I also saw that Hunter had pulled on a surgical glove while I'd been thinking about yesterday's service. The bruises on Albarez's throat told me that Hunter hadn't been willing to leave his 'end' to chance.

As he pocketed the glove, I purposely kept my eyes averted from the fresh corpse and held out my hand for him. "Are you ready to head out?"

His nostrils were flared from exertion. "I'll never let anyone stalk you again, moonlight."

"You can't promise that, Hunter."

"I can."

"You can't," I snapped then sucked in a breath to calm myself down. This was coming from a good, if fucked-up, place. "Look, I'd appreciate it if no one ever used a sex tape of us to get us to act, but we follow enemies around; we take pictures too. Just no sex tapes. Please."

He blinked at me but repeated, "No sex tapes."

I frowned at his reaction. "Why do you say it like that? Was there one?"

"No."

My sigh was relieved. "Good. Okay, let's go." My hand was still outstretched for him and I flexed my fingers encouragingly. He slid his into mine then hauled me into his side.

"I will never allow anyone to hurt you again, Aurora. Do you hear me?"

"I do." I also knew it was an impossible promise to make. But he wanted to keep me safe. He wanted to protect me. We didn't live in that kind of fairytale world. I did *not* wear rose-tinted glasses. "I understand, *amore mio*." I cupped his cheek. "Thank you for wanting to keep me safe."

His brows lifted at that. Not my gratitude, but I'd guess the term of endearment. I didn't really do those. Much like I didn't do hugs with anyone who wasn't him.

Thanking God that he didn't reply, just pressed a kiss to my forehead, I let him maneuver me around until we were ready to leave. On the way out, Giovi was waiting.

"Deal with the body," I ordered.

"The records?"

"Hunter dealt with them on the flight from Vegas."

He nodded and drifted away to do my bidding.

Our guards moved around us into a formation that was becoming second nature to them when we were together, two factions marrying because of us—it'd be cute if this was a romance novel.

He was silent as we left the hospital, and I decided to let the silence drift until we were on the plane. I'd come to recognize how useful a small space was when we were forced together for hours at a time. We could be pinned down and be made to talk about things that were uncomfortable topics for us both.

On the ride to the airfield, I checked the headlines for any updates.

News of the deal Louis Deloix, AKA Crayon, Alberto's killer, had cut with the DA had sent shockwaves across the nation.

The idea that a Macmillan, one who worked in law enforcement, could hire a hitman to take out a mafia Don in prison had me wondering if Hollywood would be taking notes and making a movie adaptation.

It didn't help that there was conjecture as to *why* Robert would do such a thing. Mostly, there'd been speculations about Marcus's disappearance and whether or not it was mafia-related.

The Macmillans really needed to hire a better PR team.

When we were finally on board the jet, and as was becoming my go-to position with him, I straddled his lap and settled in for the ride once the flight attendant informed us we'd reached the right altitude and could move around the aircraft if we wanted.

He slung his arms around my waist and I pushed my forehead against his and just settled in, letting him take the time he needed to focus.

After a while, he drawled, "Did I tell you Luc finally gave me the big brother speech the other night?"

"Over the phone?"

"Yup."

"Did you shake in your boots?"

"I told him I'd slice a 'V' into my own cheek before I hurt you."

That had me squirming on his lap. "I'm sure he approved *that* message."

"He did. I was glad to see him and Stan at Bert's funeral. It was good of them to attend the service."

"You're family. Of course, they were there." My tone was staunch before it softened. "How are you doing, sweetheart?"

His head rocked back against the rest. "Bert was always larger than life, Rory. If a man like him can…"

"We all die, Hunter," I said before he could finish. "That's just how it is. We have to make sure that we leave footprints behind when we're gone. Alberto did that. He left many. And I know that he wanted you to do the same. That was his end goal." I cleared my throat. "Well, that and making the Macmillans suffer for putting you under pressure all these years."

His mouth connected with mine. "Why do you always call him Alberto?"

I shrugged, though internally, I sighed at his changing the subject. "I don't know. I just do."

"We'll leave footprints together, Aurora. Many, many footprints."

I caressed his cheek, this man who had shed blood for me. "I know we will, Hunter. I know we will."

HUNTER

I HADN'T BEEN BACK in Rome in years, and neither had Rory, so that was why we were turning this business trip into a short honeymoon.

Four days away from the States—it felt like a lifetime and as if it were over already.

A feeling that was facilitated by the fact that the moment we stepped into our hotel, after driving through the main streets of the Eternal City, both our phones lit up with messages from Rachel.

A video of a sleeping baby popped on our screens with Rach whispering a voice-over: "Meet Sommer, guys. She's too busy sleeping to care about who you are, but I wanted you to know you're both going to be godparents when I eventually get around to having her baptized."

I checked the time and hit call, immediately putting us on speaker. Aurora had already watched the video twice by the time Rach answered, "That was fast!"

"We just checked in. Congratulations, *Mama*," I teased, pronouncing it the Sicilian way with the slight stress on the second 'M' in the word.

Her chuckle sounded frantic, but I figured that was to do with pushing a person out of her body. "Thank you, Hunter. Is Rory there?"

"She is. She's watching that video you sent again. She likes kids," I mock-whispered into the phone. "But pretends she doesn't."

Rach snorted. "She doesn't pretend. She just knows that's not what people expect of her. I think she likes the idea of them, just not the bodily fluids and the torn-apart vagina."

"Great imagery, Rachel," I retorted with a grimace but my brow puckered at the insight.

Was she right?

I thought about Aurora's meager interactions with Saverina and realized that she'd been as in awe of her niece as she was with Sommer's video, but she'd hid it better.

I thought that was probably to do with the enmity between her and Jennifer though, and not her reaction to children.

She wasn't maternal but that didn't mean she didn't like kids.

"Did I stun you with my wicked wisdom?"

"You did," I agreed, moving over to Aurora so she could greet our friend.

As I approached her, through the window, I saw the top of the *Altare della Patria,* one of my favorite monuments in the city. A modern forum, its pure white marble gleamed in the sun.

From this distance, I saw the roof of the portico and the statues of the goddess Victoria, her wings widespread, as she stood behind one of two chariots, or *quadrigas,* as they were known.

"Rach, you did good."

She laughed. "I didn't. I nearly had a meltdown. In fact, no, I *did* have a meltdown. But she's here now."

"You never have to do it again," Rory promised her, being her ever-reassuring self.

"No, I don't. Thank God Rex got that vasectomy."

I winced. "If I needed proof that he loved you…"

Rachel hooted. "He's done plenty more than that."

"Nothing less than you deserve."

She sniffled. "Don't make me cry. My hormones are whacked."

"I can't believe we're in Rome," Rory complained with a sigh.

"You did not just complain about being in Italy," Rachel chided.

"We should be with you."

"I'm a mess. A literal mess, Rory. I don't want to see anyone. I can't even look Rex in the eye yet, so speaking on the phone is more than enough for the moment."

"Why can't you look Rex in the eye?" I queried, looping my arm over Aurora's shoulder.

"Because I can't." Her sniffle had morphed into a sniff. "Anyway, you two should go and do honeymoon stuff. I'm just going to cry a bit, get that out of my system so Rex won't wake up and freak out that I'm freaking out when I really just need to cry."

Rory's voice was the most tender I'd ever heard it. "Of course you do. You cry, sweetheart, and if you need me, don't worry about whatever we're doing or what time it is, just call, okay? I'm always here for you."

Rachel's swallow was audible. "Thank you, Rory. I-I needed to hear that. I know I'm being dumb—"

"You are *not*," I said sternly. "The same goes for me, Rachel. If you need to talk, I'm here, Rory's here, you get two for the price of one."

A watery chuckle sounded in my ear. "You guys are the best. So, godparents?"

We shared a glance.

"I think we can manage that," I agreed.

"What about the Sinners?" Aurora queried warily, though I saw her excitement at being asked. I was well aware that Luc had zero idea how his not asking her had hurt her. Badly.

"Rory can be godmother, and if Rex wants one of his brothers then that's okay too," I soothed. "Now, come on, *Mama*, go cry some and rest up."

"Yes, sir!" Rachel's laughter sounded less water-logged this time. "Oh, before I go, Rory, I managed to get Chad out. It took some wrangling but if you send over the bail—"

"Rachel, you're not talking about this now, are you?"

She groused, "It's important. *Chad* is important to you! Speak with Parker. She can arrange everything while I'm—"

"Rachel, don't you dare think about work," Rory reprimanded. "Go and chill. We love you, and remember that when I cut the call now so you can't start up the conversation again!"

When she did as promised, I saw the relief in her gaze at Rachel's last words.

My lips twitched. "She knows you too well."

"She does," she admitted on a sigh. "I'm glad Chad will be out on bail soon but she shouldn't be thinking about that stuff when she just gave birth."

Because I agreed, I rubbed her shoulder as she texted Giovi and arranged for him to send the money for bail over. With that task complete, I then watched as she turned off her notifications too.

"Ready to catch some Zs before the meeting this evening?" I asked when she was done.

Turning into me and placing her phone face down on a nearby stand, she nodded. "We should have honeymoon sex."

"You look really into the idea," I teased as she yawned.

"I'm sure you could *make* me get into the idea." She spoiled her pout by yawning again.

"Come on. You've been sleeping like shit since the christening."

"Of course I have. Martínez is pissed that we withheld his niece from him, so only God knows how he'll retaliate now that he owns the *Reyes'* turf.

"Then there's the fact that Jennifer thinks I ruined Saverina's christening on purpose. Chad was in jail, Alberto's funeral needed arranging and—"

I didn't allow her to continue. "Baby girl, the world is always going to keep on spinning out of control. We can only close the door behind us when we get home and take a deep breath then accept that what we have between us is all that really matters."

She peered up at me, those cocoa-brown eyes drilling through to my very soul. "Hunter?"

"Yes?"

"I need to tell you something."

My brow furrowed. "Hit me with it."

Her tongue peeped out to smooth along her bottom lip. "I-I love you."

I smiled at her. "I know you do."

She slapped my arm. "Don't be a jerk."

"Hey! I'm not!" I teased, aware humor lit up my eyes. But fuck, the relief at hearing her say those three words was more immense than she probably knew. Recognizing that her pout was turning sulky now, I pressed my lips to hers. "You know I love you. I loved you when you were getting mad about Stan, Luc, and me not having to deal with periods, and I loved you when you dealt with my bullies for me. I loved you when you married another guy, and I loved you when you shut me out. Me loving you isn't news—"

Her arms tightened around my neck as she hauled herself into me. "I don't deserve you."

I settled my hand between her shoulders, and while I had no intention of starting something when we both needed the sleep more than we needed an orgasm—now I really knew I'd grown up—I growled in the voice she'd recognize as D's, "Never, *ever*, say those words to me again, Aurora. It took us a long time to find our way back to this point, and there's no denying it was awkward and tough, but we're here now and we deserve each other."

Against my chest, she nodded, and because I knew she was exhausted, I didn't force her to tell me she understood and that she agreed. She didn't need me to be D. She needed me to be her husband.

"Let's get some sleep."

I picked her up and carried her through the penthouse and placed her on the bed.

Moving over to the windows, I stared down at a city that owned my heart even if it wasn't in Sicily, and I closed the curtains, shutting it out because this was our cocoon. Our bubble. Not even the Eternal City could intrude upon it.

She'd switched on the lights by the time I turned around, and I watched her wriggle out of her dress and toss it on the floor then shuffle under the covers. By that point, her hand was outstretched for mine with an order that was imperious.

I grinned at the sight, only too content to obey, and stripped out of my suit. Only when I was in my boxer briefs did I kneel on her side of the bed.

"Scoot over," I ordered.

"Bossy," she grouched, but she complied, shuffling a bare two feet to the left to let me in.

I wasn't going to complain. Her cleaved to my side was how I wanted to nap, and it seemed that we were in complete accord.

She loved me.

She'd said the words.

Was it any wonder I went to sleep with a smile on my face?

40

AURORA

TO SAY our meeting with the Sheikh was not going according to plan was a definite understatement.

I shot the man a cool glance then stared up at the guard who was pressing a gun to my temple. "If you think this is a smart way to hold a business meeting, Your Highness, then you're incredibly foolish."

The older man rubbed his lips with a napkin that he proceeded to toss down on the table. "Few would dare speak to me like that."

"Aren't you fortunate that one of those *few* is here now?"

"Aurora," Hunter reprimanded with a hiss.

I arched a brow at him, trying to shield him from my fear.

I refused to believe that we'd finally shared our feelings for one another only for us to die later that same day.

The guards we'd brought with us were all unconscious on the ground, making me think that some of the Sheikh's security detail were ex-Mossad from their skills, and we were utterly on our own. That meant I had Hunter's talents with a computer and my wits to bargain with.

The Sheikh leaned forward as he reached for a glass of water. "I'm simply to believe this new change in the council?"

"Do you not read the Tribunal?" I retorted. "Alberto's death was publicized widely, as was his funeral, *and* the fact his murder was paid for by the ADA of the state. If you consider yourself well-read, then I fear you're failing."

His eyes narrowed upon me. "You do not know when to hold your tongue."

"You could always cut it off." I nuzzled my temple against the gun. "But why bother when you're going to blow my head off?"

"If my men are going to make a mess, then why should I spare you any pain?" was his calm reply, but I saw my lack of fear surprised him. In Arabic, he drawled something to a man who appeared from another room. Unlike the Sheikh who wore traditional dress, he sported a very tailored suit that reeked of Savile Row.

As he passed the Sheikh a tablet, the stranger studied whatever was on there and mused, "Your identity is *not* Aurora Valentini."

"That is my true birth name."

"Not according to this." He showed me a picture of my Italian passport then. I hid a grimace when he switched screens and let me see a news article.

NY's DA's hard stance on the Italian mafia decimates upper ranks!

For all the other bluster, I recognized *this* was why we were being held at gunpoint.

It made sense.

I'd been shortsighted in thinking it wouldn't bite me in the ass at some point, especially when dealing with overseas 'businessmen' who weren't aware of the minutiae.

If my head was going to get shot off anyway, I reached for the glass he'd filled with wine before the pretense behind this meeting burned to dust.

Taking a deep sip, I sighed with pleasure. If my death *was* in the cards, it was being anointed with a beautiful Sancerre.

"We're meeting in Rome. My one-time role as New York's DA has no jurisdiction here, as you know. I've had quite a few last names over the years, but Valentini was the first one I was graced with. My brother is Luciu, the Don of the *Cosa Nostra.*"

The Sheikh's eyes darted from the glass in my hand to the gun at my temple. "I have heard of Luciu."

"Feel free to give him a call," I mocked. "He'll be more than willing to fill you in on my real identity."

"What other last names have you had?" he questioned, ignoring my mockery. "Who is Fitzwilliam?"

"My maternal grandparents were English landed gentry. My mother was the last of their line and she wed an impoverished Sicilian.

"In order for the Fitzwilliam name not to die out and in exchange for money to raise their children in more affluent circumstances, my parents agreed to change our last names.

"I kept mine, my brothers changed theirs later in life. As for other last names, I've been a Macmillan."

He frowned. "I know this name."

"They're up there with the Kennedys and the Lindenbourgs. I was married to the eldest son, Marcus. Fun fact, he's the brother of the ADA who had my husband's grandfather killed.

"Finally, and the name that I'll die with whether that day is today or fifty years from now, is Valentini-De Laurentiis."

I didn't need to look at Hunter to know he was furious with my blasé tone. Undoubtedly, my ass would pay for it later, but at least there'd *be* a later. Well, there had better goddamn be.

"You are very brave to lie to a man like myself."

"I'm not lying. I haven't told you a single lie. I *was* the DA of New York. I'm not anymore. I'm the Consigliere of the *Cosa Nostra* and the Camorra—"

"A woman holding the role is unlikely. To be holding it twice over? Even more ridiculous. And to be an ex-DA is to strain the depths of possibility."

Ha.

"I live to strain the depths of possibility. It might seem ridiculous but it's true. Don't worry. You're not the only person I've disappointed with misaligned gender roles."

"Aurora, for God's sake," Hunter intoned starkly. "Sheikh, I don't appreciate you holding my wife at gunpoint. Keep the guns aimed at me, but I must insist that you—"

"You must insist that I *desist*?" the Sheikh mocked. "A new, inexperienced Don travels to Italy with a member of the American justice system, a woman he claims is his wife *and* his Consigliere?

"Surely you can understand my inability to believe what I'm hearing. This is better than one of my daughter's romance novels." He said something in his native tongue that had the men around him chortling. "This stinks of a set-up. An elaborate one, I grant you, but…" His mouth turned down at the corners.

Here was a man whose ego weighed more than his body.

"How would you like us to prove ourselves to you?" I asked quietly, aware we were running circles around each other but that he'd yet to ask his guards to pull the trigger.

"It is an interesting dilemma," he concurred as he drummed his fingers against the dinner table. We were in the back room of one of the few Michelin-starred restaurants in the city, and even if he did blow our heads off, I knew there'd be no raised brows at such an occurrence. "My assistant assures me that you are not whom you say you are. Yet a woman so secure in her position is intriguing considering the situation she finds herself in."

"If you contact my brother, he will clear this up," I stated, maintaining eye contact with him.

"Or my Capo," Hunter inserted. "Brunu was my grandfather's man. His trust in me is absolute."

The Sheikh's attention flickered between us. "Only a wife would have a man wrapped around his finger the way you do," he drawled before he held out his hand, snapping something in Arabic at the man in the expensive suit. "I *was* aware of Alberto's passing. But I was *not* aware of whom he'd entrusted the Camorra to." To the assistant, in English, he stated, "I want to speak with Mia Raleigh."

Hunter shot me a look, one that told me exactly how pissed he was. A freedom he was only comfortable in enacting because he knew Mia Raleigh would prove we were whom we said we were.

I didn't have it in me to be concerned about what the repercussions of this meeting would be.

Not right now.

Instead, I took a deep sip of Sancerre and inhaled it as the Sheikh got through to Alberto's right-hand woman.

Without having to say a word, communicated via a single glance that had both guards reacting, the guns were no longer butting up against our temples. They stepped back and drifted into the shadows, leaving me to rock my head from side to side to ease the strain on my neck.

"I should have attended the meeting with you," Mia apologized; I wasn't sure who that was aimed at. I hadn't even expected to hear her voice but the Sheikh had put her on speaker. "It was *foolish* not to."

Hunter's mouth tightened, which made me wonder if she'd suggested it to him when he'd attended the shadow council meeting prior to Bert's funeral. Her emphasis on the word 'foolish' was also suspicious.

Not wanting him to lose his temper, I murmured, "For an initial meeting perhaps it would have been wise, but it's unusual for the leader and his second to be so poorly treated upon ground that is foreign to both factions."

Mia was silent, as were Hunter and the Sheikh. The latter placed his phone on the table before reaching for his glass of water again. The ice tinkled against the sides as he took a sip.

"You are correct," he said eventually. "My sincerest apologies. There were far more diplomatic ways of dealing with this matter."

I slowly dipped my chin at him. "There were, but can I say that, *'I have concealed nothing, I have dissembled nothing?'*"

The Sheikh considered me. "A student of philosophy?"

"I'm a student of many things. We should have approached you with the truth first. My past is complex but I am here as a Consigliere, not an actuary of United States law, something that I only upheld to avenge my family."

He peered at me. "The downfall of the Fieris?"

"Not solely at my hands, but some part of it, yes."

"Interesting." He collected his phone from the table. "I appreciate your verifying the identities of your leaders, Ms. Raleigh."

"You could have acted earlier. I can only imagine what my Consigliere constitutes as 'poor treatment.'"

Hunter argued, "Don't be rude, Mia."

The Sheikh smirked at him. "Mia was born rude. As was I." He cut the call without a farewell.

"You know her," I mused.

"Intimately."

My brow furrowed as I pieced what had happened together. "You thought she'd attend this meeting, didn't you?"

A chuckle escaped the older man. "A wise woman indeed." That was the only answer we got. "Now, down to business. You wish to remain my sole client, do you not?" He bridged his fingers together. "Then we should discuss terms."

41

HUNTER

AVICII - ADDICTED TO YOU

"OH, GOD!"

Her scream sent sparks of electricity through my being as I pulled out of her moments before she was about to come. My seed dripped down the folds of her sex in a manner that should have been obscene but was hot as fuck.

I'd edged her four times and had come in her twice already—I was enjoying it too much.

"Please, fuck, Hunter, please. I'm sorry!" she cried.

It surprised me that I enjoyed her misery too.

I always focused on glutting her with pleasure, but her behavior at the meeting with the Sheikh called for more serious punishment.

Denial.

And I didn't see why I should have to deny myself this time, either.

I moved away from her, not going far but watching her body heave as she chased an orgasm I wasn't going to give her.

Unlike the last time I had her restrained on a coffee table, she was bent over it, her hands and knees bound to the table legs, and she'd been there for over an hour.

What could I say?

She'd scared the ever-living fuck out of me. That alone necessitated a punishment.

"Hunter, please!" she called out. "Please! I said I'm sorry!"

I picked up the bottle of water I'd left on a dresser earlier, and once I'd rehydrated, I sat on the armchair nearest to her.

It was awkward for her to hold her head up and back, but when she saw where I was sitting, she tried and whimpered again, "Please."

I knew what she was asking for, and it wasn't H2O. I grabbed her chin and carefully angled her head so that I could trickle some water into her mouth.

"Swallow," I ordered when she shot me a mutinous glance.

Relaxing after she'd drank some water too, I watched her as she panted her way down from the orgasm I'd led her toward.

"Good girls get to come," was my mild rebuke.

Five words.

Harmless words, mostly.

Nothing cruel or vitriolic, but she groaned at them. "I am a good girl," she said with a sniffle.

"You antagonized him. You *purposely* antagonized him." I shook my head as I thought back to the meeting.

While it was annoying that Mia Raleigh and Lindsay Newton had been correct about one of the shadow council attending with us, something Mia could have fixed by speaking with the Sheikh ahead of time, a mistake Mia would suffer for failing to anticipate, mostly I was pissed that I'd put Rory in danger.

The odd part was, of course, that even with a gun to our mutual temples, I hadn't been scared for myself. Not at all. Just her.

I scratched my jaw as I looked at her, pinned down and at my mercy. I'd never have imagined wanting to put her through this, would never have thought that I'd *punish* her by denying her orgasms…

Leaning forward, I ran my hand over the back of her head, unable to deny us both the connection. If it lessened the punishment and took away the 'teaching moment' then so be it.

She shivered at my touch, but it morphed into a deep-body shudder when I wrapped her ponytail around my wrist and tugged her head up and back again.

"You do not endanger what belongs to me, Aurora."

"I didn't mean to. I knew he would react—"

"I don't care. You baited him. Who do you belong to?"

My wife swallowed. "You. Always you."

I dropped to my knees and pressed my mouth to hers. For a moment, I just let her feel that link between us build before I bit her upper lip. The move had her jolting. I always went for the bottom one, and that was intentional. The upper was to shock her. To jerk her into a reaction.

I tested the resilience of the soft flesh with my teeth, hard enough that she whimpered. I left stinging nips around the outer edge of her Cupid's bow, lining them with those small bites. When I pulled back, they were bright red with little marks left behind.

"Are you empty, Aurora?"

It was a trick question.

Her dazed eyes stared at me for an endless amount of time, then she whispered, "No. I'm full of you."

"Correct answer," I crooned. "Remember who you're talking to, Aurora. Orgasms are *earned*. Understood?"

She whimpered. "Understood, Hunter."

It was late. Dawn was approaching. So I unfastened her bindings and helped her onto her feet. She was weak, her limbs wobbly from the sustained position, so I picked her up like she was a child and walked us over to the bed.

Settling her on top of me once I lay flat out on the sheets, I ordered, "Put me inside you."

Her eyes were dazed as she grabbed my cock. "How are you still hard?" she keened.

"Got the libido of a teenager after years of being D," I informed her, playing with her curls as she shivered and sank onto me. I let the ends of her locks tickle her nipples, then I encouraged her to blanket me.

As I stroked a hand down her spine, gentling her and settling her down for the night, she surprised me by whispering, "I want you to leave Mia Raleigh to me."

"You shouldn't be thinking about business," I said disapprovingly.

Her face nuzzled into my throat. "What she did was tantamount to betrayal."

I didn't necessarily disagree with her but all I said was, "Go to sleep, Aurora."

"Only after you promise you'll leave her for me to handle."

My jaw worked. "There'll be repercussions if you kill her."

"There'll be repercussions if we don't. That kind of disrespect can't be tolerated."

She was right. My answer was brisk. "Okay. Now go to sleep."

Aurora tensed at my concession, then as if we hadn't just been talking about the death of a high-ranking official in our faction, her pussy clutched in response to my order as she mewled miserably, "Yes, Hunter."

Sleep was the last thing on her mind.

42

HUNTER

IT WAS ON the Piazza Navona, behind Bernini's *Fontana dei Quattro Fiumi, Fontana del Moro,* and *Fontana di Nettuno* that we received the news the First Lady had been murdered in a Brooklyn graveyard of all places.

In a busy coffee shop where the java was like tar and delicious for it, where the world converged as tourists bustled from hotspot to hotspot and locals hurried as they led their lives amid the guests who brought eclectic energy to the Eternal City, we heard the other, less publicized news.

The leader of the Irish Mob, Aidan O'Donnelly Sr., had also died.

I wasn't an East Coaster. My faction wasn't based there. But even I knew what that meant.

A new dawn for Manhattan and, with it, the potential for war.

As she finished reading Luc's message to her, I snagged a hold of her fingers, kissed her knuckles, and told her, "Whatever comes, we'll handle it together."

"Luc, Stan, and I have been waiting for a Summit to be called." Once she dumped the cell on the table, she reached up and rubbed her brow. "I didn't want it to be like this."

"Summits are important?"

"Sometimes, I forget how seamlessly you've managed to slip into this role that it comes as a surprise when you're in the dark about some things." She shot me a weary smile, not realizing I was actually preening at that compliment. "They're rarely called. We wanted O'Donnelly to back our right to be there as the new leaders of the *Cosa Nostra*."

"He hadn't done that yet?"

"He was a prick." At my snort, she huffed out a laugh. "He really was. Only his family will mourn his passing," she predicted. "And even they won't all be sad to see him go."

Her bottom lip trembled. I was hyperaware of her reactions out of habit by this point, so I spotted it like she'd thrown herself to the ground and started screaming.

"That won't be how you die."

It seemed ridiculous to me that I had to say that, but Aurora felt things harder than people knew. Than people *cared* to know. Her brothers included.

She swallowed. "You don't know that."

"I'm your husband."

"He had a wife. Sons."

I twined my fingers around hers. "I won't let you lead your life in a way that results in you being hated more than you're loved."

"Being hated keeps you safe."

"Not by your family. You have to let them in sometimes, Aurora. It'll be easier with any kids we have. They won't let you erect any barriers between you."

She choked on my words. "Kids? Plural?"

I hitched a shoulder. "Despite what you said, a part of me doesn't know if you truly want them, then I look at how you reacted to Saverina and those goo-goo eyes at Sommer and I think, even if you hide from the fact you want them, you were supposed to be a mom."

"I'm older—" She hesitated, but there was something strange in her eyes… Was that hope? "It might not be so easy."

"We can adopt. Plenty of kids need a home, and I don't think any adoption agency in the country would dare say no to us."

That had her rolling her lips inward to hide a smile. "We'll just terrify them into giving us a kid?"

"Yup," I agreed with a wicked grin.

Her laughter was so much fucking better than the dread that had shadowed her eyes. Aurora tended to view herself like some kind of monster. She wasn't.

"I might be a crappy mom."

"I might be a crappy dad. I didn't exactly have a good role model, Rory," I said dryly. "Of the pair of us, at least you had a good influence. Your parents were the best."

She bit her lip. "I knew he beat you."

"Spare the rod, spoil the child," was my bitter retort. "We *won't* be living to that adage."

"Do you think Bert beat him?"

"Probably. Those kinds of practices are ingrained from experience. It's probably why I struggled with your needs, then, when they became my needs, I found it difficult to adapt."

"Do you think he hits your mom?"

"I don't know. He's obsessed with her, that's for sure. Possessive to the max. I don't think she'd push her luck with him, but she loves him the same amount of crazy."

"You know you're nothing like him, don't you?"

I hitched a shoulder. "I figure you'd kill me if I hurt one of our kids."

For some reason, that made her shiver again. "You would *never* hurt them, Hunter. If you don't want me to think that I'll die miserable and alone, then I'm not going to let you think that you'll beat our kids just because that's something you learned from your father."

"That's a compromise I can get behind."

She blinked at me, a light dawning in her eyes as she realized I'd manipulated her into that. Not that she chided me for it. If anything, she changed the subject. "Manhattan will be nuts for a while."

I knew what she was saying without her uttering the words themselves—it wouldn't be so easy to split her time between Vegas and New York.

"Then we'll just have to figure something out."

For a moment, insidious insecurity slithered through my veins. It snaked inside me, making me wonder if she was using this as an excuse to pull away because I'd scared her with my truth. If she really did believe I'd hit any kids we had—

No.

I was being dumb.

The last couple days were proof of that. How we'd made love on the terrace that overlooked the frenetic city, how she'd whispered she loved me as we bathed together, how she'd studied me when she sketched me (for pleasure, not as stress relief) when we sat down for breakfast one morning…

"Sometimes," she whispered, breaking into my stupid thoughts, "I wonder how much easier it would have been to have stayed in Sicily.

"For us to get together as teenagers, to live and love on the island, and to raise a family together there. To live on the beach and to exist from holiday to holiday, to—"

I tightened my hold on her hand. "An intellect like yours, Aurora, would be wasted on island life. You were meant for more, *riggina mia*. You were always meant for more, and now that you're mine, I'll give you the world," I promised her, pushing aside those latent wishes of my own.

They were cravings I felt too. Needs I had to set aside. We weren't lucky enough to have that life but we had each other.

That was blessing enough.

Her pensive stare concerned me until she bowed her head. Then, she surprised me. The smallest of smiles curved lips that I'd tasted, *savored*, bitten, and nipped. "You know what that means, don't you?"

"What?"

"If I'm your queen, then you're my king."

I just smirked at her. "Like I'd forget something as important as that."

43

HUNTER

WHEN I WALKED into my office at the *palazzo,* I'd admit it came as a surprise to see Mia Raleigh tied to the visitor's chair.

Brunu, Adrianu, Luca, and Matteo—the usual suspects—hovered at the edge of the room, clearly ordered to be there but not engaging in whatever my Consigliere was up to.

And it didn't take a rocket scientist to figure it out even if my brain was on a delay at the sight of her in an Armani pantsuit I'd set out for her this morning.

The things that tailoring did to her ass—chef's kiss perfection.

"Tell me why I should let you live."

The command had me smiling to myself as I moved deeper into the room and settled behind my desk to watch the show.

I didn't think Aurora ever got her hands dirty, but Mia had pissed her off enough to take action. She was also angry enough that she hadn't even looked at me once since I showed up.

"I sat in Rome with a gun to my temple because you didn't think to warn the Sheikh about who I was? You didn't think that telling him my position was sanctioned by Alberto was a wise option?

"With friends like you, Mia, who the fuck needs enemies?"

She had a point.

After our meeting with the Sheikh, and after I'd punished Aurora for getting mouthy with the man, I'd promised to let her deal with Mia. I hadn't expected the immediacy of her response but it was warranted.

We could have died.

Mia could have prevented that with a single phone call.

Aurora was correct—who needed enemies when you had friends like Raleigh on your shadow council?

Duct-taped into position around the chair, I had to wonder if she'd been dragged in and restrained on site or if she'd been transported here like this…

As I cast a look at the *stiddaris* stationed here, I wondered who'd breached the shadow council's security.

The sound of a slap rang around the room. Mia hissed under her breath, her first response to anything Aurora had said or done since my arrival, as her head whipped to the side.

"Answer me, goddammit."

"You're Bert's choice, but that doesn't mean you're the smart choice. Your loyalty is split between two factions," Mia spat.

"And what? You'd have been a better choice?" Aurora countered.

"I was Bert's right-hand woman. I don't need to be Hunter's Consigliere to hold a position of power—" Her words came to an abrupt halt as Aurora slapped her again.

"Why didn't you contact the Sheikh?"

"I told Hunter that he would be difficult. If he chose not to heed my warning—"

"I doubt Hunter thought we'd be made to sit with guns to our heads as our backgrounds were combed over." Aurora grabbed Mia's nose and pinched it closed. One hand clapped over her mouth as she loomed over the other woman. "You nearly got us killed. In this other faction that my loyalty is split between, that earns a person a death sentence."

I didn't know if Mia's reaction was from the lack of air or Aurora's words but her head started to whip from side to side. Aurora was stronger than she looked though, because she followed the motions and didn't let up.

"Just a twist of my hands and I can snap your neck," she crooned. "Matteo's been giving me some hints and tips."

Mia squawked at that, eyes flooding with fear—Matteo's rep was renowned in the Camorra.

"Tell me why I shouldn't let you die for disrespecting us. For *betraying* us."

Mia sucked down air as Aurora let her go. "He had to learn—" *Gasp* "—that I don't give out advice for—" *Gulp* "—no reason."

"That's bullshit and you know it. Shove your ego up your ass." Aurora's hands made to return to their earlier position but Mia whipped her head away.

"I didn't think the Sheikh would react that way! I swear! I know he's paranoid but I didn't think he'd—"

"That would have been a cold comfort if we'd have flown back to the US in coffins, wouldn't it?" Aurora snarled, her words riling her up enough that she hit her again, slapping the woman hard enough to split Mia's lip.

When blood spurted, she growled, "I'm the only one who knows where the Anjou ruby is that Bert bequeathed you upon giving birth to Hunter's heir."

Aurora froze at that. That was when Mia made a mistake—she smirked.

"What use would the Anjou ruby be if I were dead, Mia?" The smirk faltered. "How would my brothers get the ruby if I was in a coffin and couldn't grant Hunter his heir? And what use would any of Alberto's plots *be* if Hunter was dead because you didn't think to warn the Sheikh, a man who trusted you, about who and what we were?"

Aurora's response stunned me. I knew how important those goddamn rubies were to her family, but at that moment, she proved that her loyalty was with me. With us.

I never questioned the fine line of her position because I knew that I was as important to her as Stan and Luc were, but at that moment, it registered *why* Aurora had taken the role of my Consigliere.

To keep *me* alive.

Bert's work for sure, but the realization settled deep.

She chose me.

She kept on choosing me.

And, I knew, she always would.

Mia, her ploy evidently having gone awry, broke into my thoughts by whispering, "I-I'm sorry. I underestimated—"

"You think I'm in the habit of accepting such piss-poor apologies?" Aurora demanded.

"No! But I promise I—"

"You need to tell me why you shouldn't die for your treachery."

"I have never let Bert down—"

"You did when you put Hunter in danger."

Mia whispered, "I-I won't let him down again."

"Who? Bert? The Don whom you claim to be the right-hand woman of?" Aurora sneered at her. "How quickly things change when someone dies."

"No! I was behaving rashly. I wasn't thinking—I'm mourning Bert! I'm sorry. Truly."

"Where's the Anjou ruby?" It was the first time I'd spoken, and I felt everyone's attention veer onto me. But my focus was on Mia and Mia alone.

She swallowed. "I can tell you how to access it."

I cast a look at my wife. "This is her first strike, Aurora." She heard the order in my words. "She lives today. But there won't be a second chance."

Mia whispered, "Thank you, Don. Thank you. I promise I won't let you down!"

"No, you won't," I intoned grimly. "Now, get my wife her goddamn ruby."

There was no way in hell I was making her wait until we had our first child.

Aurora had earned a reward, and sometimes, those rewards weren't always orgasms.

44

AURORA

BEING BACK in the US was a culture shock, one I didn't appreciate.

Italy wasn't my home. *Sicily* was. But it was close enough that my blood seemed to pine for what I'd only experienced for a handful of days.

That was why I never went to the estate.

It was my choice.

I knew, point blank, that if I returned home, I'd never willingly come back to the States.

My brothers didn't understand that, but then, if they knew my logic, they'd be surprised.

Aurora didn't feel things so strongly, if at all.

Aurora didn't pine.

She didn't long for anything.

She was hard as nails. She busted balls. She was conniving and cutthroat.

Her soul didn't weep for the brine-scented air that rolled in off the Catanian coast and flooded each of the rooms on the estate.

Her heart didn't mourn for the lack of traffic, the quieter days, the simpler life.

If the culture shock was raw in Vegas, that was nothing to New York where things were more treacherous than ever.

"Ma'am!"

My brows rose at the shout outside the office door of *Russu.*

After the meeting with the Sheikh and O'Donnelly Sr.'s murder, I'd taken to carrying a gun with me, one I doubted I'd ever use, but I slipped it out of the slimline holster I wore on my shoulder and palmed it under the desk to be on the safe side.

"You can't go in there!"

Giuseppe didn't sound scared, more annoyed, and whoever it was he shouted at wasn't listening because the door slammed open and in strode Grainne Ledger on high heels that defied gravity and wearing a scowl that'd shrivel any man's ballsack.

Giuseppe was a Messina, so it wasn't a surprise he didn't appreciate being shoved around by a woman.

He was another reason for my gun.

Luciu insisted that if we alienated the Puglisis and Messinas who *weren't* involved in the siege—those who claimed to be in the dark about the head of their houses' actions—we'd be encouraging a mutiny.

As the history buff, I knew the annals of the past drove him, and because I wasn't an idiot and could listen to reason, one of all our guards, minimum, was from the Puglisi and Messina lines.

However, *because I wasn't an idiot,* Chad was now a part of my newly-formed Stidda too. As were a couple other ex-military vets from the homeless squad who'd become a part of my inner circle.

"Grainne," I greeted, opening the desk drawer and sliding the gun inside it. "I didn't expect to see you here."

Grainne, Manhattan's Divorce Maker, shouldn't know about my double life, but that she'd worked it out came as no surprise. She was one of the most ruthlessly intelligent women I'd ever come across. And *Rachel* was my best friend.

"No, I suppose it would come as a shock seeing me here," was her snide reply as she glanced around the office.

"You can leave us, Giuseppe," I instructed.

"Ma'am, she isn't on the list!"

I almost laughed at his whining. "I know she isn't but she's a friend."

That snagged Grainne's attention. As Giuseppe departed with a huff, Grainne arched a brow at me as she strode over to my desk and took a seat opposite me. "This suits you more."

"Than?"

"The DA mask." She angled her head to the side. "You're not concerned that I know *what* you are?"

"I won't be blackmailed."

Grainne smiled. "I know. Leverage is another matter entirely though, is it not?"

Shrugging, I asked, "Want a drink?"

She released a heavy sigh. "Please."

The depth of her weariness caught my attention. I studied her as I dipped down and opened the bottom desk drawer where Luc's Armagnac was stored.

Well, if Hunter was right, the Armagnac he bought for me. Ironic seeing as I loathed the stuff and only drank it out of a desperate need to feel numb.

Retrieving two cut glass tumblers, I placed them on the desk and slid one over to her once it was full of amber liquid.

She reached for hers. "Aren't you concerned about an enemy ratting you out to the cops?"

"I stick to the shadows and stay out of sight."

"That isn't always possible."

"Perhaps. If someone does approach the authorities, then I'm sure they'll reach a sticky end sooner rather than later." I smiled at her. Her poker face was strong, but I saw her tiny flinch. "Plus, I have friends in high places."

And they were getting higher.

"Only wise in your position."

I hummed. "Why are you here, Grainne?"

"Violence against sex workers is on the rise."

Her statement had my shoulders slumping. "I know."

"Rumor has it that Red is a Sicilian creation."

A woman like her knew more than she let on. A woman like her learned things that would make the president look out of the loop.

"It is. And no. I've tried to cut production. It's too profitable."

"And what does the fate of a bunch of sex workers matter when dollars and cents are on the table?" she asked bitterly.

I took a sip of my drink. The liquor burned as it went down. "Horrifically true. Why are you here? To get me to stop making it? Like I said, I tried—"

She shook her head. "I'd never be so naive. We had an incident at Queens of Heart this past week."

"I know."

An Irish foot soldier had killed his hooker. Aidan O'Donnelly Jr. had contacted Luciu at an ungodly time of the morning to demand he explain how a Sicilian drug was being sold on Irish streets.

That was why I was here so late. We'd had a council meeting earlier—meetings that now ran far smoother than they ever had before, seeing as Puglisi and Messina weren't around to slow things down.

For the first time, Grainne's voice was anything but smooth and polished. It was croaky and rusty with emotion as she rasped, "I loved that girl like she was my own."

"I'm sorry, Grainne."

I meant it too. Klara's death still weighed heavily on my conscience.

Owning the commissioner because of her murder didn't provide me with half the satisfaction that it should, knowing that it came with the price of her losing her life.

"Thank you." She shot me a tight smile. "We need to do something about this drug."

"I genuinely don't know what. It's being sold on our streets but I banned patrons in our stables if they're showing signs of aggression."

She bridged her fingers over her stomach. "You're turning money away?"

"The council are being men. I'm hitting them where it hurts."

"Why not just stop production?"

"A single tab is worth over two hundred dollars as of today's market rate." I shot her a weary glance. "Weight for weight, it's worth more than gold." I took another sip of my drink. "You can always turn patrons away too."

"That doesn't solve the problem. It just pushes it onto someone else's door," she griped. "But you're right. I'll implement that policy as of tonight."

"Early onset signs in regular users are hyper-perspiration," I advised her. "You can't stop the one-time users. There's no way of knowing beforehand. But once they're five or so tabs deep, it's easier to spot."

"What else?"

"Nothing that's visible, unfortunately. Their hearts race and their irritability is increased, hence the aggression." I shrugged. "We've hired more guards for our stables."

"I have too. Not enough for how many girls we run, though," she said uneasily before she got to her feet. "Some inventions would be better being tossed out."

"On that, we can agree." I stood too. "I really am sorry, Grainne. About your friend."

She tightened her lips as her gaze darted from mine. She startled me by reaching out and tilting my notepad toward her. "He's beautiful. You have a different muse now?"

I blinked at her statement then realized I hadn't returned to the Met once since Hunter and I had gotten together.

Not a single time.

How the hell did that only just register *now*?

My brow furrowed as I stared down at the sketch. It was half Hunter's face, about the size of a credit card. A doodle, but still clearly my husband.

When I didn't answer, she prompted, "He's a Dom?"

I stared at her. "More leverage?"

"No. I like to think women in business can be friendly, Aurora. I know your past, sure, but you know of mine too, don't you? Information *is* leverage, but it can also be the foundation for a friendship.

"With all my cards on the table and all yours laid out flat too, and with both of us firmly on the opposite side of the law, there's no need for us not to better acquaint ourselves, is there?"

My mouth rounded at her statement. "You mean that?"

Her shrug was elegant. Her brutally tailored suit jacket barely even wrinkled with the gesture. "I seldom say things I don't mean." She tapped her nails against the desk. "I'd imagine a Sicilian dungeon is out of the question. If you need to… explore things in a safe environment, Queens of Heart is always open to you, *friend.*"

With that, she made to sweep out of the room. Before she did, I rasped, "I'm sorry about O'Donnelly."

She paused in her tracks. "Did you attend the funeral?"

"No. My brother did."

Grainne half-turned. "He wasn't my O'Donnelly."

I knew that. She'd loved his younger brother and O'Donnelly Sr. had been pivotal in their split. For all that…

"You were friends though. Close friends."

"By the end, yes." Her gaze was stark. "Only the good die young, Aurora."

"I doubt that's true."

She hitched a shoulder. "You can answer that when you get to my age. Goodbye, Aurora."

"Goodbye, *friend.*"

She nodded then departed with as much grandeur as she'd entered.

It was only when I'd plopped back in my seat, as inelegant as she was elegant, that I realized she'd left a card beside Hunter's face.

I knew her number and this wasn't the one I'd been given years ago when we met up as DA and informant.

Was this her personal line?

As I flipped the card between my fingers, an unerring urge filled me. One that I'd never have sought to quench if it weren't for her offer. An offer that enticed me more than I could say. But it was Grainne and, call me a fool, I trusted her. That trust had grown over years of working together, and there was no need for that not to extend into a personal relationship…

In my experience, Doms changed in dungeons. Another side of their character was exposed. The prospect of opening up Hunter's nature was too tantalizing for words. It was also frightening...

Temptation, thy name is woman, I thought wryly.

A knock sounded at the door. "Yes?" I called out.

Giuseppe informed me, "Your next appointment is here."

"Who is it?"

"Cin Black?"

My brow puckered in confusion—who the hell was she and how had she gotten onto my agenda? Only one way to find out: "Show her in after you pat her down."

45

HUNTER

TWO WEEKS LATER

"CAN YOU BELIEVE THE AUDACITY?" Aurora shrieked as she stormed from one side of our room at the *palazzo* to the other. "He was selling Red under *my* nose to the Russians!"

"Who was?" I'd admit I'd gotten lost halfway through the conversation because she was wearing my jersey and with every stride, her tits bounced and…

I was only a man.

A man who'd been away from his woman for far too long.

"Aren't you listening to me?" she groused, spinning around to shoot a glower my way.

"I'm listening," I retorted, propping myself up on my hand. "But you're wearing my jersey."

"So?"

"So, that's better than silk lingerie and nudity."

"Better than nudity?"

"You're literally *wearing* my name, Aurora. What do you think?"

Her lips curled into a pretty smirk. When she twisted back and around so I could see my name, she peered at me over my shoulder. "Does things to you, huh?"

Her coyness had me hiding a grin. She wasn't often playful and I didn't want to discourage her—for a woman so bold, I didn't think she registered how sensitive she was sometimes.

"My dick is too worn out to react but my eyes are in full working order."

She heaved a sigh. "I hate that I have to leave today."

Hence the reason my dick was out of order. Two days of acting like we were rabbits and I'd need a nap after she left.

I held out my hand for her. "I hate it too." As she trudged over to me, I coaxed, "So, tell me again who was selling what to the Russians?"

"Giuseppe Messina."

The name had me scowling. "Wasn't he one of your Stidda?"

"He was."

My brain finally kickstarted into gear because she'd been in danger and we hadn't known it. "Chad's still on your detail, right?"

"He is. As are Lynx and Sebastian. One of them is with me on a twenty-four-hour rotation."

"Good."

Their loyalty was born from her compassion. From her willingness to see what society couldn't—that homelessness wasn't a disease. That it had a root cause.

I knew she was starting up a similar project here in Vegas. God only knew we had a horrific number of people living out on the streets.

"The Irish were the reason you knew Red was being sold to other factions outside *Cosa Nostra* territory, right?"

"Yeah. One of their foot soldiers killed a hooker. That's how O'Donnelly Jr. learned what was going on."

"He knows about Giuseppe Messina?"

She snorted. "No. Of course not. As it stands, it could be anyone. Someone could have bought Red in bulk and any moron looking to make a fast buck could have been the dealer."

"Then what made you go hunting in your ranks?"

"Because no one buys Red in bulk. I have details of every purchase. Only one of our people would have inside access."

"So you went hunting?"

"So I went hunting," she concurred. "Stan's dealt with him. Another Messina bites the dust. Luc's right about needing to keep our enemies close but fuck, I wish we could blast them all off the face of the earth."

With the *Reyes'* leaders literally blasted off the face of the earth thanks to Martínez, I knew where her jealousy stemmed from. Still, I asked, "Stan's back at work?"

"Kind of. He hasn't stopped acting like the nutty professor. He looks as if he hasn't slept in months."

"Maybe he hasn't." I thought about what he'd told me but simply said, "He seems to have a goal in mind."

"*Se*. Stan never could hold true to a deadline without the appropriate encouragement. I just don't see why…" She huffed out a breath as she clambered onto the sheets beside me. "None of us are ill. None of us are presenting any signs of illness, either. And I know he's not working on medication for Currau because only a transplant will help him."

"How's the miserable old bastard doing?"

Her nose crinkled as I slipped my arm around her waist and hauled her into me so we were spooning. "Same. I'm surprised he's lived this long, to be honest."

"Round-the-clock care in luxurious conditions? Of course, he's living. He must be costing you a small fortune."

"He's worth it."

I hid another smile as I pressed a kiss to her temple. "And you say you're heartless."

"My heart's there," she argued, "but only for family." Her hand tangled with mine. "Hunter?"

"Yes?"

"When you're in New York next week…"

When her words waned, I prompted, "Yeah?"

"Can we go somewhere?"

"Of course." I frowned at her hesitation. We didn't go out that much when we visited each other. Mostly, we stayed in or dealt with work. Dates—we should definitely go on more of those. "Where?"

I expected her to say a nightclub or to go for a wine tasting. A regular date. Maybe even dinner with her family where we could tell them about our marriage. Instead:

"There's a sex club in Irish territory. I'm friendly with the madam. I'd like to go there. I-I visited earlier this year. I don't have good memories of it. You've switched out most of my bad ones about being a submissive so far. Why shouldn't we work through this one together?"

Her words stirred me like nothing else could. So vulnerable but so strong. So willing to be open with me when, in the past, she'd been so closed.

Was I jealous she'd had some kind of scene without me? Sure. Was that rational? No.

I wasn't going to punish her for coming to me with this when I was the one being illogical. If anything, her openness deserved a reward.

"We can do that, baby girl." I ran my nose along the side of her jaw. Unfortunately, my gaze caught on the clock on my nightstand. Our time together was running out. "I need to mark you." And pick out her clothes for the rest of the week.

She shuddered. "Hunter?"

"Yes, Aurora?" My dick had no business reacting to either her shudder or her breathy whisper.

"Can you mark my pussy?"

I froze. "Getting whacked on your ass still makes you cry," I said carefully. "Your pussy—"

Her voice was tiny. "Please?"

My eyes closed as I ran my nose down her jaw again. *The week had been more stressful than she'd disclosed.* "Whatever you need, baby girl. Whatever you need."

46

HUNTER

DAMIEN RICE - AMIE

BY NATURE, I wasn't a fan of sex clubs.

By nurture, I'd grown accustomed to them.

Sugar & Spice & All Things Nasty had become a home away from home some months when Sunny had driven me to distraction.

So, it was with relief that I entered Queens of Heart with Aurora and not alone. That I wasn't going to end the night spilling my cum into my fist. That I'd be the one engaged in the scene, not simply a voyeur.

Not that anyone would be watching us.

The first thing I did when a hostess showed us into a private room was to close the curtains on three sets of windows that allowed strangers to peer inside. The immediate lessening of her tension was palpable.

I didn't have it in me to be annoyed with her. This was her idea, her suggestion, but she was undoubtedly nervous.

Because I wasn't sure where the anxiety was based, I rumbled in what I knew she classified as my 'D' voice, "No one sees what belongs to me."

Her nod, when it came, was shaky. Her tongue peeped out to swipe across the swell of her bottom lip. "Rules change in a dungeon."

Ah.

Of course.

"They evolve," I concurred before dismissing, "but basic tenets don't." For some reason, that made her flush. Wanting to see how far it extended, I prompted, "Undress for me, Aurora."

We'd come in the middle of the day and she wore an outfit that was more suitable for a board meeting than a dungeon. Not that Queens of Heart was exactly a dungeon, more of a fancy sex club with rooms for hire by the hour with a disturbing nod to Lewis Carroll, but as I stared around the room, I tried to piece apart what I was going to do with her.

I'd watched too many Doms with their subs not to envisage Aurora and myself in those scenes, but I thought about the conversations we'd had—D and Sunny as well as between her and me—and I knew I wanted something that resonated with us both.

Oral sex was something she enjoyed, but my patience didn't always extend that far.

Not unless it was a punishment.

I wanted in her cunt. That was my fucking home. It was where I'd craved being.

Her mouth was a delicious substitute, but it wasn't the *crème de la crème* like her pussy was.

We'd had sex earlier this morning though. With her bent over the bathroom vanity as I fucked her from behind.

I let my gaze drift over the spanking bench, the St. Andrews' cross, the bed that came complete with a multitude of restraints already fastened to the posts, and I felt the weight of the gift in my pocket.

Turning back to her, I saw the pink diamond locket nestled between her breasts and wondered if we were ready for this. She literally *wore* my ring. Around her neck. Not her finger. No one in the outside world knew we were dating, never mind 'official' yet.

I'd thought her telling me 'I love you' would be the next step, but life had gotten in the way and had derailed that plan.

Would my gift lead to the next step?

I wanted the world to know she was mine.

But more than that, I wanted *her* to know it too.

I wanted the truth of my ownership to sink into her very bones—

There went my dick.

My thoughts fueled my next moves and I knew exactly what I wanted from her.

It was fitting that we did this here.

That first porn video that had made me think that *maybe* I had it in me to give Aurora what she wanted and to need it in return.

The fantasy that unlocked it all.

She was used to me talking. We did that a lot. Always had. So, my silence unnerved her as I moved forward, stalking her until she either shuffled backward or bumped into me. Her throat bobbed and her nervous gaze made everything in me stand to attention.

I didn't want her fear.

But that wasn't what she gave me.

The hitch in her breath, the dilating of her pupils, the tremble of her lips—she wanted what I was offering even if I was surprising her.

I maneuvered her to the other end of the room where the cross was fixed.

"When I had my 'Eureka' moment about your needs, I was still stuck between a rock and a hard place. My father used to hit me— we've discussed that—and I never heard him hurt Mom, but it wasn't outside the realms of possibility.

"It was only when we talked about them that I realized that could be what held me back all this time. The fear of becoming 'him.' But the year I decided to learn all there was to this lifestyle, it began with one single video."

Her tone was dubious. "Porn?"

"Yes. It got me hard. So, to commemorate that moment, we're going to reenact it."

Her throat bobbed again. "Okay, Hunter."

Slowly, I shook my head as I breathed, "Sir."

Her whimper drove me fucking wild. "Yes, Sir."

Sweet fuck.

I ground my teeth together as I finally pinned her to the cross.

When her back collided with it, she jerked in surprise because her focus had been totally on me—exactly where I wanted it.

"Are you going to ask me about what I watched?" I whispered.

"No, Sir." Her lips parted. "Can I kiss you, Sir? Please?"

I placed my hands on the arms of the cross and loomed over her. "Why are you asking, Aurora?"

"Because I love your mouth," she admitted. "Because I want to taste you, Sir."

"You'll taste me and you don't have to ask anymore, do you?" I purred, tilting my head to the side as I ran my nose along the line of her jaw.

She smelled of the perfume she wore for work and need.

Yes, that had a scent with her.

I continued in that vein, trailing along to her throat. I fluttered my tongue along the sinews there, enjoying how her breath kept catching and how close it was to my ears so I got the surround sound version. I moved down to where her throat connected with her shoulder and I tested the resilience of her flesh by biting her. No real warm-up. No sucking. Just a bite.

She jerked in response.

Every inch of her nakedness rubbed against me—nirvana.

Fucking nirvana.

I moved around to her other side and graced her with another bite. Harder this time. Wanting it to sting. She moaned like I'd sucked on her clit.

My little masochist.

Sometimes there were perks to her needs.

I laved where I'd bitten, prodding each mark my teeth had left behind, then I moved down her body.

Heading to her tits, I sucked on her nipple, dragging my signet ring over the softness, shifting to the side to nip the inner curve so that I'd see it if I looked down her shirt later on.

That bite had her staggering into the cross for support. Her hands clawed at her sides as I graced the other with teeth marks that matched.

Down and down, I moved. Biting her belly here, gracing her hip with another there. One on her inner thigh, another on her calf. By the time I was kneeling before her, she was arching up and onto her tiptoe.

I stared at her from the floor, wondering if she knew that though *she* normally kneeled for *me,* she owned me as much as I did her.

None of this happened without her trusting me. Without her giving me this part of herself.

When I stayed there long enough for her to notice, she blinked bleary eyes at me. Her mouth worked as she frowned at my position, and I could tell that the submissive in her didn't like it.

Good.

I needed her to react.

I needed her to see, to *know*, to understand.

Once she did, I reached into my pocket. "I was going to do this afterward, but I don't want to. This feels right. This feels good." Her confusion was clear, something that wasn't aided by the endorphins I'd triggered in her bloodstream that were evidently muddling things. "I'm ready for the world to know about us, Aurora. But first, I want *you* to know who you belong to. Who belongs to you too. I want you to feel it, Aurora.

"I want, when you're ashamed of who you are, of what you need, you to touch this and to remember that you are loved. For what you are. For who you are. That I loved you before I knew this side of you and that I loved you after I knew. There is no part of you that is not adored. That is not cherished—"

"Hunter," she sobbed, sniffling as she reached up to wipe her eyes. "What are you doing to me?"

My lips quirked at her interruption as I opened the thin box in my hands. "I'm trying to collar you, baby girl." Her hands shook as she swiped her cheeks this time. "There was an auction lot at Rachel's gala, and I couldn't resist snagging it. Custom made. For you. Will you wear it?"

She sagged to her knees in front of me. "Yes. Of course. Yes. Please. Thank you." It was a tight fit with both of us so close to the cross, but we made it work. Her leg straddled one of mine as she reached with trembling fingers for the box. I thought she'd pick it up, but she didn't. Instead, one finger trailed over it with a delight that wasn't feigned.

"I wanted it to match your other necklace," I said softly. "But this isn't made of platinum, sweetheart."

She peered at me. "No?"

"Titanium. This is forever, Aurora. See the lock?" Her eyes drifted to it. "I have to screw it into place. *Forever.* That's what I'm asking for, Aurora. Nothing less than *always.*"

Her eyes closed. "I want to be your always, Hunter." I just knew that my grin lit up my whole face. "Put it on me, please, Sir."

I picked up the chain. "I wanted it to be delicate. Discreet. Elegant. Just like you. So you could wear it for any event, at any point in your life, and always be proud to wear it. Always be proud to be mine."

"*Se. Pi favuri.*"

That she spoke Sicilian at that moment just sealed the deal for me.

The collar consisted of two chains that were twined together and that met in the middle in a circle that never ended.

At the back, there was a permanent lock that was etched with our initials, and a small teardrop pink diamond hung suspended from it— one that matched her locket.

I placed it around her throat, setting it into position, then I dug into my pocket again for the tools I needed to fix it there permanently.

When her fingers slid up to touch it, she looked at me and whispered, "I needed this, and I didn't even know it."

Smiling, I leaned forward and pressed my mouth to hers. She crumpled against my chest, sinking into me as I supped from her. Gentle where I was rough earlier. Tender where I'd been harsh with my bites.

She was mine.

Forever.

Thank fuck.

As she sank into me, clutching at me, letting me pillage her mouth, sample everything she had to give, I pulled back and nipped her bottom lip, hard enough to make her eyelashes flutter open.

When I had her attention, I rumbled, "Are you ready, baby girl?"

A soft, happy sigh gave me my answer.

"Words," I prompted.

"I was born ready, Sir."

I knew it was a joke, but it was semi-true.

Eyes twinkling, I got to my feet and I set to work. She stayed silent, her gaze tracking my every move as I restrained her how I needed to.

Her ankles were fixed to the cross, splaying her thighs even in her kneeling position. I looped rope through the cuffs at the upper arms of the cross and used that to bind her wrists in place, allowing just enough give for her to move forward how I needed, but not to bring her hands together at the front. I placed some toys on a nook in the wall behind the cross for this purpose, then, I looked down at her.

My moonlight.

My Aurora.

"Now, baby girl, beg for my cock."

47

AURORA

HUNTER AND D were two different masks.

If anyone could understand that, it was me.

If anyone could appreciate that, it was me.

D demanded that I beg for his cock.

Hunter had offered me his collar.

Somehow, the two of them belonged to me. Somehow, this was actually happening.

I sometimes felt as if I bore the weight of the world on my shoulders. Or, at least, my family's world.

At that moment, the weight around my neck superseded the burden of the choices I'd made in my life, and it took away everything else. Stole it away. Gave me something to focus on. Something that was mine. For me.

"Now, baby girl, beg for my cock."

My eyes clenched closed at his words because, sweet Lord, what he could do to me with that voice.

Head tipping back, I whispered, "I need your cock, Sir. I need it so bad. I'm empty. So fucking empty. I need you to fill me. I want your cum. I need that too. In my mouth, in my pussy. I want you so much, Sir."

He hummed throughout my words and gifted me with a tease—he slid down his zipper and pulled out his shaft.

Distracted, I wondered if he was one of those Doms who'd strip off and walk around the dungeon in the raw or if he'd stay mostly clothed.

I'd have my answer soon.

"You didn't say 'please,' moonlight."

There was a thread of warning in those words. One that had my eyes flaring in distress.

"I'm sorry, Sir. So sorry. *Please.* I need your cock. Can I have it, please, Sir? I want to taste it. Please, give it to me."

I put every ounce of need I possessed into that plea.

He rarely let me suck him off. Which, now that I knew was what had started him down this road, was insane to me, but it wasn't like I had a say in how a scene developed. That was all him.

My arms were already feeling the pull from the way he'd restrained me and my knees knocked against the marble tiles—submission was glorious. It wasn't always comfortable, it wasn't always pleasant, but it was freedom in the flesh.

He gave me that.

My Hunter.

My Dom.

I knew he was using me as his personal porn flick as he jacked off. I could see his gaze lighting up when it touched upon a bite mark, watched his eyelids turn heavy when he studied my cunt.

"Please, Sir?" I mewled. "Please?"

He dragged off his shirt, revealing abs I'd licked and worshiped. His navy loafers came next, but his black jeans remained on.

"Can you take everything I have to give, Aurora?"

My eyes rounded. "I want to, Sir."

Another hum lit my insides up. I could feel the slow slide of my arousal gathering as my body prepared itself to be filled. I didn't even have it in me to mind that he wanted in my mouth and not my pussy. I just wanted his cock in any way I could have it.

He licked his lips as he dropped the hold on his shaft. Then, his feet a good ten inches away from my knees, he placed his hands on the cross and leaned over me.

"Take what you need, moonlight."

His urging had me doing as bid but he was just a scant out of reach. As I tugged on the ropes binding me to the cross, I got what he wanted—he was making it difficult for me.

He was making me work for his dick.

I knew, right then, right there, that if he touched my clit a single time with his finger, I'd explode.

I wiggled around, my bindings making it harder than it should be, but eventually, after straining and shuffling, he lowered deeper into what was, essentially, a standing push-up. When my mouth opened, saliva already gathered in preparation, I greeted him home.

His groan was delicious. Orgasmic in and of itself. It set me alight and soothed my frazzled nerves. It was everything I needed and nothing I'd ever allowed myself to have.

He fed me his cock.

There was no kinder way to describe it.

Going too far so I gagged. Not pulling back when I needed air. He fucked my mouth, literally. Impaling me on it. Forcing me to breathe through my nose, making me blink up at him through wet eyes, and what I saw made me work harder to please him. Made me want to fulfill every single one of his fantasies.

His expression was one of tortured bliss.

A man who'd been waiting years for this moment and one who was finally experiencing it.

He looked as if I'd taken him to heaven.

Me.

Me.

Aurora Valentini.

No one else.

This imperfect being who was loathed by more people than she was liked had given him *this.*

The pride in me stirred, and I refused to let him down. I worked hard to relax, not to gag when he went a smidgen too deep. I breathed in air while I could as I sucked the tip of his shaft upon his retreat, tonguing the slit and swallowing his pre-cum.

As I worked, frantically, I whispered, "Can I have your cum, Sir, please? I want it. I want—"

He shoved his dick into me to shut me up.

How long he worked me over, I had no idea. Air was precious, his pre-cum slid down my throat, my jaw was coated in saliva, and my cheeks loaded with my tears.

I felt used but not abused.

I felt like his living fantasy.

His walking desire.

He pulled back, as far as he could, almost to the point where the glans was out of the reach of my tongue. His piercing acted like a bull's eye—one I wanted to target.

"Do you need to come, Aurora? Are we still green, baby girl?"

Was this a trick question? How could I be anything other than green? And how could I need anything but an orgasm?

I stared up at him with wild eyes. "Yes, Sir. Green, Sir, *please.*"

God, those words tasted as good as he did.

I hadn't realized how difficult it had been without being able to utter that title.

He was Hunter, but he was also my Dom.

My Sir.

My everything.

Something in his expression made me wonder if he could see that. If he could sense my love. My devotion. It was forged on a lifetime of knowing him and of failing him. Of enduring a half-life without him.

He broke into my thoughts by stepping closer. He angled his hips toward me all while he tucked his foot underneath me and pressed his denim-covered shin against my cunt.

"Get yourself off," he commanded. "Don't suck, just hold my cock in your mouth. Do you understand, moonlight?"

The denim was coarse. "I do, Sir." It felt good. Weird. Oddly cold. Rough. But I could work with it.

He fed me his cock again.

My vision blurred as I worked on not sucking him, on holding him in my mouth as he'd requested, then with that done, I started to grind against him. His shin was hard and obviously bony and fuck, the pressure was just right.

Perfect.

As the rush of impending orgasm overtook me, I yelped around his cock when a stinging sensation hit my outer thigh. I jerked in surprise at the loud *thwack* too. I angled my head so I could see what he was using, but his fingers came to my chin to hold me in place.

Another hit.

And another.

Sharp. *A tap.* Stinging. *A tap.* Burning. *A tap.* Fuck. *Ow.* Good. *A tap.* So good. So fucking painful. *A tap.* So delicious. *A tap.* Oh, God. *A tap.* Fuck.

My eyes drifted shut as I screamed around his dick.

"Eyes on me!" he barked around a loud groan as I felt his cum pelt the back of my throat.

And I exploded.

I burst.

I shattered into a million stars.

All while I stared up at him, not really seeing him, just letting him watch me fly as I trusted him to always ensure I landed safely.

48

AURORA
HOWIE DAY - COLLIDE

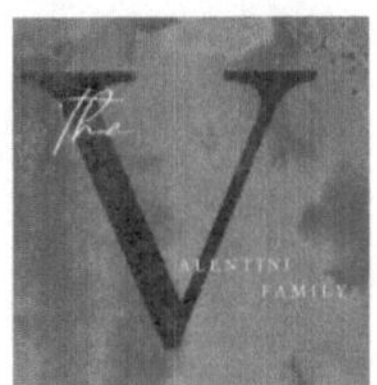

"I DIDN'T KNOW they had baths here," I slurred as he maneuvered us into the water.

"How well do you know this club?"

I held up a hand and flipped up three fingers.

"Is that a curse I didn't learn in Sicily?"

Turning my face into his throat, I mumbled, "Been here three times. I think I can see colors."

He chuckled in my ear as he started petting me. His hand cupped my head, stroking me, soothing me, and bringing me back down to earth.

I didn't want to descend. I liked it up here. *In here.*

But life, as it must, began to intrude.

My cell buzzed.

His rang.

His watch vibrated, and mine pinged.

Both of us sighed, especially as we both knew he'd be returning to Vegas tonight.

I didn't know how we'd make this work, but I knew we would. We had to.

We had to.

I didn't want to get dressed, but I did.

I didn't want to leave Queens of Heart, but I did.

I sure as hell didn't want to get into my car where Giovi was waiting with updates.

Before I could climb inside, Hunter tugged on my hand. One hand went to my new collar, the other cupped the back of my neck, and he kissed me.

This time, I needed to be grounded.

I needed to feel the depths of my new reality, a reality where he'd seen all my masks, knew them well but liked the woman beneath—the real Aurora.

His Aurora.

Yes, work called. Yes, the *Cosa Nostra* never slept and the Camorra was just as bad as a teething baby. But I had him now. We were together. This was a burden we shared.

And as I sank into his kiss, I reveled in the moment. I relished my new truth—I truly was his.

The real me.

Forever.

49

AURORA

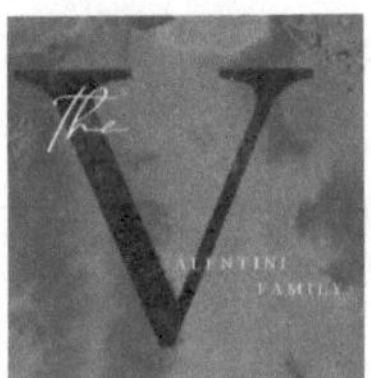

"ARE you going to be rude again?"

"No," I pshawed. "I wasn't rude before. I had business to take care of. Business doesn't stop because a baby is being welcomed into the church."

Matri's mouth tightened. "Don't let your brother hear you say that."

"He's about as religious as I am," I mocked. "I don't think he'll be too pissed."

"Your father was a believer."

"Which is why Luc had his child christened, and why, if I ever have a kid, they'll be christened too." I arched a brow at her disapproving look. "It's only recently that you've started to go to church of your own volition. It might be your thing, but it's not ours."

"It helps," she said stiffly.

It didn't take much to figure out how. "More than rehab?"

"No. Not more than. Just… It's a constant."

My brow furrowed. "*Matri*, if there's anything you… I'm always here. You know that, don't you?"

"I do. Via email. Not always by phone." Her hand reached out for mine, and she patted my fingers, but I saw the teasing glint in her eye and knew she was joking with me. "You'll try today? For me?"

"Jennifer and I don't have much in common," I said wearily. "But that doesn't mean that I won't be cordial now that she's Luc's wife."

"You weren't cordial when she was my fiancée."

I merely sniffed at Luc's sneaky entrance and wished, like hell, that Hunter was here. That he wasn't in fucking Vegas where he was needed because of an emergency council meeting regarding an impounded shipment from Sheikh Hashim, and that I didn't need to be here for this brunch and to coordinate an NYPD raid that was going to take place in *Russu* tonight—thank you, Commissioner Kingston for that particular piece of intel.

The parting was only getting harder.

I hated it.

It surprised me how much I did.

"Fiancées can still be jilted," was my answer.

"Wives can be divorced," Stan remarked.

"What is this? 'Gang up on Aurora' day? Don't make out like you didn't marry a viper, Luciu. She's just as cutthroat as I am."

He shrugged. "I never said she wasn't."

"But what he's saying is that you're worse."

I glowered at Stan. "Charming."

He winked at me. "I try."

"And fail."

Matri patted my hand. "Please, make an effort, sweetheart."

I made no promises, just leaned over and pressed a kiss to her cheek. Shoving Luc in the arm and punching Stan in the shoulder, lips twitching when he sniffled like he'd done when we were kids before he winked at me, I left the living room and headed for the kitchen.

Needing a moment, I reached for my phone, but before I could text Hunter, my brothers had swarmed inside too.

Scowling at the pair of them, I demanded, "What do you want?"

Luc held out his hand. "You said you were bringing the Anjou rubies with you today. *Matri* clung onto you like an octopus the minute you walked through the door." His fingers beckoned me in a silent 'gimme.'

My scowl morphed into a smirk. "Ask nicely."

Stan chuckled as he leaned against the table. "Pretty please with sprinkles on top?"

I grinned. "Come on, Luc. You can do it."

He huffed. "You're the one still keeping secrets from us."

"So? That means you don't have to say 'please' and 'thank you?' Because I'm secretive?" I scoffed. "Hate to break it to you, *frate*, but I've been keeping things from you since I was thirteen. It's a hard habit to break!"

"You say that like it comes as a surprise," he complained. "Okay. *Please*. I want to see the rubies."

Satisfied, I tugged the boxes out of my pockets. They'd been bulky and had weighed down my jacket so it was a relief to set them onto the table. I watched as both of them snagged one.

Luc opened the case holding the 'earbobs' and Stan opened the one with the anklet.

For a moment, no one said anything.

These rubies meant the world to us. The extents we'd gone to were ridiculous for pieces of corundum, bits of the earth that sparkled prettily. But at that moment, we were nearer to our goal.

When the Valentini queen drips in the blood of the earth, only then will the family's star continue to rise.

"They're beautiful," Luc rasped.

"They are," Stan agreed, his thumb dragging over the links in the anklet that were Moorish in design.

"We're getting closer, *frates*," I said softly.

Luc shot me a look. "How did you get these? And don't say that we shouldn't ask. How much did they cost? We deserve to know."

He did deserve to know, but the price was exorbitant—they cost me secrets.

Secrets I shouldn't have from them, but that I guarded nonetheless.

The irony was, of course, that Hunter and I were going to share the truth about our marriage today, then he'd got called back to Vegas.

Goddamn work.

It never stopped.

"Hunter's grandfather gave them to me," I admitted on an exhalation.

Stan frowned. "In his will?"

"In a sense."

"Be specific, Aurora," Luc demanded, his tone suspicious. "No one, certainly no Don who's been around as long as De Laurentiis, would give something like this away for nothing."

"It was a deal," I replied, folding my arms across my chest. "He gives me the rubies if I agreed to work with Hunter."

Luc scowled. "Work with him, how? As his attorney?"

I cleared my throat. "No."

Stan tilted his head to the side. "What aren't you telling us, Rory?"

"I'm acting as his Consigliere."

Luc gaped at me a few times, but Stan was the one who asked, "That was the price De Laurentiis demanded for the jewels?"

Not in so many words... "Yes."

"And you didn't think to discuss this with us?" Luc growled.

"I didn't need to. What I do in my spare time is my choice. If I choose to help—"

"Another fucking faction!" Luc inserted.

"That Hunter leads," Stan corrected, elbowing Luc in the side. "This is Hunter we're talking about. He's one of us. His grandfather, not so much, but Hunter? *Se.*"

Luc huffed at that but he didn't argue.

"Alberto told me that Hunter would get himself—"

"You spoke to him before the old man died?"

Uneasily, I studied Luc. "I did."

"What aren't you telling us?"

"A lot, Stan," I admitted. "But this is what I can share. Alberto told me that he was sure Hunter would get himself killed once he took over as Don. He wanted me to stop that from happening. He loved his grandson."

"And you love him too." A smile kicked up around his lips. "I think it's smart," he declared after a couple moments.

"Smart?" Luc snapped. "You're fucking—"

"Smart," Stan repeated. "Hunter's family. With Aurora acting as Consigliere for both factions, we're united, *stronger*. We're Sicilians and we own the East and West Coast." He shot a narrow-eyed glance at Luciu. "That means we're bigger than the Irish."

That had Luciu shutting up. It also had me hiding a smirk at Stan—never let it be said that he hadn't inherited our capacity to manipulate people. It just didn't come out as often.

My twin heaved a sigh. "Aurora—"

"You won't get me to stop working with Hunter, Luciu," I drawled, leaning back against the table. "So don't even try to convince me otherwise."

His mouth tightened. "I was going to say that you need to tell the council. They should know."

"After Hunter helped us get Stan back, I don't think there'll be a problem. Maybe if Puglisi and Messina were around, but they're not." I retorted pointedly.

His nostrils flared. "They still need to know."

"I'll tell them the next time we gather together."

Luc shook his head. "You're playing a dangerous game, *soru*."

"It's the only kind of game I know how to play," was my silky response. "Now, I need the restroom. Excuse me, please."

Stan grabbed my arm and tugged me into his chest. "Only you'd be able to stand as the Consigliere for two factions, *soru*. I'm proud of you, but don't burn out, *capisci*?"

I smiled at him. "*Capisci.*"

Luc just huffed. "I don't approve, but it's Hunter," he conceded. "And if you keep him alive, then I'll forgive you."

Rolling my eyes at that, I tossed over my shoulder as I drifted from the kitchen, "Gee, *thanks*."

This time, I escaped and didn't allow them to follow me. The need to connect with Hunter was real and raw. That whole conversation could have gone differently if Stan hadn't taken my side. If both of them had chosen to forget Hunter's ties to us.

Relieved that a chasm hadn't cracked open between my siblings and me—years of being cut out of the family was long enough—I read

Hunter's last message to me the second I'd closed the bathroom door behind me.

Hunter: *Have you killed anyone yet?*

Me: *Anyone? Or just Jennifer? The family seems to think that she's an angel and I'm a demon and that I'll rip her wings off.*

Hunter: *She didn't come across as an angel.*

Me: *But I come across as a demon?*

Hunter: *Only in bed.*

Me: *LOL.*

Me: *I can handle that.*

Hunter: *So can I. ;)*

Hunter: *Babe, I'm sorry I can't be there. I know this is the first get-together since the wedding and everything.*

I shouldn't enjoy it when he called me 'babe,' but I really freakin' did.

Me: *I mean, I wish you were here. I kind of always wish you were here…*

Me: *This distance is starting to suck.*

Hunter: *Probably because we've already dealt with it for years as D and Sunny.*

Me: *Probably.*

Hunter: *Got a solution?*

Me: *No.*

Hunter: *Me neither.*

Me: *Can you make it to Thanksgiving?*

Hunter: *TBH, I thought you'd never ask. I wasn't even sure if you celebrate it.*

Me: *We didn't use to but Matri's not going to complain about an excuse for the family to get together. Plus, you and Jennifer are American so I guess we'd better get used to the holiday.*

Hunter: *You want to tell them then?*

Me: *Yeah. Give them something to be thankful for, that you've taken me off their shoulders?*

Hunter: *I wouldn't put it like that lol. They're fucking lucky to* *have you. I wish you'd been on the Camorra's side from the start. Bert wouldn't have had to do what he did to fix shit for us.*

Me: *I doubt it. I'm not an evil genius.*

Hunter: *Aren't you? ;)*

Me: *:P*

Hunter: *Heard from BDSec btw.*

Me: *Oh! Good. Spill.*

Hunter: *Nothing to spill. They haven't been approached for any of the deaths you've pinpointed—by client or sniper.*

Me: *I guess that would have been too simple a solution.*

Hunter: *Probably.*

Me: *What did they require as payment for the info?*

Hunter: *For me to get into an argument with this guy on Tiktok.*

Me: *o.O*

Me: *What guy?*

Hunter: *This guy who talks about women like they're property. They want me to quote Germaine Greer at him.*

Me: *Will BDSec let me handle that on your behalf? I think I'd enjoy that.*

Hunter: *Lol. We can only try. They'll just give me something else to do if they're 'dissatisfied.'*

Me: *There speaks the voice of experience lol. :P*

Hunter: *You bet. This is quite tame for them. One time, they cut off all the lights at my place and reregistered my utilities to some convict in an Uzbekistan jail. That was NOT fun.*

Me: *Jesus!!*

Me: *I want to hear more, but I'd best go. I disappeared into the bathroom like twenty minutes ago. They'll think I got lost down the toilet.*

Me: *BUT, I did tell Luc and Stan about being your Consigliere.*

Hunter: *Trust you to throw that in at the last minute.*

Me: *:P Unintentionally at the last minute. I just remembered.*

Hunter: *Yeah, why don't I believe that?*

Me: *You should. My ass is literally on the line now lol.*

Hunter: *This is true. A paddle per word of bullshit. New law.*

Me: *Lol?*

Hunter: *No lol. I mean it. ;)*

Me: *Shit.*

Hunter: *Uhhuh. Anyway, did it go down all right?*

Me: *Relatively. They want me to tell the council.*

Hunter: *That's not unexpected.*

Me: *You're probably the one who'll bear the brunt of their annoyance.*

Hunter: *I can deal with them.*

Me: *My hero. ;)*

Hunter: *You know it.*

Hunter: *Speak later?*

Me: *Please. <3*

It was dumb. So dumb. But I tapped onto his profile picture, enlarged it, then raised my phone to my lips and kissed his mouth.

With a heavy sigh, I got to my feet and started to make my way out of the bathroom. Upon unlocking the door, I happened to overhear:

"Yeah. With that guy who showed up on our wedding day. He arrived late to the reception."

"He was hot."

"He is. His name's Hunter. But how they were kissing…" A tongue clucked. "I'm telling you that was no ordinary kiss."

My brows rose. Jennifer was talking about Hunter and me with… whom?

I stepped over to the door I knew led to her office where she was talking with someone... speaker on.

"What did he do? Stuff a ball gag between her lips?"

"Might as well have. Trust me, Aurora was *not* in the building."

"You mean… subspace?"

"I think so. I've only read about it."

"He's a shitty Dom if that's the case. Isn't that the whole point of aftercare? To bring them back down to earth before they part?"

"How much BDSM romance have you read?"

My eyes widened.

"More than you," the other woman joked.

Jennifer pshawed, "Doubt it. Maybe she's a Dominatrix."

"That was a fast graduation."

"I could see her using a whip in court. Getting everyone in line, you know? Head to toe in latex."

"Make up your mind," was the other woman's retort. "Is she the one being tied to a St. Andrew's cross or is he?"

Surprised, I reached up and touched my collar.

She sniffed. "I'm telling you that wasn't an ordinary dynamic."

"Babe, I trust you with my life, but you don't know shit about D/s relationships."

"And you do?!"

"Aidan's got his quirks."

Aidan.

Jesus, Jennifer was talking about my sex life with Savannah O'Donnelly.

"No way he's a fucking Dom."

"I never said he was! I'm just saying that there's more nuance to that kind of relationship than a scorching hot kiss outside a sex club."

"What were you doing at Queens of Heart, anyway?"

"Nothing fun, sadly. I was just stopping by Aoife's for some hibiscus tea and that new Bundt cake of hers—have you tried it yet?"

"No. Like, boring Bundt?"

"Nah. When does Aoife make anything boring?"

"True. I need to try that."

"You do," she agreed. "Whatever, I was heading home—have you noticed the police blockades have finally gone, by the way?"

The capture of the First Lady's murderer had been all over the news… Personally, I smelled 'cover-up' but I was cynical by nature.

"Yeah, thank God. They were a major pain in the ass."

"They were. Anyway, that was when I saw them. It had to be, like, an afternoon quickie or something. They were kissing and pulling away then went back to kissing. It was pretty sweet. If anything about that viper could be considered sweet."

I narrowed my eyes; she totally had my brother whipped. We'd even used the same goddamn noun to describe one another!

"Does it matter?"

"Not really. I just... She's such a cunt."

The feeling was mutual, bitch.

"Does it make it better you knowing that about her?"

"Maybe. Fucking bitch."

"What has she done now?"

She huffed. "Nothing in particular. She just looks at me and I feel like a piece of shit."

I wonder why.

"I think you're projecting."

"I doubt it."

"I don't. Luciu wouldn't allow her to get away with that. He's too protective."

She sighed. "True."

"Maybe she doesn't know how to get close to you. It's not like her life has been easy the past couple years, is it?"

"Stop being logical. And rational."

"Let me guess, Aoife told you the same thing?"

"No. I haven't spoken about this with her."

"Why not?"

"Because she'd tell me to play nice and I know I should for Luc's sake but I, just, she pisses me off. It's to the point where we'll either be enemies for a lifetime or something will happen and she'll become another BFF. Or maybe that's just my hormones talking." She heaved another sigh. Paused. Clearly expected a response. Then prompted, "Savannah? Are you even listening to me?"

A soft hum sounded in the background. "Aidan started playing basketball with his brothers."

"So?"

"So?! Have you seen my man?"

"He's not as hot as Luciu."

"Suck on my donkey dick, bitch."

"Nah, I'd prefer to suck Luc's."

"Sucking more would have stopped you from getting pregnant again so fast—"

That was when I tuned out.

I had my justification for the family 'requesting' I play nice with Jen.

She was pregnant.

Again.

Had Luciu never heard of condoms or something? Jesus Christ.

Someone grabbed my shoulder—the man himself.

"Are you eavesdropping on my wife's private conversation?"

I could tell he didn't know whether to be concerned or amused but I was neither.

"You got her pregnant again? She just gave birth, Luciu. For fuck's sake, have respect for your wife and ensure that she has the time to heal from one traumatic experience before pushing her into another. What the hell is wrong with you?"

"It's not my fault—"

I didn't let him finish. "It never *is* the guy's fault. It's not always on the woman to handle precautions.

"Would it kill you to rubber up? I am so fucking mad at you right now. To let her go through this again after—" My brow furrowed. "I'm disappointed in you, Luciu. Really disappointed in you. You didn't give her the time or the space to *heal.*"

"I don't appreciate being lectured to by my sister, Aurora. You have no right to judge—"

"I have every right to judge!"

"What the hell's going on here?" Jen's head popped up between us. "Were you eavesdropping on me?"

I slid her a glare. "I heard you talking about me and my sex life!"

"What are you arguing about?" she sniped.

This woman just waltzed into our world and was somehow handed it on a platter.

Was it any wonder I found it impossible to like her?

I'd had to strive for over a decade to be taken seriously; I'd had to earn my place. She did nothing apart from look pretty and was suddenly worthy of the Anjou rubies.

Rubies that my family had shed blood for.

Rubies that we were certain would help us ascend to our rightful place.

But… she was a woman.

My sister-in-law.

Not a rival. Not an enemy.

She was Saverina's mother and was carrying another Valentini.

I sucked in a breath. "We're arguing about you. About the fact that you're pregnant, and you only just gave goddamn birth! My brother should have left you the hell alone to get over it—"

Jennifer's tension disappeared. "You're defending me?" A smirk creased her lips as she shot Luc a cocky look. "From the big, bad Don?"

Luc growled under his breath. "Fi!"

Her lips quirked. "What? I'm the innocent one here, Luc! Your eight-pound baby tore me to shreds and you couldn't wait to get back inside."

Her jovial tone told me the complete opposite had happened.

Letting my hands flop in the air, I muttered, "There's no hope for you two."

"I'm sure it's the same with that Hunter guy from the wedding reception, hmm?" A soft smile danced on her lips and she reached out to touch my arm. "Thank you for defending me, but Luc needs your defense more than I do."

"Too much information." I looked down at the fingers perched on my arm then back up at her. She frowned then slowly slipped her hand away. A quick glance to the side saw that *Matri* and Stan were standing at the door watching us. Silently, I told myself, 'She's not a rival. *She's family.'* "Truce?" I might have choked on the word.

"You're going to break bread over *this*?" Luc groused. "Un-fuck-ing-believable!!"

"Language, Luciu!" *Matri* chided.

Jennifer, her gaze watchful, ignored them and nodded at me. "Truce."

50

HUNTER

GET YOU THE MOON (FEAT. SNOW) - KINA

WITH MY FINGERS bridging hers as she settled against me, I relaxed as my least favorite Disney movie played on the TV—*Cinderella*.

Still, it allowed me to zone out.

The week had been long. Hell, the month had been too. In fact, the entire goddamn year felt never-ending, but next week, it was Thanksgiving and I'd be spending it with the Valentinis. Not here in Vegas. Not with Bert.

My jaw worked as I staved off a surge of emotion that shouldn't have blindsided me seeing as I'd been compartmentalizing since his death.

Reaching up, I rubbed my eyes, unaware that Aurora was watching me. Unaware that she could see I was breaking down for the first time since Bert's death.

She shuffled against me, separating our hands so that she could slide her arms around my waist as she breathed, "I'm here, Hunter. Let it out. Let it out, baby."

The words were sweet, but I didn't want to let it out. I liked this crap bottled up but—

"Next week will be my first Thanksgiving without him." Did I sound like I was choking on the words? It felt as if I were.

"I know," she whispered.

"Then, it'll be my birthday and Christmas then New Year's."

"I know."

My eyes burned. "It sucks."

"It does."

"Life sucks."

"It *really* does," she agreed gruffly.

"I wish I could bring him back." I buried my face in her hair. "I hate that he died the way he did to protect me."

"To protect *us*," she countered.

"He did it for me."

"You can't honestly believe that. Not when he's the one who orchestrated our marriage.

"This, *us*, was as much a part of his plan as Crayon infiltrating the correctional facility to kill him, Hunter.

"He wanted us together, and he wanted us to have a life that was free from the constraints of the past. Accept that, sweetheart, and you'll understand your grandfather's actions a lot better.

"You were his future. *You* were what mattered to him." She patted my chest. "Do you know what my one regret is?"

"What?" I choked out, her words hitting me on the raw.

"That I didn't get the chance to know him. He seemed like an awesome guy and whenever you want to talk about him, I'm here. I'd love to learn about how you two got so close." She pressed a kiss to my chest this time. "I know the first holidays without that person you love are difficult, but you won't be alone. We'll make new traditions together. It won't be the same, and it won't make up for his absence, but—"

I cupped the back of her head. "What kind of new traditions?"

She stilled. "Um."

"Um?" I knew I sounded unimpressed.

"We could always start Thanksgiving with breakfast in bed."

"Interesting." I dug my fingers into my eyes as I forced myself to focus on what Bert wanted for me—*the future*. "Eggs Benedict?"

"If you want."

"I want."

"Okay, then, how about… I promise not to start an argument with Luc and Stan?"

I snorted. "Impossible."

"Hey!"

"It is. No false promises or I'll have to punish you for lying."

She huffed. "I could promise to *try*."

"No. You three argue. It's what you do. It's your love language."

That had Rory tipping her head back to look at me, a frown puckering her brow. "Our love language?"

"Yes." I tapped the tip of her nose with my finger. "You're all terrible at communicating so you bicker."

"We don't bicker."

"You do. You bicker and grouse and complain then, in the blink of an eye, will kill for your family.

"It's quite interesting. With you, especially. You find it difficult to relax around them so you're more persnickety than usual."

Tension throbbed through her for a second, then she released it on a sharp breath. "You're right."

"I know I am. I just never understood why you find it hard to relax around them."

She nibbled her bottom lip and, for the longest time, I thought she wasn't going to reply. Her gaze returned to the TV and I thought she was just watching the flick.

As my mind wandered back to Bert, she whispered, "You can't tell them. Or *Matri*."

Startled, I just blurted out, "Why not?"

"It'll hurt them."

"I won't share anything with them you don't want me to."

Her fingers tangled in my shirt. "After *Patri* died," Rory whispered, "our whole world imploded. It changed us.

"You know that.

"But, for me, it made me realize that I never wanted to feel so powerless again." She hesitated. "I was the one who convinced them to take this path."

"Which path?"

"Taking over New York. Bringing down the Fieris."

"I know Luc would argue with you about that."

"He would. Because I was convincing. I made him think that he wanted it.

"He was grieving, Hunter, and I exploited that grief."

"You're being tough on yourself," I argued.

"I'm not. Stan was on shaky ground for a while, and Luc was just as lost, and I gave them a purpose. But I promised myself that I'd never ask anything of them that I wasn't willing to do and that I'd dedicate my life to attaining our goals.

"I think, along the way, the guilt crept up and the deeper down that road they traveled, the blood they shed, and the crimes they committed, it just got worse—"

"Aurora," I disregarded. "You know how much they love you, don't you?"

Her gulp was audible. "Love doesn't come into this. I manipulated them."

"They manipulate you too. That's how shit rolls when you run a business with family." I reached for her chin and gently tapped her bottom lip with my thumb. "You need to lighten up on yourself, Aurora. You need to realize that they were grown men back then.

"Yes, even Stan.

"It's unpalatable for me to say this because I felt coerced into my role too, but it's my decision to stay here. To be the Don of the Camorra. Just as it is for them to be the Don and the Capo of the *Cosa Nostra*.

"We're here because we choose to be. That is on us. No one else. Do you understand?"

She didn't answer but I sensed that I'd given her some food for thought.

That was all I could do.

"Now, tell me more about these new traditions we can make together, hmm?"

51

AURORA

"WHAT ARE YOU LOOKING AT?"

I stared at Stan over the kitchen table. "You have eyes, don't you?" I glanced at the Little Debbie cupcake in his hand. "You'll spoil your dinner."

"What am I? Four? I think I can manage a couple cupcakes—"

"*And* three pounds of turkey and potatoes?"

He smirked. "Consider it a challenge."

As I rolled my eyes, he rounded the table and studied the headlines in front of me.

One declared:

'Chicago Senator dies in a car crash.'

Another:

'Florida Congressman suffers freak reaction to peanuts. "We didn't know he was allergic," *says grieving widow.'*

"Sucks to be a politician in this country," he mused.

"These murders are happening more often."

"Murders? Hardly. They're accidents."

"Jesus, Stan. Stop being naive. You, more than anyone, know how easy it is to make a murder look like an accident."

"That's inaccurate. Our pigs don't care if a body looks like it was murdered or if it died in an accident. They just want to eat whatever we feed them."

I elbowed him. "Stop being facetious."

He chuckled at me, but his expression grew serious as he took in the headlines, flickering his gaze between them and me. "What do you think is going on?"

"I'm not sure to be honest." At his scoff, I shook my head. "No, seriously. These aren't the only officials who've died this year but this recent spate is mostly in the US. There was the British prince and the—" I scowled when I realized he was looking at my neck. "What?"

He reached over and touched my collar. I froze, a flush creeping up my cheeks, then he murmured, "There comes a point when you just have to embrace who you are, *soru*. It's about time you were able to do that. I'm glad Hunter is that for you."

I blinked at him. "I don't know what you're talking about."

The tender, and unexpected, moment disappeared in a flash—*thank God.* He shot me a smug grin before he took another bite of his snack, "Yeah, sure." His wink was obnoxious. "Why are you looking at this on Thanksgiving anyway?"

"We're only celebrating for Hunter and Jennifer."

"So? It's nice not to be on the clock. You should be chilling too."

I admitted, "I find it difficult to switch off—"

"No shit, Sherlock."

Scowling, I continued, "Plus, I think this craziness needs..."

"What?"

"I think Luciu should call a Summit."

"The O'Donnellys are the unofficial heads right now. Is it wise to go behind their backs on this?"

"Luciu is friendly with Aidan O'Donnelly. He could put in the request personally."

"Isn't he still pissed about the Red situation?"

"Who could blame him?" I sniped. "What, with one of Messina's foolish nephews selling it to the Russians who used it to get his foot soldiers hooked?"

We only knew that side of things because Aidan's wife, Savannah, had surmised as much with Jennifer.

"No, Aidan isn't pissed anymore." I twisted around and found my twin standing in the doorway watching us both. "We broke bread over brunch."

"Better than breaking heads, I suppose. Are you sure? When you gave me the lowdown on that meeting, I didn't think it sounded positive."

Luciu shrugged. "It was fine."

"I thought he'd call a Summit after his father died, but he hasn't yet."

He peered at the headlines. "What's this?"

"Am I the only one of us who reads the news?"

"I have a newborn and a busy business without wasting the hours I'm *not* sleeping on trash journalism."

Though I huffed, Stan retorted, "You're also the only one with the freaky brain who'd tie these things together." To Luc, he said, "She thinks these are murders and they're related to the death of that prince who died in Scotland."

"So you *did* hear about it?" I mocked.

"Yeah, but I just thought it was some rich, old white guy who died from gout."

"Can you die from gout?" Luc questioned.

"Let's focus, people," I snarked. "There was a suspicious death of another prince—"

"Maybe this shadow assassin is anti-royalist," Stan said helpfully. "It's a good time for our line to be ancient royals and not modern ones."

I shot him a stern look.

"You really think this is something we should bring up to the Summit?"

"I do," I told Luc. "I think it's a problem. Either that, or one of the factions is orchestrating it and we should know about it. Targeting politicians should be a sanctioned move. Who knows who we have in our pockets?"

"I could see the Irish killing politicians," Stan mused. "They got deeper into that New World Sparrows' conspiracy shit than we did."

"To be fair, their ranks were infiltrated with the fuckers," Luc excused. "That's bound to cause a grudge."

At that, each of us nodded.

We all understood *vinnittas*.

"If you think this is important, I'll contact Aidan tomorrow, Rory."

"I think it's for the best." When I saw both of them were studying the papers, I cleared my throat. "While I have you…"

At my waning words, Stan shot me a look. "While you have us?"

"I kind of need to tell you something."

Luc quipped, "Are you warning us that you're going to tell *Matri* you're officially dating Hunter instead of gaslighting her into thinking you're just friends?"

My lips thinned. "No."

"You're not telling her? Dammit, Rory, that's cold. She loves him—"

"I'm not officially dating him," I snapped.

"You broke up with him?" Stan queried, drawing another cupcake out of one of his pockets. "Does he know? He's really happy watching football in the living room."

Patience. "I didn't break up with him."

"Then why won't you tell *Matri*?" Luc demanded with a frown.

"Because I'm not dating him," I argued, and before they could interrupt, *again*, I blurted out, "I'm married to him!"

For a second, neither said a word. Then, at the same time, both of them burst out laughing. Stan even started slapping his goddamn thigh as if I were funnier than an *SNL* skit. Luc roared with laughter, loud enough that Jennifer popped her head around the door, brows high at the noise coming from here—it probably sounded like a bunch of hyenas had overtaken the place.

"What's so funny?" she asked me, cradling Saverina in her arms.

I motioned at my face. "Do I look like I'm laughing?"

"What is it, Luc?" Her lips started twitching at how hard he was chuckling.

My twin had a contagious laugh, all the more potent because he rarely, if ever, laughed like this anymore.

"Rory just told…" He sucked in a breath, chortling through it before he gave up trying and just started sniggering.

"She told us—" Stan broke off to cackle.

"I told them Hunter and I were married," I said flatly.

"Oh!" Her confusion was clear. "Why's that funny?"

"You tell me."

We hadn't discussed me doing the big reveal on my own, but it was Thanksgiving, Hunter was with family again, and I wanted them to know he was *truly* family, bound to us now.

Much as Jennifer was.

I reached up to tug on my locket, opened it, removed my ring, then slipped it onto my finger.

That stopped their laughter in its tracks.

Eyes big and round, they stared at the wedding ring. For a moment, they said nothing. Did nothing. The silence was all the more potent for their amusement of before.

Then, Luc barked, "I'll kill him."

"Not before I get to him first," Stan spat.

Both of them took off, snarling under their breaths, leaving me to smirk at their antics.

"Aren't you going to go after them?" Jennifer queried, her tone concerned as she watched them storm down the hall.

I wafted a hand. "They fight him because they know they can't fight me."

She tilted her head to the side. "Because you're a girl?"

That had me sneering. "Because they know I'll beat them."

52

CUSTANZU

WESTLIFE - I WANNA GROW OLD WITH YOU

IF MY SISTER thought she was fooling anyone by pretending not to be head over heels for Hunter, she was absolutely insane, but love looked good on her.

It eased the strange ache in my heart to know that Aurora, the only sibling who'd always been alone while sitting in a room full of people, was now a cog in the wider machine of the Valentini family—one that was vital to its very existence. Not for business, not for her contacts, just for being herself.

Accepted by us, by Hunter, and by the council who didn't even care that she was the Camorra's Consigliere and just thought it'd be good for business.

She deserved that level of trust.

She'd earned it.

"You're looking sappy. Have you been drinking Averna Amaro?"

I squinted at my new brother-in-law who'd been a part of this family almost as long as I had. "No."

Hunter snorted. "Bullshit. You're getting maudlin."

"I'm always maudlin. It's my baseline."

"Since when?"

That was a very apt question. I frowned at him, slurring, "You know what? I don't have an answer for that."

His brows rose. "You need to go sleep it off?"

"Nah. I'll just eat some more."

"You already packed away thirds," Hunter said around a chortle. "I'm thinking you're missing out on being a competitive eater."

"They ain't got nothing on me."

"We'll only know if you actually take part in a challenge, won't we?"

"Are you encouraging my drunk brother to do inappropriate things?"

This time, I squinted at Luc. "What kind of inappropriate things are we talking about here?" I waggled my eyebrows.

Luc cast a glance at Hunter who'd stopped giving me his full attention when Aurora laughed at something, wait for it, Jennifer said. *Matri* was sitting in the middle of them on a loveseat, clearly in place to umpire the conversation, but it didn't seem necessary.

Because it was Christmas Day? Were they calling a peacetime effort?

Ever since we'd had this weird brunch before Thanksgiving, the pair had been cordial.

It was odd.

Personally, I preferred it when they were sniping at each other. I liked some explosions with my meals, worked better than Tums for digestion.

Luc, spying Hunter's focus had shifted, followed along until he was watching his wife too. Saverina was in her arms, and beneath the poopmaker, there was another baby, one who was just sleeping, lying in wait to cause havoc.

This time, it'd be a boy.

I knew it.

I also knew what they should call it—Damien.

I bet it'd have glowing red eyes too.

Matri tapped her knee as she giggled at whatever they were discussing, and it was such a surreal moment to witness.

My mother had been perennially unhappy since my father's death but here she was, happy, *relaxed,* the glow from her stay in Sicily long faded but still giving her a golden tint rather than a pasty white one like most of us here.

"It's a shame we couldn't get Currau to attend, isn't it?" Hunter asked softly. "I know that would have made Aurora's day."

"Least we know we come by it honestly."

He shot me a quizzical look. "Come by what honestly?"

"Our obstinacy," I retorted.

A bustling noise surged from the kitchen as the door opened and in waded Evangeline. She didn't pay us any attention. Instead, she walked over to Jen and made grabby hands for Saverina. Evangeline loved kids. Maybe because she didn't know if she'd be able to have them? Wasn't fate a fucking asswipe?

It was difficult watching her talk to my sister and SIL. Hard seeing how at ease she was with *Matri.*

Sitting on that loveseat was family.

How I wanted her to be family.

How I wanted her to be fucking mine.

She was too young for me. Too naive. Too hopeful. I was jaded. A brutal monster who had done the worst shit imaginable to keep his family safe, to keep them strong.

But just because I didn't have her, didn't mean I couldn't save her. Didn't mean I couldn't give her the life she deserved.

As I watched her, I wondered how it was that Luc and Aurora didn't know she was sick. If they'd known, they'd have mentioned it to me.

Evangeline and her mom might be the 'help' in some people's eyes, but not to us. They weren't family but they were trusted, and in this world, that meant we were close.

Friends.

Ha.

God, the idea made me want to scoff. I wanted more from Evangeline than friendship.

The baby was in her hands, tucked against her chest, held tightly in her arms. Her gaze clashed with mine, unexpected and all the more shocking for it. I felt the connection like a lightning bolt shooting deep into my soul.

For a moment, the whole goddamn world froze.

For a moment, we were the only ones in the room.

And for a fucking moment, I wasn't a recovering addict who'd gotten his father killed, I wasn't a monster reared in bloodshed and *vinnittas,* and she wasn't an innocent who deserved more than the hand she'd been dealt.

She looked away from me to laugh at something one of the women said. One of her hands reached up to rub her chest. The gesture was absentminded. The flash of pain on her face wasn't.

My brothers chatted around me, business as always on their minds, while the women discussed whatever the hell could connect three such diverse characters, and I just watched her.

Always fucking her.

Would this need ever die?

Would the wanting ever stop?

A part of me didn't want it to. A part of me knew I deserved to be tempted.

My hands curled into fists at the thought.

Maybe it was because I was watching her; maybe it was because I knew her expressions as well as I did my own. I saw the crumpling of her features, saw the faint tremor as she shivered, then her knees were buckling and she was dropping to the floor.

It happened in a split second.

Everything was fine, *normal,* then nothing was.

Saverina wailed at the abrupt movement as Evangeline's knees gave out, but Jen grabbed a hold of her before the baby was in danger, and Evangeline didn't even hit the floor before I was there, literally flying across the room to catch her.

But I was too late.

I always was.

53

AURORA

"WE SHOULD HAVE MET SOONER than this." I spoke up, sick of listening to the political bullshit that was being tossed around the table.

Meeting in a warehouse that was freezing cold wasn't my idea of a good time. I didn't give a damn how many space heaters were in here, The Victoria would have been a better option.

I was too cold to even give a shit about this being our first official Summit. We were surrounded by the Triads, the Irish Mob, and the Russians, although the latter had barely made it on time.

The leader, Maxim Lyanov, looked exhausted—as if he'd been burning the candle at both ends.

In our world, who didn't? But after the clusterfuck that had gone down in Russia, I couldn't blame him for his exhaustion. In his position, I'd be dead on my feet too.

My words drew everyone's attention my way. Luciu, apologetically, said, "My Consigliere, gentlemen,"

I was the only double dose of X chromosomes around this sorry table, and it was a wonder anything got done if they prevaricated this long and this hard.

"What do you mean we should have met sooner?" the Triad Dragon Head, Zhao, queried.

"I requested a Summit after Thanksgiving," Luciu inserted.

"Why?" Lyanov asked wearily.

"Because there's been a spate of murders of foreign and national officials. Now, there's been this bomb in Moscow," I stated as if he didn't know about the explosion already. "It's too coincidental."

"What does that bomb have to do with anything?" O'Donnelly Jr. asked.

"*It's in Moscow,*" I reiterated. "That's the motherland of the Bratva. It's practically a declaration of intent."

"Intent of what?" Lyanov questioned.

"Should you even be here, Lyanov?" the Dragon Head drawled, peering at his manicured nails. "Hasn't Moscow turned its back on you?"

"I'm still the head of the Russians in New York."

The leader of the Triads smirked at him. "For how long?"

"For as long as I can hold it," Lyanov snarled. "I may no longer be Bratva, but my Forgotten Boys are more powerful—"

Zhao sniped, "*Boys* are exactly what they are—"

"Gentlemen," O'Grady intervened, breaking up the stirrings of an argument. "Now is not the time for this. I've already assessed the situation and agreed that Lyanov still controls the Russian faction. For the moment." Those three words were damning. "Now, I'd like to hear what the Sicilian Consigliere has to say."

O'Donnelly tipped his chin at me so I continued, "I don't know what kind of message the bomb was supposed to send. That's why I think the Summit was urgent. I've been studying this for a while now. The foreign murders have a different pattern from the national murders. But both have to be related to the New World Sparrows."

"Why?"

"Because they're officials who, purportedly, are good people who don't deserve to be murdered, via peanut or otherwise." I shot O'Donnelly Jr. a disparaging look. "I'm of the belief that someone around this table is behind the deaths.

"If you keep on targeting American politicians, it's going to kick up a stink. Not only that, but some of them might be on our payroll.

These kinds of kills need to be organized. There should be a discussion first."

Silence settled among us, and with every passing moment, I felt the distrust grow. I knew my background would have been checked and double-checked. I knew the men I'd had sent up who belonged to these factions would trigger grudges, but O'Donnelly Jr. didn't look at me as if I were trouble.

He looked at me as if he were a man who knew to respect a woman's brain.

With a wife like Savannah O'Donnelly, it was no wonder.

His fingers rapped the table in a rhythmic pattern that made my heart feel as if it were jumping around in staccato bursts.

"The syndicate of Sparrows needs taking down. The Eastern, Old World, and New World trio need to be eradicated from the face of the earth, and there's only one way to do that."

I frowned as I pieced together what he was saying. "You're taking out Sparrow politicians and…" My eyes flared. "You want to take over the New World Sparrows!"

"How the fuck did she piece that together?" Stan muttered to Luc in Sicilian.

O'Donnelly Jr. hitched a shoulder. "There'll be more deaths as we sort the wheat from the chaff. Whether they're on your payroll or not is of no interest to me.

"The Sparrows are a blight on our world. One of the only reasons I'm allowing you in this Summit, Aurora Valentini, despite your colorful history, is that you were not one of their minions." O'Donnelly Jr. looked around the table. "You don't have to like it. You don't even have to agree with it." That was aimed at Zhao. "But you will deal with it because they're a parasite, and they're willing to use our factions as hosts."

I frowned at him. "How do you know I wasn't a minion?"

Stan hissed, "Aurora."

"Your cases were fair. I looked into you personally. A basic part of the Sparrows' endgame was to trap men into being their patsies by fitting them up for a crime they didn't commit. You rarely prosecuted those cases."

O'Grady studied me. "Why is that?"

I shrugged. "I couldn't tell you without knowing a specific case."

O'Donnelly Jr. chuckled under his breath. "There. Right there. You don't know the specifics because you did your job and you weren't anyone's puppet."

"I targeted mostly *Famiglia* foot soldiers," I said unapologetically. "And I tossed a few of your men in—" I glanced around the table. "—to make sure my reputation didn't seem skewed toward unfair treatment of the Italian mafia." I shot O'Donnelly Jr. a smile. "If you'd be willing to discuss this situation, I'd be happy to strategize with you."

Luc waved a hand. "I'm a strong strategist, but no one can play politics like Aurora."

O'Donnelly Jr. frowned at me. "Why would you be interested? I'd be the new head of the Sparrows. No one else."

I hitched a shoulder. "Because it seems like fun."

"Fun?" O'Donnelly Jr. repeated blandly.

My smile turned wicked. "Shaping the future of this country and the global stage doesn't seem like fun to you?"

His eyes narrowed upon me, then he tipped his head in assent. "Any other business?"

And that was how I got my in into taking down the biggest secret society the earth had seen since Galileo walked the globe...

54

AURORA
ROBBIE WILLIAMS - ETERNITY

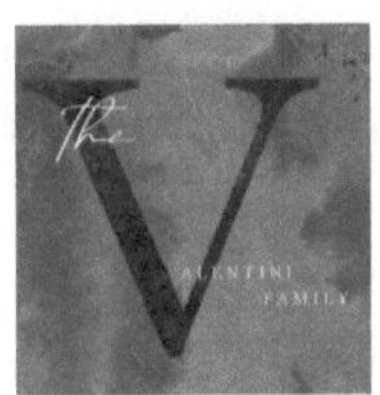

A YEAR LATER

A GIDDY LAUGH escaped me as Hunter hauled me onto the dance floor. His arms slipped around my waist as mine curled around his neck.

"You look gorgeous," he muttered in my ear.

"I have good taste," I retorted with a chuckle. "It's just been rusty since you took over my wardrobe."

Our lips collided as the music started but instead of melting, I froze when a Dean Martin song played in the background.

We were alone on the dance floor—this was our *first* dance. He'd told me to leave the choice to him, and he'd picked this?

I almost pouted.

Then, his arms dropped and his mouth hovered beside my ear. "You didn't think I'd forget, did you?"

Frowning in confusion, I waited, much as our guests did, as he plucked something from his pocket. Well, *two* somethings.

The sight of the AirPod cases had me frowning, then he passed one to me before he opened it and slipped the buds into his ears.

"Trust me," he said with a grin.

I did, nudging the Anjou earrings aside so I could insert the buds as I watched him nod to someone in the crowd. My eye roll told him he was on shaky ground. Dean Martin for our first dance. Seriously?

No offense to Dean but—

The beginning of a song trickled into my ears.

I closed my eyes as a smile stirred on my lips.

He remembered.

The song I always cried to. The song that Robbie Williams had performed by special request of my husband when he'd played at the Gallinaro. And the song which Hunter had serenading us while he proposed to me for real.

'Eternity.'

As Robbie Williams, my teen crush, sang about summer dreaming and hoping his woman found her freedom, my *adult* crush and the love of my life danced me around the floor. We waltzed to Dean Martin, the song that everyone was hearing, but no one knew this private tune.

Our song?

It had to be now, didn't it?

Tears prickled my eyes as we swept around the ballroom floor. He dipped me low and lifted me high. Holding me close with a promise that I felt in his arms—he'd never let me go.

As Dean Martin came to an end, people joined us on the dance floor. They clapped and cooed their congratulations around us, but it was only when the song finished that I whispered, "Thank you, Hunter. Not just for this, but for bringing me peace. For loving me as I am. And this song choice is pretty nifty too."

His lips quirked, then he pressed them to my ear, murmuring, "Loving you is the easiest thing in the world, Aurora. As for the song, it's not exactly music fit for a Consigliere and a Don's wedding dance, but I knew Stan and Luc would help us out."

My head whipped to the side at that admission, where I found my brothers shooting me dopey grins and tucking their phones back into their tuxedo pockets.

I couldn't help myself—I shot them one back.

Feeling myself being steered toward the edge of the dance floor, a quick glance around let me know why—his parents were waving us over.

Getting my in-laws here had been simple, but Hunter hadn't been happy about their attendance. Bert was the only family he wanted at our service and reception, and I was good at what I did but I couldn't make miracles happen.

There were two empty seats at our wedding table for him and my *patri*—it wasn't enough, but it was all I could do.

"Think we can sneak up to our room without talking to them?"

I snorted. "No."

"We've already argued twice today," he pointed out.

"They're leaving in a week," I attempted to reassure him.

His grimace told me it didn't work. "So are we," he remarked. "I'll kill your brothers if they mention we're going to your estate for our honeymoon. They'll expect us to visit them if they know we're on the island."

"I don't think Luc and Stan will say a word."

"Why not?"

I sighed. "They asked why you guys weren't getting along. I probably shared too much."

His brows lowered. "You told them he used to hit me?"

"Not in so many words."

"Not in so many words but that was still what they'll have picked up from the conversation?"

My nose crinkled. "Sorry?"

Arms tightening around me as he swayed me into another dance—only because he was trying to avoid his parents still—he rumbled in my ear. "You can make it up to me later."

Relieved that he wasn't mad, I kissed his cheek. "I will. I promise."

As we journeyed around the dance floor, he murmured, "I knew this day would come but, sometimes, my faith was tested."

That drew my attention back to him. "I never imagined it would, and yet, it was always bound to happen." I reached up and cupped his cheek, my gaze darting off the camellia he wore in his boutonniere—red for love, passion, and desire. I now knew that the pink camellia he'd given me when we first got together had symbolized 'a longing for someone.' "Thank you, Hunter. You're giving me love when I never expected that. You're giving me a shot at a future that's more than work." I let my thumb trail across his bottom lip. "I don't deserve you but—" I yelped when he cut me off.

His mouth stopped the flow of my words as he dipped me low again, swooping me backward in a move that had the crowds cheering.

"We were born for this. Here. Now. We deserve each other."

I stared up at him with my heart in my eyes and whispered our truth, "We deserve each other."

55

HUNTER

DON'T WORRY BABY - THE BEACH BOYS

I LET LOOSE A TIRED, jaw-cracking yawn as I stepped into Bert's *palazzo.*

It was late. Ridiculously late. Three AM late which meant I'd missed putting Custantinu down to bed and reading him a bedtime story.

Some days, those simple acts of fatherhood were the only things that kept me from feeling like I was a monster. Some days, being Aurora's husband was the only thing that kept me from falling off the edge.

Violence was addictive when you were determined to keep your family safe, and there was no one more determined than I where Aurora and Tinu were concerned. Now, she was pregnant again, my instincts were back to being on the rampage.

It didn't help that we split our week between New York and Vegas where our powerful factions attempted to tear us to shreds in the name of business, but we made it work.

We had to.

There was no alternative for us.

She was it for me.

I was it for her.

Yawning again as I headed into the family quarters, I moved down the hall toward Tinu's room. I only opened the door, not wanting to disturb his sleep, and saw him, butt in the sky, face in his pillow, snoozing away.

A smile creased my lips, one that was joyous and filled with gratitude. It took away the feeling of blood coating my hands from the night's business.

Gently shutting the door, I stepped toward our suite. My heart skipped a beat as it always did when I thought about coming home to her.

My moonlight.

When I made it inside, I saw she had the low-level nightlight on just in case Tinu came barreling in after a bad dream.

The first time that had happened after he moved into his own room, he'd almost knocked himself out on the bed frame.

When Aurora had settled him back down, I'd slammed a hammer into the damn thing until it was ripped to shreds, and had it replaced with a padded head and footboard by the following evening.

No one and nothing hurt my family.

Not even inanimate objects—Aurora still teased me about that.

The warmth of home began to fill me when I saw her, cuddled on her side, the duvet around her in a cocoon that somehow covered none of her—I knew she liked the comfort of the down but got hot easily late in her first trimester.

I dragged off my necktie, gaze locked on her when I saw something on the nightstand.

My eyes flared.

Her controller was on there, sitting in front of the shadow box that housed her 'Sunny' mask. My 'D' mask was on my nightstand—we'd gotten sentimental in our old age.

Aurora rarely played the games I'd introduced her to, but on the nights when she did, the controller went on the nightstand, and that was our code.

Our silent code.

Fuck.

I'd been exhausted when I walked through the front door. Now I was exhilarated.

As I stepped closer to the bed, she released a soft sigh and gently tumbled onto her back. Her pooch peeped out from one of my football jerseys, revealing the taut skin of her bump, streaked with lightning from where Tinu and now another baby made their home, and a pair of CK panties that ran low on her hips.

My mouth watered at the sight of her.

She'd made me realize that there was nothing deviant about wanting her like this.

What we had together could never be that.

In my eagerness, I stripped out of my clothes, flinging them onto the floor without giving a damn where they landed before stepping over to the side of the bed.

Allowing my fingers to smooth along her calf and higher, I watched as she released a soft breath but didn't respond. I trailed them along her inner thighs, gently following the line of her panties on her hip.

A tiny frown furrowed her brow, but she didn't stir.

I hesitated between wanting to wake her up and enjoying these moments of silence, of appreciation.

I wanted her to wake up overloaded with pleasure.

I wanted to enjoy exploring the trust between us as she gave herself over to me in her most vulnerable state.

It had taken three years to reach this point. Three years of constancy and love to let her put aside the trauma of her past and to have faith that I wouldn't abuse her limits.

Jaw clenched, I ran my fingers along the front of her panties. I dipped one deeper, pushing between her folds, and darted a look at her, watching her reactions.

A soft sigh drifted from her lips and she wriggled slightly, one leg shifting to the left.

I stilled again, not wanting to wake her yet, and watched as her breathing regulated and she fell asleep once more.

Tugging the crotch of her panties to the side, I stared amid the shadows at her folds and felt my mouth start to water.

The sense that this was wrong always froze me in place, but I cast a look at that controller, the code we used for her to tell me when she wanted this, and I nuzzled my nose against the top of her pubis.

Trailing down, I let my tongue flutter out and gently flickered it over her clit. Her legs spread wider in response, and I cast a quick glance at her face but saw only mild annoyance, as if a mosquito were buzzing her ear.

The thought made me grin to myself and it also pricked my pride. I gently sucked on her clit then let my finger rub along her folds until I found her slit. I circled the entrance as I tasted her, then I moved away, letting the digit trace her gate as, with my other hand, I dragged the jersey higher so I could see her breasts. They'd always been a handful, but now they were a cup bigger at least.

Tomorrow, I'd fuck those beauties. Tonight, I had *this*. The biggest offering of trust of them all.

I could feel my pulse pounding along my shaft and I gripped it hard, needing some relief even though I knew I wouldn't get any outside of her cunt.

Growling under my breath at the thought, I stopped fucking around and pinched the panties at her hips so I could carefully start to drag them down her thighs.

Whenever she shuffled around in annoyance, I paused. Each time, my heart pounded, the strangest excitement filled me, and I waited with bated breath for her to settle down.

When her panties were abandoned on the bed between her feet, my dick was leaking pre-cum and I could feel the heat in my veins making sweat bead on my brow.

I carefully clambered on the mattress, but this disturbance was one too many—she rolled onto her side, legs closed, huffing sleepily as she nestled her face into the pillow.

Sometimes, I wondered if she was really asleep. If she was playacting. I didn't know how I felt about that, but it didn't stop me from going out of my way to keep her relaxed.

Game plan shifting, I settled next to her, her back to my chest. We were so used to sleeping with each other in this position now that she actually leaned into me, sighing with relief as if she could sense, deep in her slumber, that I was home.

Love filled me as I pressed a kiss to her shoulder and gently started stroking the outer edge of her thigh.

Carefully, in slight increments, I lifted it until it was resting on mine. I tipped my hips forward so my dick was between her thighs and I started to rock back and forth, eyes closed as I savored the exquisite sensation.

She was wet. Fuck, she was so wet.

Elation poured through me as I began to tunnel through the tight gap between her thighs faster. She moaned because, with every thrust, I rubbed her clit.

When I thought I was about to cum, I reached over and added pressure to the tip of my cock from the front and in I popped. Into the sweetest place on earth. My fucking reward for doing shit I didn't want to do to keep my family, my *world,* safe.

As I pushed into her, I felt the sudden jolt of awareness as she awoke for real. No slight sighs or huffs of annoyance.

"Hunter?"

My name had an urgency about it, and I acted swiftly to put her at ease. "Moonlight. What a welcome home."

She instantly sagged into me, but I didn't let up. I let my fingers do the talking as I reached for her clit and started to rub it from side to side, just how she liked.

Aurora groaned, deep and long, as she rocked back into me. Allowing me to thrust faster into her now that the angle was better.

As her cries echoed around the room, my heavy grunts entwined with them.

Heart pounding, body shaking, her pussy clutching at me, I exploded, cum drenching her cunt with everything that I had as I continued thrusting through the aftershocks, fingers still teasing her clit until she burst around me too.

Gritting my teeth at how fiercely she clamped down around my shaft, I burrowed into her, face hiding in her throat for a handful of seconds until I reached up with my still slick fingers and gently stroked her collar.

"*T'amu*, Hunter," she breathed drowsily, relaxing as she tumbled back to sleep.

Like I was an empty well, the words filled me up.

There were many parts of my life that I didn't like, that were unexpected and violent and not what I'd ever want for myself, for her, or Tinu for that matter, but she made it bearable. She gave me a reason to wake up and a reason to hope that, one day in the future, we'd have built somewhere better, somewhere brighter for our children.

As I curved a hand over her swollen stomach, the promise of yet another resting peacefully in her mother's belly, I whispered, "I love you too, Aurora."

Though my body was still racing in the aftermath, my heart and soul relaxed, at ease now that I was home, with my family, with my forever.

56

HUNTER

A THOUSAND YEARS - CHRISTINA PERRI

I SLAMMED my hand down against the desk when Tinu opened the door to peer through the gap he'd made. "No."

He scowled at me. "You don't know what I'm going to ask!"

Ignoring him, I stared down at the headlines.

Murray, Garcia Eugenio, and O'Donnelly stand up in the last Democratic Primary debate.

"Are you even listening to me?"

"I'm not and I know exactly what you're going to ask." My cell buzzed—*Crayon*. I hit disconnect and sent him a text telling him I'd call him back later. Gaze drifting to the pouting teenager in the doorway, I retorted, "You *are* going to college. You're going to major in whatever the fuck you want, General Studies even, you're going to graduate, *then* you can make massive life-changing decisions."

"Mom said—"

"I don't care what Mom said!" Well, that was a lie.

"Hunter!"

I didn't even heave a sigh when I heard Aurora's hurt tone. Instead, as she stormed in, wearing the Gucci dress I'd picked out for her this morning, leaving Tinu over by the door, I folded my arms against my chest—she wasn't about to coax me into this.

"No, Rory. He's going to college."

"What makes you think we're not on the same page?"

"The fact that you're negotiating on his behalf?"

She huffed. "Tinu can negotiate for himself."

"So, you're here, why?"

"Because."

"Great argument," I drawled.

Tinu whined, "Mom!"

"If you're old enough to get married, Tinu, then you're old enough to stop whining at your mother."

A smile curved my wife's lips as her fingertips toyed with her collar. "He has a point, son."

Custantinu scowled at us both. "You're *ruining* my life."

"Ruining? More like saving it," I snapped.

"You're proving him right, Tinu," Alessandra, our secondborn, mocked, laughing from her position over by the door to my office.

We still lived in my grandfather's *palazzo,* which meant we had ample room for the whole family not to be in here all the damn time. Yet Lyra soon made an appearance, as did Fenella.

We'd been blessed with three children, but Fenny was a kid Aurora's charity had saved from the streets and who we'd brought into our family.

Eight years old and somehow Social Services had failed her.

It still killed me to think about what she must have gone through out there.

She was a De Laurentiis now, though. That meant she was untouchable.

"How am I proving him right?" Tinu snarled at his sister.

"You're behaving like a brat." She sniffed. It was disconcerting how much she took after Aurora when she pulled those stunts.

"He's destroying everything."

"No, I'm not. I'm just telling you to graduate."

"I love her, Dad."

Aurora's gaze tangled with mine. She was still as hard as nails, and together, we'd made the Camorra a ruthless, stream-lined organization that kept the underworld under control. But there was a softness to her that only made itself known when our kids were around.

I understood—I was a putz for them too.

"I don't dispute that you do, Tinu." If anyone knew that young love could last the ages, it was me.

"YOU NEVER UNDERST—" My son stopped shrieking at me long enough to blink. "What?"

I had to hide a smile. "I said I'm sure you love her. I'm pretty sure she loves you because only a woman in love would deal with an eighteen-year-old who has temper tantrums and is still undecided about college."

He glowered at me. "What's the problem then? Is it who she is?"

"It doesn't help," I retorted. "You know her father doesn't like us." *'Doesn't like' read 'hates.'*

My kid hitched a shoulder. "He likes me."

"God only knows why," Lyra muttered as she waltzed over to me and kissed me on the cheek.

She was a daddy's girl, which meant I spoiled the fuck out of her and didn't have it in me to care. Unlike Tinu who always answered back at every goddamn opportunity, she was my angel.

I rubbed a hand over my face as Aurora inserted, "There's no reason they can't get married, Hunter."

"It's not like I'm not an adult," Tinu inserted bitterly. "I shouldn't need your permission."

"You don't need it," I countered, watching him bluster at my words. "It's if you want me to keep on paying your way that you need it.

"You want to go out into the big, bad world, son, you do it. You get to make your own choices but it's on your dime.

"If you like wearing thousand-dollar sneakers that look like they've been in a dumpster for five years and don't want to worry about rent, well, nothing truly comes for free."

Aurora cleared her throat, making sure she had my attention as she glared at me to shut up. "If Tinu agrees to go to college—"

I narrowed my eyes at her. "Is Angel out in the corridor too?"

Tinu shuffled on his feet. "Maybe."

"Bring her in here," I ordered.

Aurora made the smart decision of rounding the desk and placing a hand on my shoulder. Immediately, my tension died. I didn't like being angry with her, hated being angry with my kids, but sometimes, they drove me around the fucking bend.

A small girl made an appearance in the doorway. She was petite, all onyx curls that gleamed in the light from the hallway. She looked *nothing* like Kingston or Martínez. She was shy. Also unlike them. Timid.

Their secondborn for my firstborn—who'd have imagined it?

My son placed his arm on her shoulders, hovering protectively around her much as I did with his mother. The difference was that Aurora liked it, whereas Angel needed it. Aurora wasn't shy, never had been. Angel, on the other hand, exuded it.

My tone, as a result, was softer than anything I even used with Fenella, my youngest. "Angel, do you really want to get married? You're both so young."

She swallowed. "I love him, Mr. De Laurentiis. I-I know he has tantrums and you're right about his bad taste in sneakers, but he's a good man. *My* good man."

At my side, Aurora sniffled.

Christ.

I slipped my arm around her waist and tugged her nearer to me. I knew she'd accepted Angel as a daughter-in-law because she didn't just let me hold her close, she perched herself on my knee. She only did things like that around family.

When her cell buzzed, from the corner of my eye, I saw Saverina's name on the Caller ID.

Our niece was thick as thieves with Aurora, much to her father's dismay because my wife was intent on making her the next Dona of NYC.

When the call wasn't accepted, a second later, she texted:

Saverina: *DAD is being such a JERK!*

"What about your parents? I won't go against your father, not when it's his daughter's happiness at stake. I know what I'd do for my girls," I warned.

Martínez, for all that he'd gone legit back when Aurora and I had first gotten married, for all that he'd turned his turf around, was still a force to be reckoned with.

Angel bit her lip. "He respects your family, Mr. De Laurentiis."

"Doesn't he want you to go to college?"

"He does." She tipped her chin up. "He wants me to get an MBA."

I knew enough about kids to register that wasn't what *she* wanted. "And what do *you* want to do?"

Her cheeks turned pink. "I want to be a paleontologist."

My brows rose because my son was a jock, much as I'd been.

"He likes them nerdy," Lyra teased.

"Shut up, Lyra," Tinu barked, making Angel jump.

I frowned at my daughter. "There's no need to be mean."

Her shoulders hunched at my disapproval.

Focusing on Angel, I queried, "What are you going to study? Business or paleontology?"

"He's paying for my tuition." The spark in her eyes died, turning flat. "So I'll be aiming for my MBA."

Drumming my fingers against the desk, I mused, "Tinu, if you want to marry Angel, I give you my permission on the proviso that you attend college." I knew why he'd been sulking—his school of choice, Stanford, hadn't picked him up on a scholarship for the football team. But I knew my son too well. For all that he'd started celebrating my decision, I drawled, "I will cover your college fees, and Angel's paleontology classes too, whatever postgrad studies she'd like, and you can even be a walk-on for Stanford's football team, *but* if you quit school early, I'll expect full repayment with interest."

Aurora chuckled, clearly approving of my method. "Not a bank's interest rate, either."

Tinu's eyes rounded at my offer. "I HATE YOU BOTH! Why do you have to ruin everything?"

Angel shushed him, but there was humor in her eyes now—the girl understood a smart business deal better than my son did. Maybe paleontology would be wasted on her. "I'll make sure he doesn't quit, Mr. De Laurentiis."

I believed her. "I'd like to meet with your parents, Angel. Do you think they'd be amenable?"

Martínez and I hadn't shared breathing space since before he'd burned down the *Reyes'* compound twenty or so years ago.

She nodded. "I'll talk with them."

My office swiftly vacated once the show was over. Aurora led them out, unaware they trailed after her like she was the Pied Piper. Even Lyra, my shadow, traipsed after her when their mom was at home.

I looked around my office at the sudden emptiness and felt disconcerted at the silence—it was deafening.

My gaze caught on the ink sketch that I'd had framed and which hung pride of place above the mantelpiece.

It was of the family at the Valentini Estate, back when the kids were little. I was at the head of the table peeling apples while Aurora managed to wreck the pastry dough for the pie we'd intended (and failed) to bake.

Our kids were around the table, all apart from Fenella as this was back when they were really young.

Each of them was working on their own project—Tinu on his art (he was just like his mom), Alessandra on her diary (she wrote pages and pages about her every waking moment), and Lyra drawing dot-to-dot because she'd only just started to sit upright.

Aurora still didn't like her art being displayed, but I'd convinced her with this one, just because it reminded me of the sketch her mom had sent into a competition and that had been published in a magazine.

A sudden urge for Catania hit me, and the one perk to being a Don? Though I had work to do, a veritable mountain of it, just like I knew my wife-cum-Consigliere AKA my Oracle had also, we were the king and queen of our world and there was no one to chide us for playing hooky.

That was why I called our pilot and arranged for a flight to Sicily then hunted down my family to tell them where we were spending the next couple weeks.

While the kids were still under our roof, before our little birds flew the nest for good, taking us to the home of our hearts seemed like a smart step.

And if we added a new little bird to our nest—Angel—then it was only fitting, seeing as she needed to be introduced to the land of our ancestors...

AUTHOR NOTE

Dear reader,

I want to let you in on a little secret…

Hunter and Rory are in a DD/lg (Daddy Dom/little girl) relationship. :) I just didn't tell you until you finished the story because Daddy books get a hard rap! Personally, I love them, but I never like to make my readers uncomfortable so I decided to write the dynamic without overtly using the labels that put people on edge.

Anyhoo, with that confession out of the way…

This provided some inspiration for Aurora's collar. :)

This provided inspiration for the carbon rod 'flogger.'

This provided inspiration for the bracelet 'whip.'

Don't forget the second THE ORACLE hits 500 reviews, I'll be dropping a bonus scene in my Diva reader group and on my Discord server!!

You can join here to read it when it happens: www.facebook.com/groups/SerenaAkeroydsDivas or here: https://discord.gg/TJp9Pz7MNJ

If after reading Hunter and Rory's story you are interested in finding out how we reached this point, start with Filthy and follow the reading order you can find here:

https://serenaakeroyd.com/my-books/the-five-points-mob-collection-universe/
Much love to you all,
Serena
xoxo

THE CROSSOVER READING ORDER
WITH THE SINNERS & VALENTINIS

FILTHY
FILTHY SINNER
NYX
LINK
FILTHY RICH
SIN
STEEL
FILTHY DARK
CRUZ
MAVERICK
FILTHY SEX
HAWK
FILTHY HOT
STORM
THE DON
THE LADY
FILTHY SECRET
REX
RACHEL
FILTHY KING

REVELATION BOOK ONE
REVELATION BOOK TWO
FILTHY LIES
FILTHY TRUTH

RUSSIAN MAFIA
Adjacent to the universe, but can be read as a standalone
SILENCED

FREE BOOK!

Don't forget to grab your free e-Book!
Secrets & Lies is now free!

Meg's love life was missing a spark until she discovered her need to be dominated. When her fiancé shared the same kink, she thought all her birthdays had come at once, and then she came to learn their relationship was one big fat lie.

Gabe has loved Meg for years, watching her from afar, and always wishing he'd been the one to date her first and not his brother. When he has the chance to have Meg in his bed—even better, tied to it—it's an opportunity he can't refuse.

With disastrous consequences.

Can Gabe make Meg realize she's the one woman he's always wanted? But once secrets and lies have wormed their way into a relationship, is it impossible to establish the firm base of trust needed between lovers, and more importantly, between sub and Sir…?

This story features orgasm control in a BDSM setting.
Secrets & Lies is now free!

CONNECT WITH SERENA

For the latest updates, be sure to check out my website!
But if you'd like to hang out with me and get to know me better, then
I'd love to see you in my Diva reader's group where you can find out
all the gossip on new releases as and when they happen. You can join
here: www.facebook.com/groups/SerenaAkeroydsDivas. Or you can
always PM or email me. I love to hear from you guys: serenaakeroyd@
gmail.com.

ABOUT THE AUTHOR

I'm a romance novelaholic and I won't touch a book unless I know there's a happy ending. This addiction is what made me craft stories that suit my voracious need for raunchy romance. I love twists and unexpected turns, and my novels all contain sexy guys, dark humor, and hot AF love scenes.

I write MF, menage, and reverse harem (also known as why choose romance,) in both contemporary and paranormal. Some of my stories are darker than others, but I can promise you one thing, you will always get the happy ending your heart needs!

NAMES & CHARACTERS OF INTEREST

MAIN CHARACTERS:

HUNTER LACHLAN -

Grandson of Alberto 'Bert' De Laurentiis, new Don of the Camorra.

AURORA VALENTINI -

Consigliere of the *Cosa Nostra*, twin sister and sibling of Luciu (Luc) Valentini, the Don, and Custanzu (Stan) Valentini, the Capo. Legal surname is Fitzwilliam. (Maternal grandparents' family name.)

SIDE CHARACTERS:

RACHEL LAKER - Best friend of Hunter and Aurora, lawyer to the *Cosa Nostra,* Old Lady of Rex, Prez of the Satan's Sinners' MC.
    Jennifer Valentini, née MacNeill - Wife of Luciu Valentini,

friends with Aoife O'Grady (wife of the Irish Mob) and Savannah O'Donnelly (wife of the Irish Mob.)

Lodestar - Lone wolf who found refuge with the Satan's Sinners.

Alberto 'Bert' De Laurentiis - previous Don of the Camorra.

Lauren Valentini - Mother of Luciu, Aurora, and Custanzu. British.

Custantinu Valentini - Father of Luciu, Aurora, and Custanzu. Sicilian.

Currau Valentini - Great-Uncle of Luciu, Aurora, and Custanzu.

Brunu - Capo of the Camorra.

Paulu - Consigliere of the Camorra.

Giovi - Foot soldier of the *Cosa Nostra,* works with Aurora.

Grainne Ledger - High-profile Madam, affiliated with the Five Point Mob (Irish.)

'Fieri' family - Arch-nemesis of the Valentini family. The previous leaders of the *Cosa Nostra* until their eradication. They worked with the New World Sparrows.

ORGANIZATIONS:

CAMORRA - SICILIAN MAFIA on the West Coast. Ruled by the De Laurentiis family.

Not to be confused with the *Cosa Nostra,* who are ruled by the Valentinis and which governs the East Coast.

Five Points' Mob - Irish Mob, allied to the Valentinis, ruled by the O'Donnelly family.

Satan's Sinners' MC - a motorcycle club in West Orange, New Jersey. Allied to the Five Points. Led by Rex, the Prez.

Russian Bratva - Allied to the Five Points and the Valentinis. Led by Maxim Lyanov, the Pakhan.

New World Sparrows - often abbreviated to NWS. The members are known as Sparrows.

One of three global secret societies of criminals hidden in plain sight, mostly known for sex trafficking. Having infiltrated every aspect of US society, from the government to the courts to law enforcement agencies, they've escaped justice for their heinous crimes for decades.

Éire le chéile go deo - often abbreviated to ECD. The members are known as *cheiles*. An Irish organization dedicated to uniting Northern Ireland with the Republic and removing the British from their land.